The Curse Is Come Upon Us

Tales From Hawthorn Lane

~Libris Two~

Kristina Schram

Mischief Maker Media

Published by Mischief Maker Media (USA)

First printing: February, 2018

Cover Design, Interior, Technical Expertise: Mischief Maker Media
Cover Photo of Witch Woman & Interior Icons from iStockPhoto

ISBN: 978-1-939397-29-4

Visit Kristina Schram at: www.KristinaSchram.com

Acknowledgements

A big thanks to my mom for pushing me to get this second book done, in a year where I felt like getting nothing done.

Thanks also to my beta readers: Elizabeth Schram, Ian More, Dan Unzen, and Heather Duane. You keep me honest. Mostly.

For all the cursed…

Chapter One

I set out at the darkest hour of night, when most of Hawthorn Lane's residents are held captive deep within their dreams, pulled down by the weight of their unconscious mind, unable to move or even sense a shadow passing by. It was a moonless eve, with a warm breeze that would conveniently make it difficult to track my scent. But even with the wind on my side, I was grateful that the breach triggered only when someone attempted to enter Hawthorn Lane from the Alterworld, and not the other way around. Those who chose to leave the village were able to do so without notice, and if I were going to escape, I needed all the help I could get.

Even so, as I made my way through the maze of towering black firs that populated Fell Forest it bothered me knowing that Kyran Van der Daarke, the newly returned Count of Castle Daarke, could follow my movements. Along with being able to enter locked doors without lifting a finger, assessing and tracking blood origin and quality was a special ability of his, and my blood seemed to hold a particularly strong draw for him. I both liked that, and didn't.

But he should be fast asleep at this late hour, and I should be able to get away before he had any idea I was leaving. *Should* being the operative word here.

My footsteps made no sound on the carpet of thick moss and old pine needles covering the forest floor, and I moved swiftly and surely despite the pitch black all around me. My night vision has always been excellent, uncannily so, now that I thought about it. And if my eyesight failed me, I could always use the sparks I had recently learned to shoot from my fingertips.

Cutting myself off from the other villagers this past week had come with one positive side effect—it forced me to confront my fey. I was supposedly an Omni-Fey, the most powerful of all fey, and after some initial misgivings, I found myself embracing my new persona as a magical being. I realized I really liked having the power to make things happen. I liked that I could control the elements, and, if I wanted to, other people. After years of being oppressed by others, the temptation of having power over them was irresistible.

On the more fanciful side, I loved the way the sparks looked, shooting from my fingers like tiny stars. I'd yet to make anything truly great happen since the night I'd pushed back the waters and cleared the skies, but that didn't surprise me. My mentor, Missy Thornback, a witch and retired brew maven, had often talked about the trick to making magic. At the time I hadn't known I was fey, but I took in everything she'd told me like a child eavesdropping on adult conversations. What it boiled down to was knowing how to connect to one's inner core, and then being able to connect that core to the rest of the world—to other people's core, to nature's core; in short, to the very essence of power. Doing magic requires self-confidence and self-knowledge, two traits I've never possessed in great quantities, unfortunately. So my progress, while moving forward, was advancing slower than I'd like. I was missing something, an element Missy would call my 'glister,' or my spark, and I'd yet to figure out what that element was.

Too bad it hadn't come to me before my attempt to make a break for it while sneaking through a forest of magical creatures.

My night vision held true, however, and I was able to discern that the Fernie Brae wasn't far now. Many times I'd accompanied Lady Faylan, Hawthorn Lane's no-nonsense overseer, to Ware-Port Day, a monthly exchange of goods that takes place at the border between the village and the world of non-magicals, a.k.a. the Alterworld. Still, I was nervous. I'd often gathered delectables at night in Fell Forest, but the wood remained foreign to me, populated as it was by enigmatic and unpredictable fey. I'd only recently encountered one—a centaur named Rialban of the Fell—and he had been kind to me when I'd taken a tumble in the forest. But I sensed that if I crossed him, he'd make short work of me, leaving my carcass to the messenger birds, or other, less kindly, scavengers.

When the spirit orbs began to pop on, one after the other like flash-bulbs, I knew I was nearing the Fernie Brae. The only other indication that the border was close was the slight blurring of the air between two massive oaks, the tall trees illusioning the effect of a doorway. I was almost there. My heart beat a little harder and my mouth went dry.

This is it.

I spun around a few times, taking in everything that I could, sights, smells, sounds, delaying my next step, not wanting to leave Hawthorn Lane just yet. Truth be told, not wanting to go at all. I would miss so much here—the quirky villagers, the sense of living in another time, the feeling of magic in the air, the intrigue of my job as a gatherer.

Even worse, I felt like I was abandoning Ilia Van der Daarke, Kyran's young, and way too innocent niece, to the dangers of Hawthorn Lane, not to mention leaving her alone to deal with her awful mother, Kyran's sister, Melaina. But I had unfinished business in the Alterworld, and besides that, if I didn't leave, I felt quite certain the curse on the village, the one that soured love affairs and tainted relationships, would never be lifted. I couldn't remove it, so I had to remove myself in order that others would have a chance to try. I had no choice but to go back home.

My eyes blinked rapidly as hot, painful tears threatened to erupt. I hadn't cried once since that day six years ago when I'd decided to run away from home and stumbled upon Hawthorn Lane. For survival reasons, I had hardened myself nearly to the point of callousness, and my armor had served me well. But from the moment I'd determined to go back, I'd spent a lot of time suppressing a nearly overwhelming urge to cry my eyes out. My entire body and soul rebelled at the idea of returning to my perpetually angry mother, to my depressing Aunt Nimair and my scheming sister, Eudrea, or to my cheating ex-boyfriend, Dallen.

But it was a necessary evil. Because, as it turns out, Dallen hadn't cheated on me after all. My younger sister, Eudrea, had manufactured the little drama, using magic to bewitch him. Somehow or other she'd discovered she possessed powers and had used them on him. As I'd only just learned about mine a little over a week ago, she had the jump on me. It would not be fun going back to that.

At any rate, Dallen had begged me to believe him, and I hadn't. More than that, he'd been the first person in a long time who actually seemed to want to be with me, despite my standoffishness and the countless little tests I'd perform to see if he would cut and run like the others had. He also stuck around despite my warnings about my crazy mother (who actually ended up liking him quite a bit—probably more than she liked me). Simply put, I owed him a lot. He'd been a nice guy, and even though I wasn't at fault for thinking he'd betrayed me, I needed to atone for the fact that I hadn't given him a chance to make his case. I needed to apologize for doubting him and for running away. It might seem like a small thing to most people, but I had to make things right with him, or I wouldn't be any better than the rest of my trash family.

But that wasn't the only reason I had to go back. For years now I'd had this terrible fear that my mother would find out where I'd gone and come after me. Every time there was a breach my heart started to hammer, and I would think, *She's come. She's going to force me to go home.* It was never her, but I couldn't stop worrying and that worry had been growing stronger with every passing day, as though if I didn't go back, trouble would come to me, and in the worst form. It was a feeling that took all the pleasure out of my life, and I had to do something to make it stop.

What would happen after my reunion with Dallen and my family, I could only guess. Would I stay in the Alterworld? Would Dallen, if he'd remained single, want to pick up where we left off? Would I return to him if he did? I didn't know. I only knew that I had to do this. If I were lucky, he'd be married with five kids, and Mother would be dead, and I could return to living my life without either encumbrance hanging over my head.

Straightening my shoulders, I wiped my eyes and stepped forward. *Courage, Lorelle,* I said to myself, then began to stride toward the oaks. *Go quickly and get it done with.*

I was a mere three or four strides from the two oaks when I heard a cracking sound behind me. I spun around, looking about with a lump in my throat. Rialban of the Fell might have been friendly, but there were others who might not treat a trespasser so kindly, especially one this close to the border.

The sound of footsteps came from straight ahead of me, light and sure, followed by the swoosh of branches being pushed aside with great force. Whoever it was wasn't trying very hard to proceed quietly. Damn my luck. Not only was I wearing the clothes I'd had on when I'd run away from the Alterworld, I was standing in the middle of fey territory, alone and unprotected but for the dagger strapped around my calf.

I reached down and pulled out my knife, which, even though I was leaving, I couldn't quite give up, and pointed it in the direction the sounds were coming from. I should have moved quicker, I realized too late, and put distance between myself and the border. At the very least this would have extinguished the orbs, allowing me to hide in the darkness. But I was stuck now. I could already see the nearest branches moving. My predator was only feet away from where I stood, my dagger at the ready.

Like an actor pushing through the curtains on a stage, a large form emerged from behind the feathery branches of two cedars, and advanced on me with stately grace. My eyes widened in surprise. "Rialban?"

The centaur stepped forward and the orbs bobbed a little in his presence, as though bowing to him. He made a formidable figure, his human torso rising up from his powerful horse body like a phoenix from the fire. In the shadows cast by the orbs, his powerful muscles and shorn head looked as though carved from marble.

"I have come to see you home, Mistress Gragan," he announced in his thick Scottish accent.

"You're escorting me to the Alterworld?" I asked in disbelief.

His eyelids flickered. "Do you consider that vile place home?"

Vile place? Interesting slip. "It's where I must go."

"I'd never guess you to be one to run from your responsibility."

I frowned, sensing where this was going. "And what responsibility is that?"

"Your duty is to break the curse that has buried us beneath its evil weight for far too long. It is not only your duty, but should be your desire, as well. For how could you wish this blight to continue to ravage this world that you hold so dear?"

My fingers tightened around my dagger. Not for the first time I wished I could tell the truth about who had laid the curse on the village a hundred years ago, and it hadn't been my great-grandmother, Elowina Gragan, as everyone thought, but Lady Faylan, our oh-so-respectable overseer.

But I'd thought it over, and had reluctantly decided that I couldn't tell the truth. One, because it would harm Juletta, Lady Faylan's sister, and she'd had a hard enough time of it as a Desolate. And two, as much as it hurt me to admit it, Hawthorn Lane needed Lady Faylan. She knew her job and she did it very well. She protected us from intruders and fey-hunters, plus she had yet to teach her knowledge to anyone else—job security at its best—so we needed her to keep working.

It was a conclusion I hadn't liked coming to.

"You don't understand, Rialban. I have to go. I have business in the Alterworld I must attend to."

"Count Van der Daarke wants you to stay."

From what I'd learned through reading a tome on fey, written by our resident sage elf, Professor Ballylee, one quality of the centaurs had always stood out to me…they were an independent and proud sort who bowed to no one. "What do Count Van der Daarke's wishes have to do with you, Rialban?"

"They have everything to do with me."

"Are you saying he's your master?"

The centaur drew himself up to his full height of eight feet. "No one commands Rialban of the Fell, and it would be in your best interests to remember that, Mistress Gragan."

"No, no. Of course not," I soothed, tucking away that bit of information. "But I can't see why his opinion should matter to you when you are your own master."

"We've come to an understanding."

An understanding? How? When? *Why?* "While I respect that, know that Kyran Van der Daarke and I have no such understanding, so I have no need to do as he says. I'm leaving."

"You are no longer your own liege, Mistress Gragan. Not until the curse is removed. You possess the power to make things right, and the sooner done, the sooner you can take care of your other business."

"You don't understand. My other business isn't some silly fancy I'm pursuing. It involves a promise, one that I need to hold to or be forever in its debt. I'm sorry, Rialban, but I must go."

"I'm sorry, too, Lorelle." He gave me a slight bow.

Stupidly thinking he was acceding, I turned around and stepped forward. But before my next foot could touch the earth, Rialban was upon me. Luckily I heard him coming and at the last second I leapt to the side, narrowly avoiding his reaching hands.

"Stay back!" I wielded my blade and it flashed dully in the greenish glow of the orbs.

Looking down at me, he chuckled. "Silly lass. You think that tiny blade can take down someone of my size and strength?"

"I don't have to take you down, I merely have to hamstring you."

A barely discernible eyebrow rose in appreciation. "That would be effective. And how do you propose reaching one of my legs?"

"Through sheer determination."

He threw back his head and laughed, and I took his distraction as a sign from the heavens to make my move. Having once been caught in a bar fight at *Puck's Pub*, which I might have accidentally-on-purpose started, I'd learned the beauty of the tuck and roll, which I put into action now, launching myself into a diving somersault.

I was underneath Rialban now and what I saw gave me pause. Let's just say the centaur—not to put too fine a point on it—was hung like a horse. It was a bit distracting. But then Rialban reared up, exposing me and I quickly rolled back out. I wasn't really going to hamstring him; I simply wanted to divert him long enough to get myself across the border. As long as he didn't follow me, I'd be home free.

Jumping to my feet I pointed my dagger at him, then slowly began to back up. "Leave me be, Rialban, or I'll turn you into a gelding."

If I'd impressed him with my hamstring plan, I'd put the fear of Lorelle in him with my threat of castration. "So you're willing to fight dirty, Mistress?"

"Let's just say I'm willing to strike a low blow."

"As am I." Before I could react, he swung his rump around and whipped me with his braided tail. I staggered back, giving him the opportunity to seize hold of me and lift me onto his broad back. He swung around and took off so fast I could only wrap my arms around his muscular torso and hang on for dear life. Glimpsing back, I watched as the orbs blinked out, one after the other, extinguishing like my hopes.

With each stride taking me away from the border, my anger grew. I was furious at being manhandled in such a demeaning way, furious that I was being dictated to by the likes of Kyran Van der Daarke. Before leaving, I had thought I might miss him most of all, but I'd been deluding myself. He didn't care for me. He was setting himself up as Lord of Hawthorn Lane, and if he managed to end the curse on this place, he'd be hailed as king of my adopted home until his dying day.

The bastard had pulled the wool over my eyes more skillfully than a hangman.

By the time we reached my cottage I was ready to scream out my frustrations loud enough for the entire village to hear, or at least take out my fury on Rialban's sweaty torso by pummeling him with my fists. Or better yet, my dagger.

But when he came to a halt outside my home I only slid to the ground in silence.

"Do not attempt to leave again, Mistress Gragan," he ordered as I opened the gate.

I turned back. "I won't forget this, Rialban."

"See that you don't."

My words had been meant as a threat, but he'd purposely taken them the wrong way, turning their meaning back on me. "I didn't mean it that way," I tried again.

"This I know."

"Oh, go away."

"It's been a pleasure, Mistress. Until we meet again." With a chuckle and a mocking salute, he turned and galloped away.

I watched him go, a roiling rage growing inside me. How had Kyran done it? How had he convinced this daunting centaur to be his lackey? However he'd done it, he'd moved awfully quickly, using his position as Count to make the fey here his own. I didn't like how he'd already insinuated himself into the village, making numerous connections as easily as a spider weaving its labyrinthine web. Within a fortnight Kyran had become a part of Hawthorn Lane in a way I hadn't managed to achieve in all my six years. Oh, how I envied him, and my jealousy felt like a ravenous snake eating its way through my core.

Fine. So be it. Lady Faylan could have the man, and be welcome to him.

When I re-entered my cottage, still warm from the fire I had let die down to coals, I refused to admit that the sense of relief washing over me was so very welcome. I also would not acknowledge how good it felt to change out of my human clothes and back into my fairy tale nightgown, old and worn, yet more beautiful than anything I'd ever owned in the Alterworld.

So here I was…back where I'd started. I hadn't wanted to leave and Kyran had given me the best excuse not to go. He wouldn't let me.

I both hated him and wanted to ravish him with my gratitude.

Damn the man.

Chapter Two

Kyran arrived the next morning, bright and early, and when I didn't answer his knock, a few moments of suspenseful silence hung in the air like errant mist. I thought he would leave, as he usually did when I didn't answer, until an ear shattering blast sent me flying to the floor for cover.

When I peeked between the balusters of my loft's railing, I saw that one large pane of glass in the conservatory no longer existed. Knocking a few shards out of the way with his elbow, then pushing aside the fern fronds blocking his way, Kyran stepped through the opening as nonchalantly as though entering through my front door. He was a big man, nearly a foot taller than me—and I wasn't exactly tiny—and typically serious looking, as though the weight of the world had settled on his broad shoulders. His dark hair and dark eyes lent to his gravity, and there were times I thought him a cross between Heathcliff's brooding, passionate disposition and Darcy's stiff and respectable one.

Grim help me, if that was the case.

"What are you doing?" I cried from my perch.

"Your door appears to be broken," he answered, wiping bits of glittering glass off his black woolen cloak. Although he was American, he'd been raised in English boarding schools and spoke with a British accent, which I admit I found rather delicious.

"It's not broken!"

"Then why has it not opened for me once in an entire week?"

I pointed to the bar my next-door neighbor, Doolin Fiersen, had installed for me after he'd fixed the cottage foundation. "Because of that."

"And who ordered it put in place?"

"I did."

"That sounds broken to me."

"You're paying for this, you know. I don't have extra Goldenars to be throwing around cleaning up after one of your temper tantrums."

That sent his pompous attitude scurrying. "I am *not* having a temper tantrum."

"You broke my glass pane because you weren't getting your way. That constitutes a temper tantrum."

"I broke your glass pane because you're the one behaving like a child, hiding from me for an entire week."

He might have a point there. "Where did you learn to do that sort of magic?" I asked, wisely moving on.

He didn't look triumphant, which is what I'd expect after such an impressive show, only deadly serious, his hands in fists, his chest rising and falling as though he'd been running. I was starting to think that this was Kyran's way of keeping a lid on the simmering pot that was his temper. "Avice has been helping me this week. After the ball I decided to take her up on her offer."

"I see." I did see. What I had feared had come to pass. Avice Montrose, my mage friend and a seductress of all, had won him over. But why did I care? I had no claims on him. Didn't want to have any. He was a social climber, an ambitious politician willing to step on people to scramble his way up the ladder, and besides that, I was leaving.

So there.

"I'll clean it up."

"You're damn right you will."

"And then we need to talk."

"I have nothing to say to you."

"Well, I've plenty to say to you." He turned and focused his attention on where the pane used to be. With a wave of his hand, the air took on a shimmering quality, then the glass flew into the air and backward, reforming the pane like a movie in reverse. The feat was quite remarkable, and I was impressed with Kyran's skill. I'd been under the impression that he wasn't all that good at magic, an impression *he'd* given me. "You were running away from me," he said when the pane was whole once more. His back remained facing me, his shoulders stiff and slightly hunched.

"I wasn't running away from you," I yelled down at him. "You know nothing about it."

"I know you were up to something."

"But not why, and you aren't going to know why. It's none of your business."

"Ridding the village of this curse is my business...it's been *made* my business...and I can't do it without you."

So I'd been right. He was only pretending to want to be with me to show the villagers what a big, powerful deal he was. Even so, I knew I should tell him about Dallen and what I had to do—it would simplify things. How could he argue against such an unselfish act on my part? But his manner was so damn imperious right now that I didn't want to tell him anything.

I resorted to being annoying. "I can't marry you."

"I told you, Lorelle. We'll deal with that issue when the time comes."

"No, we won't deal with it when the time comes, because it's not going to happen. There's an impediment." My dramatic statement made me sound like a character out of a Jane Austen novel, but I didn't care. Unfair as it was to Dallen, that's what he was to me now. An impediment.

Kyran swung around, his dark eyes flying up to find mine. "What do you mean there's an impediment? I was told you were not attached to anyone here."

"Who told you—?" I broke off. Royalton, of course. That big-mouthed faerie was going to be hearing from me soon. He worked at *Fawn's Fashions* and loved to gossip. "I'm not attached to anyone. Not here." I stopped. I'd meant to stay silent about my intentions, and here I was about to give away the whole damn farm, along with all the cows and chickens, too.

Kyran strode toward the ladder to my loft and was up it in a flash. I turned and raced to my bed, tucked into a nook built in the wall, and jumped inside, thinking he wouldn't dare follow. Crouched on my hands and knees, I watched him warily as he stopped near the top of the ladder and looked around, his eyes touching on everything as though recording the scene to play back at a later time.

His gaze took in my old dressmaker's dummy, complete with the ghoulish head I'd fashioned for it, which I used to hang my clothes on for the next day. At the moment Twiggy Squared wore my French muslin gown, and with surprising panache, I might add. Kyran's eyes moved on to an old wardrobe, so big and heavy it would likely never see the outside world again. I had a hard time imagining how someone had got it up here in the first place, though magic had probably played a big part. A French-style vanity table was home to my few bits of jewelry, a silver hairbrush, and a spritzer bottle of my favorite perfume, a homemade mixture of rose and patchouli. Attached to the table's back was a dark mirror. An assortment of leering faces encircled its frame, and their disapproving countenances humbled me every time I viewed my reflection. Paintings of all shapes, sizes, and subjects, ranging from shadowy landscapes to Rubenesque portraits of female beauties to Dali-like macabres, colored the dark walls. Some might find the artwork a bit off-putting, but I found it welcoming, especially when viewed in the warm, flickering light from my candle.

And then there was my bed. Tucked, cave-like, into the wall, and filled with a soft down mattress covered by thick, colorful quilts and numerous pillows, it was a cozy little nook. Two carved figures, a man and a woman reaching out to each other, stood on either side of the opening, destined never to meet up. Come to think of it, it was a terrible thing to have flanking the entry to my bed. But in my case, sadly ironic.

"Don't come up here," I warned. "You'll hit your head."

He glanced up at the loft's low, slanted ceiling. I could walk around easily enough, but he had an extra foot on him that would put half his head through the roof.

"Who is the impediment?" he demanded.

"I told you…this is not your business."

"I'm making it my business." He climbed up the rest of the ladder, and keeping to his hands and knees, crawled toward my bed. What should have looked awkward at best—this great hulk of a man on all fours—instead came across as predatory, like a panther stalking its victim.

I clutched a pillow to my chest, remembering his kiss at our last meeting, its intensity and heat, and how easily it would be to submit to it, body and soul. "Stay where you are. You've no right to be up here, and you had no right stopping me from leaving Hawthorn Lane."

He paused in his steady movement toward me. "So you really were going to go away?"

"Don't play the innocent with me, Kyran. It doesn't suit you."

"I've no idea what you're talking about."

"You sent your new best friend after me. Does that jog your memory?"

"I wasn't aware I had friends here. Other than you."

His words, entirely unexpected, made the insides of my nose tingle. He thought of me as a friend? "Oh. Well, you know…Rialban."

"Ah, yes. Rialban of the Fell. We've spoken. I like him."

"Well, he certainly likes you. What did you tell him about me?"

"I told him nothing, Lorelle. I don't discuss you with other people. I merely get them to discuss you with me."

Of all the nerve! He was stealing my tricks from me. "He said you wouldn't want me to leave Hawthorn Lane, so he was making sure you got your wish."

"He's right, but I didn't ask him to do that. On the contrary, I would've gone after you myself if I'd known what you were attempting to do."

Well, then…I kind of wished he had known. Wouldn't that have made for an interesting chase?

"If you didn't know I was leaving Hawthorn Lane, then why did you think I was running away?"

"I felt your essence moving away from me, like a string tugging at my heart." He touched his chest, his expression bemused. "The sensation woke me up, so I knew this wasn't simply you doing your gathering thing. Something was different this time. I was about to pull on my boots and go after you, to try to talk you out of whatever it was you were planning to do, when I sensed you coming back. The tugging stopped and the pain went away."

Pain? "Didn't you wonder why I changed my mind?"

"I did. But now I see you didn't return of your own volition." His expression was nettled, as though he didn't like that I was forced, which was a point in his favor.

"I do have to go, Kyran. Damn the curse, and damn Rialban, I'm leaving."

Kyran began crawling toward me again and soon was at the entrance to my bed. I pushed myself back into a corner. I wasn't afraid of him, I was afraid of what I wanted him to do. It had been a long time since I'd been with a man, and my hormones were all screwed up, making me do things and think thoughts I might otherwise have avoided. His hand reached out and grabbed hold of a corner of quilt sticking out, and the gesture was as intimate as if he'd laid a hand on my breast. He began to pull, dragging me toward him.

"I'm asking you not to go."

I dug my heels into the mattress, but it didn't help. "You don't understand," I ground out as I moved steadily toward him.

"Then explain it to me, and use small words so I can understand why you're doing this to me." We were now inches from each other and electricity crackled in the air between us. I found to my annoyance that I'd missed the strange phenomenon that happened whenever we were near each other, which I'm afraid might say something damning about my state of mind.

"If I explain my reasons for wanting to leave," I answered, "then you really won't let me go." It was true. If he knew I was going back to Dallen, then I wouldn't be able to help him break the curse. For some inane reason, he was fixated on me being the one to do it with him when I felt sure so many others, more willing than myself, could take my place. Maybe it's because I'm an Omni-Fey, and would one day make a powerful ally.

He released the quilt and leaned close to me, his dark eyes boring into mine. My heartbeat pounded all the way up into my head and I found it hard to catch my breath. "You can't leave me here alone."

"Alone?" I scoffed, fighting against his allure, his magnetism. "Hardly. There are plenty of girls eager to fill my shoes. Girls who fit the requirements of the curse." Girls who had much more to offer than I did.

"No one can fill your shoes, Lorelle."

"Oh, please. I'm not Cinderella."

"No, you're not." He pushed away from me, taking with him the electric pulses. "All right. Then give me a week."

I peered at him suspiciously. "What are you talking about now?"

"Give me one week, and then you can go."

I narrowed my eyes. "You won't be able to change my mind, you know."

"Melaina has moved into the castle."

I blinked. This conversation was hopping around like a kangaroo on crack. "I'm not surprised. I can't see her leaving until the curse has been removed."

"She and Renwick are always fighting. I had to get out. That's a big reason why I joined Ilia in her magic studies. I couldn't bear to listen to them going at each other for another minute."

"You don't go alone?" Which meant no hanky-panky with Avice. A thrill, like a tiny ballerina, pirouetted through me.

"Ilia and I serve as protection for each other. Avice can be a bit, um, demanding."

Protection for each other. I liked the sound of that more than I should, but the rest of what he was saying, other than that Avice could be demanding, made no sense. "So your sister and cousin are fighting and you had to get out of the house. What does this have to do with my leaving Hawthorn Lane?"

"Please…just say yes. And in one week, if you still want to leave, I won't stop you."

"What about Rialban?"

"I'll make sure no one stops you."

I regarded him warily. "If I were to stay—and I'm not saying I will— what do you plan on doing?"

A small smile played about his lips. "I won't be doing anything to you…unless you want me to."

I decided not to respond to that. He was very good at playing me at my own game—distracting me from the original topic. But now it was my turn. "I suppose all that fighting between Renwick and Melaina reminds you of your parents."

He sighed and rubbed a tired hand over his face. His jaw was shadowed, but smooth; not even the stress of his sister could keep him from maintaining his high-born image. "My sister is a very angry woman, and she takes that anger out on anyone within striking distance. I've done my best to make sure Ilia doesn't get hit in the crossfire, but our meals together are trying. It's like Melaina brings a sword to dinner, and we don't even have shields to protect ourselves. Renwick slips out whenever he can, coming home late and very drunk. I can't say I blame him, but I'm envious of his ability to come and go as he pleases."

I snorted. "And you can't come and go as you please, *Count* Van der Daarke?"

"If Melaina can't go after Renwick or Ilia or me, who do you think she'll go after?"

My first thought was an associate of mine, and Kyran's new employee. "Josepha, I suppose."

"She holds his being a wood elf against him." It surprised me that Kyran had noticed, though not that Melaina had already learned the hierarchy of Hawthorn Lane. Poor Josepha. He'd worked so hard to move up the ladder, and getting a job at the castle had been a big step up for him. Yet he still got treated like dirt. "He's quite adept at staying out of her way, which isn't easy being how much he does for me. But Melaina and Sinead have had more than one run-in."

"I hope Sinead gave her what for." Sinead Fiersen, who was working along with her sister Gemma and brother Conor up at Castle Daarke, was the eldest daughter of my next-door neighbors, the Fiersens, and not someone to be trifled with. "That girl could hold a grudge and beat you over the head with it, all without breaking a sweat."

"And then some," he replied with a small smile, "but I'm afraid Melaina will go too far one of these days."

"You could ask her to leave. You are the heir, not her."

"And risk having her blow up the castle on her way out?"

I'd only interacted with Melaina once, but that sounded exactly like something she would do. "All right," I gave in, feeling again that delicious surge of relief. "I'll stay. For one week."

"And you can't tell me why you must go?" he tried again. While I liked his tenacity, it had a way of weakening me, and I needed to resist. Though I had a sneaking suspicion that my continued resistance had less to do with being noble, and more to do with wanting to defy Kyran. Simply put, I didn't like being bossed.

"It has to do with my past. That's all I can say."

He gave a brief nod. "Then I won't push it."

"No one here knows what it is," I persisted, "so don't bother snooping around."

He gave me a serious look. "I won't."

"Good." I paused, wondering why he was giving in so easily. "Well, then I guess I'll see you in a week to say my goodbyes."

"In a week? I don't think so. I'm taking you out to dinner tonight."

"No, you're not!"

"It's at *Chez Chantilly*."

My stomach rumbled. "It is?"

"I'll pick you up at seven."

"No…I'll meet you there."

"Be ready for me here at seven."

He was back down the ladder and out the door before I could curse the bloody aristo out for routing me as easily as though I were a child.

Chapter Three

What is Kyran Van der Daarke up to? I wondered as I pulled on my wellies and went out to feed the chickens and gather eggs. I was strangely glad to see the tough little buggers, though they greeted me as always, with pecks at my boots and clucks of annoyance that I hadn't come sooner. The scent of lilac drifted through the air and I breathed in deeply, taking in the kelpish odor of the nearby brook, the warming black soil of my garden, the sweet apple and peach blossoms. After a long, hard winter, spring was here at last.

Feeling lighter than I should, knowing I'd been granted only a temporary reprieve, I began to hum an old Gaelic song I'd picked up from Missy Thornback, who liked to sing as she prepared herbs for the potions she'd taught me to make. Her voice matched her dried and wizened appearance, though I found I liked it that way. Even so, I hoped my voice was a bit more pleasing as I launched into the words that told the story of a woman forced to leave the land she loved to marry a wealthy man far from home. It seemed appropriate for my situation, other than that Dallen wasn't wealthy. The chickens didn't try to attack me, so I thought maybe I sounded all right. Of course, judging by how they ignored me when I called to shut them up at night, they could all very well be deaf.

The clapping came as the last word faded away. "That was lovely, Lorelle."

I spun about. "That's Miss Gragan to you."

Renwick laughed. "I think we're past that, don't you?"

I was glad for the robe I'd donned to ward off the cool air of this early May morning. Renwick Van der Daarke, cousin to Kyran and Ilia, was too much of a rogue to be allowed to see me in my nightgown, nearly transparent it was so threadbare.

"What are you doing here?"

His jovial smile cut and run, soon replaced by a familiar forlorn expression that I knew presaged a request. "I need a place to stay." He indicated with a shiny black cane, which he didn't actually need, the worn, brown leather bag at his feet. Renwick was quite the fashion plate, and today he wore a jaunty outfit of heather gray spats and matching bowler cap, and a dark green overcoat over a pale green vest. He was growing out his beard, which gave him a rakish, almost satyric look. I liked it, although it made him look older, and I wondered just how old he actually was. He looked to be around my age, which was twenty-four. Yet I'd always thought of him as way too old for Ilia, who's a young eighteen. In turn, I thought of him as way too young for Melaina at thirty-six. If I had to guess I'd say he was the type of person who adapted to whatever age he felt worked best for him at the time. Which fit with how Lady Faylan had once described him…as very adept at blending in.

I threw the rest of the feed out to the chickens, took my time filling their water bowls, then marched past Renwick, a basket of still-warm eggs in one hand. I'd learned that with sweet talkers, it was essential not to give in to their charm, or at least hold out against it for as long as you could.

He picked up his bag and hurried after me. When we reached the cottage entrance, he paused. "May I come in?"

"Wipe your feet first."

He used the fanged boot scraper to clean off the soles of his black leather boots, and I went inside. I set the eggs on the table, then built up the fire to take the edge off the cold that had settled into the cottage overnight. I could tell from the hesitant shuffle of Renwick's steps when he came inside that he wasn't nearly so sure of himself as he liked to present, which made him a touch more appealing in my eyes. In the short time I'd known him, I'd come to realize there were two sides to Renwick Van der Daarke—the charming, self-assured man, and the uncertain boy I was seeing now.

"Sit at the table," I told him.

He had left his bag by the door, so he pulled out a chair and sat down, upright and stiff. "I had to get away," he said after a moment's silence.

"Are you hungry?"

His forehead wrinkled in thought. "I am, rather. It's a bit of a hike down the mountain."

"Tell me what happened," I prompted him, as I began to prepare a hearty breakfast for the both of us. I had a feeling it was going to be a long day, and I was going to need the sustenance.

He heaved a forlorn sigh I'm sure was meant to encourage my sympathy, though it only served to make me want to burn his rashers. "Melaina and I can't stop fighting. It's always been bad, but we'd always make up afterward, and that was great." He grinned, his shoulders slowly relaxing. "But now we don't even have that."

"How awful for you."

"No need to be sarcastic," he rejoined, sounding hurt.

I brandished my spatula at him. "Do you think you're the only one around here with problems, Renwick?"

"Of course not. But at least you have your own place. You don't have the shadow of a family name hanging over you."

Oh, yes, I did.

"Oh, boo-hoo. You have a family name that means something around here, a castle to live in, and plenty of culinary delights to eat. What's the problem?"

He banged a fist on the table, making the silverware I'd just set jump like grasshoppers. "I don't have my freedom, Lorelle. That's the problem!"

"Then earn it."

"How?"

"You're high-born, Renwick. That gives you a leg up on most people, and you should be able to use that to your advantage."

"You're high-born, too."

Ah, yes. I'd been trying to forget that. Having always thought I was one of the lessers, the idea of being an uppity-up was taking some getting used to. "It's not the same. I never knew about my ancestry, so I couldn't ever use it to my advantage, and I certainly never lived like gentry. Being high-born didn't get me this place. Hard work did."

"Yes, well, I always knew I was high-born and it didn't help me one bit. Throughout my entire childhood I was made well aware of how we weren't high-born enough." His lips twisted into a grim smile. "Isn't it funny that the current Van der Damns—as my grandpa liked to call them—never knew about my side of the family? Yet we always knew about them. I've grown up hating them, Lorelle." He stuck out his bearded chin defiantly. "I admit it. But then Melaina found me, and well, I didn't hate her. Not at first."

I set a plate in front of him, the fresh eggs were perfectly sunny, the rashers crisp (and not burnt), and the warmed toasted mulled wine muffins I hadn't been able to make myself throw out because, of course, I hadn't wanted to leave, smelled delicious.

"This looks amazing!" Renwick threw me a glance of admiration.

"Oh, it's just a little something I threw together." I admit I was showing off a bit, but an audience is an audience, and I was not immune to attention from a man with golden-brown eyes and matching golden-brown curls that would make a woman squeal with envy as she spiraled a lock around and around her finger. Not that I thought about doing that, or anything. I joined him at the table and we both tucked in. "So you hate Melaina now?" I picked up where he'd left off.

"Hate might be too strong a word, but I have disliked her for some time now."

"How long?"

"Since coming here to Hawthorn Lane. Since I first saw you."

I pointed my egg-laden fork at him, determined not to let his implied flattery go to my head. "You know, it's kind of creepy that you spied on me. I suppose you peeked through the conservatory windows." I didn't like it that someone had been watching me and I hadn't known it. It made me feel vulnerable, as though he'd read my diary, or my mind.

He laughed, stretching out his legs. "Like I could see anything through that jungle. Rest assured I could only see bits of you, like a ghost passing by. I envied you your little place here." He glanced around, his eyes appreciative. "It's not very big, but it's yours."

"Not entirely," I said, relaxing a bit. He'd been more interested in observing my cottage than me, which was a bit vexing when I thought about it. "I still owe on it." And once I left I'd be defaulting on my loan, meaning Lady Faylan would get my cottage back. I didn't like that at all, but could see no alternative beyond finding a buyer, which I didn't think would be possible in a week's time.

"It's far more than I've ever had for myself."

"Well, you're not moving in with me, if that's what you're angling for. The last thing I need is to give Melaina more ammunition to use against me."

He smiled. "Well, it was worth a try." He took a sip of spiced lemon-lime fizz. "Actually, I thought you might know someone I could stay with."

"Have you ever heard of a thing called *getting a job*?" Really, what was with these high-borns always looking for a handout?

He jerked upright, his elegant features sharpening with anger. "I've been working since I was eight years old. I started with a newspaper route and then moved into the food service industry. I don't have any ready cash, and it would only be until I can pay my own way. Whoever I stayed with, I'd work off my debt or pay them back. I don't want *charity*."

I held up a conciliatory hand, somewhat chagrined by my erroneous judgment. "Okay, okay! Sorry. You just don't strike me as the working type."

He preened in a half-mocking way. "It's a carefully cultivated image I like to project."

"The idle rich man?"

His smile was lazy. "Exactly."

"You do it well."

"Thank you." His smile turned into something more than friendly, and it made me a little uncomfortable, even though I was quite aware the smile was just a part of how Renwick functioned, coming as naturally to him as breathing.

"I know someone who could use a hand around the house in exchange for room and board."

He reached over and grabbed my hands, his eyes lighting up like a child's. "You're a lifesaver, Lorelle! I knew I could count on you."

I enjoyed the moment for as long as I dared before pulling my hands free. "You can thank me if it works out." I pushed back my chair. "You wash the dishes while I get ready for the day, and then we'll go."

He stood and saluted. "Yes, Madame."

"That's Mademoiselle to you."

He laughed and began to clear the table, looking rather more at home than I'd have thought he would. While he worked, I went to clean up and dress, donning a serviceable cambric dress of deep blue and pale rose, and my best walking boots—it was a two-mile trek across the moors—and then I strapped on my dagger, a habit I wasn't sure I could ever break. My long, black hair pulled up into a bun and dove gray gloves donned, I was ready to go.

When I descended the ladder, I found Renwick in the conservatory, studying my deadly cactus with raised eyebrows. "Ready?" He nodded and headed toward me. Picking up his bag at the door, I handed it to him. It was light, but then, I suppose he truly didn't have much in this world to call his own. "Come on, then." I grabbed my hat and donned it, shoving a deadly skull-head hatpin through it and my bun, then put on the rucksack I'd packed earlier and pulled the straps tight for the journey.

I locked the door and we headed out. The sun had risen, bright and strong, and I was glad for the wide-brimmed hat to shade my pale skin and sea-blue eyes. The hat was also useful protection against the wind that swept across the moors. My favorite time to visit the heath was late summer when a carpet of heather bloomed into an impressionist painting.

Sadly, I'd yet to catch sight of the infamous Moor Riders, though I remained ever hopeful. Ever since I'd seen Fitzwilliam Darcy, played by the lovely Colin Firth, riding his mighty steed in *Pride and Prejudice*, I'd had a thing for a man on a horse, especially when he's galloping at great speeds across a wide-open stretch of land. The Moor Riders, a band of ethereal creatures on horseback, are as elusive as ghosts, maybe because they tend to ride only during violent storms. Little else is known about them, but I imagine they make a most impressive sight astride their black horses, silhouetted against a dark sky, capes flapping and the sound of pounding hooves loud as thunder claps.

After scanning the open heath, I checked the skies for messenger birds, but no ravens or falcons dotted the blue expanse. Either I had become old news, or something bigger was brewing in the village. I wasn't sure what to make of either case. I was relieved to no longer be the subject of gossip, but I didn't like not knowing what that 'something bigger' might be. I wondered if it had anything to do with Kyran and his wish to keep me around for another week. I felt sure he was up to something that involved me, and I didn't like being in the dark about it.

A sort of beaten down path cut across the moor, which made walking easier, and as we trekked along it, I told Renwick about Missy Thornback, the witch I hoped would take him in. She had retired some time ago, leaving me to take on the task of brewing, and now lived in a tree house, of all things, in Wuthering Wood. I realized as I spoke that I was looking forward to seeing her. With all that had been going on it had been a while since my last visit, and I felt guilty that I'd planned to slip away without even saying goodbye. Now I could.

"Matron can be a bit cantankerous, but she's basically harmless," I ended my description of the old witch with a white lie.

"Do you like her?"

I peered at Renwick sideways, noting his keen attention. "I do. But I admit she took a bit of getting used to at first. She'll keep you hopping, I can tell you that much." She'd do more than that, but I felt it would be a good penance for what he'd done to Ilia and Kyran, pretending to want to marry one and making the other think someone was out to kill him. Renwick Van der Daarke had been a naughty, naughty boy and needed to be on the receiving end of a bit of punishment to make amends.

"Keep me hopping?"

"Oh, yes. She's very old, you know how that can be, and she's a witch, but you might be able to learn some things from her."

"Oh?" He perked up. "What sort of things?"

"Magical things, of course."

"Ah, yes. About that, Lorelle. I've been feeling different these past several days. About a week ago a strange sort of energy started growing inside me, and now it sits in my chest"—he pressed his fist to his heart—"and kind of pushes, as though it's trying to come out."

A tingling sensation spread through me. "You're saying you feel more powerful?"

He nodded, squinting up at the sun. "I never felt much of anything growing up, but when I met Melaina and learned what we actually are, I started to feel something spark in me. While my grandfather loved to complain about the uppity Van der Damns, the old git never once let on that we were fey. Like it was some kind of secret." He kicked at a tuft of grass. "But this past week, well, it's like I've got a current running through me. And I can do things. Simple things, but never anything I could do before. Like this." He waved his hand at a patch of heather and it suddenly began to grow, rapidly lengthening into vines that covered my foot and started up my leg.

"Renwick!" I cried, when the vine was about to enter forbidden territory.

He gave me a mischievous smile, then waved his hand and the heather retreated, soon returning to its normal size. I stared at him, feeling a little unnerved, and a little excited, too, though the excitement might have been from nearly getting felt up by a plant, which, come to think of it, is pretty pathetic.

The unnerved feeling had to do with a pattern I was beginning to see lately…Kyran's little magic show this morning, Renwick's ability to grow horny plants, the sparks I could now shoot from my fingers like sparklers on the fourth of July.

Something was going on here.

His eyes went from the heather to mine. "You see?"

I grabbed his arm. "I do see, Renwick, and now I'm going to give you some advice, free of charge. Keep what you can do to yourself. Don't flaunt it, and never use it on anyone here…not that they can trace back to you anyway. The fey here are very touchy about their magic, about magic in general."

Maybe that was because none of the villagers were very powerful. But once Melaina and Lady Faylan had revealed the existence of the curse and what it had done to them all, Hawthornites began to claim that it must have blunted their magical abilities, as well. And maybe they were right.

Now the opposite seemed to be happening. Magic was returning to Hawthorn Lane, and as much as I wanted to believe this was a good thing, I couldn't quite manage it. It felt like handing a bomb to a group of children and leaving them to figure out what to do next.

And I think we all know how that will end.

Chapter Four

I'm not sure Renwick took in even a bit of my advice, staring at his fingers in wonder and murmuring, "That's the best I've ever done. Maybe it's you, Lorelle. Maybe you're good luck."

"I'm not good luck, you dolt." Off to my right I spotted Atermorte Cemetery rising up like a lost city in the desert. "There's one of my favorite haunts," I said to change the subject to one less dangerous.

He peered across the way. "A cemetery?"

"It's really more like a small city. I'd stay away from it if I were you," I warned. "The caretaker, Cutter Flint, is a bit odd, and someone as pretty as you would set his teeth on edge."

Renwick laughed. "Pretty as me? Why, coming from you, does that not sound like a compliment?"

"There's such a thing as being too pretty, Van der Daarke."

"Then this Cutter Flint must hate you."

I cocked an eyebrow at him. "Oh, he does." But certainly not for my looks. If I were that terribly gorgeous I'd be fighting off my admirers with a broomstick. But no, the only workout my broom got involved sweeping the floor.

"Lorelle Gragan, I swear you grow more paradoxical by the day."

I gave a little bow. "Thank you."

"That wasn't a compliment."

"It was to me, pretty boy!" I picked up my skirts and started to run. "Come on!"

We ran for about a mile, until Renwick begged for a rest, and I reluctantly slowed to a walk. I loved running, but especially on the moors when the wind bellowed and blew against me like a live creature. There was a wondrous power to the elements, and knowing what I did about my fey now, I felt a connection to the world around me even greater than before. It was heady stuff, and I wondered how far I could take my new powers.

The woods were close now and Renwick, though out of breath from our run, was obviously in awe at the sight before him, his eyes as wide as his gaping mouth. I had always felt strange visiting the wood, sensing the fey who lived here somehow knew I wasn't one of them. But I realized with a rush of relief that I could now come and go anywhere in Hawthorn Lane and not have to worry about getting found out. Not that it mattered anymore since I'd be leaving soon, but still...I no longer had to feel afraid or somehow *less than*, and that to me was worth its weight in Goldenars.

Wuthering Wood reminds me of a fairy tale forest, like those found only in books. The wide, solid trees stretch so high you'd swear they could catch a comet in their branches. Some of the residents live on the ground, but most live up in the trees. Missy Thornback is one of the tree-dwellers. She's a witch and can fly—a good thing being that she's as old as dirt and climbing a ladder can be a bit of a challenge. I'd always chosen to climb, of course, giving the excuse that I liked the challenge of it. Though sometimes I took the lift, especially on the days I brought goods for Matron. Maybe one day I'd be able to fly up to the little tree house on my own. That would be a good day.

Stepping from the open moors into the dark wood has always been a bit intimidating, but even now, when I no longer had to worry about being found out, I felt a shiver of anticipation. A reverent sense clings to the place, much like you'd find while sitting alone in an ancient cathedral. Renwick seemed to feel the same way, growing quiet the moment we entered the cool realm. On my previous forays to the Wood, I'd always noticed a low-pitched humming noise pulsating throughout the place, and today was no exception. When I'd mentioned the strange sound to Missy Thornback, she'd given a resigned sigh. "It be how the Woods talk to each other. At first the burble drove me round the bend, up the wall, and over the other side. But I've grown used to it, though maybe I shouldn't have."

"It's this way," I gestured to Renwick, and led him down a path that meandered amongst the massive tree trunks like a serpent. Nothing in this place was straightforward, not even the trails. It didn't help that I felt watching eyes on us as we walked along, but I couldn't see anyone.

After about a quarter mile, I stopped. In front of us, high in the trees, stretched a virtual metropolis of houses, connected to the trunks and limbs not by iron spikes but by an ingenious webbing of ropes and planks.

"This is where you want me to stay?" Renwick wondered aloud as he stared up at the houses fifty-plus feet in the air.

"I hope you like heights."

"I don't like falling."

"Then you'd better watch where you put your feet."

He squinted. "I guess being up there would make it harder for Melaina to find me."

"That it would. Of course, there's always the cemetery and Cutter."

"I think I'll take my chances here."

"First things first. We'll have to get Matron to agree to take you on."

He stroked his bearded chin. "Not a problem. She won't be able to resist my charm."

I laughed. "We'll see about that."

I headed toward Missy's tree house, set near the front of the neighborhood. All the houses were shaped like mushrooms, though I'm not sure why. It's not like anyone would mistake them for the real thing. But I like whimsical creations, so I accepted them, and have even come to appreciate their strange appearance so high up in the trees.

When I arrived at the foot of Missy's oak, I tugged on a rope that set off a clanging bell inside the house. A few moments passed, then a hunched figure shuffled out onto the balcony. I waved. "Greetings, Matron."

"Where the hell ye been?" she shouted down at me.

"In trouble."

She snorted. "Oh, the cheek of ye! I'm not surprised, I'll say that right now." She leaned further over, squinting, then grabbed an ocularscope attached to an accordion arm mount to get a better look. "Who've ye got there?"

"I've got a favor to ask you," I said, swerving around the question.

"So ask it."

"My friend here needs a place to stay."

"Do he now? Well, bring him up for a closer look and we'll see about that."

I glanced over at Renwick, then indicated the ladder. "After you."

It was a sturdy ladder, but went straight up, like maintenance ladders on bridges. After a moment's hesitation, he looped his bag over his arm, tucked his cane into his belt, and grabbed hold. When he was a fair ways up, I lifted my rucksack into the air. Matron clapped her gnarled hands in delight, then lowered the lift. When it hit the ground I climbed aboard, and soon was passing Renwick, a grin on my face.

"Hey!"

"Only room for one, and since I've got the goods"—I showed him the rucksack—"I get the ride."

He scowled. "I could've gone after you."

"This is a test," I called down to him. "To see if you can manage."

"I can manage!" I gave him a thumbs-up. He gave me a scowl in return.

Missy Thornback was waiting for me at the top. The lift worked on a system of pulleys and gears and a bit of magic, so she was required to power it. Hence the need for a ladder, which was a good way to keep people from leaving before she was done with them. Matron was also a necessity if you wanted to use the ladder. Without her magic, you'd likely end up either falling to your death, or having to go back down once you reach the illusioned part. A large section of the ladder is missing, though you can't tell until your hand goes through air. The section will only become whole when Matron commands it. It was a great security measure.

I stepped off the lift and handed her the rucksack. "I thought you could use some jam."

Her cracked face brightened. "Oh, Lorelle, ye don't know how much I've been craving yer jam."

"Bread, too," I added.

She undid the clasp and peeked inside. "Oh, now ye've gone and done it." She pulled out the bottle of *Ambrosia Potation* I'd brought her, a twinkle in her old eyes. Well, at least in one of them. Her left eye had been damaged while she'd been brewing a particularly dangerous potion for a local potentate. The good eye was black as coal, the other a yellowish white, which did nothing to improve her looks. Unlike Lady Faylan, Missy Thornback looked every inch her age. But then, I had a feeling Missy Thornback was as ancient as the universe, probably older, actually.

"I made it myself. Should help with your rheumatism."

"Ah, yes. Me rheumatism." She winked at me. "So what's the story with handsome?"

Renwick's head appeared through a hole in the deck, followed by his slender form. "This is Renwick Van der Daarke," I tossed my head in his direction, "and he needs a place to stay."

She clapped a wrinkled hand to her chest as Renwick stepped off the ladder. "A Van der Daarke in me humble abode? Well, the things ye live to see. So the castle ain't good enough for the likes of ye, eh, whippersnapper?"

He pushed back a handful of wayward curls. "It's a bit stifling, I must admit."

She let loose a deep cackle and the sound echoed around the wood like shouts. Any fey nearby who wasn't already watching our every move would be now. "Should we go inside?" I indicated the way.

Missy limped forward, pushing the round wooden door wide, and I followed after her, with Renwick behind me, ducking low. Everything was built lower and smaller than it would have been for your average person. Missy wasn't exactly what you'd call tall, but she wasn't quite a dwarf, either. Age had shrunk her, seemingly compressing her spine half an inch every year, though her girth fought the process, expanding at the same rate. Missy Thornback liked her victuals and potations.

When we were inside her crammed little home, I made the proper introductions as she unpacked the bag of goods, piling her booty onto the already crowded table. "Matron Thornback...Renwick Van der Daarke. Renwick, this is the esteemed Matron Thornback."

He bowed low to her. "A pleasure, Madame Thornback."

Missy threw a sidelong glance at me as she handed back my rucksack. "Quite the charmer, ain't he?"

"He can be," I replied, as I pulled the straps over my shoulders.

"I'd work hard for you, Matron, and I'd only need stay long enough to earn the money to get a place of my own."

Missy popped a monocle she kept on a silver chain around her neck into her good eye. "Who ye running from, laddie?"

He glanced over at me, and I shrugged. "I didn't say a word."

"Someone who doesn't want to let me go, Matron."

"Ah. In a high fettle, is she?"

"Very high."

"Well, I do be needing some help round here." She looked around her messy house with a frown. Stacks of books stood like towers around the main living area, and on every surface some sort of dried herb, glass bottle, or mixing implement took up space. Missy might have retired, but that didn't mean she didn't still dabble. I just hoped she'd be careful and not lose sight in her other eye—her memory wasn't always what it should be and certain ingredients simply shouldn't meet up in close quarters. "Some organizing is long overdue, wood needs to be fetched and herbs gathered, and then me bit o' earth needs tending."

"You'll take me on, then?" Renwick asked, trying not to look too eager.

"We'll call it a trial run, shoog. I've a little space up in the tower. Ye can lay yer head there."

"I appreciate it."

I smiled to myself. I'd known all along that Missy Thornback would take Renwick in—she needed the help. She was a hopeless hoarder and finding dried toads under her cast-iron stove or live grasshoppers in her teapot wasn't an unusual occurrence. But more importantly, the witch had an eye for pretty boys. Hopefully this time she'd keep her hands *mostly* to herself. The last time she'd had a helper things had ended badly. It had taken two months to convince her to change the less than agreeable elf working for her back from a hedgehog to his normal form. "Ye want to come off all prickly, cheeky devil?" she'd asked him. "Well, then I'll make yer dreams come true, see that I don't."

And *bam*, he was a hedgehog.

I believe that was the strongest magic I'd seen in Hawthorn Lane. "Why don't you go check out your new digs?" I said to Renwick, nodding at a little staircase. "I need to talk to Matron for a moment."

He received the hint agreeably enough. "Sure." His long strides took him up the stairs, two at a time.

When he was gone, I turned to Missy, my voice low. "What have you heard?"

She indicated a chair, and after removing a rough-looking black cat and a stack of books, I sat down simply because it was easier than standing. The tree house had a tendency to sway in the breeze, and it was mostly lovely, like being in a giant rocker, until a storm came, that is, and then it was more like a ship in a hurricane.

"Cuppa?"

I shook my head. "I have to get back soon."

She poured herself a cup of her typical brew, a stinky mess that I avoided whenever I could get away with it. I'd swear some of her beverages could burn a hole in your gut before you could even say *ow*. "I've heard ye're an Omni, shoog."

I pulled in a breath. "Did you..." I lowered my voice even more. "Did you know I was one before this?"

She shrugged. "I knew ye were something special, but I also knew ye had no sense of it."

"I didn't mean to keep things from you, Missy."

She waved that off. "Oh, child. I knew why ye did it, and I let ye keep yer secret." She knew and hadn't told, bless her dried up old heart.

"Why didn't you tell me you knew?"

Her good eye shifted. "Well, ye see...I didn't really know what *exactly* ye were, and truth be told, ye were so private, I didn't want to pry."

I fixed her with a stern gaze. "What's the real story, Missy?"

She sighed and took a slurp of her brew, and its pungent odor, which might come from the rat-tails she used, made her warty nose wrinkle. "All right, ye got me. I did know what ye were, which be why I tried teaching ye what I could. All secret-like, though, cause I figured ye wouldn't need me anymore if ye knew ye were fey. And not just fey... the most powerful of them all. I was gonna tell ye, but the time kept slipping by, and well, I kept putting it off."

I wanted to be mad at her...all those years of worry on my part, but I couldn't quite dredge up the necessary emotion. "So you didn't tell me because you wanted to keep me around?"

She flicked a guilty sideways glance at me. "I'm a selfish old besom, ain't I?"

"No argument here."

"Hey, now!" She wagged a thick finger at me. "No need to be so sassy."

"You deserve it. I worried a lot about that!"

She shrugged. "I can't help who I be." It was her standard response whenever she was backed into a corner.

"Fine. Then what can you tell me about my great-grandmother, Elowina? She was an Omni-Fey, so it would be highly unusual for me to be one too, right?"

"Tis a strange thing, to be sure, two in such a short span. I never knew yer great-gran, though. Before me time, I'm afraid."

I cast her a doubtful glance. "I didn't think anything came before your time."

"Now listen here, ye fine madam! I'm not as old as all that." She glared at me over her cup. "I lived elsewhere before I came here. I'm an international traveler, I'll have ye know."

She hadn't been here? Damn. I was hoping she'd be able to tell me something about my family before they went so wrong. "So do you think I truly am an Omni-Fey? Because I'm not so sure, and neither is Lady Faylan."

"Lady Faylan," she spat the name out. "That one likes to be in charge, don't she? So she'll be doing her best to undermine ye. Ye're a threat to her now. I think ye've always been one."

She didn't know the half of it.

"So you *do* think I'm an Omni-Fey?"

She fixed me with her one-eyed stare, the other eyeball peering off to the left. "I ken a lot of things, lass. I do. And what I ken about ye is that there's something inside ye I've never yet encountered. Whether that be Omni or otherwise, I ken not."

I leaned back, making the chair creak. "I'm not sure I like the sound of that."

"Well, ye'd better get used to it. And ye'd better get used to being fawned after and feted. Word is out. Whether or not ye're a true Omni-Fey, ye have the blood, and for most that's enough. They'll be after ye."

"If they're wielding sticks, maybe."

"Is that why ye're trying to leave?"

I stared at her. "You know?"

"Of course. But it won't stick."

I wasn't so sure about that. "I have to take care of something back in the Alterworld, and now seemed a good time to go. The villagers are angry with me because I won't marry Kyran Van der Daarke and break the curse."

Missy leaned forward avidly. "Is he as fetching as they say? More handsome than the devil himself, I heard tell."

I lifted a shoulder. "He's not bad. Renwick's his cousin, you know."

"And he's a fine kettle of fish, ain't he?" She licked her dry lips, leaving behind a tealeaf.

"Be careful with him, Missy," I warned. "The woman he left—Melaina Van der Daarke—she's trouble."

Missy frowned. "I can handle meself."

"I know that, but she's vindictive. She pretended to be dead to get her brother to come here, and she treats her daughter like a leper."

"Oh, aye. I'll be careful, shoog. But it don't hurt to look, do it?" She gave a lusty cackle and slapped her knee.

I laughed. "As long as that's all you do."

Of course we both knew perfectly well that's not all she would do.

Chapter Five

R enwick joined us after a few minutes and I stood to take my leave. Pushing in my chair, I fixed Missy with a stern look. "Be good."

She cackled. "I'll be good when I'm dead."

"If I don't see you for awhile, well, know that I'm thinking of you."

Missy's one good eye looked me over. "And I you." She patted my arm. "Go with the gods, child." I nodded and turned away, tears threatening to well up.

"I'll see you out." Renwick took my arm and steered me onto the balcony, basically giving me no option but to go along with him.

When we were outside, I removed his hand from my arm, then stepped onto the lift. When I was settled, I turned to face him. "Good luck, Renwick."

He smiled. "You think I'll need it?"

"Oh, I know you'll need it."

The smile faded. "What's going on?"

"Oh, Renwick!" I laughed. "I can't believe you're this naïve."

"What do you mean?"

"I mean, you'd better watch your ass around Matron."

His eyes widened in surprise. "You think she'll try to hurt me?"

"No." I grinned evilly. "I mean literally watch your ass around her. She's a grabby one."

My meaning finally dawned on him. "You can't be serious. She's old enough to be my *great*-grandmother."

"You dated your cousin, Renwick. I don't think now's the time to start being choosy." He scowled and I snorted with amusement. "One last bit of advice." I signaled to Missy, who was watching us—of course—to lower the lift. "Find a job that will give you long hours. Matron is very persistent." With a laugh and a wave, I left him watching me descend at a rapid pace, his expression uneasy. "And find a way to bar the door on your room!"

He shook his head, then pivoted, leaving me to descend alone with a smirk on my face. Lesson delivered.

As I neared the ground, I realized something strange...I wasn't alone in my descent. Schooling my expression to one of indifference, I let my eyes flit about, taking in all the lifts following me to the ground. When mine was about a foot from reaching terra firma, I jumped off. My stalkers did the same. Once they hit the ground, they began marching toward me with frightening purpose. Others, appearing from behind trees, joined the swelling crowd. There had to be a good fifty fey by the time all was said and done, their sheer number cutting off my escape routes. I was trapped.

When they had surrounded me like a noose, they stopped and stood watching me in silence. Each boasted numerous tattoos, which resembled the henna markings one might see with Mehndi, an ancient body art. I wondered why they would mark themselves in this way, and what the markings meant. Number and type of kills? I glanced up at Missy's house, but neither she nor Renwick were anywhere to be seen. Apparently she wasn't wasting any time getting to know him.

The circle contained a good number of fray elves—warriors distinguished by their leather uniforms and ever-present bow and quiver of arrows—a few centaurs and fauns, a handful of dwarves, and the rest were dryads, who appeared, not from behind the trees, but from the trees themselves. The dryads were a seemingly sexless group, their long robes disguising their slender forms, and their sharp features seemed neither overtly masculine nor feminine. Some wore braids of ropy vines in their long hair, the color of spring leaves; others sported crowns of branches. I suspected that the vines and crowns sprouted from their skin, which was a shade or two lighter than their hair. This was my first meeting with dryads, and all I could feel at the moment was exceedingly wary.

The humming seemed louder today, though maybe that was because there were so many fey all gathered in one small space, and only feet from where I stood. Feeling threatened, I took a step backward, ready if need be to use my dagger to fight my way through the crowd and retreat to Missy's ladder.

A dryad, dressed in shimmering white, and boasting a fine rack of branches, stepped forward, and I checked my urge to flee. The dryad looked to be one of those types used to being obeyed without question. If that were the case, the misguided creature wasn't going to like me very much. Obeying without question was a bad habit I'd dropped the moment I came to Hawthorn Lane, and lo and behold, was, if not liked for my defiance, then respected for it.

"Welcome to Wuthering Wood, Mistress Gragan." The dryad had a cool, whispery voice that reminded me of the sound of leaves rustling. "I do apologize for our previous lack of welcome. I can only say that due to our uncertainty about you we were remiss in our manners. However, in our defense, we cannot be too careful here in the wood. Fey-hunters like to come this way to reach the village, as we are farther removed from Lady Faylan and her Mage Patrol. So it behooves us to be cautious."

I wasn't sure I believed this. For six years they had needed to maintain this caution with me? What had they seen in me? My peculiarity? Almost as important, had everyone else in Hawthorn Lane seen it too? Was this why I'd been tolerated but never embraced? Was this why I couldn't get a date?

I didn't voice these questions aloud for the same reason I didn't bother to ask why the Woods lived here where they were less protected. They wouldn't tell me. My guess is that those who chose to live here had more to hide than the village fey. Or perhaps they didn't trust the village fey. Either motive was equally likely, and equally disturbing.

"What changed your mind about me?"

The dryad's nostrils quivered delicately, as though an odd smell had drifted below them. "We have heard you possess roots in Hawthorn Lane. Deep ones."

"And that I might be Omni-Fey, as well?"

The dryad gave a single nod. "We had heard that, yes."

"I see." I could have pointed out their hypocrisy—accepting me only when I showed I might be a potentially useful ally—but I wasn't about to ruin this new state of affairs by being confrontational. Besides, they way outnumbered me. "Well, it's a pleasure to meet all of you. Wuthering Wood is a beautiful place. You must be proud of it."

"You're very kind. We do treasure the wood, and we are honored that you would grace us with your presence."

"I came to visit Matron Thornback."

"Yes, we know." *Of course you do.* "A fine mage."

And what exactly did she tell you about me? I wanted to ask, but refrained. I like plain speaking, and it has its place, but I've found that silence serves me better in situations like this, when I couldn't expect the same plain speaking from my associate.

"Yes, she is."

"And you brought a friend?" What should have been a statement was politely presented as a question, inviting me to answer. I declined. Time passed in silence and I felt a growing tension that I refused to defuse with words, even though the heavy quiet sent nervous twitches up my arms and into my chest...my fight or flight response was kicking in, and I was beginning to ponder which one I'd have to use.

"Domina Gragan!" someone shouted from the crowd, finally ending our deadlock of silence.

"My name is Lorelle," I corrected the anonymous shouter. "Lorelle Gragan."

"You do not understand," the dryad spoke up to explain. "It is our wish to call you Domina, and would be our honor."

"Does it mean something?"

"It means ruler."

Ruler? Well, that was certainly more palatable than harridan or traitor. "But I'm not your ruler," I pointed out, rather needlessly. "I'm not the ruler of anyone, nor do I wish to be."

The dryad's expression was unreadable. "It's a title that fits better than mistress, though, do you not agree?"

I did not agree, though I admit I liked how Domina bore an uncanny resemblance to the word dominate…and dominatrix. I've always liked whips. "You may call me what you wish," I decided to back down. "And what may I call you?"

"I am Asherley Rowan." The dryad bowed stiffly.

"Pleased to make your acquaintance, Asherley Rowan." Unfortunately, the unusual name did nothing to solve my problem of gender identification. Pronouns did make conversation easier, but I supposed I was just going to have to deal with my confusion, there being far worse things in life.

"Likewise, Domina Gragan," he returned the compliment.

The others continued to regard me with unblinking stillness and I started feeling uneasy again as silence fell over us like a net. Behind the hush hovered the ever-present buzzing, a swarm of bees in the distance.

"Domina Gragan!" It was the same voice as before, and he was louder this time.

I straightened to my full height, scanning the crowd for him. "Yes? What is it that you want?"

The fey creature, wearing a red toque similar to what a French voyageur might have worn centuries ago, pushed forward through the crowd. A wood elf of slight stature, he was holding a tiny child in his arms. "He has come to harm."

I could see that without being told. The child's typically brown skin was pale, its freckles nearly white. His eyes were closed, the sockets dark like bruised indents in his sallow face. His unmoving head rested against the rough wool of his father's shirt. "What happened to him?"

He pointed up at a tree branch. "He fell."

The tree branch was a long way up. "I'm so sorry."

He thrust him forward. "Please help him."

My eyes focused on the reddish black split marring the elf's trembling lower lip. "I'm not sure I can." I met his eyes, pools of agony, and felt an urge to run. "My potions are at my cottage, but I'm afraid they'd do no good in this case."

"Ye're an Omni-Fey, Domina," he said in a voice raspy with grief. "Ye've the power."

I looked around at the crowd. Their expressions had changed now, from blank-faced impassivity to avid expectation. "I've only just found out what I truly am, sir. Though whether I'm actually an Omni-Fey or not, the point remains that my powers are untrained. I could do more harm to the child than good."

"I do not think any more harm can come to the lad," Asherley pointed out matter-of-factly.

I glared at the dryad, feeling set up. The wood fey were testing me, using an innocent victim for their deadly experiment. If I failed to save the child, I would be outcast once more, maybe even called a murderer for letting him die, either because I didn't have the power, or didn't understand how to use it correctly. But if I succeeded…well, that would start me down a road from which there'd be no returning.

"I'm not sure what I can do." I glanced down at the still child whose innocent face reminded me a little of Ilia. I let loose a pent-up breath. "But I will try."

I pulled off a glove, and with a trembling hand, reached out and touched the child. His skin was cold and I thought I was too late to help him. But I did not retreat. My fingers made their uncertain way down from his pallid face to his heart. He looked so vulnerable, so close to death that my heart filled with a compassion I hadn't allowed myself to feel in a very long time. Pulling in a steadying breath, I called forth the sparks, and they responded instantly to my command, leaping from my fingers and onto the child's skin like hungry beasts.

The boy's father gasped and jerked him backward, out of my reach. "What's this?"

"It's what I can do. It's all I know," I explained, looking to Asherley.

"Let her continue," the dryad commanded with an imperious gesture.

The wood elf fixed me with a fierce gaze, but he stepped forward without a word, presenting his child to me like a sacrifice. Such an apt phrase for the situation. I sensed Asherley was using the child for his own motives, and if the boy died, so be it. He would have his answer about me.

I mentally scolded myself. I'd already slipped up and given the dryad a pronoun.

I took another deep breath and decided to try something different. With a flick of my fingers, I pulled the sparks together into one steady stream, letting the compassion I felt grow inside me, then reached down to touch the boy's heart. A golden river flowed into his chest, filling it with a bright light that highlighted his lungs, his ribs, his weakened heart, more clearly than an x-ray. The fey around me gasped in awe, and I blocked them all out, focusing on directing my energy into the child until he was filled with a luminous radiance.

Suddenly the elf spasmed, nearly throwing himself out of his father's arms. I pulled back in alarm and the light went out. Each one of us held our breath as we watched the child twitch and convulse. Then his body arched once, as though electrocuted, before falling limp.

Time passed with only the distant call of a falcon and the whisper of leaves to fill the heavy air around us. I had failed.

But then the child's eyes, dark as black walnuts, flickered open. "Papá?"

"Jaimen!" The elf hugged the boy tight, then started sobbing with relief. "He speaks! He lives!" The resulting cheer rose upward like birds in flight, filling me with a strange triumph. I'd found my 'glister,' and because of what I'd done, the boy was going to be all right.

Asherley's expression was hard to read. "The rumors are true, then."

"I'm still not sure what I am—"

"Domina Gragan, *we* are sure," Asherley interrupted, giving me a regal bow, the long branches on his head sweeping the ground.

I patted the boy, now sitting up in his dad's arms, his large eyes on me. "Always watch where you put your hands and feet when climbing, little one. That way you won't accidentally slip on a bird's nest."

He stared at me, then nodded solemnly.

"Thank ye," the father said, his cheeks flushed, his eyes wet with tears as I pulled my glove back on. "Ye've returned my life to me."

"It was a pleasure. He will grow to be a fine elf, and an even better climber, now that he knows what to watch out for."

"What can I do for ye in return, Domina Gragan?"

"Nothing. Truly. I was glad to be of help. But I'm tired now. I should be going home."

In truth, I wasn't tired at all. Instead of feeling drained as one would expect, I felt more potent than ever. It's why I'd spent hours playing with my sparks, shaping them into balls, throwing them around my dark cottage like a light show. The power of my magic was an irresistible siren, and I found myself answering its call like a lovesick sailor. It's also why, when faced with the potential of seeing other people, I'd decided to don gloves. The allure of using magic, of showing off my newfound powers like a child desperate for attention, might be too strong for me to resist.

"I shall escort you to the edge of the woods," Asherley offered.

The crowd, which had felt hostile before, had changed perceptibly toward me, like night turning to day, their smiles and excited chatter filling my senses as we passed by. Many reached out to touch my arm, a strand of hair that had slipped from my bun, a wisp of my gown. I felt quite sure that if they thought they could get away with it, they'd pluck whatever they could off me for a talisman, leaving me naked as the day I was born.

I both liked the attention and despised it, and knew with foreboding that this was my new world…where adulation held a seductive charm that could pull me from my quiet life, and force me into a position I could only keep hold of by doing bigger and better things.

The wood folk were about to follow us, but Asherley turned and spoke to them. "Go back to your homes and return to your work. There is much to be done this day." They went, reluctantly, and only after I lifted my hand to them in farewell. Then the dryad and I walked on together. At the edge of the wood, Asherley turned to me.

"Thank you, Domina. You have returned one of ours back to us."

"Are you going to tell the village fey about what happened? I'm not sure I'm ready to have this get out." Why couldn't I shake the feeling that I'd just been part of a stage production and had played my role perfectly? As though every word and every gesture I'd made had been laid out long before I'd arrived? I was being manipulated, I felt, but by whom?

The dryad held out his pale, slim hands in a helpless gesture. "I cannot stop them from talking. I might speak for them, but I am not their commander."

Why did I not believe him?

"Well, maybe you can talk to them, ask them to keep this to themselves." It was a futile effort, I knew, but I wanted it on record that I made the request.

"I can try."

"Please do." I stepped out of the wood, then turned back to the dryad. The sunlight had turned his pale green skin nearly translucent, as though he were a mirage. "My friend is Renwick Van der Daarke. He came here seeking refuge. Will you provide it for him?"

Asherley smiled, knowing that doing this favor for me would relieve the Woods of their debt. "It would be my honor."

"Very good. Goodbye, Asherley Rowan."

He bowed. "Until we meet again, Domina Gragan."

"Until we meet again," I answered, and hoped that wouldn't be any time soon. Not only were the wood fey a strange group, I suspected that Asherley Rowan had ambitions involving my newly discovered magical abilities.

Chapter Six

While asking for Asherley's protection would lighten Renwick's burden, which I didn't particularly want, it would add to Melaina's, which I particularly did, so the loss of an IOU was worth it. Anything was worth it to stick it to the woman who'd called me stupid more times and in more ways than a schoolyard bully. A part of me couldn't believe she and Kyran were brother and sister, but after discovering how ambitious he was, I could now see the connection. It seemed Ilia, Melaina's daughter, was the odd Van der Daarke out, but then again, she might turn on me, too. I hoped not. She was the one and only shining beacon I could see in this dark and treacherous world.

Feeling warm under the increasingly hot sun, I pulled off my gloves and shoved them into my rucksack, then began my trek across the moors, enjoying the wind billowing about me. The fresh air combined with the invigorating aftereffects of using my magic left me feeling like I could rule the world. I felt like I could fly! I started to run, my dress flapping around me like wings. Buoyant, I turned my face toward the sun and blue sky, but what I saw up there made me stutter to a halt. Six ravens flew overhead, all of them upside-down. Everyone in Hawthorn Lane knows what that means…that magic is afoot and big things are about to happen. Based on the strange twists and turns my life has been taking lately, I wasn't so sure I liked this omen.

I wrapped my arms around me and looked about, searching for anything amiss, and my gaze landed on Atermorte Cemetery. Standing outside its elaborate entrance was the death wraith himself, Cutter Flint, his rangy frame hunched and his eyes turned my way as though he were waiting for me. A scarecrow of a creature, I found him beautiful, his black cape always flapping behind him as he strode along, his strong beak of a nose often stuck in a book of dark poetry. When he wasn't reading poems, he was scribbling down inscriptions, as he was in charge of writing all the epitaphs for the departed. The color of his hair is as blue-black as the wings of a raven and his eyes just as watchful. One of many things that fascinates me about Cutter is that he likes to collect old prosthetic body parts—hooks, wooden legs, glass eyeballs—and hang them from tree branches in the cemetery. Best not to ask where he gets them, even though I think we all know.

Cutter Flint does not like me, has never liked me, and I'm not sure why, though I'd always believed it had to do with my not being fey. Despite his antipathy, I had never let it stop me from going into the cemetery. Like Haunted Hollow, I'm drawn to the place like a vampire to blood. I know perfectly well what my obsession says about my psyche, and I don't give a tinker's damn. Atermorte Cemetery is a wondrous place, a sprawling maze of moldering mausoleums, lichen-encrusted tombstones, life-like statuary, and cave-like sepulchers. Mourners often bring offerings to their loved ones, ranging from the sedate—flowers, wreaths, locks of hair—to the more macabre—animal skulls, vials of blood, poisonous plants, weapons—and nearly every gravesite in the cemetery has been decorated with such mementoes at one time or another. What's not to like about such a place, I ask you?

To enter the cemetery, you pass through a wrought-iron gate lodged beneath a tall archway. The iron had at one time been coaxed into all kinds of shapes, from bones to scythes to skulls split in two, all virtually screaming the message, *Welcome to Death.* The entrance connects to a wall that surrounds the cemetery, and the entire structure resembles an ancient structure one might find hidden deep beneath riotous jungle growth. Spiky hedges, dark trees, and sinewy vines grow like mold, quick and silent, both inside the graveyard and surrounding it. Beyond the walls, the light is always muted, as though the gloaming never ends, giving the orbs that reside there something useful to do by helping to light the way.

With its stone passages and cobbled walkways, Atermorte Cemetery has evolved into its own little burg. Rumor has it that beneath the cemetery winds a network of tunnels that leads to the village proper over a mile away, with the mausoleums serving as entrances. Infused with the potent smell of death, the cemetery is a wild world unscathed by light. I come here whenever I'm feeling especially dark, or when I want to entertain myself by annoying Cutter.

Usually he greets me with a scowl, and sometimes throws black sparks at my head if I get too close to him, but today he did something strange. He beckoned to me. Curious, and feeling daring, I picked up my skirts and quickly made my way to the cemetery. With each step, the walls seemed to grow exponentially higher and longer until close up, the place was overwhelmingly massive. I thought it must be a trick, an illusion, and I liked that about the cemetery. Imagine having the power to make yourself look bigger than you really are. I glanced down at my hands. Maybe, just maybe, I had that power.

"Good day to you, Cutter Flint."

He nodded, his long black hair flying upward and outward from the strong breeze off the moors. Actually, his hair was often flying upward and outward, and breezes were always stirring up around him, and I couldn't help thinking he had a wind devil that followed him.

"Mistress Gragan." Was I imagining things or did he sound somewhat pleased to see me?

I gave him a saucy smile; I was looking forward to setting him on edge. It's both a pleasure and payback to poke people who don't like you. "Lovely weather we're having."

He squinted up at the bright sun. "If you say so." Cutter's voice is a raspy thing and makes him sound as though he's speaking to you from the other side. It never fails to send delightful shivers down my spine.

"I do."

"Then it is a day to behold."

"It is, indeed." I eyed him, and he eyed me back. For once his twig-fingered hands were free of books and he looked oddly vulnerable without one to hide behind.

"I thought your thirst might be deep," he said after a moment.

I licked my lips, dry from the wind, from my performance with the elf boy. I nodded. "It is deep."

"I would like to quench it." From anyone else, I'd think that this was a come-on, and a none-too-subtle one at that, but this was Cutter, and Cutter did not like me.

"I would like it to be quenched."

He motioned to me. "Step into my world, Mistress Gragan, and see what is on offer."

Said the spider to the plump, delicious fly...

My curiosity, among other things, most definitely aroused, I stepped past him and into the cemetery. He typically barely spoke to me, much less invited me to do anything with him, and I was all aflutter with anticipation at finding out what he might be up to. Once across the threshold, the light instantly dimmed and I could make out the orbs floating above my head. I stopped and waited for Cutter to take the lead. He swooped past me and I could smell his scent, a peculiar mixture of smoky ash and dry dust combined with the earthy smell of vetiver oil. I breathed in the captivating scent as it swirled around me, finding it as intoxicating as I'd always done. It was one of the reasons I liked visiting the cemetery, just to catch the scent of Cutter Flint on the wind.

I followed after him and he led me down a cobblestone path at a fast pace. In the past, I could walk beneath the orbs without incident, but today they pulsed as I passed, then began to follow me.

"Cutter?" He didn't respond, being too far ahead, so I called his name again. Something in my voice must have caught his attention and he spun around, his cape whipping about with him. I pointed at the orbs, bobbing nearby. They were clustered together instead of staying put along the path like good little orbs. "What are they doing?"

His brow, which jutted out over his piercing green eyes and was typically smooth as river stone, creased in bemusement. Then his eyes fastened on mine, and his mouth actually twitched into an approximation of a smile. "Come!" He whirled about and took off again, and I had to hurry to keep up with his long legs.

After ten minutes of fast-paced walking, we arrived at what appeared to be the center of the cemetery, and stopped before a small stone building with the name Flint carved over the entrance. Compared to the other grand structures, this one looked rather plain, unadorned as it was by the seemingly requisite elaborate carvings and winged statuary the others boasted.

Cutter pulled a large skeleton key from his cloak and unlocked the cast-iron door spotted with green and black lichen and rusted in spots, but still solid. With some effort, he pulled open the heavy door and waved me inside. The orbs made to follow, but Cutter put up a hand to stop them. "One only. Who shall it be?"

A small greenish orb zipped ahead of the others and through the door, and I had to laugh. "Apparently that one doesn't believe the saying that good things come to those who wait."

"Aber is but a child, and unacquainted with restraint."

"Well, in this case, his impatience serves him well." I stepped past Cutter and into a heavy darkness lit only by the bobbing orb. "Hello, Aber," I called, my voice hollow in the small chamber. "Have you come to play with us?" The orb bobbed up and down even faster, like an excited child. "I'm excited, too. I've never been in here before, or in any sort of mausoleum, for that matter." The orb made a motion, like nodding, just as Cutter shut the door with a clang. A frisson of fear knocked along my spine like bony knuckles as he locked the door, trapping us together inside the grave. But my fear walked hand in hand with exhilaration. Deep down I believe all of us feel a thrill at confronting the unknown.

"Follow me, Mistress Gragan, and I will take you to my lair."

I am about to enter a death wraith's lair. Today is a good day.

In the middle of the empty room—no caskets here—an iron trapdoor enticed us to open it. Cutter unlocked the door, lifted it up via a head-sized iron ring, and set the door backward on the floor with a clang that echoed through the darkness like the tolling of a bell. He motioned to me and I stepped nearer. The orb had already disappeared down the hole, and when I peered into it, I saw a steep set of stone steps spiraling downward into a black expanse. There were no railings, no walls, just open space on both sides. I took my first step into the hole, anticipation fluttering in my stomach like the beginnings of life. I carefully descended ten steps before stopping to wait for Cutter.

Is he going to close the door after us? I wondered, watching him carefully. He was. Like an alligator's mouth, the trap door slammed down, and after locking it, Cutter went ahead of me. The stairs were meant for only one person at a time, and he had to squeeze past me. As he did so, I felt something in my chest, a sort of pull from him, like an inhalation. It was the allure of death, I realized, and was glad the draw was resistible, if only barely so.

Cutter went on ahead and we descended deep into the earth, going round and round for quite some time, until at last the stairway began to straighten out. The smell rising up as we made our way downward was a mixture of Cutter's own scent and something darker; I felt as though we were making our journey through a sídhe before sinking into the underworld of the ancient gods, the Tuatha Dé Danann.

Maybe we were. I nearly giggled with glee.

Finally, stone walls appeared, almost from out of nowhere, and on them hung hundreds of mirrors, some ornate, some plain, some quite large and others no bigger than a hand mirror. After we'd passed a number of them, Cutter stopped to face me, his expression blank. "What is it that you see, Mistress Gragan?" he asked with a sweep of his hand. "In these mirrors of mine?"

We had been moving too quickly for me to catch much of anything, so I turned to the mirror in front of me—a tall piece, its tarnished silver frame shaped like a skull—and leaned forward for a closer look. I had expected to see my own reflection, but before me played a scene of a man kneeling down before a guillotine. His long hair was a matted mess, and his clothes filthy, though I could see they were of fine quality. A bloody basket waited to catch his head. He was shaking, but remained silent as he waited. "Vive la Libertad!" someone in the crowd shouted, though I could see no one, only the man. Then the hissing of the guillotine as it plummeted, a dull thunk, the man's head dropping, blood spraying, then cheers. Angry, hateful, jubilant cheers.

It seemed very real, not just some movie or television show. I turned to Cutter, who was watching me closely, his green eyes glowing in the light of the orb. It seemed a strange contrast, such vivid color in one so dark. "Is this the actual French Revolution?"

"I was there, you see. I go where I am needed."

I indicated the other mirrors. "All death scenes? All real?"

"This is my memorial to the fallen."

"Was that man anyone special?"

"All men are special. All women. Children, too."

"But why do you show him in particular?"

"All Revolution deaths I witnessed reside in that mirror." Just as he said this, another image appeared. This time it was a woman. I turned away.

"Why did you want me to see this, Cutter?"

"To determine if you *can* see it, Mistress Gragan." With that cryptic remark, he turned and headed down the stairs once more, leaving me to follow after him, my curiosity growing with each step. We were close to the bottom when a particularly grand mirror, its border composed of all sorts of odd-looking creatures, caught my eye. An image of what looked, strangely enough, like the inside of *Fawn's Fashions* flickered in and out. Then the mirror's surface went black, and nothing more could be seen.

Soon after, the walls parted ways to reveal a large, open space. Cutter snapped his fingers and there was a gentle poof, followed by the sudden illumination of hundreds of glow torches. Lit by an unusual golden phosphorescence, they lent an unexpected celestial aura to the cavernous room. Every inch of the chamber contained something strange... piles of human skulls, stuffed birds and animals, and jars filled with a matter whose nature I wasn't sure I wanted to ascertain, green and yellow and distorted as they were. Delicate pencil sketches of both angelic and demonic creatures, along with more mundane drawings of skulls and crosses, papered the walls. Even the books stacked on the floor and lining the shelves, which rose all the way up to the cathedral-like ceiling, looked old and mysterious, as though if I were to open one something either very terrible or very wondrous would fly out.

An entire dead tree 'grew' over in one corner, its black branches reaching imploringly to a sky it would never see again, and I wondered how Cutter had managed to get it in here. Branch by branch, then painstakingly pieced back together like dinosaur bones? Perhaps, as there was a full set of such bones lurking next to the tree, a raptor, judging by its sharp teeth and long tail.

Cutter obviously liked collecting things, as evidenced by the numerous instruments of death spread around the room. A dark corner housed what looked like a real gallows, complete with a rope that was regrettably frayed, a full-sized guillotine, bloody head basket included, a two-sided ax hanging on the wall, a gibbet sporting a rusted hanging cage. No one was inside it... for the moment.

There were notes and pages of writing on the table and nailed with miniature spikes to the stone wall. A pipe organ, whose pipes resembled bones, and which maybe were, took up one whole wall. Now I knew the source of the melancholy music I sometimes heard on clear summer nights when sound travels as effortlessly as water running downhill.

When we reached the blackened stone floor, a pale gray pentagram carved into its center became perceptible. Cutter left me and headed toward a round table in the middle of the room. Numerous carafes filled with dark liquids dotted the scarred surface, and I felt quite sure none of them were tea. He picked up a carafe and carefully poured its contents, which sparkled as it fell, into a black crystal skull goblet, then handed the cup to me. I took it and peered into its depths.

"It is *Ombra*," he explained.

"I've never heard of *Ombra* before, and I've heard of them all."

"It is, shall we say, an unusual drink. It means shadow, as in 'bere un'ombra'."

"Drink a shadow?" I translated. Sounded good to me.

"Nunc est bibendum," he toasted. *There is drinking to be done.*

"Salus," I returned with a wry smile as I lifted my goblet to him. *To your health.*

We both drank at the same time. The libation was potent and delicious and I realized too late that it might not be a good idea to accept a drink from a death wraith. But the deed was done and if this were the end for me, I might as well enjoy it. I took another deep drink, then peered at Cutter over the rim of my goblet.

"I thought you didn't like me."

"My behavior toward you had nothing to do with like or dislike. I have learned to avoid succumbing to strong emotions and the best way to make that happen is to distance myself from the object of my sentiments."

"So why the change?" I took another drink, then set my goblet down, already feeling a shadow growing inside me.

"You are the one I have sought for longer than one should have to seek."

"I've been here for six years, Cutter," I said dryly, not buying it. "What's changed?"

"Your true nature has at last been revealed to me."

"And what nature is that?" I asked cautiously, wishing now that I hadn't drunk from his cup.

"Why, you are a death wraith, of course."

Chapter Seven

"A death wraith?" I echoed, shaking my head. "I don't think so."

"The truth cannot be altered."

"Oh, yes it can. People do it all the time. Look, Cutter. I'm not a death wraith. I just found out that I might be of Omni blood, but I don't really even know that for sure. What I do know for sure is that I'm not a death wraith."

One moment he was standing at the far end of the table, the next he was by my side, the rapid movement taking my breath away. I took a step back, but he grabbed my hand, pulling me close. His touch was cold, though it felt strangely soothing on my skin, which had grown warm despite the coolness of the underground lair. "Omni is everything…life and death and in-between. You are all things at once, Lorelle"—it didn't escape me that he'd switched to using my first name—"and stronger than any one alone."

"But how do you know this, Cutter? I'm no different than before." That wasn't entirely true, I realized the moment I spoke. Nobody can be the same once they've done magic.

"Before I saw only the life and beauty in you, and I had no choice but to turn from such an intrigue or pay a price for my attraction. But now I see your true nature. I sense it in you. I smell it." He leaned close and breathed in deeply. "Ah, yes. There it is. Thanatos."

Being told one smells like death isn't as flattering as you might think. "Why don't you smell like death?"

"Oh, but I do, Lorelle. Earth to earth. Ashes to ashes. Dust to dust." Vetiver, ash, dust—all composed his alluring scent. He was right. He did smell like death.

"Do others smell it on me?" It might explain why they avoided me.

He shook his head. "Only our kind."

Oh, stars. I could smell it on him, had always been able to. "Even if I were one of your kind, Cutter, what makes you think I'd be interested in you? You've treated me like a nonentity for the last six years. One doesn't forget that sort of thing. No one rational, anyway."

"I had good reason, but I will redeem myself."

I looked up into his intense eyes. Such a vivid green in a creature of death struck a discordant note, and for the first time I wondered who Cutter Flint truly was and what had brought him seeking sanctuary in Hawthorn Lane. What was he running from? What would a death wraith have to fear?

"I should be going," I said quickly, feeling a bit out of my depth, literally, as I had to be at least a quarter mile underground. Too much was happening at once, and I, who was used to being left alone, wasn't sure how to handle all this unfamiliar attention. It was nice to be noticed, but not in this way. Not when I'd done nothing worthy to earn it.

I stepped away from Cutter, anxious to be far from this place. But he didn't let go of my hand, raising it to his mouth instead. Just before his lips met my skin, he turned my hand over, pushed up my sleeve and kissed my wrist. A sharp tingling sensation, almost like a burn, ignited where his lips touched flesh.

Startled, I pulled my hand from his grasp and stared at my wrist. On the pale skin, superimposed over blue veins, was a skull. "What the hell is that?"

"A memento mori."

"I know perfectly well that I must die someday, you sadist. I don't need a reminder. Take it off."

"This one possesses a different meaning, Lorelle. It shows that we are connected."

"We are *not* connected, Cutter Flint. Now remove this brand, or I'll brand your entire face." I lifted one hand and let the sparks fly.

He watched them shoot upward with interest before returning his gaze to me. "I cannot remove it for it is no longer mine to remove."

I stared down at the skull in dismay, then at him. "You put it on me, you can take it off."

"Me paenitet, but I cannot."

"It sorrows *you*? I'm the one left with a tattoo that I don't want." I threw a shower of sparks at him, but he didn't flinch. "You told me you were going to redeem yourself with me. This isn't how you redeem yourself! You'd better figure out a way to remove this tattoo, Cutter, or I'm going to remove you from this world." If one can do that with a death wraith.

His eyelids lowered slowly, then opened again, and he licked his lips as though he'd just savored an exquisite wine. "I shall do my very best to please you."

He didn't mean a word of it, or at the very least we had different definitions of what it meant to please me, which meant I was stuck with a skull tattoo on my wrist. I spun away. "Come on, Aber. Show me the way out." Aber flew down from the ceiling, where he'd been communing with the phosphorescent lights, and zipped up the stairs.

"I will show you the way."

"You go play with your organ, Cutter Flint, and leave me alone."

I mounted the steps with determination. Aber flitted ahead of me, and we made our way past the mirrors and back up the spiral staircase, which seemed endless. I didn't have to turn around to know Cutter was behind us, following like a shadow. It was just as well he was coming, as I needed him to unlock the doors to let us out. I didn't say a word, but neither did he as he performed the necessary tasks to free me from his lair.

I made it to the gate, but not without a flock of orbs in tow, keeping themselves between myself and Cutter. Just before I stepped through, I turned around. "Thank you for watching over me." The orbs bobbed up and down. "Be safe, and don't let him"—I pointed at Cutter— "push you around."

"When again will our paths cross?" he asked as I stepped from the darkness into the light.

I peered at my wrist with its new tattoo. "When I'm dead." I didn't stop to take in his reaction, just turned and ran, wanting to distance myself from the death wraith who had so arrogantly marked me for his own.

Feet pounding and arms pumping, I bolted for home. I needed to eat a good, filling meal, then I would sit quietly and think through everything that had happened to me today. I had a feeling serious reflection was crucial to my future well-being.

When I arrived at the cottage, I half expected to see Avice waiting for me, as had been her habit before the Van der Daarkes showed up. But she was not there. My brow furrowed, and I, so proud of my self-sufficiency, had to admit that I missed her. I recalled the day when it had been her and myself, Kyran and Ilia, when we'd shared bread and tea in front of a roaring fire, and it had felt like we were a family, safe and comfortable and connected to one another. Connected in a healthy way, that is, not by an unasked for fetter such as the one Cutter had forced on me.

Once inside my cottage, I prepared a hearty meal of cranberry brioche and a Chanterelle and boar bacon omelet. I found I was ravenous and devoured every last bit, washing it down with wild grape juice and peony, a drink that would calm my nerves and marshal my scattered thoughts.

As I cleared and washed up the dishes, I contemplated what I must do next. Yes, I'd told Kyran I would stay for another week, and if nothing went wrong I would. But what would I do in the meantime? I didn't know. What was his angle, anyway? I was tempted to not make an appearance at *Chez Chantilly* for dinner, just to show him he wasn't the boss of me, but I knew I would go. I had to find out what he was up to. Besides, courtesy of Avice, I'd dined at *Chez Chantilly* several times, and I absolutely loved their decadent food.

I wondered if, while we dined, I would hear all about Renwick's defection. It was likely, though I certainly wouldn't share my part in his escape. If I said something to Kyran, Melaina might twist it out of him. Or maybe he'd simply tell her, which I couldn't blame him for doing, especially after what Renwick had done to him. Best to keep my mouth shut and play it by ear, as was my typical modus operandi when it came to unpredictable situations.

I wasn't sure what to think about what had happened in Wuthering Wood with the elf boy, Jaimen, or what to even say about it if asked (because of course the story would get out). Had I really saved him, or had his recovery simply been a coincidence? Whatever had happened, it was clear the wood fey had changed their tune about me, even before I'd encountered Jaimen. But why? Was it because they'd heard I was an Omni-Fey? It seemed the only reasonable conclusion. But even if I were an Omni, I'd always been one, so I hadn't changed. I was the same old Lorelle, only now I was *officially* someone to be reckoned with. I wasn't sure I liked that. Yes, I wanted to be accepted, even sought after just a little bit. Who doesn't? But I wasn't sure I could trust this sudden change of heart toward me. It smacked of duplicity, and maybe of something bigger going on that I didn't know about.

Even Cutter Flint, who'd gone out of his way to avoid me whenever I entered the cemetery, had done a complete turnabout. In fact, he seemed to be actively courting me. What did he think he was going to get out of this 'connection' he thought we had? Little Cutter juniors? Mini-Lorelles? Was procreation even possible for a death wraith? I'd always thought they weren't exactly of the living, though Cutter seemed quite solid to me, his skin cold to the touch maybe, but his breath warm and his body firm.

I put the last dish away and headed to a nearby bookshelf to find the book Professor Ballylee had given me as a gift—probably because I was one of his rare visitors. We would sit for hours and drink fizzy blood-orange phosphates while discussing all sorts of topics, from the influence of the Alterworld on young fey to the growing threat of fey-hunters. The book contained loads of useful information about the different kinds of fey—a far bigger variety than I'd ever imagined existed—and I'd read through it before, but didn't remember everything. I realize now that it had been a very kind gift for a girl who'd had no clue what she'd gotten herself into. I made a mental note to say good-bye to the professor before I left Hawthorn Lane for good.

The book, *Fey or Foe: The True Nature of the Magickal*, was massive, its paper thick and rough. On the cover a protruding face peered out at me, its expression changing every few seconds as effortlessly as a Face Dancer. I carefully opened the book and flipped my way through the pages of tiny gothic script, accompanied by elaborate and beautifully drawn illustrations, near to the end to find wraiths. It seemed even the fey prefer alphabetical order.

After a bit of searching through the different kinds of wraiths, I finally found *Death Wraith: Vassal of the Grim Reaper* and began to read. The description was a little convoluted, but the gist of it was that a death wraith is one of many assistants to the Grim Reaper, who apparently can't be everywhere in the world at once. If the Grim Reaper actually shows up at your demise, it is a privileged death indeed. The death wraith serves as a sort of caretaker and keeper of the dead, possessing a connection to them that the living do not. Individuals become death wraiths when their soul gets caught on the cusp between life and death, supposedly because they embrace the idea of dying too eagerly. So what had happened to Cutter Flint to inspire his obsession with departing this life? Had it been what compelled him to come to Hawthorn Lane? Whatever the reason, he was now neither alive nor dead, but stuck somewhere in between, until he resolved what had ensnared him.

I turned my arm over and studied my new tattoo for clues, but it was merely a plain old skull and gave away nothing. Leaning down I sniffed at it and inhaled the scent of vetiver, ashes, and dust. For as long as I bore this tattoo, I carried Cutter Flint with me. The idea both unnerved me and sent a little buzz through my stomach. To be wanted, whatever the reason, is a powerful allure, and hard to resist.

I am wanted, therefore I am.

Nonsense, I scolded myself. One can exist without the acknowledgement of others, right?

Unsure how to answer that loaded, and perhaps somewhat pitiful, question, I read through the rest of the book's report until my eyes caught on the word *Brand*. I skimmed through the description, then re-read it again, more carefully this time, my anger growing with every word.

When a Death Wraith sets his brand on another of his kind, it cannot be undone, except through an act of sacrifice. Be it blood spilled or life given, the sacrifice must be great.

Holy hell. That bastard was going to pay for this.

I slammed the book shut and stared off into space, my chest heaving with fury. *How dare he?* I wasn't cattle, to be branded his property simply because he felt like it. Branding shouldn't even be done to cattle, or any creature, unless the little deviant wants it, of course. Just because Cutter held this delusion that I was one of his kind didn't mean I had to suffer for it. I might be Omni, but I felt quite certain I wasn't a death wraith. If I truly had been responsible for Jaimen's recovery, then I'd helped someone return from death. If I was interpreting the role of a death wraith correctly, then this sort of behavior was quite the opposite of what they can do, or even were allowed to do.

"I am not a death wraith," I said aloud, my whole body trembling with indignation.

Seeing that my fingers were trembling I sensed I needed a break from my growing wrath, and the best cure for pique was hard work. I stood and shoved the book back into place, then spent the rest of the afternoon stirring up batches of *Dewel-Juice*. I hated waste, and the dew I'd gathered on May Day would soon lose its efficacy if not properly prepared. I'd meant to make the juice before I left, but it had slipped my distracted mind. Now I was grateful for something to do. I'd already let the dew sit in glass bottles in the sunlight, which allowed the dregs to settle, then strained out the residue three times before leaving the remaining liquid to sit again. All I had to do now to finish the potent *Dewel-Juice* recipe was mix rowan dust and dried blackthorn berries into the dew and bottle it up.

As I worked, my thoughts turned to a topic a little less incendiary— my own feyness. It was becoming quite obvious that I'd always possessed powers, but had never known they existed. I should have guessed, though. My uncanny vision and hearing ability, my speed and agility, my innate sense for gathering both information and delectables. I'd simply thought everyone could do what I could do, even while acknowledging at the back of my mind that perhaps I could do a bit more than the average person. My fey might also be why all the coaches at my school had wanted to recruit me to play for them. In the sixth grade I made starting striker for the 'A' soccer team, even though I'd never played before. I played for one glorious month before my mother ended that dream. Too much money, she claimed, when I told her I needed cleats and shin guards to keep playing. When the coach offered to buy them herself, Mother said I didn't have time for useless activities and told the coach to leave me the hell alone or she'd make her life a nightmare. After that, coach and all the other coaches at school stopped talking to me. So did a lot of kids. That's when I learned how to go it alone.

From *Fey or Foe* I'd discovered that most fey can only do a few things well—mages can fly and cast a wide range of spells. Elves, along with possessing excellent hearing and the ability to do simple charms, are often good at one particular skill, typically one upon which their livelihood depends. While faeries are hard to categorize, they excel at enthrallment, transfiguration, and glamour. As an Omni, however, I should be able to do all these things well. But what did that mean exactly? I was excited to find out, though wary. As a child I'd read too many books and seen too many movies that warned of the perils of possessing great power, oftentimes leading to an outcome involving immolation of some sort.

Finished with the juice, I wiped my hands on a towel and returned to the bookshelf. It was time I learned a little more about myself. I pulled out *Fey or Foe* and opened it to about the middle, then paged my way to the O's. Omni-Fey, I soon discovered, had its own, very large section. I read through it, feeling a growing sense of excitement. There were so many things I could do! Spells, flying, augmentation of powers, energy sourcing, mind control, healing, possession, and more. Better than any superhero, or villain.

I had the potential to do so much good, but also the potential to cause a lot of harm. The book made it very clear that training is essential for Omni-Feys, starting very young. I was twenty-four and already set in my ways, no longer a moldable child. I was beginning to realize that I was like a spark and the rest of the world a cardboard box full of gasoline-soaked rags. I could light the whole bloody world on fire if I wanted to…or even if I didn't want to. A dangerous part of me found that sort of power deliciously appealing.

To avoid destroying the earth and everyone on it, including myself, my best and only option was to seek training. It was very late in the game, but I was a fast and motivated learner. I didn't think I had a choice, anyway. Doing magic to save my cottage from flooding had set things in motion, and I couldn't turn back. I had a feeling that if I didn't learn to control what I could do, my powers would consume me, and in turn, everything I touched.

But the list was so long. Where to start? In a perfect world I knew which of these skills I most wanted to conquer…I wanted to learn to fly. I wanted to be able to soar like the ravens and falcons passing over my head countless times a day. I wanted to skim the treetops and touch the moon. I wanted to feel the freedom of the air and sky, the wind rushing past me. And after encountering the strange behavior of the wood fey and Cutter Flint, I wanted to have the ability to quickly escape from danger when it arose, as I had a feeling it would. Flying could do all this for me, and more.

There was one person I knew who could teach me to fly, and that was Avice Montrose, best friend and current competition—if you could call it that—for Kyran Van der Daarke. She was already training Kyran and Ilia. All I had to do was join them.

Question was, would Avice let me?

Chapter Eight

A s I readied myself for my night out with Kyran I still hadn't made up my mind about consulting Avice. I wouldn't put it past her to say no, merely to keep me away from Kyran. The rejection part wasn't my big worry, though I wasn't keen on it. My big worry was the idea of having to rely on her for something. Avice keeps track of favors like a bookie with bets, and I didn't like to be beholden to anyone.

Staring at myself in the mirror, my eyes roaming over my black Morticia Addams-like gown with its hypnotic sapphire shimmer, I finally decided I would ask her. What did I have to lose beyond my dignity? Besides, I had a week of nothing better to do. Plus, if she said yes, I would get to see Ilia and make sure she was doing okay. The fact that Kyran might be there had nothing to do with my decision.

I donned my silver Celt torque and matching tree of life bracelet, which effectively covered my new skull tattoo, and studied my reflection. Tilting my head to one side, I realized something. I looked different. Grander, somehow, or maybe more majestic. I looked queen-like. I laughed and made a face at myself. If I let my head get any bigger, it'd pop off like a dandelion's.

As it was nearing half past six, I grabbed a silvery shawl and headed outside to walk into the village. It was time to find out what Kyran was up to. But when I turned from locking the door I spotted the Van der Daarke carriage already waiting outside the gate, though I can't say I was entirely shocked to see it there. Josepha, Kyran's new driver and my wood elf friend—not to mention Ilia's crush—gave me a cheery wave, then turned and knocked on the carriage roof. The door swung open and Kyran unfolded his long form from the carriage. At six-four, he was a sight to see. He had quickly adapted to Hawthorn Lane's more formal, antiquated style of dress, and the dark cloak and top hat he wore made him look both elegant and formidable.

I folded my arms. "I told you I'd meet you there."

"Did you?" He opened the gate and strode toward me, his steps long and quick, his eyes on me, dark and intense.

It was all I could do to hold my ground. "You know I did. I yelled it loudly enough. You could've heard me all the way into next week."

"This way you won't have to walk."

"What if I fancied myself a walk?"

"I've heard you already had a long one today. Or was it more of a run?"

I blinked. Did this man have eyes everywhere? Or had he purchased his own messenger bird to spy on me? "Is that so?"

"Did something scare you at the cemetery?"

I relaxed a little. Whoever, or whatever, had spotted me, it had been after I'd delivered Renwick safely—well, *successfully*, anyway—into Matron's hot little hands. I gave a small laugh, keeping it light. "Of course not. I often run. I like to pretend I can beat the wind." Which is true, and maybe someday soon I'd actually get my wish. The thought made me smile.

"I wasn't spying on you," Kyran was quick to point out.

"Oh?" Such power in those two little letters, though I threw in a skeptical eyebrow arch to drive home the point that I wasn't swallowing his fabrication.

"Melaina was."

My mistake. Then I recalled another way he could track me, all on his own…through my blood. "Why would she waste her time on a simple gatherer?"

He gave me a wry look. "I wager the term simple has never been applied to you, Lorelle. Anyway, I told you she wouldn't rest easy about this curse and now that—" He paused, took a step closer. "Now that Renwick has run off, she's out for blood."

I pretended surprise. "Renwick's run off?"

"They had a bad fight, and then this morning he was gone." He studied me closely. Such scrutiny made it hard to stay still, to maintain my composure, though in similar situations with others I managed to handle myself just fine. "I don't suppose you've any idea where he might be?"

"Renwick's a big boy. I'm sure he's fine."

"You didn't answer my question."

"I didn't feel the need to, the answer being obvious." I pressed a hand to my stomach, then fluttered my eyelids, as though lightheaded.

Kyran grabbed my arm to steady me, and a shockwave rippled through my body, leaving me to question my motives. I could have picked numerous other methods as a means of changing the topic, all of which didn't involve Kyran touching me. And yet I'd chosen the faint.

I never could behave.

"Lorelle?" His dark eyes scanned my face. "Are you all right?"

"I haven't eaten in a while," I replied in a shaky voice that wasn't altogether feigned. The electric pulses, far from dying down, had increased, weakening my resolve to stay strong against Kyran and his crafty ways. "I must be hungry. All that running, I guess. Then I spent the afternoon working on an elixir and it's late…"

"You work too hard."

I laughed. "I just need to eat more, that's all."

"Come." He pulled me along with him. When I couldn't keep up with his long strides, he seemed to think it was due to weakness and not from the fact that he was a giant. With one quick movement, I was up off my feet and in his arms. The hot forks of lightning heating me up from the inside out made me truly woozy and I decided to just go with it, telling myself to enjoy the ride. Seeing I was 'indisposed,' Josepha jumped down and held the coach door open. Kyran managed to maneuver me inside without knocking my head against the doorway, then slid in after me. "Quickly now, Josepha," he said, a tone of amusement in his voice, "before our Lorelle fades away before our very eyes."

Damn him. He was on to me. Josepha winked at me, then shut the door. I heard him clamber up to the driver's seat, making the carriage sway a bit, then we started off toward *Chez Chantilly* at a sedate pace.

"I would've been fine," I mumbled in annoyance. We were sitting very close, my knee nudging his outer thigh.

"I know. But I wasn't about to take any chances with you."

Was he being flippant, or did he mean it? Damnit, I couldn't tell with the man.

"How thoughtful you are." I fanned my face. It was hot in the enclosed quarters. Too hot. "Can we open a window?"

"Of course." Although he had a window on his side, Kyran reached across me, his scent and nearness tempting me to grab hold of him and never let go, and pulled down my window, allowing the cool night air to rush in. I leaned back and let it wash over me.

We didn't speak again, which was exactly what I needed to ready myself for the ordeal of our upcoming meal. I knew Kyran was going to interrogate me, and I knew I was going to need a clear head to sidestep his every lunge and thrust. It didn't escape me, of course, that nearly every other female in this village would welcome Kyran's lunges and thrusts.

I quickly leaned out the window, sucking in cool, fresh, much-needed air.

At last we pulled up outside *Chez Chantilly* and I thought maybe now I'd be able to breathe normally again. The chicest restaurant in town, it was located on the periphery of the village proper and built into the side of a hill. The space had originally been intended as a mound tomb, but no one knows if it was ever actually used for that purpose. When the owners, Alindra Abu and Fogle Peveril, maestro elves, had been looking for a place, they found the tomb and opened it. It was empty… of bones anyway.

While adding on and preparing the space for their restaurant, a few unexpected visitors showed up, and all of them dead as the dirt being dug up and hauled away. Rumor had it that their bones had once resided in the tomb, but had been stolen to be used for spells. The more outgoing spirits of the lot are a faerie ballerina called Peretta, a man who'd once been a werewolf and answered to Gangus, and a depressed pixie named Bloo. There were others, but these three took top billing. Not only did I find them amusing, I realized that if they showed up at our meal, they could serve as a good distracter, if needed. They can be quite the divas, taking center stage whenever they're feeling particularly neglected.

The carriage pulled up to the front entrance and gently rocked as Josepha jumped down. He first opened the door for Kyran, who came around and opened the door for me. I can open my own door, of course, but despite it being a bit pretentious on my part, I rather like being waited on. Back in the Alterworld I'd heard far too many women complaining about always having to do the waiting on. If both sides did it, fine. But that often wasn't the case. She'd bring home the bacon, fry it up in a pan, then wash the pan, and deal with the children, laundry, and housecleaning, too, while the man watched television and drank beer. Maybe things are better now over there, but I'd bet good money women still carry the majority of the burden. I wasn't going to be that woman. I'm an independent, hard-working kind of gal, and someone opening my door for me isn't going to change that. So I was going to let myself be waited on and enjoy it for the luxury and rarity that it is.

I slid out, looked up into Kyran's solemn eyes, and smiled. Kyran isn't much of a smiler, but when he does smile, it gets you right in the chest. He smiled back at me in return, a real one that sent a hot liquid bolt through me, then turned and offered his arm. I accepted it, got my jolt, which I suspect was becoming to me like coffee to a caffeine addict, and we walked toward the entrance to the restaurant while Josepha drove off, taking the carriage to the village stables to wait for us. He would hang out there with the other drivers, sharing a cheap but hearty ale stew purchased from the owner, Tabby Rose, and drinking and playing cards. It was a great place to gather information, but I was glad that tonight it wasn't my destination.

"Count Van der Daarke, most felicitous greetings!" Fogle Peveril, co-owner of *Chez Chantilly*, exclaimed, and his long, curved nose nearly touched the ground as he gave an excessive bow. Standing just outside the entrance, his potbelly thrust outward as he beamed affably at us, bejeweled hands outspread. He was short, but grand, with full red cheeks and tufts of white hair sticking out from beneath his dark pink beret. His partner, Alindra, stood half a foot taller than him and ran the place with an iron fist. Fogle was more the 'people person' of the operation, while Alindra wouldn't even notice you standing in front of her, especially if she was in the kitchen. Food was her passion; people were not. Well, unless you made the mistake of criticizing her food. Then *you* would become her passion, and not in a good way. More like a "I'm going to hunt you to hell and back and make you sorry you were born" kind of way. "I received your message and set aside our best table for you."

Kyran nodded. "Perfect."

Fogle turned to me, his red cheeks growing even rosier. "Mademoiselle Gragan, it is a great honor." He clasped my hands in his warm, pudgy ones.

I regarded him suspiciously, but was careful to keep my skepticism hidden. Typically Fogle hardly noticed me, at least not in Avice's shadow. I'd always thought that would be par for the course until I died, but apparently not, even when I had a Count standing next to me who cast an even bigger shadow than Avice did. It appeared Matron was right. People were going to fawn over me, not because I'm this super awesome person who can do no wrong, but because I might be Omni-Fey.

"It's a pleasure to be here, Monsieur Peveril," I said, pulling my hands from his eager grasp. "What's on the menu tonight?"

"Come inside and see all we have to offer!" He ushered us into the restaurant, glancing back at the passersby watching our interaction with avid curiosity. He nodded at them importantly, then scurried after us.

The interior of *Chez Chantilly* is best described as cavern chic. Thick roots covered the walls like a trellis, and hundreds of lit candles dangled from the woody tendrils growing from the dirt ceiling. The original tomb hadn't been small, possibly the size of my cottage, but it had been enlarged during the renovation, going downward a good fifteen feet and outward to encompass a kitchen and more seating area. Large mirrors throughout made it look even bigger. A small stage had been built for entertainment, and the lyrical sounds of *Mad Hatter*, the group that had played at the *Danse Macabre* ball, regaled us as we stepped inside.

As we descended the stairs I looked around, taking in the other diners and the dark setting of the place. Most of the tables were not yet filled, as it was still early for Hawthorn Lane, and I was just fine with that. Those patrons already seated glanced up at us, then stared openly as Fogle led us to our table in the middle of the room. Gracing each tabletop was a serpentine vase that held a single monkshood, a beautiful, though poisonous, purple flower; its presence convenient for those whose dates aren't going well, or, on the other side of the coin, serving as a foil for any break-up plans.

"I feel like we're center stage," I said to Fogle, unable to keep the displeasure from my voice. I do not like center stage. It's a place one goes when you want to be looked at, like Avice, not to look about, like I wanted to do. But to give Fogle credit, this was regarded as his best table.

"Oh, dear!" Fogle wrung his hands. "Is that bad?"

Kyran pulled out a velvet chair and nodded at me to sit. "It's perfect," he said. I glared at him, but decided to go along, even though he'd given me the chair that left me with my back to the door. Making a scene is not my thing, either, but I could see why people do it. To get your way. He scooted my chair in, then sat down across from me.

Fogle hovered over our table, rubbing his stubby hands together, his numerous rings clicking against one another. "Would you like to hear the daily specials? Alindra has outdone herself tonight!"

"We'd be delighted," Kyran replied graciously, as it was obvious Fogle was nearly bursting to share them.

I nodded my agreement, and the maestro elf launched into a recitation that made my mouth water. From whisky-pickled oysters to spiced oeufs en cocotte, all the specials sounded delicious. "Now, I shall bring you the menus and you shall make your choice. Perhaps drinks first?"

"I'll have the *Lightning*," Kyran said. "Lorelle prefers *Dark Spirits*, isn't that right?"

"Actually, I'll take a carafe of the *Stygian Spumante*. It better fits my mood tonight." A dark 'white' wine, it was a juxtaposition that matched my feelings of late of being neither here nor there, one or the other.

"Excellent choice," Fogle beamed. "Your *waiter*," he gave a quick sideways glance at Kyran, "shall be here soon with your drinks. Regretfully, I must return to my station at the door. We're booked solid this evening"—he just barely restrained himself from giggling with glee—"and my customers expect me to be there to greet them." His round little body swelled with self-importance as he scurried off. I had a feeling being "booked solid" was a result of Fogle letting the entire village know Kyran Van der Daarke was eating at his restaurant tonight.

When the elf was gone, Kyran unfolded his black and violet linen napkin and laid it across his lap, then leaned forward. "You can stop scowling at me, Lorelle. I'm doing this to help you. If others see us together they'll think you're doing everything you can to help undo the curse."

"I don't give a rip about the curse," I hissed. "And they can bloody well see us in a corner."

"Such manners," he tsked. "You really do need to eat."

I sighed. He was playing the game better than I was. Calmness begets information, a motto I would do well to remember. "You're right," I replied sweetly.

"And you don't need to pretend with me. I know there's something going on with you. Some reason you're mad at me. I'm quite sure I deserve it, but do me the favor of explaining first what it is I'm guilty of, will you?"

This was new. Getting information in Hawthorn Lane is a lot like performing a dance one has never danced before—lots of missteps before finding your rhythm. Kyran's approach was a refreshing change, and I decided to take him at his word. "Why do you want to rid this village of its curse so badly, Kyran? Really and truly?"

He shrugged casually. "Because it's a *curse*?"

"You can do better than that. I want to know…what are you getting out of it?"

He leaned closer, so close I could touch his lips with my own. I wondered how he would react if I kissed him as he had kissed me the night of the ball? It was tempting to find out. "I get to escape from the hell it has put my family through for generations, that's what. And since it was your ancestor who began all this, I would think you'd be falling all over yourself trying to set things right."

"So you're saying you're doing this for altruistic reasons," I said, ignoring his pertinent though untrue statement, "and that coming out of it looking like a hero doesn't factor in?"

"Who's going to look like a hero?" came a familiar voice from behind me, and I jerked backward, away from Kyran.

I turned to see a waiter approaching us, a tray of drinks in hand. "Renwick? What are *you* doing here?"

Chapter Nine

Renwick smiled as he set our drinks on the table. "Good evening, Cousin. Good evening, Lorelle." His eyes found my cleavage and seemed intent on burrowing into the dark crevice between my breasts. I made a gesture that conveyed, *My eyes are up here, buddy*. He was only pretending interest to irritate Kyran anyway.

He reluctantly dragged his gaze up to meet mine. "I'm to be your waiter for this evening."

Leaning back, Kyran looked Renwick up and down, one dark eyebrow raised in disbelief. Dressed in the black violet velvet the *Chez Chantilly* staff wore, Renwick looked quite dapper. I had to give the guy credit. He'd found himself a job *really* quickly. But with the proper incentive (horny old witches), I believe people can perform miracles. I'm sure it helped that Fogle couldn't resist hiring a Van der Daarke. What a coup for the elf. No wonder he'd taken a peek at Kyran when he'd told us our waiter would be coming with our drinks. He wanted to see if Kyran approved. Judging by Kyran's irate expression, he did not.

"Do you have any idea what you've done?" he hissed at Renwick.

"Did I bring you the wrong drinks? A thousand apologies."

"Stop being a toad. You know perfectly well what I'm talking about."

"I've gotten a job. That isn't against Van der Daarke law, is it?"

"Of course not. I'm simply not sure why you had to do it at Ilia's expense."

"She can take care of herself."

"So you're saying she should run off like you did?"

Renwick's eyes scanned the restaurant, spotted all the curious faces turned in our direction, including Fogle's, and leaned toward Kyran. "You know your sister, Cousin. She won't be happy until everyone is drowning in misery like she is. What did you expect me to do? Let her drag me down with her?"

Kyran reached out and gripped both sides of the table. "I expected you to have more courage."

"I did have courage," Renwick growled. "I left her knowing she'd want to kill me once she tracked me down. Yet I stayed here in Hawthorn Lane instead of slinking off to the Alterworld. I won't have her dictating my life any longer. I don't belong in that castle anyway. I'm not one of you, and thank Grim for that!"

Kyran slowly relaxed his grip. "Not so fast, Cousin. You're a Van der

Daarke whether you like it or not, and that means you and I will work together to figure out what to do about my sister. You brought her here, after all."

"I'm not moving back, and I'm not getting back together with her."

"No. I think both would be unwise, and change nothing."

Renwick looked surprised, and wary. "What do you want me to do, then?"

"For now I think all we can do is wait and see what she's planning. Though I'm afraid your keeping a low profile is out. She'll find out soon enough where you are."

Renwick smiled and handed us our gravestone-shaped menus, the top displaying the amusing epitaph, *Each Bite is Like a Little Death*, on it. "My circumstances require I work."

"I could give you the money."

For a moment Renwick looked tempted, then he glanced at me and saw me watching him with a knowing smile. "No, thank you, Cousin. I must do this on my own."

"She will find you, you know."

"I've made an arrangement that should hold her off for a little while."

"At least a week?"

"I think so."

"Fine." Kyran opened his menu and began to scan the contents, topic apparently dismissed.

I glanced at Renwick, who stood poised, quill pen and notepad in hand. "I'm going to need a few minutes," I told him. He nodded and pivoted, striding away to another table to wait on a faerie couple, who were, of course, staring at us. I turned my attention back to Kyran studying his menu as though he hadn't a care in the world beyond choosing the perfect appetizer. "Why do you want him to be out of reach for a week?"

He looked up at me. "No particular reason."

"I don't believe you." What *was* he planning? And what did Renwick have to do with it?

"Then you tell me what my reason might be."

"I don't know, but I'm pretty sure it has something to do with this scheme you have going and why you want me to stay around for a week." I leaned forward. "Don't you think I should know what it is you're up to?"

"I don't. The game pie looks good. What are you getting?"

"What? Oh." I scanned the menu, found my usual. "The roast partridge." I set down the menu. "I should know what's going on, Kyran. The more soldiers we have united against Melaina, the better."

"That sounds good, but I believe I'll get the game pie. More filling, I think, and today I'm famished."

"Are you listening to me?"

He set down his menu and matched my bent-over stance. "I listen to your every word, Lorelle. I just don't always agree with you."

How infuriating he was being. "I've found that people who don't agree with me tend to be fools with a death wish."

Kyran opened his mouth to answer when a hullaballoo broke out near the doorway. His expression was hard to read as he watched what was going on behind my back, and I turned to see Avice gracefully making her way down the steps, even while wearing cloven-heeled shoes, her arms thrown wide as she seemingly regaled the entire room with an amusing anecdote. She had Ilia and Juletta in tow, and both were looking in our direction as pointedly as Avice was ignoring our presence. Her early arrival told me she'd known we were going to be here. But had Fogle been her source, or Kyran?

When Avice reached the main floor, she swayed her way to our table, her sunset blue eyes looking everywhere but at us. She was wearing a tight-waisted, low-cut, nearly see-through gown of will-o-the-wisp organza. Strategically placed pixie lights accentuated her curves with daring accuracy. When she reached the table, she stopped abruptly, a calculated act that set her red curls dancing, and let out a little screech of surprise. "Oh, dear! I didn't realize my *usual* table was taken." She flicked her head back at Fogle hovering behind her, his eyes wide with both agitation at offending his best customer and feverish anticipation at the thought of the impending drama this little contretemps might stir up.

"I'm so terribly sorry, Mademoiselle Montrose!" he cried. "I didn't realize you were coming tonight. You always let me know!" Judging by his reaction, he obviously hadn't been the one to tell Avice about our dinner reservation—not directly, anyway.

Kyran stood up. "Avice. Good to see you." He took her by the shoulders, which were plump and bare, and leaned down to kiss her on both cheeks. Avice made sure I noticed, giving me a triumphant smirk that said, *Game on, contest won, and award ceremony about to commence!* "I was not aware you were coming, either, or I wouldn't have asked for the best seat in the house." He motioned to the table. "Lorelle and I will move and let you ladies take center stage. You all look so lovely, the whole room should be able to see you." So Kyran hadn't been the one to tell her, either. Unless this was some sort of ruse on their part. Though why they would pretend ignorance in front of me was unclear.

Ilia cast me a quick sidelong glance. Her long, golden hair was pulled back in a tight bun, which did nothing to soften her sharp features and protruding front teeth, and I thought she looked unhappy. I felt guilty I hadn't gone to visit her. It wasn't her fault that I was in a bad place, or that she had a mother no one wanted to be around.

"I think that would be just the thing," I said. "How kind of you, Avice. You know I don't like being out in the middle of everything."

The smirk turned into a grimace. "This is the greeting I get, Lorelle? I haven't seen you for a whole week!" Was I mistaken or did she look hurt? "We could join tables, couldn't we, Fogle?" She fluttered her long lashes at him and he sucked in a deep breath. Not even Fogle, who preferred his love interests to be decidedly less feminine, could resist Avice's allure.

"Not tonight," Kyran said in a tone that brooked no argument. "I need to speak to Lorelle about something private."

"Surely it can be shared with friends?" Avice purred, grabbing his arm and pressing her breasts against it.

He patted her shoulder gently, then removed his arm from her grasp with impressive dexterity. "I'm afraid not, Avice. For everyone's protection, you understand."

"I do not understand!" she cried.

"Just sit, Avice." Juletta steered her into a chair that faced the crowd. "I'm hungry." She winked at me as she took a padded chair. "Not having eaten for a hundred years, it seems I'm making up for lost time." She looked lovely in an aubergine silk that brought out the blue in her eyes. It was a little strange seeing her looking so fresh and alive when at our last meeting she'd sported fangs and rotting flesh. Like her sister, Lady Faylan, she had maintained her youthful appearance despite being over a hundred years old, and I wondered if there was a family secret, beyond an age-cure, that kept them looking so young.

Kyran pulled a chair from another table and held it out for Ilia to sit. Avoiding my eye, she sat down, her expression remote. I felt a pang in my chest. I wanted to say hello to her, but she was obviously upset with me, and the greeting stuck in my throat. I couldn't blame her for being mad. During one of the hardest times of her life, I'd abandoned her to indulge my own self-pity at the choice I had made to leave.

My two friends in Hawthorn Lane, and both of them hated me right now. Maybe it was best to go as soon as I could. Though perhaps a real friend wouldn't dash off at the first sign of trouble. It was something to consider. I had very little idea what real friends acted like, never having had one other than Avice (and perhaps Dallen at one time), so I wasn't exactly sure how healthy our friendship was. Though I suspected it could use some work.

"Enjoy your dinner, ladies." Kyran bowed, picked up our drinks, and nodded at Fogle. "Another table, then?"

I turned to wave, but Avice ignored me, her full lips pouting beautifully. Juletta was already perusing her menu, and Ilia quickly grabbed one and placed it before her, blocking her face from view.

"Of course, Count Van der Daarke," Fogle fawned. "You are most gracious!"

"On the contrary, I simply found that like Lorelle, I prefer something a little more *private*." The look he gave me when he said this sent shivers up my spine. What was he up to now?

Fogle showed us to a little nook, complete with its own black velvet curtains that one could pull shut for complete privacy. Kyran gestured for me to sit with my back to the wall, thank Grim, allowing me to easily survey the room. He slipped into the dark space opposite me, his presence undetectable by most of the patrons in the room.

"Is this to your satisfaction, milord?"

"Yes, it is." He sat down. "Could you let Renwick know we're ready to order?" It was a masterful stroke designed to show the elf he didn't give a damn that his cousin was working as a waiter.

"Naturally, naturally." The round elf spun around. "Ah, here he is now!" His eyes flew to the entrance, which was filling up. "I'll leave you in his obviously capable hands."

"What can I get you?" Renwick asked when he arrived, looking straight at me as he spoke.

"I'll have the crab apple-stuffed roast partridge."

"Excellent. And you, Count Van der…Daarke?" Renwick flashed me a mischievous grin.

"I'll have the game pie, with a side of fried sourdough bread, and a carafe of *Dark Spirits*."

"Your wish is my command." Renwick gave us a slight bow, if a mocking one, and left to go place our order.

"What can you see?" Kyran asked after taking a drink.

I took a sip of wine, savored its spicy charm, then looked around. "The place is filling up very quickly. I don't think I've ever seen it this busy."

"Do the others see you?"

I took another sip. The *Stygian Spumante* was delicious and the nook warm and dark. If this were a real date, I'd be in heaven. "They do, and I'm pretty sure they know I'm with you." In addition to my fine-tuned hearing, I can read lips quite well, so it wasn't hard to see the other patrons' mouths forming the words Count Van der Daarke and Lorelle Gragan over and over.

"Excellent."

"The Iverich family just arrived," I went on. "Ah, yes. There's Charlton." He was the eldest of the faerie family, and the heir apparent to their successful business, even though I wasn't sure he wanted to inherit it. He also looked as though he'd rather be anywhere but *Chez Chantilly*. Where I'd always thought of him as rather a dry stick, after we danced together at the ball, I found myself both feeling sorry for him and kind of liking him, two feelings I pretty much never experienced in regard to high-borns. But it couldn't be easy bearing the weight of your family's entire welfare on your shoulders, so I cut him some slack. Trailing after Charlton came his mother, Coriana, his sister, Enchanté, and a sulky faerie who looked as though he'd been rode hard and put away wet. "Looks as though Hanover is back from the Alterworld. He's the youngest Iverich," I explained. "No Wexford, though." Wexford was Charlton's father, and a bit of a bastard. Well, more than a bit. He was an entire bastard.

"I heard he's ill."

"Oh, he's always ill. More likely he didn't come because he and the little missus had an argument."

Kyran set his glass down and leaned forward, one eyebrow raised enquiringly. I liked that he wasn't above enjoying a good gossip. "An argument?"

"I'll bet Coriana wanted to come here tonight and he didn't. The children have no say in the matter, so they had to come. But Wexford does his own thing, and I'm sure he opted out. Coriana must be up to something."

Kyran looked satisfied, though I didn't know why. "And who else has come?"

My expression no doubt soured. "Baroness Arie, along with her little entourage." Which included Fan and Dawn Ravenna, the two snotty high-elf proprietors of *Fawn's Fashions* and little sycophants, apparently. Coldly attractive in a pale blue gown of *Satan Satin*, and with her thick brown hair done up in its usual snake-like coils around her head, Merceen Arie was the epitome of hauteur. She was merely the owner of a perfumery called *Scentsibility*, yet acted as though she were queen of all she surveyed. Like Lady Faylan, I wondered if Merceen had 'borrowed' the title baroness to impress people. I wouldn't put it past the conniving elf. I was also pretty sure she had her sights set on Kyran. He was quite a catch, and one of the few villagers who could hold his own with her. As much as she liked to be the boss of everyone, I had no doubt her ultimate fantasy mate was someone who would take charge and give her a good old spank when she'd been naughty or, more fittingly, disgustingly nice.

"Good," he responded smugly.

I fixed my attention on him. "Why?"

"Because I want all of them to know we're together."

I took an indelicate swig of wine. This night was not going as I'd planned. Though, come to think of it, I'm not sure what I'd planned beyond showing up and trying to wrestle out of Kyran his motives for keeping me around another week.

"This all centers around the curse, of course."

"Of course."

"Well, you've got your wish because your audience is coming to us."

Chapter Ten

"Who specifically?" Kyran demanded, though he didn't turn around to see who was approaching. I was tempted to say Fan and Dawn, both of whom had him in their sights, as well, but I decided to go with the truth even though it wasn't nearly as funny.

"Coriana Iverich and Charlton. I like him. Her I can't stand. She's a high-born *snob*, and Grim knows I can't stand those."

Sensing I was aiming my poisoned dart at him, Kyran's jaw hardened as he slid out of his booth chair and stood to greet Coriana. I reluctantly followed after him. "Madame Iverich," he said smoothly as she floated her way toward him. He took her hand and bowed over it, then nodded briefly at her son. "Charlton."

Coriana looked supremely pleased with herself, her flaring nostrils filling up with the aroma of success. She was one of those faeries so ethereal you felt like you could pass your hand through her body and not feel a thing. She always wore silver and white, and the colors matched her long, done-up silver hair and silvery eyes, and her pale, nearly translucent skin. Today she looked more lively than usual, two red spots highlighting her angular cheekbones and her hands fidgeting as though not knowing quite where to go. I already figured she was up to something and her behavior confirmed my suspicion. She typically was quite reclusive and rarely left her sprawling estate, but when she did, you knew it was for something she was scheming to attain.

"Count Van der Daarke, how lovely to see you. I spotted you when I came in." Which was impossible as he was hidden in the booth. But she'd seen me. "I thought I'd stop by to say hello before dining."

"I'm glad for the opportunity to see you again, Madame Iverich."

"And you, as well, Mistress Gragan." She peered around Kyran. "How lovely you look." Her practiced eyes scanned me from head to toe and in doing so she couldn't quite contain the contempt she felt for me. I knew she didn't like me—I was poor and not faerie—but I also knew she wasn't going to take the chance of losing out on acquiring an Omni as a possible connection. If it was true that I had come from a powerful, high-born family, as well, then even though I wasn't pure-bred faerie I might pass muster as a spouse for one of her two boys. "You know Charlton, of course." She practically pushed him forward.

"Hello, Charlton," I greeted cheerily, partly because I wanted Coriana to get her hopes up so I could dash them—the three times we had encountered each other, she not only had ignored me, but had literally turned her back on me—but mostly because I thought it might tick off Kyran. He was playing some sort of game with me, and winning, and I didn't like it.

"A pleasure to see you again, Lorelle." Charlton took my out-stretched hand and kissed it, his lips cool and dry against my skin. As was typical with Charlton, he was impeccably dressed in pale gray tails and a dark heather waistcoat. His light brown hair was shaped into perfection, his silvery eyes watchful.

"Dinner with the family, hm?" I poked. "And Hanover has come home for a stay. How fun for you all."

His eyes, a dimmer version of his mother's silvery orbs, glinted coolly. "A real treat," he replied dryly. "We should get together some time, shouldn't we? You must be running low on Effervescence. I could stop by and sort you out."

"That would be lovely," I replied, allowing him to hang onto my hand for longer than necessary, seeing Coriana and Kyran's eyes fastened on us. "I rather need sorting out at the moment."

"Absolutely!" Coriana practically yelled. "You two really *must* get together." She looked rather wild-eyed, and a part of me actually felt a little sorry for her. She and her husband, Wexford, didn't get along, which is why she spent so much time building her never-ending house. Being that she and Wexford pretty much hated each other, I'd think she'd want me to get together with Kyran and end the curse, thereby fixing their relationship. But then, maybe the hatred went so deep that she didn't know how to function without it.

Lady Faylan appeared at the top of the stairs at that moment, and calmly surveyed the room. She spotted me, and the company I was keeping, and her blank gray eyes blinked once, slowly and distinctly. *What is the world coming to?* I wondered with a smile. The upright, uptight overseer of our little village never indulged in anything that might be frivolous, and *Chez Chantilly* was the epitome of frivolous.

Yet here she was…

Her high-necked, dark blue gown was slightly fancier than the usual prison warden look she liked to effect, and her hair not so severely pulled back. Had she come with Kyran's seduction in mind? If so, she was going to have to do better than this. Like show a little ankle, or something.

Seeing my attention diverted, Kyran turned, and when his eyes found her, a satisfied expression crossed his features. I realized why she had come now…because she knew he was here with me. But why was he looking so smug about it? Because he wanted to make her jealous? Because he wanted the sole credit of breaking the curse? Or because he wanted her to know he was with *me*?

I know which one I'd choose.

Seeing our distracted gazes, Coriana's head swiveled about, a strange expression, almost a nervous one, creasing her face when she saw Lady Faylan. She quickly turned back to us. "Would you care to join us?" She waved her hand toward her table, another coveted spot almost at center stage, but not quite. That had to grate on her. In her mind, the Iverich family ranked high above Avice. Unfortunately for Coriana her lack of patronage did little to elevate her status with Fogle, a business elf, through and through.

"You're too kind, Madame Iverich," Kyran replied, "but Lorelle and I have business to discuss. Some other time?"

"Of course." Her glance darted back to Lady Faylan and a secretive look narrowed her eyes.

Charlton squeezed my hand and I realized he was still holding it. "Can I come by tomorrow, Lorelle?"

"That should be fine. Come in the morning."

Kyran stepped forward, his hand held out to Charlton, forcing us to part ways. "Good seeing you, Charlton. Perhaps when you're done with Lorelle, you can stop by the castle. I have a little project I'm working on that needs your expertise."

Charlton took Kyran's hand and shook it. "It would be my pleasure. I look forward to discussing it with you." He looked anything but excited at the prospect, but I suppose when you're in sales you have to dissemble. "Enjoy your evening." With a bow to me, he and his mother left us, Coriana giving me a stiff nod in farewell. I refused to curtsy to her, but I returned the nod as regally as I could. One corner of her mouth tilted upward in a tiny smirk, indicating that I'd somehow managed to do it wrong. Damn her icy eyes. Really, that woman could do without that stick permanently lodged up her arse.

Kyran and I sat back down and I was relieved to see Lady Faylan join the Iverich family at their table. I wasn't sure I wanted to duel with her this evening. Being rebuffed by Ilia and Avice had knocked me back more than I cared to admit. It was a weakness on my part, and not one I felt sure I could fix.

Our return was good timing, as our food arrived just then, Renwick delivering it on a black tray carved into the shape of a medieval shield. He laid our dishes out before us with the expertise of someone who had done this before, and I decided he hadn't been exaggerating when he'd told me he'd been working from a young age.

"Will that be all?" he asked when the table was set.

"One moment." Kyran leaned back against his seat, his jaw tight. Renwick seemed quite talented at setting his cousin on edge. "What will you do if Melaina shows up here tonight?"

Renwick's demeanor matched his cousin's stiffness. "I shall cross that bridge and deal with that troll when I come to it. But for now I have a living to earn. The quicker I can change my circumstances, the better." He glanced quickly at me, then spun away to tend to his other patrons.

Kyran and I ate in silence for a few minutes, each savoring our meal. The partridge was perfectly moist, the apples soft and sweet, with a hint of tart. Kyran offered me a slice of his fried sourdough bread and I accepted, slathering it with bacon butter. After taking a drink, Kyran set down his glass and fixed me with a determined look. "I own Fell Forest."

I glanced up from my plate, startled. "What?"

"That's why Rialban stopped you from leaving."

"You own the *entire* forest?" I paused. "Of course you do. You're a Van der Daarke, and your kind likes to acquire things."

"Yes, we do," he admitted easily, "and according to ancient laws because I own the forest, I can dictate to the creatures who inhabit it."

"Ah. So Rialban thought he'd get in good with the landlord?"

"Something like that."

"Really? Because he told me he stopped me because I have a responsibility to end the curse."

"He's right about that."

I gripped my fork tightly. Lady Faylan's lie was making my life increasingly difficult and I wanted desperately to tell the truth and clear my name, ending this charade. And yet for motives I wasn't quite sure I understood, I held my tongue. "What's the real reason you want me to stay for a week, Kyran?"

He gave me an innocent look. "Real reason?"

"Don't play dumb with me, though you're really quite good at it." I tilted my glass at him, then took a sip.

"I simply need a little more time."

"To do what?"

"I can't tell you."

"Why not?"

He glanced around the room. It was at maximum capacity, and more people stood waiting at the door. The loud buzz of voices filled the cavernous space, nearly drowning out the ethereal sounds of *Mad Hatter*, which I'd much rather listen to over Avice's obvious attempts to show how good a time she was having without Kyran Van der Daarke and Lorelle Gragan's presence. If she'd only stop looking this way, she'd make her point more effectively.

"What do you think of Charlton Iverich?" he asked.

I shrugged noncommittally. "He's tolerable for a toff, and stop changing the subject."

"And why does Renwick keep giving you conspiratorial looks?" he went on, ignoring my command.

"I don't know. Maybe because he and I are conspiring?" If Kyran could dangle his secrets in front of me like a rack of ribs before a starving man, I could do the same.

"What do you mean?"

I sighed. Did I tell him now? He'd find out my role in Renwick's escape soon enough. But did I care if he found out from me versus through the grapevine? Yes, I determined after a moment's reflection, I did. Better to seize control, I decided. "He came to me."

His face darkened with a rush of blood. "What do you mean, he *came to you?*"

I realized how that might sound, like a lover in a romance novel visiting his mistress in the darkest depths of night, and laughed. "He wanted a place to stay."

"With *you?*"

I laughed again, feeling the wine going to my head. "Is that so hard to believe?"

"So he's staying with you?" Kyran gripped the edges of the table. "In your cottage?" He was so angry, he was making the table shake. No, wait. That wasn't him. The whole room went quiet as the shaking grew all around us, a sort of low-key vibration that could only mean one thing. I closed my eyes and inhaled deeply. Yes, most definitely. It was a breach.

When I opened my eyes again, the quiet broke like shattering glass and everyone began talking at once. *Someone has crossed the border!* made the rounds quickly, followed by, *Two crossings in such a short span...who could it be this time?* Strangely, no one sounded afraid. In fact, excitement and anticipation appeared to be the dominant emotions.

"What was that?" Kyran demanded when the shaking stopped.

"That was a breach. It means someone has crossed the border."

Was this the big change that the upside-down birds had heralded? I suppressed a shiver.

"So that's what I felt the night we arrived in Hawthorn Lane. But it didn't happen when Melaina came, did it? I would've remembered that."

Kyran Van der Daarke did not miss much. I liked how quickly his mind worked, if only he wouldn't apply that astuteness to me.

"No, it didn't," I said briefly.

"So it's someone from the Alterworld?" I nodded grimly. Unlike the others in the room, I felt only dread. "I wonder who set it off this time."

I watched Lady Faylan rise and make her way up the stairs, a grim expression hardening her features. I frowned, watching her go with a nagging twitch in my gut. "I don't know, but Lady Faylan appears to be looking into it. I'm sure it's nothing, though."

"All right, then." He accepted this answer quite easily, which, while not a lie, also was not my opinion. "Let's get back to Renwick."

I mentally shook myself, forcing my mind to return its focus back to our conversation. "What about him?"

"I can't believe you're letting him stay with you."

"But I'm—"

"Even knowing what he did to me and Ilia?"

"But you don't—"

"I thought we were in this together."

"In this *together?*" I echoed.

He raised an imperious eyebrow. "It certainly doesn't sound that way."

"Would you please let me speak more than three words in a row?" I yelled at him.

"I won't allow it!" He threw down his linen napkin, but before he could continue, someone burst into the restaurant, obviously winded. It was a member of Lady Faylan's Mage Patrol, a group of witches and warlocks either working for her or apprenticing under her, and who also served as a security force for the village. As soon as the villagers noticed him and went quiet, he drew himself up importantly.

"My fellow Hawthornites…the breach is unsanctioned!"

Chapter Eleven

A vice, of course, screamed, and so did a number of other patrons, not all female, thank Grim. After the screeches died down, the sound of twittering voices soon filled the void.

"What exactly does that mean, an unsanctioned breach?" Kyran demanded, turning from the chaos to grab my hands.

The shock jolted me out of my daze. "It means someone has entered Hawthorn Lane without permission."

"Is that cause for panic? We entered without permission. Didn't know we needed it."

"Your breach was unplanned, but not unsanctioned—your family name earned you your free pass. When we feel the breach, Lady Faylan assesses the danger, then lets us know within a short time if we need to go on alert. We have to be careful about anyone entering our world without warning. They could be fey-hunters, you see."

"And fey-hunters are...?"

"They're Undesirables, either trackers pursuing a fugitive who's hiding out here, or outlawed fey, like vampires and werewolves, who capture other fey to use them for their powers. Our blood is very powerful, you see." It was the first time I'd included myself as a fey, and it felt amazing. "Sometimes, though, it's just a wild animal. Let's hope it's that."

A frown creased his forehead and his grip tightened on my cold hands as he looked me over. "Are you all right, Lorelle? Because you don't look it."

I forced myself to smile. "I'm fine, Kyran, just a little surprised. Everyone here is always worried about fey-hunters, it comes with the territory, but we've never had a real threat in the six years I've lived here."

"Would an Omni-Fey be a particular attraction to outlawed fey?"

His question startled me. Moments before I'd been thrilled to be fey, now I realized that with the good comes the bad. The very bad. "I suppose it might."

"So you could be in danger?"

I pulled in a deep breath. "I'm fine, Kyran. I'm sure it's nothing."

"I'm going to go track down Lady Faylan and find out what's going on."

"Right now?"

"I'll be back. I'm done eating, but you're not. Order us dessert when you've finished."

He was gone before I could think of a sensible argument to stop him from going to her. I sighed and finished my meal, mutinous thoughts running amok inside my head. What if this was it? What if my mother had finally found me? I felt sick at the idea, though it was certainly plausible. If Melaina had rooted me out, so could any fey. But would it really be so bad if my mother did find me? It was a question I had yet to ask myself and it was a long time in coming. I couldn't quite come to terms with the knowledge that I wasn't a child, that she no longer had a hold over me. Even so, she'd insist I return home and make things right with Dallen, and while I'd already planned to do that, her hectoring would make everything harder. Plus, she was a horror, and I didn't want her here sullying my home with her evil.

I grabbed my drink and took a big swallow, not knowing quite what to do, but feeling an overwhelming desire to run, like I'd done that night six years ago. I looked around the room, searching for answers to who the Undesirable might be, listening closely to the others as I had always done. Soon whispers about the intruder came to me like the beginning rumblings of a storm, and woven into them was confirmation of something I'd already been noticing. Magical powers in Hawthorn Lane were growing stronger.

Let the intruders come…I could take them out with one flick of my wrist! bragged a young mage.

I don't know what's going on, but ever since the ball I've been feeling really powerful, a faerie observed. *I tried transfiguration and afterward not even my mother recognized me! I feel like I could do anything, even take out a fey-hunter!*

I can't believe I was able to resist his charms, when I'd never been able to before. This came from an attractive elf. *The intruder would be no match for me!*

So it was true. The Hawthornites' magical abilities were strengthening, and with this increase in power came a worrisome rise in arrogance. At least with the younger fey.

I went to take another sip of wine, realized my glass was empty, and borrowed some of Kyran's *Dark Spirits*, my thoughts whirling like a tornado. If powers were increasing here, then my mother's would grow as well. When I went back home, she might make me do something I didn't want to do, just as she'd always done…until I'd run away.

I looked up and saw Dawn Ravenna making her way toward me, a predatory smile on her perfectly molded elfin face. Her controlling older sister, Fan, watched us from a table she was sharing with Merceen, her sour expression making her look as though she'd just smelled something terrible, like Merceen's perfume. It appeared that Fan had found herself a new friend. Ally, anyway. I wasn't sure Fan or Merceen did friends. One could only guess at what they were bonding over, though hating me was a good place to start.

"You must be feeling mighty pleased with yourself," Dawn announced, coming to stand by our table. Instead of her usual over-the-top gown and hairdo, she wore a style that, while still elaborate, was simpler and far more becoming than her usual circus clown attire, and served to distinguish her from her sister.

"A little bit, yes," I replied with a small smirk.

"Hilarious. You know, what's happening to you is really unfair."

"I totally agree."

"I mean unfair to me, you old besom. Without doing anything to earn it, you get granted insta mega-status and the hottest bachelor in the village." I laughed inwardly. For a brief, mad moment I'd thought Dawn was going to sympathize with me.

"Do you want him for yourself?"

She gaped at me. "Uh…*duh!*"

"You're welcome to take a leap at him."

"And get stoned by the entire village?" She looked around, checking to see if she had an audience. She did. "No, thank you. Much as it pains me to say this, you have to be with him, Lorelle. Besides, I'd like to see what my life could be like without a curse making everything a misery. And maybe my sister will finally stop treating me like curdled toe jam stew."

"Lovely image, Dawn." She gave a little curtsy. "But what if our being together won't break the curse? We're both high-born, and the curse states we must come from two different worlds. Remember?"

She wrinkled her perfectly narrow nose with its perfectly symmetrically shaped nostrils. "Oh, that's right. I find it so easy to forget you're one of us, Lorelle. I wonder why?" She regarded me with a wicked gleam in her eyes. "I'm sure there's something else that differentiates you two, like your sex appeal. You and Kyran certainly come from different worlds in that department." She looked me over with a practiced eye. "I really don't know what Oren sees in you."

"I know exactly what your brother sees in me."

Her immovable brow attempted to furrow into a frown. "What?"

"He envies the fact that I don't have you and Fan as sisters."

"Guffaw, guffaw."

"Just think…if I were to marry Oren, *you and I* would be sisters."

Dawn looked horrified. "I'd rather wear a burlap sack and parade around the village square."

"That would be a good look for you. Peasant chic."

"Oh, now you're just being mean." She leaned forward, her eyes bright. "This was fun, Lorelle." It was, rather. It was also nice to see that Dawn could hold her own when out from under her sister's critical gaze. "But now I want to ask you to do something for me. It's the reason I came over in the first place, actually, but I got distracted by your gargantuan nose."

And now the fun was over. "What do you want, Dawn?"

"Say something flattering about me to Renwick, there's a good girl. He's looking particularly yummy with that new beard."

"And in return?"

"A new gown."

"Make it two."

She narrowed her eyes, thought for a moment. "Deal."

"He's coming right now," I said. "Maybe you could talk to him yourself?"

Her magically enhanced eyes widened. "Are you mad? I can't chase after him! He'd think I liked him."

"But you do…"

"Of course I do, but I can't show it. It would be unseemly, and besides, if I threw myself at him, it'd be my luck that I'd miss and end up face down on the floor." She brandished a delicate fist at me. "So just do it."

I held up my hands in surrender. "All right, all right. I'll put in a good word for you."

A rosy glow that made her look less like a robot and more like a living, feeling creature spread over her face. "You're not nearly as awful as people say, Lorelle. Ciao!" She fluttered her fingers at me, then glided away, the epitome of grace.

Renwick approached, his eyes on Dawn's retreating form bright with interest. When she was seated, he turned his attention to me. He leaned low, his mouth near my ear; his breath and a small patch of his beard tickled my skin, giving me goose bumps. "What's happening, Lorelle? What's an unsanctioned breach?"

"Someone crossed the border without permission," I answered. "It could simply be an animal or a young wood fey who's wandered off and gotten himself lost."

"You don't think it's either one, do you?"

"I'm not sure…" I stared at my glass, full of rich red liquid, tempting me to take it in, and it occurred to me that Kyran had ordered a carafe of my favorite drink on purpose. That sneaky bastard. What did he think was going to happen? That he would get me drunk and haul me off to Professor Ballylee to marry us, so he could save the day? If that were the case, he had another think coming. Hawthorn Lane weddings don't go off like that. Any excuse to celebrate turns into a full-blown, village-wide event. Weddings here are as good a reason as any for a party and *no one* gets out of going through the whole crazy charade. The Executors even make you follow the old 'crying of the banns' ritual, and for three whole weeks, because each cry constituted a reason to celebrate. So if Kyran thought he was going to win this battle so easily, he was sorely mistaken.

Still maintaining his closeness, Renwick glanced around. "Where's Kyran?"

"He went after Lady Faylan."

"That witch?"

I lifted an eyebrow. "You don't like her?"

"I know the type. She's an underhanded schemer, just like Melaina. She let me in when I first came here, didn't she?"

"I believe she did," I replied cautiously, wondering how much he knew about her, about what she'd done.

"I think she was planning something the whole time," he went on. "I think she was setting me up."

Like Dawn, Renwick was turning out to be more astute than I'd given him credit. It was easy to think he only did what Melaina told him, but he was showing he had a mind of his own. My sense of caution grew, but my desire to gather knowledge could not be quenched so easily. "Why did you go along with Melaina, Renwick? Why did you pretend that you wanted to marry Ilia and let Kyran think someone wanted him dead?"

He leaned closer, his lips nearly touching my cheek. I squirmed a little, both uncomfortable and annoyingly aroused. "As you might recall, I didn't try all that hard with Ilia." I did recall; he'd seemed far more interested in me. In fact, that part about him hadn't really changed. For some reason, he felt obligated to continue the charade, and I pulled back, putting space between us. "As for Kyran," he went on, unfazed by my defection, "I guess I was mad at him because he's Kyran Van Perfect Man and had everything I wanted, so it was rather entertaining taking him down a notch."

"Your family's big on the nicknames, aren't they?"

He shrugged. "If the shoe fits…"

"So do you still feel that way about your cousin?"

"I don't know. Sometimes."

"But he didn't do anything to you."

His eyes narrowed. "You know, Lorelle, I have the feeling you brought me to Matron on purpose. This is your way of getting back at me for what I did to Kyran, isn't it?"

"Of course it is," I replied smoothly. "It's how we do things in Hawthorn Lane. Eye for an eye. That sort of thing."

"I didn't actually hurt anyone, Lorelle."

"And you aren't getting hurt. Just learning a lesson about cruelty."

"I'm not that kind of person, you know," he said, his lips thinning with frustration.

"Then here's your chance to prove it. I believe in redemption, Renwick, though it often isn't an easy belief to maintain." I thought of Dallen, of what I needed to follow through on with him. I was so tempted to simply forget he existed. So terribly tempted. Not because of him, but because of his connection to my old life, to my mother, to all the things I wanted to forget.

"But I do like you, Lorelle. That part wasn't an act."

I regarded him. "I know."

He laughed. "No false modesty?"

"I think you like me for a specific reason, Renwick, and it has nothing to do with my feminine wiles." In fact, he was starting to remind me of Oren, drawn to me because the freedom of my life compared to living with his two sisters was very alluring to him. He didn't know that I paid a price for the life I led. "You're not attracted to me, you're attracted to my lifestyle."

He swooped in again, his eyes fastened on mine. "Oh, I don't think that's all I'm attracted to." He held my gaze for what seemed like a long time, then Avice's screeching laugh broke us apart.

"I think we'll have dessert," I said calmly. I still didn't believe he truly desired me, but it was rather fun playing with fire. He was a dangerous man to be around, both because of how Kyran felt about him and because Melaina claimed him as her property. I didn't truly desire him, either, but fun was fun, and dueling with Renwick was turning out to be quite fun.

He straightened up, a lazy smile on his face. "As it's the only dessert I can remember, how about the golden chocolate soufflé?"

"Sounds perfect." I paused for a moment, sensing an opening. "Say, what do you think of Dawn Ravenna?"

"The younger sister at *Fawn's Fashions*?" I nodded. "She's all right. She'd be better if she were able to wriggle out from under her sister's thumb."

"I agree, and I think she's trying to do that. It isn't easy escaping from someone who has power over you," I added pointedly.

"Touché. So why do you bring her up?"

I shrugged. "I happen to find her an interesting paradox, rather like you."

He regarded me silently for several seconds. "Did she put you up to this?" he finally asked.

"Do you think anyone can put me up to anything?"

He laughed. "Probably not." He turned to go, but about faced when I called his name. "Yes?"

"Don't skimp on the fudge sauce."

"As you wish, *Domina* Gragan."

Damn. He'd heard about that. Which meant the story was already spreading. But who was doing the spreading? Matron? The witch did love to gossip. Little Jaimen's father? He had good reason to want to share the news of his son's recovery. Asherley Rowan? His motives were less obvious to me, and likely less benevolent.

Renwick laughed and left me to finish my meal alone. As I ate I stared at my tattoo and thought about painful ways to murder Cutter. Luckily Peretta, the resident faerie ballerina ghost, distracted me from my growing fury when she stole a faerie's wine glass, chugged the contents, which ended up as a puddle on the floor, then twirled off. When she noticed me watching her, she flashed me an unrepentant grin. I gave her a thumbs-up, which she returned before flitting on to the next table. I glanced about the dining room to see if I could spot any of the other ghosts. Ah...there was Bloo, hovering in a corner near the ceiling, sulking and plucking the petals off a bouquet of flowers she'd probably stolen from someone on a date, the colorful bits floating downward like confetti and landing in an unsuspecting warlock's white beard. Gangus was creeping about amongst the tables, large ears cocked as though listening in on conversations. Probably was. He was one snoopy ghost.

When I was done eating, a young elf arrived to clear the table, leaving our drinks. He seemed rather surly, banging the plates and scowling, but I put it down to having a crappy job. Despite myself, I drank some of the *Dark Spirits*. I would regret it in the morning, but at that moment I didn't give a damn. Right now I needed to feel powerful, because this had been an unsettling day and power has a way of steadying a person.

The same elf delivered the dessert with two spoons, along with a folded note, his every move demonstrating his disdain. I was starting to feel like his anger was personal and was glad when he moved on to the next table. When he was gone, I read the note.

I'm not the only one who needs to lock my door at night.

I glanced up at Renwick, but he was busy with another table, joking and laughing with a beautiful faerie. No one seemed to find it strange that a Van der Daarke was working as a waiter, which was strange in itself. Hawthornites thrive on imposing hierarchy, contesting positions of power, and stirring up drama. Renwick's story possessed all three elements, so something was going on. I was about to tune in to the conversations around me when Kyran darkened the entrance. My traitorous heart leapt upon seeing him, breaking my concentration. He was just so tall and imposing, so commanding and self-assured.

I took another drink.

After crossing the floor and returning all the greetings coming his way, he sat down, bringing with him the invigorating freshness of the outdoors and a faint hint of magic, a scent reminiscent of an incoming storm. "That looks delicious." He picked up his silver dessert spoon, a naked woman entwined about its handle, and scooped up a bite. The mound disappeared into his mouth and I watched him intently, taking in his pleasure with interest. Here was a man who kept himself tightly in check, and yet, when the moment called for it, could let himself go without regret.

I wondered if he was like that in bed.

Damn you, libations.

"Did you find anything out?" I asked, my voice a little wobbly.

"Not yet."

"Has Lady Faylan sent out scouts?"

"She has. Given her interest in me, I thought she'd tell me more, but she was evasive. She even encouraged me to go back to the restaurant, finish my meal, and not bother myself with the matter."

"Maybe she doesn't want you taking over."

"Taking over? Why would I want to do that?"

I cocked an eyebrow. "Why, indeed? This place is a mess. No one in their right mind would want to run it."

"I certainly wouldn't want the job."

No, like all high-borns, you want the devotion of the masses without having to do much to earn it.

"Me, either." I spooned up a mouthful of dessert, savoring the rich chocolate flavor and a hint of spice.

"What's that?" Kyran nodded at Renwick's note, which had been left exposed when I went in for more dessert.

I grabbed it. "Nothing. Just a joke."

"Then you won't mind if I read it?"

"I—"

"Great." He snatched it out of my hand, and I cursed my alcohol-fogged mind. I should have stuck the note in my pocket or burned it the moment I'd read it. Instead I had kept it, and out in plain sight. Either I was being very stupid or some part of me had wanted Kyran to read the note.

Oh.

Well…how duplicitous of me.

As he read what was written, he went very still. "Is this a threat?" His voice was quiet, yet I heard it clearly over the babble of voices and mournful wail of *Mad Hatter*. I always seemed able to hear his voice.

"I told you. It's a joke."

"Renwick wrote it."

"He did."

"Would you care to explain the joke?"

"No."

"So you want me to make assumptions?"

"You already have, Kyran."

"I don't recall doing that."

"Well, you did."

A commotion at the door once again interrupted our conversation at a pivotal point. Lady Faylan had entered and stood at the railing, bidding us to be quiet. "She's here." I pointed. Kyran turned around and we waited, along with the silent room, to hear what the overseer had to say.

"Fellow Hawthornites, as you already know, we have experienced an unauthorized breach. Someone has crossed the border into Hawthorn Lane. Who that someone is remains to be seen. What I can tell you is that the intruder has ill intentions." A hiss of fear sparked across the room.

"Is it a fey-hunter?" someone shouted from the crowd.

"I cannot say. The trespasser's aura is a strange one, both familiar and yet not. Until I can run this creature to ground, I am putting the village on lockdown. No one in and no one out." That might make my eventual escape harder, but only if Lady Faylan set the alarm for departures. If she had any idea I was leaving I imagined she'd escort me out with trumpets blaring. "Life should continue as normal," she went on, "but stay on the alert."

"What are the ill intentions?" someone else called out.

Lady Faylan drew herself up. "I cannot say for certain, but I know those intentions are befouled by obsession. An obsession to destroy…"

Chapter Twelve

Lady Faylan, sensing she would not be able to regain her platform in the midst of all the shouting, slipped out as quickly as she'd come. Before she left, though, she made eye contact with me. There was a message in her eyes, but what it was I couldn't decipher. I do know it wasn't friendly.

"I'm taking you home," Kyran announced.

While it was an order and not a suggestion, I was too tired to point out that he was being bossy. "Yes." I smothered a yawn. "My bed sounds pretty good right now." It had been a long day, full of drama, and I was worn out. Being slightly intoxicated didn't help any. Luckily I was sober enough to realize that if I drank any more libations, I would end up tossing caution to the winds, and perhaps my clothes, as well. Now was a good time to make my exit.

"*Your* bed? No, I'm taking you to the castle."

I gave him my best gimlet eye. "No way."

"But you'll be safe there."

"I'll be perfectly safe in my cottage." My words slurred a little, undermining my assertion just a wee bit. I sat up straighter, determined to look in charge.

"I doubt Renwick will be a match against a fey-hunter."

"Renwick?" I laughed quite loudly, drawing some attention. When the observers finally returned to their own conversations after I gave them the stare-down, I met Kyran's eyes boldly. "You're being an idiot."

"Is that right?"

"Completely. I can take care of myself, you know, and besides, Renwick isn't staying with me."

"But you said—"

I held up my finger. "I said nothing of the sort. You *assumed*."

"Why didn't you correct me?"

"I tried to, you git. You kept interrupting."

His brow furrowed. "I don't recall doing that."

"They do say one's memory starts to go as they get old."

"Thirty hardly constitutes old," he said dryly.

"Oh. I thought you were thirty-five," I lied.

His eyebrows drew together so fast I thought they'd collide. "That's still not old, and I only recently turned thirty."

I threw my hands in the air. "Fine. You're practically a spring chicken." I leaned forward. "So tell me Kyran. Why did you really invite me to dinner?" I tapped the table with my naked woman spoon. "The truth this time."

"I told you. I wanted to be seen with you."

"I get that. You're doing public relations. But there's another reason, isn't there?"

A slow smile spread across his face and I suddenly felt uncertain I wanted to head down this road. "Are you sure you'll believe me if I tell you?"

"I will," I promised rashly, if a bit hesitantly. "Absolutely."

"I wanted to see you."

I stared at him. "That's it? You wanted to see me? See me do what exactly? Get stared at and talked about?"

He placed his elbows on the table and fixed me with a fond look. I went immediately on the defensive. "I wanted to see you do your Lorelle thing. Like when you play with your hair, or when you bite your lip, just a tiny bit, when you're thinking. Or when you get mad—the fire in your eyes. It's captivating."

"Y-you're having me on," I stuttered, feeling winded.

"Come home with me. I promise you'll be safe." He winked.

I inhaled sharply. He was having me on. This was all a part of his scheme, or merely an excuse to have a good laugh at my expense. It wouldn't be the first time. "Thanks, but no. I'll be fine at my cottage."

His jaw hardened. "Something's out there, Lorelle, and I've a bad feeling it's after you."

"And I think you're letting Hawthorn Lane's dramatics affect your mind. You have to learn to distinguish real trouble from the make believe if you're going to survive here."

"I'm a Van der Daarke, not an innocent. Believe me, I've had plenty of experience with real trouble, and with drama. I know the difference."

I regarded him. "Growing up with that sister of yours, I suppose you do. But I'm still not going to the castle. I'm more afraid of Melaina than any fey-hunter."

"Then let me stay with you."

"What? No!" I placed a hand to my chest. "Whatever will people say?"

"You don't give a rip what people will say."

"I know, but sometimes I like to pretend I do."

"I'll sleep on the floor."

"Not happening."

"In your bed, then?"

"Really not happening. The last time I shared a bed with someone, she hogged all the blankets."

"She?"

"Avice."

He cleared his throat. "Would you care to elaborate?"

"I might be slightly tipsy, but I still have my wits about me, and I don't kiss and tell." I smiled inwardly. Nothing had happened, of course, not for Avice's lack of trying, but he didn't need to know that.

"You kissed?"

I laughed and stood up. "Take me home, Kyran. It's been a long day."

He pulled out a leather pouch and laid a handful of Goldenars on the table. "All right, but only if you tell me if you two kissed."

I counted the Goldenars. "That's an awfully big tip."

"I've a feeling Renwick could use it. Now did you?"

"We did." It was the truth, so I guess *something* had happened the night she'd slept over, but at the time I'd been dreaming, so it was purely an accident. A lovely one, I do admit, but an accident all the same, and it stopped there, though not without some tussling between us. Avice is my best friend, but no way am I letting her sink her claws into me.

"Ahhh."

"You can put your tongue back in your mouth now. Meet me at the door. I have something to tell Avice before I go."

I stepped out from the booth and headed toward her table, feeling bold. "Hello, Ilia. I've been selfish and hiding out, but now I'm emerging from my cocoon." I turned to Avice. "Can I join your magic lessons?"

"Honing in on my territory?" she said snidely.

"I want to learn to fly."

"Oh." She did a mental calculation, the gears in her mind practically grinding as she tried to figure out which course to take. I'd read from my book on fey that to teach someone to fly involves some heavy body contact, mainly to ensure the student won't fall to her death. "I see," she said breathily.

"Are you game?"

Her tongue flicked out, licked the little nub on her top lip, then darted back inside. She looked up at Kyran, who was talking to Fogle at the top of the stairs, then back at me. "I'm in."

"Good. I'll see you tomorrow at eleven at your flat?"

"Make it the day after. I've an appointment I can't miss."

"All right. I'll see you soon then, Ilia." Before she could respond, or not respond, I turned to Juletta. "Being alive really suits you."

She threw back her head and laughed. "Oh, Lorelle! Thank you for not tiptoeing around the subject."

"You're welcome." Then I grew solemn and looked at each of them in turn. "Be careful out there everyone. All right?"

Avice grabbed my arm. "You be careful, Lorelle. If you're Omni, well, then your blood must taste like the nectar of the gods." She nibbled at her lip, as though tempted to get a taste herself.

I patted her hand. "I will. Goodnight all."

I caught up with Kyran, slightly winded at the climb. The stairs were great for making an entrance. Not so great for getting away, especially after a few drinks. Another couple had arrived as we were leaving, so we made our exit without further fuss from Fogle.

Josepha, as if reading Kyran's mind, was waiting for us outside. As Kyran's new driver, he was dressed impeccably in a slender black jacket and fitted trousers. Before this job, he had worn whatever cast-offs he could find, often resembling a hobo, but these days he was looking quite dapper. Maybe Ilia was feeling dismal because the villagers, especially the young women, were surely starting to take note of him. If I'd known how she was feeling, I would have reassured her that Josepha was a loyal bloke, but I hadn't been there for her to do that, had I?

"Win anything?" I called up to him.

He patted his jacket pocket smugly. "A bit."

Kyran helped me into the coach, using more leverage than was necessary, and we drove home in silence. I peered out into a darkness barely penetrated by the glowing streetlamps flanking the cobbled lane, and thought about who might be hiding out there.

"I'll escort you inside," Kyran said when we arrived. "And make sure the place is secure."

"You just want to snoop around a bit," I teased, though I thought my joke was probably accurate. It's what I would want to do.

"I don't have to look around. I can simply stand inside and see if I sense anything."

"I was only joking. You can come in."

As soon as we crossed the threshold, I froze. Kyran had gone ahead of me and was standing in the middle of the room, stiff and alert. "You had two visitors, but whoever it was is gone. I feel that one of them is connected to you by blood, the second, I'm not sure about. There's seems to be a link, but in some other way. A dangerous way." He turned to look at me. "Lorelle, who was here?"

Connected to you by blood was all I needed to hear to feel the fear rise up inside me. It had to be my mother. Oh, stars above. She'd found me. I'd always feared she would, and now, here she was. This was awful.

Just then the bell in the tower began to ring, *bong, bong, bong.* Silence followed, pierced a moment later by the whinny of Kyran's horses.

"What was that?" he asked, his whole body on alert.

"That was the tower bell. It's our warning system. Lady Faylan is letting the village know what has happened. Five chimes signal that an all-out invasion is happening right now. Three mean we have an intruder, so proceed with caution, go out in pairs, stay in at night, be armed, that sort of thing. Unfortunately, while Hawthorn Lane is a sanctuary, it's not a stronghold. People can hide out here, but we're not especially prepared for battle."

"We should be."

"I agree." Especially now that I knew I was truly fey. Before I'd always thought I'd be immune to the attentions of fey-hunters and hadn't gone much beyond learning how to protect myself. I could wield and throw a knife, and perform some basic acrobatic and defensive moves. But now... Well, it seemed flying lessons would come in handy, at least until I could learn better ways to defend myself. "I'm joining you for magic lessons the day after tomorrow," I informed him. "I think it's time I upped my game."

His face lit up, and I felt a responding warmth in my chest. "Excellent idea, Lorelle. But I'm still staying the night."

"And leave Josepha to fend for himself?"

He waved this off. "He'll be fine."

"He's driving a coach, which he will protect with his life if someone tries to hijack it. He's very loyal to you, Kyran, and won't hesitate to do something stupid to protect you, the family, and all your possessions."

He looked surprised. "He would do that?"

"I've known Josepha a long time. He's loyal, and he keeps his mouth shut. He's got integrity, too, and you won't find that in spades around here."

"I'll go home with him, and then come back here."

"Alone?"

"Of course."

"And you know how to fight off a fey-hunter?"

He straightened to his full height. "I've been in plenty of fights."

"And no doubt you acquitted yourself wonderfully, but fey-hunters are different. The mortal ones are a little easier to manage, kind of like fighting a ninja assassin. The immortal are much harder to handle."

His shoulders sagged a little. "I can't leave you here alone."

"I'll be all right. I've been alone for a very long time, and managed just fine."

"I'll alert Rialban and his kin, then. He can watch over you."

"If it makes you feel better, go right ahead. It won't hurt for him and the forest fey to know what's going on." I might still be mad at the centaur for fetching me like a dog, but I wasn't about to let my ire harm innocent creatures. "Tell him what Lady Faylan said about the intruder having ill intentions. He should know that."

"I really don't want to leave you here alone, Lorelle."

"Go and watch over Melaina and Ilia. They need you more than I do."

"Be that as it may, that's not how I want it to be." He pushed past me and his coat sleeve brushed my arm, leaving a tingling sensation behind. He stopped at the door. "Looks like someone gave you flowers." He nodded at my kitchen table, where I spied a beautiful black crystal vase. It held an array of spiky branches, half of which were covered in small, musky smelling white flowers. I stared at the arrangement of hawthorn branches mixed in with blackthorn, and a chill ran up my spine. It was bad luck to have either one in your home, but the two of them together seemed particularly threatening. "I've seen those in England," he went on. "Aren't they hawthorns?"

"Both hawthorn and blackthorn," I said, taking note of the differences in bark and the presence or lack of flowers, which distinguished the two.

"I seem to recall that neither were the most beloved of plants."

"Well, no. But it's more than that with these two trees. It's complicated," I finished, because it was.

"Just like you." He regarded me for a moment, as though trying to piece it all together, then turned and left me alone. There would be no kiss tonight.

Chapter Thirteen

I awoke early the next morning, hot and sweaty and out of sorts. My blankets were twisted and shoved this way and that, my hair was a mess, my eyes bloodshot. Damn nightmares had been chasing me all night, and I felt like I hadn't slept at all. Mouth dry and head pounding, I cautiously made my way to the kitchen, the overpowering smell of hawthorn flowers greeting me like a punch in the face. I could handle the scent out in the open air, but in my small cottage, it clung to the inside of my nose like a needy lover. I fixed myself a cup of chaga tea to take the edge off my mini-hangover. It was very unlike me to let myself go like this, having kept a tight rein over my emotions and thoughts my entire life, even more so since coming to Hawthorn Lane.

But now that tight control was unraveling like an old knitted blanket, and I didn't like it. I chugged down the rest of my tea, did my morning chores, one of which included ridding myself of the hawthorn and blackthorn branches, then took a long, hot bath. When I emerged, the tea had done its job and I felt more like my old self. I cooked up a large breakfast and wolfed it down as the sun rose above the forest's treetops. Morning had come.

Charlton would soon be here, I suddenly remembered. I couldn't imagine him as anything but an early riser. I dressed quickly in an empire-waist, light cambric gown, then tended to the plants in my conservatory, spending extra time on my Dancing Bones cactus, which had been damaged by Kyran's little show.

A knock at the door signaled Charlton's arrival and I was grateful for his good timing. I had just finished watering everything in sight and was loath to be alone with my thoughts, muddled and disturbed as they were. A part of me wanted to hash through the recent events and work things out in my mind, but another part didn't want to face up to the conclusions I might draw. It was not a good place to be, mentally or emotionally, but I didn't know how else to handle things.

I set down my elephant-shaped watering can and peeped out the conservatory window, then hurried to the front entrance. After lifting the bar, I unlocked the door and let my visitor in. "Good morning, Charlton."

He took off his top hat and gave me a quick bow. "Thank you for agreeing to see me, Lorelle." He stepped inside and looked around, the expression on his face one I'd seen only just yesterday in Renwick. Envy. Both men seemed to think my little abode a place of wonder, and looking about with pride, I had to agree. How many twenty-four-year-old women have their own house, run their own business, and possess the freedom to come and go as they please? Oren Ravenna also admired my independence. Could Dawn and Fan's brother be the one who'd given me the strange bouquet? On my front stoop he sometimes left various bits of flora, acquired through his wanderings, that he thought might interest me. Or were the flowers Renwick's idea of a joke? Either way, I would very much like to solve this mystery and learn the identity of my intruder. If either one had left the flowers maybe they'd also seen the person connected to me by blood. I reminded myself to ask Renwick the next time I saw him…if I saw him again before I left.

"Would you like some tea?" I offered Charlton.

"No, thank you, Lorelle." He held up a long, elegant finger. "One moment." He stepped back outside, then returned with two large pots, one in each arm. "Where should I put these?"

Two whole pots of Effervescence? That would cost far more Goldenars than I possessed. "I can't afford those, Charlton."

"They're gifts."

"Gifts?" Nobody ever brought me gifts. Well, until yesterday, and I wasn't sure a bunch of sticks counted.

"To thank you for what you did for me at the ball."

I raised a skeptical eyebrow, then decided not to look a gift pot in the mouth. I do like my hot baths. "Thank you, Charlton. You might as well set them down right there." He carefully lowered the pots and arranged them along the wall near my bookshelf. "We can sit in the conservatory and talk, if you'd like."

"That sounds good." He followed after me and sat on the green velvet loveseat while I took the nearby chair. "What an amazing room," he said, looking about at the wild jungle I barely kept in check.

"I doubt it can compare with your home, Charlton," I said with a laugh. "Surely somewhere in that place you have a conservatory?"

"If we do, I've yet to see it. But if Mother finds out about yours, I imagine we shall be getting one soon."

"What is she up to, Charlton?" I asked, getting right to the point. Tiptoeing around the faerie, I decided, wasn't the best method of gathering information from him. We'd be tiptoeing all day.

"Up to?" He gave me a sheepish smile when I didn't respond. "All right. Yes, I suppose she is rather obvious."

"I think it's best if you and I were on the same page when it comes to her plans, don't you?"

He gave a nervous cough. "I didn't come here to propose, if that's what you're getting at. Our alliance might be what my mother wishes to see happen, but I wouldn't submit you to such audacity."

"Oh, Charlton! I just meant we should have some sort of plan ourselves. She's not going to let this go easily."

"Oh. Yes, sorry." His eyes flicked about the room. "Then what do you think we should do? Because I haven't a clue."

"I don't plan on marrying, and I'm pretty sure you're not in love with me. Am I correct?"

His cheeks flushed faintly. "I don't know you well enough for that."

"Exactly, so here's what we'll do. When together, we can be affable toward each other, be seen in each other's company even. It will be reported back to your mother, and that will make her happy and hopefully keep her off your back. But you and I both know we only want to be friends," I said this casually, testing him.

"Friends," he repeated, then nodded. "That would be acceptable."

"Good. Is there anyone you're in love with?"

He shook his head, though his eyes slid away from mine. "Being made head of the family business at such a young age, I haven't had the time or energy to notice anyone or anything outside of making money."

"You poor thing," I said sympathetically. "And now you've got your brother to deal with. How is Hanover?"

He shifted uncomfortably. "Well, to be honest, Lorelle, he's the main reason I came to see you. Though I'd be happy to discuss your energy needs, as well."

I'd already guessed his brother was the reason he'd come. "I think I'm all set on that, don't you?" I indicated the pots.

He laughed. "I suppose so."

"Hanover needs an age-cure, doesn't he?"

He started. "How did you know?"

Because he looks awful. "Charlton, do you think you're the first person to cross my threshold looking for something they don't want anyone else to know about? I will give you your cure, and I will say nothing about it. People will suspect, of course, but they will not *know*. Not from me, anyway." I wouldn't even tell Charlton that this was not the first time Hanover had required my services. Though usually he sent a lackey, someone not related to him, anyway.

Charlton nodded, as though I'd confirmed something for him. "Lorelle, you are an angel."

I snorted. "Hardly that, Charlton, other than perhaps the vengeful kind."

"What can I give you in exchange? Anything you ask…"

"I want information."

His features shuttered close in a useless attempt to shut me out. "About what?"

"I want to know if your sister is happy in her life."

He looked surprised. "Why?"

"Because it strikes me that there are too many young females in Hawthorn Lane, and very likely beyond, who aren't living the life they want to live."

"Young males, too," he muttered.

"Meaning you?" I asked quietly, because this, of course, was the information I was searching for all along.

The look he gave me was filled with such pain that I left my chair and went to sit by him, resting my hand on his arm. "You hate your life, don't you, Charlton?"

He nodded, unable to speak as he fought the anguish building up inside him. His fingers were white as bone as they gripped each other, his silvery eyes haunted. "More than you will ever know."

"And if you were to simply leave home, leave the business?"

"It would kill my mother."

"I don't think anything could kill your mother."

He gave a choking laugh. "I imagine not, but she has suffered so much with my father and his, his…actions. I can't add to that."

"I know quite well what he's done, Charlton. Everyone in the village does, so you might as well be aware of that upfront. But maybe if we break this curse…well, maybe it will change things for everyone and you won't feel the need to sacrifice your life for someone else."

He glanced over at me. "Do you really think that?"

"It's what I hope."

He let loose a long sigh, as though releasing all his frustrations and fears in one breath. "Then you and Count Van der Daarke must marry."

A cold chill went through me at the iron resolve in his voice. "There are other ways of breaking the curse, I'm sure."

"We must all make sacrifices, Lorelle. This will be yours."

I pulled back from him, feeling as though the conversation, which I thought I'd been steering, had suddenly veered off course and slammed into a tree. When Professor Ballylee's book on fey had said it would take a sacrifice to rid myself of the brand, surely it hadn't meant this big of a sacrifice?

"Why are you saying this, Charlton?"

"You're right, you know," he went on calmly, looking and sounding like a completely different person. "Things have to change in this village and if it takes your marrying Kyran Van der Daarke to effect that change, then so be it. But marriage doesn't mean the end, Lorelle." He reached out and took my hot hand in his cool one, and I was glad I'd worn my bracelet to cover my tattoo. I didn't want him, or anyone, seeing it. "You know that."

I pulled my hand from his and stood abruptly. "I'll get you that elixir, Charlton. The sooner Hanover takes it the better." In the kitchen I pulled down various herbs and added them to the *Dewel-Juice* I'd prepared yesterday, my hands shaking slightly. Then I brought out my Hexbox, an ornate six-sided puzzle box that contained my most dangerous and powerful elixirs, unlocking it using a key I kept hidden from prying eyes. To get to the lock, one had to search out a series of camouflaged entryways and buttons. Once I unlocked the box, I opened one of its many tiny, rune-covered drawers, withdrew a glass vial, opened it, and added three drops to the potion. After returning the Hexbox to its place, I mixed the ingredients and transferred them to an empty bottle, which I quickly sealed with a cork and black wax. Scrawling out directions, I glued the label to the bottle and returned to Charlton, my wits thoroughly about me again.

"Here you are." I handed him the bottle.

"How much do I owe you?"

I glanced at the Effervescence pots. "Shall we call it even?" I was getting the better part of the bargain, and both of us knew that, but it was the best I could do.

He looked like he wanted to say no, but then gave a polite nod. "Of course, Lorelle. Though I really did mean to make the Effervescence a gift."

I'm sure you did.

"I think if you want to speak to Kyran you should go now."

He frowned. "Speak to Kyran? Oh, yes. Thank you for reminding me. I'd nearly forgotten. How unlike me."

Yes, how unlike you. I escorted him to the door, wanting to get rid of him as soon as possible. "I'll see you around," I said vaguely, shooing him out with one hand while I kept the other firmly on the door to shut it as soon as he was outside.

"I look forward to our next meeting, Lorelle. In the meantime, be careful. If a fey-hunter has come to Hawthorn Lane, as an Omni-Fey you would be in grave danger."

There was an ardent look in his eyes that was fast becoming familiar and growing more and more unwelcome by the minute. "I'll be careful. Goodbye." I quickly shut the door on him, and leaned against it.

I'd spent the last six years enduring a dry spell that even a desert would find appalling, and now every red-blooded male I knew seemed to have developed an interest in me. I didn't trust this change of attitude one bit and that royally ticked me off. I wanted to enjoy their attention, wanted to revel in it, but instead I had to discount it because of what I was now. They weren't attracted to me; they were attracted to my pedigree. And that made me want to throw things at all of their heads. Big, heavy, painful things.

With a sigh, I pushed away from the door and went to clean up the kitchen. Like black flies, various thoughts entered my head and buzzed about, so I finally gave up and granted them the attention they wanted. I knew Avice was mad at me—she'd caught me having dinner with the man she wanted—but why Ilia? I wanted to believe she was simply feeling put out about Josepha and his growing popularity, but I had a feeling she was mad at me. So what had I done? Had my not visiting her this past week hurt her feelings? Maybe. I really wasn't very good at this friend thing. I would have to trick her into coming clean at our lesson later so I could better understand what I'd done wrong and not do it again. I had a feeling, though, that something was going on I didn't know about…something that had to do with Ilia's mother, Melaina. Damn the woman. I wish she'd leave Hawthorn Lane and go directly to hell.

Coriana Iverich could join her, with her pretense of liking me now simply because of my newly elevated status. I also didn't like the look she'd given Lady Faylan last night at *Chez Chantilly*. Those two were up to something, I just knew it. But what was it, and was Charlton involved? After encouraging me to marry Kyran, probably not, since that's the opposite of what either woman would want. His behavior didn't make sense, though. He acted like he was interested in me, and yet was pushing me to be with another man. Then again, he *had* said that marriage didn't have to be the end, right before he'd taken my hand. Did he think I would get married to beat the curse, then be his mistress?

This was all so ridiculous, it was fast becoming farcical. If I were to marry, I would take my vows very seriously. I didn't even know who my father was and doubted my mother did, either, and there was no way I was going to pass along that proud family tradition. To marry Kyran would mean I'd have to truly love him, and right now I wasn't even sure I could trust him.

Chapter Fourteen

The following day, I made sure to wrap my tattoo, to better control its scent, before slipping on my bracelet and donning gloves. Then, rowan walking staff firmly in hand, I left half an hour early to pick up pastries at *Devil's Cakes* before meeting the others at Avice's flat. At the thought of the impending lesson, I felt a jolt of excitement in my chest. I was going to learn magic! What a rare and wondrous thing, and, like most humans, something I'd secretly wanted to do since I was a child. I couldn't wait to get started.

The previous afternoon I'd received a handwritten note from Kyran via messenger bird, casually asking how I was faring. The bird waited for me, so I sent an equally bland message back stating that I was doing quite well, thank you for asking, and would see him at magic training the next morning. In the past I might have bridled at the idea of him thinking I couldn't handle myself, but actually it was rather nice to know that someone other than myself cared about my welfare. It was a novel experience, and I decided to take it at face value.

As I walked down the main drag of Vildrey Boulevard, I spotted Lady Faylan and Coriana Iverich standing close together, near the fountain featuring the statue of the warrior elf, Arius Vildrey. Their conversation appeared to be quite intense, judging by their serious expressions, Coriana's perhaps more anxious than serious. As though sensing my presence, Lady Faylan turned her cool gray eyes on me. No smile cracked her thinned lips, no pleasure lit up her unadorned face. Coriana, following her gaze, was more receptive, raising a hand in greeting; her smile was stiff, but it was there. Without slowing my step, I returned the wave with a gracious nod.

The village square was crowded, people coming and going, busy with errands, gossiping and laughing. Though the weather was glorious, with not a cloud in the sky, my lighthearted mood darkened, as I hadn't counted on the range of reactions aimed at me as I approached. The looks I got were either adoring or foul, with only a handful that could be termed fairly neutral. Outdoor vendors turned their backs on me, a carriage driver nearly ran me down, a dwarf spat a gelatinous yellow gob at my feet.

I hurried toward *Devil's Cakes*, wanting to escape, but when I entered the bakery I found it filled with customers. The tantalizing aroma of sugar and cream and melted chocolate calmed me a little and I let the door close behind me. Jacques, the skinny warlock proprietor, was busy at the counter taking and filling orders. Around me some invisible force cleared cups and plates from the tables, like a scene out of *Fantasia*. Having never before witnessed the likes of this sort of thing at *Devil's Cakes*, I determined it to be yet another sign that powers were increasing in Hawthorn Lane.

As I took my place in line, I was either ogled or given the stink eye, just like what I'd experienced outside. What was going on? I considered leaving, but my turn had come and I stepped forward to place my order.

Jacques looked over my shoulder to an elf behind me. "What'll it be?"

"I'll have the—" I started to say.

"Sir?" Jacques said, ignoring me. "What'll it be?"

The elf looked down his brown nose at me, then stepped around me to place his order. "I'll be taking—"

"I was next," I interrupted him. I aimed my eyes at Jacques, who aimed his eyes over my head. "Are you purposely ignoring me?" No answer. "Because I need to know for sure before I make my next move."

Jacques stiffened a little and his eyes darted around the now quiet room. "I'll not serve you, Lorelle Gragan," he said stubbornly, "until you do what you're supposed to do."

"Is that what this is all about? The curse?" When no one answered, I knew I was right. "Did someone put you up to this, Jacques? Killew, perhaps?" Killew, Jacques' ample wife, rarely left her boudoir at the back of the bakery. Their marriage was not a happy one, so I could easily see her issuing this mandate to him. Or maybe Jacques was tired of being miserable and was doing this on his own.

"I don't need her permission!" he cried.

"But does she know what you're doing? Because she wouldn't like it if you did something she didn't approve of."

"I hope she do know, and I hope it royally pisses off the hoity wench."

Well, there went that threat.

Most of the customers refused to meet my gaze as I looked around the shop, but one faerie raised her hand. Dressed in a *Fawn's Fashions* gown, she was obviously wealthy and one of the village elite. "I'm not a part of this—"

I made a gesture with my hand, cutting her off. Her eyes widened in astonishment, and I thought she'd be peeved at my impertinent behavior, but instead she looked like I'd bestowed a benediction upon her, her expression lighting up. "Then this next part is not for you." I addressed the crowd. "If you continue treating me like a pariah, you will regret it. I am memorizing each and every one of your names and faces, and will, if necessary, seek retribution. So pick your poison, Hawthornites. Decide who you want to anger less. Whoever set you up to this…or me."

With that, and my head held high, I left the bakery, quivering with anger. I was ready to go at anyone who dared cross me, and I felt sure if I hadn't been wearing gloves, sparks would be flying from my fingers like geysers. Someone had started this little rebellion, or was at least fanning its flames, and that someone had to be a powerful force in the village, like Lady Faylan or Coriana Iverich, or both together. They'd looked awfully cozy for two people who had never seemed to want anything to do with the other. Damn them. If they were responsible for this sudden uprising against me, they were going to make my last week here a difficult one.

Sensing my irritable mood, the villagers, even the ones who seemed determined to either frighten me or shame me, cleared a path for me. I had brought along my staff for protection against whatever nightmare awaited me—fey-hunters, ravenous beasts, my mother—and made it clear I was not afraid to use it on anyone's sorry behind.

As I made my way to Avice's flat, I was surprised that no one else seemed particularly concerned about the breach and the three-bell warning. Judging by the number of fey I'd witnessed doing magic in the short, winding march, they perhaps felt themselves immune to any threat. In fact, they seemed more relaxed about going outside than they'd been with a Desolate on the loose, reinforcing my idea that they had discovered their burgeoning magical powers and were growing cocky. I'd call them fools if I weren't so enamored of my new powers myself.

The way was paved with polished cobblestones, thick moss growing in the dirt-filled cracks between the worn stones. I passed flower boxes filled with colorful blooms and saw bright green leaves had emerged from the thick vines crawling along the stone walls. Soon I was climbing the crooked steps to Avice's flat, a two-story affair overlooking Amore Boulevard. A surge of anticipation welled up inside me. I was so close!

I lifted the knocker, which is an actual set of knockers, and let it drop. Every time I visited Avice, I had to wrap my hand around a pair of voluptuous breasts—which I believe were modeled after Avice's own—and bang away. I had no choice in the matter. Ensign, Avice's dwarf lackey, was under strict orders not to open the door unless he heard the knocker. Its metallic sound differed from knuckles on wood, so it was easy for him to tell. Avice likes to get her kicks wherever she can.

I waited until the door swung open, then peered down at Ensign. He peered up at me, a dismal sight if ever there was one. For the record, Ensign always looks unhappy. At his most gloomy is when he is at his happiest, which is why he could serve Avice and not want to kill her. She's an old hand at making people miserable.

"This way," he said in a rumbly voice. Ensign had learned long ago never to say, "Walk this way." He had a limp that supposedly was the result of an old war wound, and many of Avice's young acquaintances couldn't resist poking fun at the old guy. I don't typically feel sorry for people, and Ensign is no exception. The one time I'd felt bad for him and tried to intervene on his behalf, he didn't talk to me for six months. I soon realized that Ensign likes to suffer, but only at Avice's hands. He won't take any guff from her lovers. So I guess that's *something?*

As we walked through Avice's flat, I thought that if there were a picture of decadence in the dictionary, it would be a panorama of Avice's rooms. Her furniture is overstuffed—a bit like her corset—with a minimum, per divan or loveseat, of two throw pillows, all of which are plump and fringed and covered in either silk or velvet. Mirrors are prevalent and have been placed in between portraits of Avice in varying states of undress. She keeps the curtains drawn and lights the place with a profusion of candles in crystal-bedecked candelabra, the resulting smoke producing a perpetual haze. Red and pink dominate the color scheme, and her personal scent perfumes the air at all times. The sheer number of classical statues, all stunningly lifelike and erotic, always makes me feel as though I've just stumbled upon a Roman orgy. Whenever I come across the term love nest—which is surprisingly often—I can't help but think of Avice's flat.

I followed Ensign up a set of stairs and into Avice's small ballroom, which she had decorated herself. The décor leans heavily toward a profusion of nymphs, thick damask curtains, plump cushions, and included a gleaming bar stocked with her favorite potation, *Lightning.* Avice holds dances here on a regular basis, though I don't usually attend them, as she pretty much only invites people who are in love with her. Not only does that make for a dull party for me, but it also implies that I'm in love with her, which I'm not. But that doesn't stop Avice from trying to get me to fall head over heels.

Ensign directed me forward, then ambled off, muttering to himself. I stepped into the ballroom and was surprised to find Kyran and Ilia already there. I wasn't late, but I wouldn't put it past Avice to invite them both to come early so that she could practice her wiles on Kyran without my interference.

Kyran stood and met me halfway. "I got your note. Did Josepha find you all right?"

"Josepha?" I echoed, seeing a strange look cross Ilia's face. "I didn't see him."

His jaw tightened. "He was supposed to give you a ride into the village."

"I must have missed him. I left early to pick something up at *Devil's Cakes*."

He looked at my empty hands, one eyebrow lifted. "Were they out of everything, or did you eat it already?"

"I didn't buy anything, though I meant to. I was going to bring pastries for everyone."

Avice sneakily glided between us and took my hands, steering me away from Kyran and toward a purple velvet settee that set off her pale blue eau de Nile gown and vibrant red hair to perfection. "Sit down. Rest a moment. Tell us what happened."

"How do you know something happened?"

She looked at me like I was a simpleton. "Because you didn't get your pastries."

"Let's just say I wasn't exactly welcomed."

"You were quite welcomed at *Chez Chantilly*," she pointed out, a little grumpily.

"Mostly." I remembered the busboy now—how irritated he'd been. "And there were people at the bakery who seemed fine with me. But there were more who weren't." And the disgruntled, I realized, had all been regular villagers—no high-borns, no wealthy, no elite. The very people with whom I'd associated myself all my life had turned against me.

Did that ever stick in my craw.

"But Coriana came to talk to you and she never does that," she breathed reverently, as though I should be impressed. "People come to her. She even left her house." Her hand squeezing mine was both supportive and a bit painful. I slowly wiggled my fingers from her firm grasp.

"She came to talk to Kyran," I amended, though perhaps that wasn't entirely true. "You didn't see the look on her face whenever she had to pretend to like me. Like she'd just taken a bite out of an apple only to find the other half of the worm."

Avice grabbed my hand again. "All your imagination, dearest. People here love you. *I* love you."

"And that means the world to me, Avice, but I don't think it's all my imagination. You haven't heard anything? Rumors?" Avice's eyes slid sideways and I guessed she knew something. I was about to order her to come clean when Ilia spoke up.

"I've heard things," she said, her lisp stronger than usual, then she snapped her mouth shut.

"What did you hear, Ilia?"

She shrugged, looking mulish. I thought she looked tired today, and thinner. She'd been doing well with gaining some weight back after her mother had 'encouraged' her to starve herself to get a man, but seemed to have slid back a bit. Her brown dress was plain and not the best color for her. I realized now that she'd worn something similarly dowdy at *Chez Chantilly*, and had a sneaking suspicion her mother was making her wear frumpy, unflattering outfits out of jealousy. The ugly duckling was becoming the swan, but not if Melaina could help it.

"Just things," she replied, when the silence stretched out too long.

Kyran sat down next to her. "What things, Ilia?"

"Yesterday I overheard someone talking at the castle…someone making a delivery."

"And what did this person say?"

"Something about how Lorelle can save a forest fey in return for a favor," she said, her tone bitter, "but she doesn't have the time to remove a curse her own family put on us."

Kyran looked at me. "What's this about?"

I gave a noncommittal shrug. "You know how people like to gossip."

"Who told you this?" he asked Ilia.

She shook her head. "Didn't see a face."

Kyran's jaw tightened, and I sensed he was about to lose his temper with the girl, so I spoke up before he made things worse with her than they already were. "Well, whoever said that doesn't know the whole story."

Ilia faced me, her back rigid and her hands in fists. "Why don't you just end the curse, Lorelle? You like my uncle. He likes you. You could save so many people, but you won't do it, will you? Because you're totally selfish."

I stared at her in surprise. Gone was the little waif who'd shown up at my door, frightened out of her mind, looking for help and leaning on me for support. Gone was the girl whom I'd thought would be my redemption. In her place was a surly teenager who was very unhappy with me. My fear was coming true—the one person I'd hoped would be on my side wasn't.

"Is the curse affecting you, Ilia?" I asked.

She glowered at me, something she'd never done before. "It's affecting all of us."

"So you think I should marry your uncle to save everyone?"

"Yes!"

"Even if I didn't want to marry him, I should still do it?"

Her lower lip trembled, but the defiant look remained. "Sometimes people have to make sacrifices."

There was that word again. Everyone was quite keen on making me the sacrificial lamb in all this. Though I suppose since they thought it was my kin who'd done this to them it made sense to blame me. Sort of. But hadn't they ever heard the saying, "Visit not the sins of the father on the child?" If not, it was about time they did.

"So if your mother had done something to someone," I said in a quiet voice, "and she couldn't be held accountable, then perhaps you'd be willing to take her punishment?"

She jerked back, as though I'd struck out at her. "What? No! That's different. She's evil and deserves what she gets."

"Like me."

Her eyes widened. "You're not evil, Lorelle, you're— Wait, no. You are! *No.* I mean, you're..." She sobbed. "Oh, I don't know what I mean!" I reached out to her and she pulled back, dashing away her tears. Straightening her features into a mask of coolness, I watched her turn herself into a little Melaina right before my eyes. "I can't do lessons today, Avice. I forgot I'm due for a fitting at *Fawn's Fashions.* Uncle Kyran?" She stood and turned to him, holding out her arm. "Will you take me there? I don't feel safe on my own right now." Her eyes caught mine, then dashed away.

Kyran glanced at me and I nodded. Ilia saw the gesture and her chin, still pointy despite her weight gain, jutted out and her lips tightened into a pout. "Of course," he said to her, standing and taking her arm. She'd been somewhat upset with me at the restaurant, but now she was openly hostile. What had changed?

"Are you coming back?" Avice asked him. "We haven't done our lessons yet."

"I'll need to stay with Ilia," he replied, his eyes on me questioning.

I looked away. "I guess it will be just you and me, Avice."

She turned toward me and licked her lips, looking far less disappointed than I thought she would. "Just you and me, Lorelle. Alone. *Together.*"

"And you'll be teaching me to fly…"

Her eyelids lowered seductively. "Oh, we'll be flying all right."

I turned back to Kyran, who looked slightly alarmed. "Goodbye, Kyran. Goodbye, Ilia."

"How will you get home?" he asked.

"Avice can give me a ride in her barouche."

"If you're sure you'll be all right." He obviously didn't want to leave me alone with her.

I pulled myself upright. "I'm quite sure."

He gave me one last look, his jaw tight with uncertainty, then he bowed to us. "Then I bid you adieu."

"Au revoir!" Avice waved as they turned and left the room, Ilia's form rigid, Kyran glancing back over his shoulder. When he was gone, I glanced at Avice. "You can give me a ride, right?"

"Oh, I can give you a ride all right."

I smacked her hand. "Give it a rest, you lusty wench."

She pulled me to her. "I've missed you so much, Lorelle. If you were ever to leave me, I think I'd die."

I let her caress my hair and run her hand up and down my back as she held me tight. I knew she was being dramatic, but what if… Well, what if she really meant it?

Chapter Fifteen

Flying lessons ended up being a total flop, and I went home disappointed. Avice had insisted on eating beforehand, "to build up our energy," she argued, and had then imbibed too much *Lightning* to be of any use. The conversation as we ate pretty much revolved around her asking why Kyran wasn't making the moves on her, followed by a swig of *Lightning*. She then demanded to know why I hadn't answered her knocks or been by to see her, followed by another slug. It was like a drinking game, but with only one person. At the time I didn't mind too much, as it kept her from interrogating me about what Ilia had said concerning my rescuing a forest fey. I wasn't ready to get into that.

When we finally returned to the ballroom to practice, she leaped into the air and flew about the room like a deranged hummingbird. "Come on up, Lorelle!"

"I can't fly, Avice. Remember?"

"Oh, it's easy! Just come on!"

"But isn't there something I should be thinking? Or doing?" I asked her…repeatedly.

"Think about flying!" she cried every time I asked, then swooped about the room, at one point adding, "I don't think I've ever flown so well. I feel like a bird!"

Eventually I gave up and watched over her until she at last drifted down to the floor and fell asleep hugging my feet, a happy smile on her face. After extricating myself, I fetched Ensign, who in turn fetched two tall, good looking footmen, whom I rightly suspected were the newly arrived Damnay twins. They picked her up and carried her away, but not before they both gave me an identical dirty look. I wasn't sure if their rancor had to do with my role in the curse, or their resentment of my relationship with Avice. Probably a bit of both.

"Tell Avice you drove me home, Ensign," I said to him. "She needs tending to, and it's broad daylight, so I'll be fine on my own. Make her drink that tisane I gave you a while back."

His yellowish, off-kilter eyes narrowed as though in protest, then he bowed. "As you wish, madam." He showed me out, but before he closed the door, he paused. "We don't all hold with that harridan up the way." He jerked his oversized head at the door.

"Thank you, Ensign. That means a lot to me." And then, even though it wasn't in my nature, I reached out and gave his shoulder an affectionate pat. "I needed that." It was good to know I had someone on my side who wasn't a high-born and had no interest in gaining my favor. Ensign might be a masochist, but he was a loyal masochist.

So what harridan could he possibly be referring to? I gave an unamused laugh. As if I didn't know. Melaina, of course. She was the instigator behind the villagers' pugnacious behavior, not Lady Faylan or Coriana like I'd thought. She must have spent all of yesterday convincing the very people I'd always affiliated with—the low-borns—to turn against me. If I were a betting girl, I'd wager she had figured out my sympathy for the working class and resultant disdain for the aristocracy, and was making sure I suffered for my refusal to dance to her evil tune.

As I marched along the lane toward home, I forced myself to keep my chin up and eyes straight ahead, ignoring the hisses and hostile looks, the snide comments and one out-and-out threat that I marry Kyran Van der Daarke, *or else*. Though I did keep my staff at the ready in case anyone decided to take things to the next level. No one did, and I admit to feeling slightly disappointed. Cracking skulls can be quite the stress reliever, or so I've heard.

When I reached my cottage, I could only feel relief at being home again, though it quickly turned to caution when I spotted something strange sitting on my front stoop. As I grew closer, my steps quick but careful, I saw that it was a large birdcage, elaborately designed in a Victorian style, and in it was, of all things, a bird. But not just any old bird. It was one of the rarest kinds—a rapture.

I kneeled down before the tiny thing. Still covered in down, the bird was likely only a nestling. But over the next several hours, it would grow from nestling to fledgling to juvenile, and finally to a full-grown adult, an impossibility for any other bird, but natural for a rapture. Half raptor, half vulture, it was a powerful creature that served as both predator and scavenger. A rapture can stalk better than any lion and find food no matter where, or in what form, it might be.

Next to the cage was a pot of *Dead Man's Fingers*, one of the rapture's favorite treats. It's a fungus that looks exactly, and disturbingly, like its name. The first time I'd seen the pale, human-like fingers poking up out of the dirt, as though reaching for help, I'd run into the village shouting that a body had been buried in the woods. After the villagers followed me back to the place where I'd found the fungus, and knowing all along what it really was, everyone had a good laugh at my expense. I wasn't allowed to forget my mistake for a good year, and even now some wiseass will bring it up on occasion. He pays for it with a black eye, but still... It was the last time I overreacted to a strange experience in this place, or asked for help.

The little bird looked up at me with pale green eyes and slowly blinked. "Braaah?"

I had the uncanny feeling it was saying, "Mother?" I slowly reached between the bars and stroked its soft, white-gray back, watching the bird all along to ensure it wouldn't rip off one of my fingers. Even the young ones can be vicious. But this one seemed content to enjoy the stroking.

"What are you doing here?"

"Braaah?"

"Who brought you?" I tried again.

This time the bird didn't answer, merely peered up at me with innocent eyes. In a short time a person would be able to communicate with the bird and use it as a messenger, as the villagers used their ravens or falcons, and the occasional stubborn crow, like poor Ilia had bought from our local con artist, Geordie Wicklow. Communication with messenger birds occurs mainly through mind work, although a few villagers prefer to do it the old-fashioned way, by writing notes. Luckily I rarely received messages via bird, claiming that I preferred people tell me in person what they wanted. But now that I knew I was fey, and once I figured out how to telecommunicate, I should be able to join in on the fun, and increase my efficiency.

If I kept the bird.

"Braaah?"

I was keeping the bird.

Secretly I'd always wanted my own go-between, and given a choice, hands down I'd pick a rapture. I'd wanted one the moment I saw an adult version at Ware-Port Day, its sheer size and intelligent gaze a thrill to see.

Having made my decision, I lifted the heavy cage and carried it inside. After setting it on the table, I hurried back outside, then scanned the area for any watchers before bending down to pick up the coffin-shaped pot holding the *Dead Man's Fingers*. The fungi really were quite creepy looking, the stalks gray, with yellowish-white tips like fingernails, and would make a nice addition to my other plants.

Even though I was glad to be given such a gift, it bothered me that I didn't know who my benefactor was. Had the bird come from Kyran as a less-than-subtle hint that I could now send him messages whenever I wanted? He was one of the few fey in Hawthorn Lane who could afford a rapture. Or had it been someone else anxious to get on my good side, like Charlton or Oren? Whoever it was, they might just be on to something.

As I set the *Dead Man's Fingers* on the table next to the cage, Gothic writing on the side of the pot caught my eye and I ducked low to read it.

Close the lid
and let it sit
From dusk to dawn
Then open it.

There you'll find
Just what you crave
A rapture's rind
From some man's grave.

If I wasn't mistaken, this was a resurrection pot. If my rapture ate the fungus, I need only close the lid for the length of a day or so, and the fungus would re-grow. The food was perfect for those times when the rapture couldn't hunt.

I turned my focus on my new pet and was only slightly surprised to find it looking bigger, with little feathers beginning to poke their sharp noses out from between protruding shoulder blades. I opened the cage and stood back, waiting expectantly. A few moments later, the bird waddled to the door and hopped up, then out, onto the table. He spotted the fungus, and turned his steady green eyes on me. "Braaah?"

"Go ahead," I urged. "They're for you."

The rapture spread its wings and I could see more feathers poking out, elongating like stretched gum. The little bird was literally growing right before my eyes. It hopped over to the fungus and pecked at it, its sharp beak easily removing a chunk from the fungus's soft meat. Within moments, the treat was gone and the last bit was making its way in fits and starts down the bird's long, curved neck. More feathers grew, its talons lengthened, and just like that, my new pet was no longer a nestling, transforming into a fledgling at a speed that stunned me.

"Mooore?" it cooed, tilting its head at me.

I blinked. Raptures could speak out loud? "Um, it has to re-grow." I reached over and closed the lid. "There'll be more later. Would you like to go outside and look for bugs?" It nodded, and I was relieved to find that bugs were adequate fare. Raptures eat the dead, the living, and everything in-between, and luckily for me, insects come in all those forms. I held out my arm. "Come." With a brief wing flap and a jump, the rapture was on my arm, its marbled talons denting my skin, but not unpleasantly. It seemed to sense my vulnerability and did its best not to dig in too deep. This was one amazing bird.

My new companion, I sensed, was male, and he needed a name. "What shall I call you?" I asked him as we headed outside. He didn't respond as he took in the world around us. He soon spotted the chickens and pushed off, into a glide. "No!" I raced after him. "Leave them be!"

The bright red rooster, spotting the attacker, puffed himself up, then launched his scruffy body at the rapture, his little legs pumping like mad. I cringed, knowing what was coming, but kept running, my feet hitting the ground with dull thuds, which came way too slowly. I wasn't going to make it in time.

Just as I thought the rapture was going to attack the clucking object hurtling toward him, he landed on the ground, then glanced back at me. "They're not for eating!" I shouted, which was true only in the sense that they weren't for *his* eating.

Rudey the rooster stopped where he was. Not quite sure what to do, he hopped to the left, back to the right, and back to the left again. All the while the rapture just stood there, taking in the odd behavior with a tilted head, then, after fully considering the situation, he gave a sort of bow. Rudey froze, stunned into disbelief. His posturing had actually worked; he'd subdued the giant!

I approached my new pet, slowly but with confidence. "Good boy," I cooed. "The chickens are friends, not food. I know that can be a hard distinction to make, even for humans, but make it you must."

He gave a sort of shrug, then flew up to land on my arm once more. Rudey, all cocky now, started to strut about amongst the hens, making victorious clucking noises as they gathered around him, looking for all the world like adoring fans. The rapture watched the fowl closely, then turned away, his eyes scanning the yard.

Working to balance his increasingly heavy weight on one arm, I made my way toward the brook. When I passed beneath one of the apple trees, the rapture jumped down, landing amongst the fallen apple blossoms. Within moments he was rooting about in the dirt, just like the chickens, and discovering all sorts of plump bugs to gorge on.

I watched him moving about, taking in his increasing size with satisfaction. The development of his strong brow, a feature that aged him considerably, was nearly finished, and his wings now rose up on each side of his body into two feathery epaulets. Like an artist making a sketch, his feathers filled in, his beak curled into a deadly hook, and his legs thickened. By tomorrow, he would be a full-grown bird, able to fly high in the sky, dive low to hit prey, and land in tight spaces to dine on carrion. In short, he'd be a super bird.

After eating his fill, he trotted around the yard, studying and taking in everything, looking for all the world like a dog on his rounds. When a half hour had passed in this manner, the rapture's wings began to droop and I held out my arm and gave a short, sharp whistle. Within seconds, he was roosted there, head held high despite his obvious fatigue. I realized it must take an incredible amount of energy to grow so quickly and figured he needed a good old-fashioned nap. With his rapid maturation, I was glad to see he had maintained the fuzzy down on his head and hoped it would always remain.

Walking around to the front of the cottage I heard a babble of voices coming from the direction of the village. I peered down the road to see a group of young fey making their way toward my place, laughing and shoving one another like children. Only two destinations lay out this way…my house and the Fiersens, and I had a bad feeling the teens weren't going to visit the Fiersens.

I stepped back and the movement caught the attention of one of the fey at the front of the pack. He pointed at me. "It's her!" After a moment's hesitation, as though drawing breath, the group started to run towards my cottage.

At the same time, the rapture went on alert, pulling up his already massive wings into a defensive position. "Daaanger?"

"Yes," I whispered as I watched the gang approach. "Definitely danger." Young, brash, and bored, I figured they were looking to prove themselves by going after an Omni-Fey. I didn't know any of them personally, and guessed they were the children of the transient prole fey who worked odd jobs around the village. They were soon huddled together outside my gate, as though wary of going any further. Uncertain of their motives, I stayed where I was, halfway between them and the cottage. "What do you want?" I called out.

"Well, if it ain't the Omni-Fey," a rough-looking elf drawled, hitching up his dirty trousers. "Or should I say, Omni-*Fail?*"

"Clever," I shot back. "But untrue."

The rapture flapped his wings ominously and the gang drew back, with the exception of the elf. He scratched at one large ear, and I noticed that its tip was missing. "Ye calling me a liar?"

"I'm calling you an idiot, which is worse. A person can stop lying, but he usually can't stop being an idiot."

The elf scowled, and his hand, which was on the gate, undid the latch. "Me da says ye're holding out on us cause ye want the villagers to pay ye to end the curse. He says ye're only gonna help the rich, who got the money for it." He pointed a thumb at his thin chest. "We don't, so we lose out."

"Again, untrue."

"Now ye're calling me da a liar?"

"I'm saying that you and your father have been fed lies"—courtesy of Melaina—"and now you're repeating them, like mindless drones."

"Is that right?" He pushed open the gate and stepped inside. I noticed one grubby hand clutched a large rock. I had a feeling his whole gangs' grubby little hands clutched rocks, with more tucked away in their grubby little pockets. Here in Hawthorn Lane stoning someone wasn't considered entirely wrong, especially if the victim deserves it, and right now, no doubt a lot of villagers felt I deserved what was coming to me.

I took a step backward. "I don't want this curse, either, you know."

He spat on the ground as though rejecting my words. "Then end it."

"It's not that simple."

"Then let me make it simple. I'm sure a little fright will make ye do what's needed, eh?"

I pulled back my shoulders. "You're challenging an Omni-Fey?"

"What've I got to lose?"

"Your life?"

"Not much of a life," he replied flatly, and I felt my heart skip a beat. The most dangerous people are those who simply don't care anymore. And this elf, with his hollowed out cheeks and deep-set eyes that had seen too much, had reached that point.

He took another step, letting the gate clang shut behind him. Our eyes locked in one final showdown. A crooked grin revealed a broken tooth and several dark gaps. Before I could retreat, he rushed at me, rock raised high. As though lifting a sluice gate, the rest of the gang poured through the gateway with the speed of a roaring river, and I turned to run, certain I wouldn't make it to the cottage in time. With a large, awkwardly perched bird on my arm, I was an easy target. I'd only gone a few feet when a rock hit my calf and I stumbled; another clipped my elbow, bruising it. But I kept going.

I was nearly to the cottage when a heavy stone hit the back of my head, bringing me down. The rapture screamed loudly in my ear, then lifted into the air just as I hit the ground. I pressed my hand to my wound as I gazed up at him in awe, stunned by his size and strength. He flapped his massive wings, turning himself about, then dove at the young fey, his sharp beak darting up and down.

The gang members started shouting, throwing their hands up to protect themselves. "We has better go, Carius!" one of them shouted, his arm bleeding.

"I'll do as I please," Carius growled. Several of the delinquents began to back up, their eyes wide and mouths open. Unafraid of the rapture, the elf took aim, but before he could release his rock, the bird swung about, his wing knocking the projectile away. A loud screech burst from his beak, the sound high and piercing as a banshee, and wary at last, Carius began to back away. Not waiting to see what happened to him, the rest of the gang spun about and fled. "I'm telling me da!" the elf threatened, his voice shaky as he took another step.

"Go ahead," I challenged him.

The rapture screeched again and Carius turned and took off, leaving the gate clanging behind him.

When the gang was gone, the rapture returned to me, landing by my side. He nudged at my shoulder and I reached out and petted his soft head. "You saved me." At that moment, his name appeared in my mind like a flame come to life. "I shall call you Edan. It means 'full of fire.' What do you think of that?"

"Eeedaan!" the bird squawked, then beat his wings in approval.

"Edan, it is." I laughed. "So it looks like you're stuck with me. Though where I'm going to put you I've no idea."

Chapter Sixteen

Whoever had given me Edan might just have saved my life, or at least saved me from serious harm. Question was, who had given him to me? I thought about the strange bouquet I'd received, and wondered if it was the same person. What was their motivation? To woo me or warn me? To these questions, I had no answer. But maybe if I figured out the why, I'd figure out the who.

I picked myself up and headed for the cottage, with Edan hopping after me. Once inside, I peeled off my gloves, tossing them on the table, then plopped down on my chaise in front of the fireplace, chilled and out of sorts. Edan sat next to me, making small cooing noises. I should start a fire, I thought. I should do something. But I couldn't make myself move.

A brisk knock sounded on the front door, and I turned sharply, the action making my head spin. Had the elf boys returned? Was it the villagers, come to force me into marriage? Or had my mother really found me?

"Lorelle?" It was Kyran, and he sounded concerned. I relaxed slightly. "Are you in there? Why is there blood on the walk?" He paused a second. "Lorelle!"

"I'm all right," I managed to push out. Hearing Kyran's voice, Edan had edged closer to me, his bright eyes locked on the door. "It's okay," I soothed. "He's a friend."

"Frieeend?"

"Yes, like the chickens." I cringed, then made a mental note never to let on to Edan that I ate chicken, or he'd think all my friends were fair game. "Go wait in the conservatory." I pointed at the glass room. Edan studied me with eyes that already looked more intelligent than a lot of people I knew, then did as I said. "The door's unlocked," I called. In my unsteady state, I'd forgotten to bolt it.

The door swung open and Kyran charged in, looking winded. "What the hell happened?" The air around him seemed to vibrate as he kneeled down and took my hand. I flinched, but soon the jolt dissipated into a gentle throb, and I was able to relax a little. Kyran looked me over, then spotted the blood on my collar. "You've been hurt." His tone was guttural, as though the words scraped at his throat.

"It's nothing," I told him. "Just a cut. I should probably clean it."

"Let me." He went into the bathroom, returning with a wet cloth. His fingertips zapped me with little pulses as he undid the buttons of my collar. I had to inhale deeply to avoid passing out. Then, with a gentleness I hadn't imagined him possessing, he wiped away the blood, stroke after tender stroke. I closed my eyes and let him work, grateful I didn't have to do the job myself. My limbs felt rather wobbly at the moment, probably from getting beaned by a rock. Though I'd been in worse situations and walked away without so much as a quivering muscle. So perhaps it was Kyran breathing on the back of my neck as he worked that was making me feel weak.

"Why did you come?" I asked after he stopped.

"I enquired after you at Avice's flat and discovered you'd gone home *alone*. After I told you not to. So I had Josepha bring Ilia back to the castle and I came here."

"You didn't have to do that, Kyran. I'm fine."

"Yes, you look fine," he said dryly. "Who did this to you, Lorelle?"

"Only young fey looking to show their courage. They blamed me for the curse, figured they could scare me into doing the right thing." I turned to face Kyran, searching his dark eyes for answers. "It's Melaina, isn't it? You warned me she would do this."

His jaw clenched into granite. "I did."

"I thought I'd be fine in daylight," I explained. "And I just wanted to get home. Away from all that…" I waved my hand in the direction of the village. "She really did a number on them, getting them to turn on me so quickly and easily. I hope it was because she used some sort of spell and not because they hate me so much."

"I want to know each and every name of every fool who slighted you," he ground out.

I stood abruptly, then swayed. He rose and caught hold of me, and I relished the delicious pain of the shocks—they brought me back to my senses. "I can take care of myself," I told him stubbornly, conveniently forgetting that not all that long ago I'd relished his concern. "Besides, now I have Edan." I indicated the conservatory where Edan waited, hunched over but ready to attack at my word.

Kyran's eyes moved to peer over my shoulder, then awe transformed his fierce expression into one of intrigue. "What is that incredible creature?" Edan made a satisfied caw in response.

"That's Edan. He's a rapture—a cross between a vulture and a raptor. Would you like to meet him?"

Kyran nodded wordlessly, then took my arm and steered me toward the conservatory. I leaned a bit heavily on him, even though I was perfectly able to walk on my own, and could only hope he wouldn't notice my hypocrisy. It was just that his arm beneath mine felt so solid and reassuring, and very muscular, I might add.

"Edan…this is Count Kyran Van der Daarke, and you will know him as a friend of mine until I say otherwise."

Edan ducked his head in a bow. "Kyran, this is Edan."

"It's a pleasure," Kyran replied, then swept low in a bow worthy of royalty.

"Braaah…" Edan purred in a pleased tone, and I knew Kyran had won him over.

"Where did you find him?"

"On my doorstep. I thought maybe you had brought him."

"Not me."

"And you didn't give me the bouquet, either."

He shook his head, looking a bit regretful he hadn't, or so I wanted to think. "So you don't know your admirer?"

"Admirer? Hardly. I thought maybe it was someone trying to get on my good side. For every fey who hates me, it seems another is trying to win my favor." My mouth twisted. "Melaina was savvy enough to go after the low-borns. They're the ones who seem to despise me now."

Knowing how much I disliked my newly elevated status, I thought Kyran would laugh, but he only said grimly, "My sister enjoys employing irony as a weapon."

"Why is she so determined to use it against me?"

"Because she knows I like you, and she can't stand me having anything good, and also because she doesn't like anyone who defies her. And you did that at the ball, in front of a crowd. She'll never forgive you for that."

"Well, she's very good at making people hate me."

"Yes, she is." He turned me about and escorted me back to the chaise in front of the fire. "Sit down." I found myself descending without making the conscious decision to do so. "Do you have a salve for your wound?" He squinted at the back of my neck. "It's bleeding again."

"In the bathroom. There are bandages there, as well. In the cabinet."

He left me and returned a few moments later with a crystal jar of aloe healing salve and a bandage. He ministered to me quietly, his caresses electric and soothing at the same time. The back of my neck is partial to human touch and reacts to it in the form of whispery shudders. I sighed softly and closed my eyes, letting him play doctor for as long as he wanted.

Too soon he was finished, though I had the feeling he'd been taking his dear, sweet time. He stood and returned the supplies to the bathroom, then came back and started up a fire. When it was blazing, he pulled the antique rocking chair that I had begun to think of as his closer to me, and sat down.

"How was your visit with Charlton yesterday?" he asked after a few moments of staring into the fire.

"Fine. How was yours?"

"Fine. Did he fulfill all your needs?" As far as loaded questions go, this one was a winner.

"I'm not sure that's possible."

"I'd hate to think you aren't being satisfied, Lorelle. Perhaps I can rectify that."

I shot him a look. "I rather doubt that."

He arched an eyebrow. "You underestimate me."

I thought about what he'd done to my conservatory, the exploding glass, the careful restoration. "Perhaps I do. Avice has outdone herself teaching you."

"Avice hasn't done anything. I've been working on developing my skills alone, every free moment I have. I've learned during my brief time here that this is not the place to be taken unawares."

"True. I'm surprised you're staying. Weren't you thinking of leaving Hawthorn Lane?"

"I said that to annoy Lady Faylan."

An amused laugh slipped out of me. "So you're definitely staying?"

His eyes met mine. "You think I'd leave you here alone?"

I turned away. I'd meant to leave him alone, still meant to. But not for selfish reasons. I was doing it to help my village. To make things right with Dallen, and salve my conscience.

"But if I'm not here," I said softly, "you could leave Hawthorn Lane."

"You don't understand. I want to stay. I like it here. I like the old-fashioned feeling, the sparks of magic everywhere, like Christmas year round. There's an atmosphere of intrigue in Hawthorn Lane I've never before encountered, and I like having a reason for getting up in the morning that involves more than making money. I feel like I can be of use to these people. But most of all, most importantly, you're here."

Well...

"But if I do go..." I persisted.

He shook his head. "Don't you see? I have to stay. I have responsibilities now, and having taken them on, I will not forsake them. I *need* to be here."

Was this him wanting to be the hero, or him being a damn good guy? I couldn't tell anymore. "So your magic is growing stronger?"

He nodded, his eyes bright. "I've never felt this way before—so connected to the world around me, so powerful and sharp. I feel like I've just awakened from a long sleep."

"Don't you find that strange? This sudden change?"

He shrugged. "It's this place." He paused. "And you."

"Me? What have I done?"

"You've invigorated me, filled me with a reason for living."

"That's a bit melodramatic, Kyran," I scoffed, thrown by his emotion. "We've only just met, and don't give me that karma crap and how it was meant to be. People and relationships are ugly. I've witnessed that nightmare first-hand. I don't know why it should be any different for you and me."

"There are people in the world who've had love affairs most only dream about having. Why can't that be us?"

My heart spasmed painfully. "Because I'm not that lucky."

He rocked back and forth in his chair, its rhythmic thumping filling the cottage. "Do you know why I want to remove the curse, Lorelle?"

"I have my theories," I replied wryly.

"It's a selfish reason."

"I know."

He cocked an eyebrow at me. "What's your theory, then? I recall that you mentioned something highly unflattering at dinner the other night."

"I think you're doing this because it will make you a hero, and you'll have finally found a place full of people who will look up to you."

He winced a little, and I wondered if I'd gone too far. "Nice to know you hold such a high opinion of me."

"That's what happens when you're raised by evil. You trust nothing and no one."

He leaned forward. "Is your mother why you're leaving Hawthorn Lane? I don't really know anything about your life, other than what my sister said…that your mother isn't the nicest person. Is she your impediment? Is she the visitor with a connection to you?"

I realized that with one statement I'd let on far more than I'd meant to, and my mind scrambled to figure out what to share with him without giving myself away any further. "There you go, getting all dramatic on me again." I stood up. "I need to see to Edan. He'll be hungry."

Edan made an affirmative noise, but Kyran didn't move. "Where is your mother, Lorelle?"

"She's in the Alterworld." I *hoped* she was in the Alterworld.

"She isn't here?"

I laughed jerkily. "Stars above, I hope not!"

"You're sure?"

"When it comes to my mother, I'm not sure of anything. But if she's here, well, that would be bad."

"Why?"

I sighed and rubbed my forehead. "Because *she's* bad."

"Why won't you tell me what's going on?" He rose up. "It has to do with why you want to leave, doesn't it?"

"Partially," I answered honestly, if reluctantly. Growing up with my mother, my aunt Nimair, and my sister, Eudrea, I'd learned not to ever give whole truths. Revealing my thoughts and feelings had a way of getting me hurt, or those around me hurt. I'd once befriended an alley cat and when Eudrea found out, let's just say I never saw Will Feral alive again. A part of me wanted to trust people and another part that felt sick at the idea.

"I think Edan is going to need a bed," Kyran said, his convoluted style of conversation once more throwing me for a loop.

My fingers, which I had unconsciously curled into fists, slowly relaxed. "I suppose he will. A nest, I imagine. An eyrie."

"I can help you make one."

"Eyyyrie!" Edan responded excitedly.

I swallowed, feeling suddenly hot and itchy. This man was determined to become a part of my life. The only answer I could truly comprehend for why was that he needed me to achieve his goal of being a hero. And yet, I couldn't quite believe that, either. Maybe because I didn't want to.

"All right," I agreed. "Because I'm certainly not sharing my bed with him."

Chapter Seventeen

We spent the rest of the afternoon building an elevated nest that fit perfectly into a corner of the conservatory. I had learned to be self-sufficient in Hawthorn Lane, but building stuff was not an area of expertise for me. I was of the 'measure once, screw up the measurement, then spend hours trying to compensate for my mistake' school of thought. It's why I had to hire the Fiersens for any building jobs, or I'd end up with crooked furniture, a leaning henhouse, and wobbly chairs. Apparently being Omni-Fey gives one the ability to do everything but construction. So, as much as I wanted to do things myself, I had learned from experience to compromise on this matter.

Luckily Kyran was surprisingly adept at building. As we worked, he told me he'd spent his holidays out in their garage making whatever he could, mainly as a means of escaping the house whenever his parents were fighting, which was often. It explained why his hands weren't the typical soft, lily-white lumps most hoity-toitys possess. As his assistant, my job was to find usable tree limbs for the platform and branches for the nest while Kyran sketched out a basic plan. Edan joined me in my hunt, hopping along behind me and rooting for bugs while I sawed with enthusiasm.

"You already cut them?" Kyran asked when he saw my pile.

I peered up at him as I finished removing the last twigs from a thick branch. "Is that a trick question?"

He laughed, and I felt the increasingly familiar warmth I always experienced around him flutter to life in my belly. "I could've done that."

"Oh, that. I thought I'd screwed it up. I cut the branches as long as I could so you could make them shorter if need be."

"These are perfect."

"Really?" I wasn't accustomed to compliments and was leery of receiving them, like they were little time bombs set to go off the second I let myself accept one. Mother never complimented me, and Aunt Nimair wouldn't know a compliment if it kicked her in the head. Eudrea would flatter me to get something she wanted, then, when she got it, would go about revoking each and every bit of praise, with relish. Dallen had been full of glowing remarks, and I'd finally been letting myself relax and accept them when I'd caught him and my sister going at it. Since then the only compliments I received were from Avice, and while they were nice to hear—better than insults, anyway—I never really believed them. I'm pretty sure she said what she did to get me into bed, and she only wanted to get me into bed because I kept refusing her.

"Really," Kyran assured me. "Do you have a wagon?"

I did. It took two trips to haul everything into the cottage and Edan got a ride with each trip. Then I played Igor, fetching tools and handing them over whenever Kyran asked. We worked well together, something I both liked and admonished myself to stop dwelling on as having any kind of meaning.

While Kyran built the platform, I worked on the nest, weaving together the sticks I'd gathered using long strands of colored wool to create a soft bed. Edan's head jutting out over my shoulder, he watched me work and occasionally made clicks of satisfaction. Several times I'd had to stop and take him outside to eat. He was still growing, but now only in size; all his adult feathers were in. The fuzz on his head, along with a ring of white down that encircled his neck like a fancy boa, hadn't yet fallen out, and I enjoyed petting him there, which he seemed to equally enjoy. I hoped he wouldn't grow much larger. He was the size of a large condor now, and already I wouldn't be able to carry him on my arm anymore.

Thanks to Kyran, the eyrie turned out perfectly. The platform, complete with a moss-covered roof and intricately woven branches, resembled something you'd find in a mythical story. Most of the sticks used to build the nest came from the apple trees, making the cottage smell like fresh-baked pie. After attaching the last limb, Kyran stood and gave the platform a good shake. Sturdy and well-built, it didn't move so much as a centimeter.

"What do you think?" he asked, turning to me, his dark hair mussed up from his efforts. His expression was almost boyish, and a fondness for him welled up inside me, surprising me—it seemed both he and his niece had the same effect on me. I wasn't sure what to make of it.

"I think it's a masterpiece."

"Braaah," Edan agreed.

Kyran's rare smile broke loose, lighting up the room. "Now for the finishing touch." He lifted the nest I'd made up onto the platform, which stood about four feet high and four feet wide. It fit perfectly. Since Edan wouldn't be able to fly up into the eyrie—his wingspan being too wide—Kyran had built a little ramp for him to climb. It was a feat of engineering I couldn't have managed myself, and I was impressed. Kyran was not the muckety-muck I wanted to paint him as, and that made me feel both proud of him and uncomfortable. I had my reasons for not wanting to get too involved with him, though a part of me wondered how rational and fair they were.

Feeling like a sentimental parent, I wished briefly for a camera to document Edan's first ascent into his brand-new bed, but as modern gadgets were banned from Hawthorn Lane due to their ill effects on magic, I'd have to make do with my memories. He looked so satisfied sitting in his nest, and I realized at that moment how much I needed him to be exactly where he was, in his new eyrie, in our home, with me.

I turned to Kyran, who was watching Edan with an equally proud and proprietorial look on his face. "It's perfect," I said. "Thank you."

"We make a good team," he replied, not looking at me. "And I don't mean in an end-the-curse-and-save-the-village sort of way."

I laughed. "I agree." I took a deep breath and made the plunge. "Would you like to stay for supper?"

At last he turned his dark eyes on me. "I'd love to."

"It won't be as fancy as our meal at *Chez Chantilly*, but it will be drama-free."

"I could go for a drama-free night."

"Drama-free it is."

We moved to the kitchen, leaving Edan to clean his feathers and settle into his nest. After all the growing he'd done, he'd likely sleep until morning. I hoped so anyway. If we could skip the 'baby' part of his growing up, where he woke every few hours for a feeding and needing to be let out to do his business, I wouldn't be disappointed.

Kyran and I worked side by side in the cozy warmth of the kitchen—me frying up Kentish fish and crab cakes, and him preparing a burnet salad. We were both quiet, with only the sounds of his knife slicing and dicing and the sizzle of butter to fill the air. When the fish and cakes were finished, a crisp batter coating them both, I broke open the bottle of *Dark Spirits* Avice had given me a short time ago. Kyran stoked up the fire, then we sat down to eat in the glow of the flames.

After a few bites, followed by a sip of *Dark Spirits*, Kyran turned his attention on me. "This is amazing, Lorelle. Where did you learn to cook?"

I bit my lip. Damn, he had a way of asking questions that forced me to talk about my past. Avice never asked these sorts of questions. She was a 'here and now' sort of gal. The past held no interest for her—or, as I suspected, it was a source of pain, and so she repressed it. She had a brother, Malen, who spent most of his time in the Alterworld, her parents were dead, and she really had no one family-wise to lean on. Whenever I tried to get her to talk more about her life, she'd change the subject, leave the room, come on to me…anything to get me off the topic of her life and onto something else.

But I had to wonder if holding back was good for a person. I no longer had to worry about being outed; I was one of *them*. I was fey. So I was safe to share some of my background. But old habits—formed in early childhood and cemented here in Hawthorn Lane—die hard. Still, Kyran and I were having a moment and he'd done a great job building Edan's eyrie. I kind of felt like I owed him something.

"We didn't have much to work with in my house, so I learned to make do with very little. Plus I had a great home-ec teacher, and when I came here, a witch—Missy Thornback—taught me a lot about using herbs, and not just for making elixirs and potions." I stopped there. It wasn't much sharing, but it could lead to more, something I didn't quite want. I quickly slugged back a mouthful of wine and waited for the questions to come.

Kyran took a bite of crab cake, and chewed it with his eyes closed. "Well, you must have been an excellent student."

"Thank you," I replied carefully, still waiting for the rest of the interrogation. When it didn't come, I bit into the crab cake myself and savored the buttery crust. It was quite good. "I enjoy cooking."

He opened his eyes and forked up some salad. "So, tell me about the Fiersens. Are the rest of them really as wild as Sinead is always claiming?" He looked at me sideways and I knew he was doing this on purpose—holding off, giving me my space. It was either very kind of him, or a trick to get me to relax and tell him more. Either way, he was only going to hear about the Fiersens.

We were both laughing after one particular story I'd related—about when Madera Fiersen had drunk too much *Lightning* and streaked through the village throwing flowers to every passerby. Doolin Fiersen was not pleased about what he called his wife's 'loose' behavior, but she seemed to have no regrets about it, reveling in the attention that circulated around her for weeks afterward. The room was pleasantly warm, my mind swirling in lovely circles, my chest light. I don't think I'd ever felt so happy, not even when Dallen and I had been dating.

And then Kyran had to go and ruin things.

"Who gave you Edan, Lorelle?" he asked in a low voice. "And that weird bouquet?"

I could feel my lips stretching into two tight lines, like someone had pulled drawstrings attached to the corners of my mouth. "I don't know," I ground out, feeling angry and upset and disappointed. "Why do you care?"

He leaned forward and placed his giant hand over mine, completely covering it, blotting it out so that it no longer seemed to exist. He could just as easily do the same thing to my entire self. Though the thought of him covering me with the tremendous length of his body, zapping me all over with little shocks from head to toe, didn't frighten me in the least. In fact, I welcomed it, and that scared me. But as he hadn't even tried to kiss me after that first time, I probably had nothing to worry about, from him or my hormones.

"I care because I'm worried about you," he said softly. "Doesn't it concern you that someone has come into your cottage uninvited? Or that you've been given a gift that had the potential of killing you?"

I was glad that he said 'had' instead of 'has' regarding Edan killing me. "Of course I am," I replied testily. From the conservatory came a warning growl. "I'm fine, Edan. Just a little annoyed." The growling ceased, but I could sense he was alert now, making sure I was okay. I liked that, having a watchbird to look after me. Especially since Kyran was right—I wasn't exactly over the moon that someone had broken into my cottage, and likely had used magic to do it. Whether or not the intruders had good intentions I wasn't sure, but I thought maybe not. Either way, it was a violation, and if Edan weren't here to protect me I'd be feeling quite unsettled right now.

"And whoever it was did come into your cottage uninvited?"

"Do I strike you as the sort of person who invites people in?" It was a dodge, but also the truth.

"No. So may I assume they came in here without your permission?"

"I suppose you may."

"And that doesn't make you nervous?"

"Of course it makes me nervous," I grumbled, then took a sip of wine. "But Edan has been a gift to me, Kyran. He'll protect me." Especially now, with the threat of fey-hunters, the menace of the angry villagers, and Melaina's wrath, I needed protection. I couldn't fly, but until I could, I had Edan to do that for me. I could only hope that would be enough.

Kyran nodded his understanding, though his jaw was tight. "I still don't like it."

"But it's done, so let's move on. Tell me what's going on with your sister. How worried should I be about her?"

His jaw tightened even more, like a turning screw. "Very. With Renwick having done a runner she's gone ballistic. This morning I thought she was going to burn down the entire castle."

"I assume she's gone looking for him, or is having someone do it for her."

"Oh, yes. And their reports are not to her liking. Wherever Renwick is, he's well-hidden. And however he's getting to and fro has so far baffled his pursuers."

I laughed. *Good.* "Do you want to have something to hold over her?"

His eyes narrowed in the dim light. "You know I would."

"Can you keep it a secret? And by that, I mean, can you block access to your mind?"

"I've been doing it since I was a boy. Never exactly realized it until coming here, but yes."

"All right. Renwick is in Wuthering Wood, staying with my old mentor, Missy Thornback. He'll be safe there for as long as he's with her."

"You brought him there," he stated flatly.

"For a couple reasons. Would you like to hear them?"

He toyed with the stem of his glass. "You do like to draw things out."

I smiled. "I have so few pleasures."

"Out with it."

"In return, I want to know why Ilia is mad at me."

"She's mad at you?"

"You didn't notice?" He shook his head. "What good are you then?" I sighed. "All right I'll tell you anyway, and you have the libations to thank for that." I tilted my glass at him. "One, I'm doing a favor for Missy Thornback. She likes young, good-looking men. Two, this is punishment for what Renwick did to you and Ilia." Kyran's eyebrows rose, but he stayed silent. "And three, I did it to annoy your sister."

"Remind me not to get on your bad side."

I raised my glass in a toast. "Damn straight."

He laughed and toasted me back. We both drank, then spent the next several minutes savoring our meal before it grew too cold to be properly enjoyed. When the quiet had gone on long enough, Kyran broke it.

"Thank you for telling me."

"You might have noticed that I'm not good at sharing."

"I noticed. What made you that way?"

I peered at him over the rim of my glass. "That would be sharing."

"Does it have anything to do with why you want to leave Hawthorn Lane?"

"It might."

Kyran opened his mouth, closed it, opened it again, then abruptly rose. "You and I are more alike than you realize, Lorelle, and I hope someday you'll see that as a good thing and not as a threat, as you do now. I can't make any promises because I'm the sort of man used to pursuing what he wants and getting it. But I'll try to respect your privacy, and give you space to make up your mind about me."

I swallowed hard. Did he really mean it? Could I trust him? I'd grown up despising his type, had been burned by so many people I should've been able to trust, and manipulated and lied to too many times to count. It was hard to set all that aside simply because one man wanted to get to know me better.

Oh, but stars above, I desperately wanted to.

Chapter Eighteen

Seemingly in accord with his statement, Kyran didn't ask me any more questions. We cleaned up, talking as we worked about Edan and how big he might end up. The rapture was in his eyrie, nodding off, though I had no doubt he could hear us, a rumble of voices in his subconscious mind, ears attuned to anything that might be off or threatening. He seemed too young to be exposed to such vagaries, but then, perhaps it was best he learn early how unpredictable and threatening life could be.

When the work was done, Kyran strode over to the door and donned his cloak. I followed him, my arms crossed in the cooler air by the door. "I feel better with Edan here," he said, deftly buttoning the top clasp—a silver bone. "So whoever gave him to you, I feel grateful to him."

"Or her."

He looked pleased. "You think it might have been Avice?"

I frowned. "I don't think Avice's mind works that way."

The pleased look fled. "Ah."

"Either way, I'm not going to look a gift bird in the beak."

His lips twitched. "Then I won't, either."

"Anyway, I'm beginning to think your sister figured out that I'm the one who helped Renwick find a hideout. It would explain the villagers' sudden change toward me. If I'm right, and she's looking for revenge, then I'm very glad Edan's here."

"As am I. So what are your plans for tomorrow?"

"Avice never did teach me how to fly. Maybe I'll go see her."

"You'll be careful?"

"I'm always careful, Kyran." Though I wasn't so sure that was true, not after my attack this afternoon. I'd been caught off guard, and I didn't like that. But I did have Edan now. I could bring him with me into the village. See how those low-born traitors liked them nuggets.

Kyran nodded, but remained quiet. I looked up, straight into his eyes, and found his expression tight with concern. "I'll be thinking about you. Good night, Lorelle."

"Good night, Kyran."

I shut the door behind him, berating myself for wanting him to take me in his arms and kiss me, kiss away all my troubles and make me forget. Yes, I admit Kyran wasn't as bad or as snobbish as I'd thought, but things were so complicated now that I didn't know what to do about us, other than keep things impersonal and distant until I could figure it out. Tonight's little tête-à-tête hadn't exactly fit with impersonal and distant, and I vowed to do better.

But I did it with an unwilling spirit.

Not long after Kyran left, Edan started making hungry noises, so I fed him everything I could find in the kitchen until he finally settled back down. Then I read for an hour, sipping *Dark Spirits* from a crystal goblet and nibbling on *Sweet Elfin Dreams* chocolate. The libation and the chocolate, combined with a tantalizing plot, helped steer my mind from things I didn't want to think about. After my encounter with those young hoodlums this afternoon, I needed to restore my equilibrium, and I typically did that through my defense mechanism of choice…escapism.

I awoke with an agonized cry in the dark hours of the morning. Sitting up straight I glanced around, relieved to find myself in my own bed, safe and not responsible for what I'd done. It had all been a dream. I groaned and scooted out of my bed nook, grabbing my robe off a beckoning, cast iron skeletal finger hook, and muttering to myself. *Damn libations.* Sometimes they released something in my unconscious that manifested itself in my dreams, something darker than I thought could possibly dwell there. Did it have to do with this damn tattoo on my wrist? The one that filled the air with Vetiver, ashes, and dust every time I so much as lifted a finger? Burn that Cutter Flint! He was stirring things up in me that I didn't want stirred.

After checking on Edan, who was still sleeping the deep and heavy sleep of adolescence, I took a hot bath to clear away the remaining bad aura, then dressed for the day. I once again wrapped my wrist and donned a thick silver bracelet to cover my unwanted tattoo, then pulled out something comfortable to wear—a soft spider silk and cashmere blend perfect for activity. Today I would make Avice teach me how to fly. After my strange dream I felt a growing need to be able to flee from danger more quickly than on foot.

After tending to the hungry chickens and gathering their still-warm eggs, I returned to the cottage to prepare breakfast for myself and Edan, who was only now waking up. As I approached his eyrie, he opened one sleepy eye. "Braaah?"

I reached in to pet his soft head, glad to see his down still remained. He was quite a bit bigger this morning, his body now the size of an ostrich's. I hoped for both our sakes he was pretty much done growing now. "I bet you're hungry."

Edan nodded and I marveled at his understanding. He wasn't just memorizing my words to deliver messages, he understood them. I didn't think the ravens and falcons possessed that kind of intelligence. But then again, this was Hawthorn Lane. Anything was possible.

I fetched the box of *Dead Man's Fingers*, thrilled to see the number of stalks had multiplied from yesterday. The fungus should tide Edan over until I could bring him outside to hunt. He ate greedily, then snuffed around for more.

"After I eat," I told him, as I closed the box and put it on a shelf in the conservatory, hidden from view. "Then we'll go outside."

He seemed to consider my words, then turned to cleaning his feathers, his sign that he acquiesced. Good, because I was starving. I quickly ate, feeling rather excited about taking Edan out. When I was done, I motioned to him. "Ready?"

"Ready," he croaked, his voice deeper than yesterday.

He waddled after me and I had a brief qualm about getting him out the door, but he folded his wings in tight and made it through without too much fuss. The day was another kind one, with a warm, dry breeze blowing out of the south. Edan let the wind ruffle his feathers, his eyes blinking in blissful enjoyment.

"Wait until you get up there." I pointed at the open blue sky over the moors. "You'll love it. Now remember, limit yourself to the already dead or the smaller rodents, all right? Avoid going after the animals of the forest…they fight back. All right?" He nodded, and I stepped back, giving him room as he extended his wings, then flapped them a few times.

After a few more flaps, he pushed off and lifted into the air, emitting a joyful screech that echoed all around me. My heart beat a little harder than normal as I watched him soar into the sky, his massive wings rising up and down slowly and steadily. He started showing off, swooping low, then lifting his head and shooting straight upward. Eventually he moved farther away from the cottage, reducing to a mere black pinprick against the blue. And then he was gone, out of my sight.

I felt a bit odd. Would he come back? Would I if I were in his position? Would I trade my liberty for a tiny handmade bed, funky looking fungi, and the company of someone who wasn't my kind? I didn't know the answer to that, so I just stood there, hand above my eyes to shade them from the growing brightness of the sun, and waited for him to return to me, safe and sound, all the while envying him his freedom. I missed my gathering missions, missed being in on things, missed being able to come and go as I pleased. I loved my cottage, but lately it was starting to feel a bit prison-like.

All my attention focused on the sky, I didn't notice the gate open and close, or the person marching toward me.

"Lorelle Gragan!" my visitor cried out in a voice pitched high with emotion.

I spun about. "Atlene?" Her stride was determined, her ebony face etched with fury and pain as she strode toward me on stocky legs, her colorful ribbon skirt swishing back and forth. "What are you doing here?"

A few feet from where I stood, she stopped and stared at me like I was stupid. "How can you ask me that, girl?"

"Did I forget to pay for something at the shop?" I asked, my mind struggling to recall the last time I'd visited her store, *Crystalline Vessels*. I mentally snapped my fingers, remembering. It had been the day of the Van der Daarke ball. I'd been distracted, so it was possible I'd forgotten.

"Forget to pay?" she sputtered. Short and round, with a wild Afro that flared around her head like a dandelion gone to seed, Atlene was the epitome of cute and spunky. The maestro elf ran her own shop, which specialized in producing crystal and glass objets d'art, and although a bit disorganized and scatterbrained, she was very good at what she did.

"Yes..." I replied carefully. "Or did I break something?" I frowned. "I'm pretty sure I'd remember that, though."

"Break something? Break some *thing*?"

I took in her belligerent stance, hands planted on her wide hips, head thrust forward, and wondered that I hadn't caught her agitation before. "What happened, Atlene?"

Her lower lip trembled and her round, orange-hued eyes regarded me with both fury and fear. "I'll tell you what happened. Oh, yes, I will." She looked around, her expression frantic. "I just can't believe, after all these years, when I've never said so much as an unkind word to you or about you, that you'd pull something like this! I've worked my stubby little fingers to the bone to build up my shop, put up with a lot of back talk from the villagers and my own family about my doing it on my own. And in one fell swoop you go and ruined everything. And not just ruined! Destroyed! And then you laughed! *Laughed*, Lorelle. Who does that?" She shook her fists at me, like a boxer ready to square off. "*Who?*"

"You're wandering, Atlene," I said gently.

Her fists gave a final accusatory thrust. "Damn right I'm wandering!"

"Yes, okay, but I still have no idea what it is I did to you. Is it the curse? Is there a relationship you're in that's been ruined because of the curse?"

She drew back slightly, her eyelids blinking furiously. "Curse? Well, yes, I suppose I could call it a curse." She shook her head with a frown, making her Afro sway. "But not that curse. You!" She unfurled a fist to point at me, revealing a finger covered in red. "You're the curse!"

I stared at her bloody appendage. "Atlene, you're hurt."

She looked down at her finger, then up at me, her face drawn. "Oh, sweet Grim, help me. I'm not so good with the blood."

Bad attribute for someone who works with glass, I thought, as I rushed to her side and caught her before she fell. Supporting her weight, I half-dragged her into the cottage and seated her on my chaise. Then I stirred up the fire before starting up the kettle. While the water was heating, I wet a cloth, grabbed my first-aid salve, and tended to the poor elf. She sat unmoving, her blank eyes staring at the flames as I administered to her wounds, mostly scratches, though she had some deeper cuts on her hands. It was a hazard of working with glass—getting cut like this, and the numerous thin scars covering her hands attested to that—but this seemed a bit much all at once.

When she was washed up and bandaged, I fetched her a cup of chaga tea, and sat down next to her. "Drink this, and then we'll talk."

When she didn't move, I lifted the cup and brought it to her full lips. When the liquid flowed from the tilted cup, she began to drink—luckily—or she'd have tea all down the front of her colorful gown. When half the cup was gone, I set it down and turned to her.

"Now, Atlene," I said briskly. "You obviously think I did something terrible to you. What was it?"

"You destroyed my shop." For once she was concise, getting to the point immediately, and her words hit me harder than the stone Carius had thrown at me.

"Destroyed your shop? When? How?"

She looked at me like I was crazy. "You were there, girl. You should know."

"Humor me, Atlene."

She shrugged her cap-sleeved shoulders. "Fine. I was setting about cleaning up a few odds and ends from the previous day, and I heard the door open and in you waltzed like you owned the place!"

"That's weird, because as far as I know, I was here in my cottage all morning."

She shook her head, her eyes fierce. "Oh, it was you, all right, and you started looking around with this smirk on your face, as though you'd found exactly what you wanted. Then you lifted your hands, and that's when all hell broke loose. Everywhere you sent your hands chaos followed. Bottles fell from the shelves, goblets exploded, vases smashed against walls. You destroyed everything. *Everything!*"

My whole body went cold. This all sounded very familiar to me. Uncannily so. "I would never do that to you, Atlene. You've always been kind to me, like you said earlier. I would never do that," I repeated feebly.

"You know what you said?" I shook my head, not sure I wanted to hear. "You said that now you're an Omni-Fey you can do whatever you want. You said to be sure everyone knows what happened and that you were the one to do it."

"So did you make sure everyone knew?"

Her forehead wrinkled. "I, well, after it happened, and you'd left, I just stood there, frozen. Frozen! My whole life ruined, and I didn't once try to stop you. I didn't even run after you when you left. I let you go." She sniffed miserably. "You see, I couldn't think, I couldn't *move!* I was a bloody coward, wasn't I?" Her eyes, miserable and pleading, found mine.

"You were in shock, Atlene. Your response was perfectly normal. But did you tell others about what I'd done?" I persisted.

"Well, it took a while, but I did move. I ran out of my shop. I think I was screaming." She bit her lip. "Yes, I was definitely screaming. Your *name*. I was chasing after you. So I was brave, after all," she said wonderingly. "I came after you, an Omni-Fey."

"You were very brave," I soothed. "And now the entire village has linked my name to what happened at your shop."

"Yes!" She pounded her palm with her fist. "Because you did it! You ruined my shop!" Her anger suddenly left her and her shoulders slumped. "Why, Lorelle? Why did you do it?"

I stood suddenly, my hands in fists, my heart beating hard. "I dreamed about this, Atlene. In the night, but it was just a dream. It wasn't real."

"You dreamed about this?"

I nodded. "It was a terrible thing to do, even in a dream."

"But you did it anyway."

I shook my head. "Impossible. I haven't left my cottage all morning. It couldn't have been me."

Her face went hard, like hot glass cooling. "If you were here, as you claim, then explain how someone who looked almost exactly like you was in my shop this morning?"

One word stood out to me. "*Almost* exactly like me, Atlene? What do you mean by almost?"

"I mean, well, I know it was you," she sputtered. "It was your face, your skinny behind, definitely you. But…"

"But?" I pushed.

She gestured at her head. "Your hair. It was different."

"Different how?"

"It was really short, like how you wore it when you first arrived."

Really short, just like my mother wore her hair. Oh, murder.

Chapter Nineteen

The unsettling thought that my mother really could be in Hawthorn Lane at this very moment churned through my mind as Atlene eyed my long, black hair. "Did you change it somehow?" she asked. "To disguise yourself?"

"If I'd wanted to disguise myself, Atlene, I would've done a better job of it...like not going as me. Besides, it sounds like whoever did this wants the whole village to believe I was the culprit."

Her eyes narrowed. "Are you saying the loser who destroyed my shop wanted me to pin the blame on you?" She smacked her plump thigh. "And like a rube I went for it!"

"You were in shock, and the person looked like me. Why would you think any different?"

"Because I fancy myself a wee bit smarter than that," she said, a grim set to her mouth. "I know I might be a bit of an airhead, but I'm not stupid!"

"Of course you're not. You run a business all by yourself."

"Well, I used to," she said wryly.

"You will again," I promised. "I'm going to fix this, Atlene."

"But how? My whole shop is in ruins. How will I live now?"

"I've an idea, but you're going to have to close up the shop for today."

She snorted. "Like I have a choice."

"And don't touch anything. Don't try to clean anything up, don't move so much as a speck of glass."

Her expression was wary. "Why not?"

"I know you don't have any reason to trust me, but like I said, I have an idea. If it doesn't work, I'll clean up your shop myself and pay for the damage. All right?"

"You don't have to pay for anything. That ass who did this should be responsible for every last Goldenar." She paused. "Who do you think did this? It sounds personal." I didn't answer, and thankfully she rushed on. "And besides that, impersonating is strong magic, as you know, and while we've some powerful fey here, who might be able to pull it off, I haven't seen anyone do anything like that for quite some time. But why can't we do it? What's stopping us?" Her forehead wrinkled perplexedly as her thoughts came full circle. "So maybe it's true about the curse—that it affected our magic." Well, almost full circle. She'd forgotten about asking me who I thought had done this, and that was a question I didn't want to answer.

"I think the blunting spell Lady Faylan cast to try and fix the curse did that."

She lit up. "Of course! And maybe, since the truth has come out, it's wearing off."

"Maybe." Atlene's theory would certainly explain how Kyran and Renwick had been able to perform magic so well and so easily, and it made sense of all the whispers I'd overheard at *Chez Chantilly*. Hawthorn Lane was coming back to life.

"You know, I've noticed changes in myself!" Atlene's voice trilled with excitement.

"Yes, me, too," I acknowledged.

She cast me a sidelong glance. "But we're still cursed, and if we're still cursed, well, that could be a problem, couldn't it? Because we're going to start doing things to each other, and not nice things."

As far as I was concerned, it had already begun. "Increased powers mixed with hard feelings and long-held resentment due to the curse... It's a bad combination," I summarized.

Atlene gave a nervous titter. "Now all we need is a match and the whole village will ignite, killing us all."

"That would certainly solve our problem. But what we really need is someone to undo the curse. Fewer deaths that way."

"People are saying that it has to be you who undoes it, but I say nonsense. Curses can be undone in many ways, but nobody says anything about *that*." She gave a contemptuous snort. "They want to blame *you* for what's happened," she said fervently, as though speaking from personal experience, "even though it wasn't even you who made the curse in the first place. You shouldn't have to be our only option, you know."

"I think someone out there doesn't agree with you on that, and maybe this little stunt was set up to force my hand." Or maybe it was my mother teaching me a lesson—*You can never escape me, Lorelle.* Either alternative was disturbing.

I reached down and pulled Atlene to her feet. "Come on. We have to move quickly on this. Go back to your shop, lock it up, and don't speak to anyone. When you hear a particular knock"—I demonstrated on the coffee table—"you can open the door. But only then. Got it?"

She nodded, her eyes sparkling. "This sounds very James Bond-ish."

"Let's hope we have his luck at finding the bad guy." I escorted her to the door. "I'll make this right, Atlene."

She beamed up at me. "I know you will." Her expression grew serious. "Though I hope it isn't too late."

"Too late?"

"To stop what's been started. I mean, it's begun, hasn't it? Like a boulder rolling down a mountainside. And we're just helpless little saplings in its way, unable to stop its momentum, and hoping we don't get flattened if we get hit."

"Translation?"

"People think you did this to me, Lorelle, and the villagers...well, there's been talk before now about you, about the curse and your unwillingness to do anything about it. They might come for you and make you do something you don't want to do."

"Don't worry about me, Atlene. I can take care of myself."

She sighed. "That's what I'd thought, until this happened." She threw her hand back in the direction of the village. "Miss Independent, that's how I saw myself. And then, *bam!* My whole life in ruins."

"But you did handle things on your own, remember? You came here, and you confronted me. And now I'm going to make things right. You took care of yourself just fine, Atlene, and I'm going to do the same."

Her mouth twisted. "Just be careful, all right?"

"You, too, Atlene."

She nodded bravely, then turned to leave. I followed her out into the yard, scanning the area for danger. But it was quiet, without so much as a messenger bird to break the silence. I didn't trust the quiet.

Atlene waved goodbye, her usually cheery face solemn, then shut the gate behind her. She'd only been gone for a minute or two when a dark shadow passed in front of the sun, its rays already hot on my face. I shaded my eyes—Edan. He'd returned. The worry I'd been feeling since he'd left lifted a little.

With a whooshing noise, he landed in front of me looking quite pleased with himself. "You came back," I said when he'd tucked his wings in.

His fuzzy head bowed to me. "Always," he croaked.

I bit my lip as a messy feeling of sentimentality rushed through me. "I'm glad." I looked him over, thinking he'd packed on a few pounds of muscle after his flight. "Are you ready for your first job?"

If birds could look excited, this one did. "Braaah!"

"Good." I pulled a pad of paper out of the reticule I wore at my waist and scrawled a quick message...*Come quickly. I need you.* "I want you to bring this to Count Van der Daarke. Kyran. You remember him, and you can track him?" Edan nodded, his bright eyes regarding me steadily. I wasn't sure how much he understood of what I said, but his questioning gaze demanded an explanation. "Something has happened. Someone pretending to be me destroyed a shop in the village, and now the villagers are angry with me." Edan puffed up, his neck and body rising upward as he looked about for signs of danger. Apparently he understood me quite well. "They haven't come yet, but they will. I need to fix this, and quickly."

"To Kyran," he squawked.

"To Kyran." I looked him over. "I don't have a carrier pouch for you yet, but perhaps you could hold this in your beak." In answer, Edan opened his mouth and I slipped the folded note between his upper and lower beak. I patted his head. "Go the way of the gods, my friend."

"Braaah." Edan stepped back from me, gave a powerful flap, which blew back my hair, and lifted off. Soon he was high up in the sky and lost from view as he disappeared over the treetops.

I headed back inside to do some work while I waited, but it wasn't easy. Everything seemed to be happening too quickly, and too much all at once. And now this…someone trying to make me look bad.

I didn't like turning to Kyran, to grow even more indebted to him, but I felt I had little choice. He was the only one I knew who could fix Atlene's shop. I'd already seen what he could do after he'd blasted his way through my conservatory, and more importantly, cleaned up after himself. I felt confident he could do this.

The question remained, though, that if it had been my mother who'd disguised herself as me and destroyed Atlene's shop, why had I dreamed I'd done it? The dream had been so real and vivid; I'd truly felt as though I'd been the one doing everything. And it somewhat bothered me the rush I'd experienced at such power, power that I had wielded.

A screech from outside signaled Edan's return, and I hurried to the door to let him in. He scooched inside, the note no longer in his beak. "You found him?"

"Braaah," he replied sleepily. I stepped aside and he shuffled past me.

"Good job, Edan." He lifted his wingtip in acknowledgement, then hopped up the ramp and into his nest. Within moments he was fast asleep.

I wish he'd stayed awake a little longer to distract me as I waited, pacing back and forth. I didn't like this feeling of being out of control. It didn't help that it was getting warm in the cottage. Beads of sweat popped out on my forehead, and the sensation that I was trapped in this place began to set in. I should've left when I could.

When the sound of hooves penetrated my thoughts, I ran to the door and flung it open to see Kyran striding down the walkway, his jaw tight with anxiety.

"Kyran!" I stepped outside, where it felt even warmer, and shut the door behind me. "You came."

"You said you needed me," he pushed out, his chest rising and falling as he approached. When he reached me, he grabbed my arms, sending a welcome jolt through my whole body. "What's wrong, Lorelle? Are you all right? Are you hurt?"

"I'm fine, Kyran," I said rather breathlessly. His touch was no longer merely electrifying in the usual sense; it was hitting me at a different level, sending a rush of arousal through me. I slowly disengaged myself…slowly, because he seemed loath to let me go, and more so because I felt loath to be let go of.

"Then what is it?"

"There's been an incident in the village. Someone destroyed Atlene's shop—she's the crystalier for the village—and she came here to confront me about it."

His eyes grew stormy, and he looked ready to take on Atlene and the entire village. "Why you?"

"She said whoever did it looked like me, but it wasn't me, not exactly."

"What do you mean?"

"My impersonator had short hair, which is weird, since I haven't worn my hair like that for years."

"Do you know who it was then?"

I looked away. "Not definitively."

"But you have an idea?" he persisted. "My sister, probably," he answered when I said nothing.

I met his eyes, tempted to go along with his assumption. Then decided against it. "Strangely enough, I actually hadn't considered Melaina. Is she that powerful? Impersonation isn't easy."

He ran a hand through his hair. "I don't know. But this sounds like something she would do. She's furious with you for not doing everything you can to end the curse. And you were right, she knows you helped Renwick, and has vowed revenge."

"But she's already gotten it, by inciting the villagers."

"She's just getting started, Lorelle."

"Great. So she certainly has motive."

"You thought it could be someone else?"

"Oh, well, yes."

"Who, Lorelle?"

"My mother."

"Your mother? Why would she do this to you?"

"When I was eighteen I ran away from home because she wanted me to do something I didn't want to do, and I ended up here. Maybe she's finally tracked me down and sending me a message that I can't get away from her."

"Is that why you're going back to the Alterworld?"

"Not quite," I sidestepped.

He regarded me for a moment. "She's that vindictive?"

"Yes. She is. Listen, Kyran, I'm afraid I need your help."

He gave me a little smile. "I shall be sure to record this moment for posterity in my journal tonight."

"Will you help me or not?"

"Of course I will."

"Even when you don't know what it is I want?"

"Especially then," he said in a low voice that made me shiver. "I've always been a bit of a gambler."

"Well, thank you," I responded, my tone measured. "Though you might regret your impetuosity. I was hoping you could do to Atlene's store what you did to my conservatory windows, but after you blew them up."

"Ah." His brows drew together as he considered my request. "Well, I can certainly try, though I'm not sure how successful I'll be. I've never fixed anything I didn't break in the first place."

"You think it will be more difficult undoing someone else's work."

"I'm not sure." He lifted his chin. "But I'm up for trying."

"I'd be forever grateful."

He blinked slowly at me. "I rather doubt that."

"I mean it, Kyran! This is important to me."

"All right. But I won't hold you to it, or hold this over your head, either."

I regarded him skeptically. "That's very good of you, though now I feel even more indebted to you."

He gave me a wolfish grin. "You don't think I became a success in business by being a sweetheart, do you?"

"Not for a moment." I paused. "There's something you should know, though, before you truly commit."

"Go on," he prompted when I didn't continue.

"I had a dream about all this, and, well, I dreamed I was the one destroying Atlene's store. I felt everything as though I were there, and it felt really good."

He frowned. "So you think it really could've been you?"

I peered up at his unsmiling face. "I don't know, but it might have been."

Chapter Twenty

"The thing is," I hurried on. "I would never engage in wanton destruction. Destruction with a purpose, absolutely. Wanton? Never."

"Maybe you had a reason to do this, albeit an unconscious one."

"Thank you for the analysis, Dr. Freud, but I don't think so, and for several reasons. I can't see why I'd want to be blamed for something like this. I like to lay low and observe. This isn't my style at all. Plus, I had this dream in the night, and was awake and doing chores well before the incident happened. So even if I had managed some sort of astral projection, the timing doesn't fit. Another point…" I ticked off a finger. "The hair thing bothers me. I never really liked my hair short, and I no longer imagine myself with a buzz cut, but back home my mother made me wear it that way. She cut my hair, even when I could've done it myself. Would definitely have preferred to, actually."

Remembering my haircutting experiences, I tried to suppress a shudder and failed. How to forget the burn on the back of my neck from the razor when it'd get too hot, the painful hair pulling when I didn't angle my head just right, the smell of cigarette smoke surrounding me like a malevolent fog, hot ashes dropping on my bare arms. All of this, with the end result that I looked like a victim of head lice. I could live with all those things, but her constant condemnation was harder to take. Criticizing everything about me, from the way I talked to the way I walked, she'd run the clippers back and forth over my knobby head and deliver her insults with a precise anger. How efficient of her to fit all her psychological, emotional, and physical punches into one short encounter. These memories I'd just as soon forget, but somehow I never quite managed to. I wondered if Lady Faylan could place a blunting spell on my entire childhood.

"For the record," Kyran put in, "I don't think you did it."

"I could have," I argued contrarily. "I'm quite the bad ass, you know."

A corner of his mouth tugged upward. "I've no doubt of that. But what's your motive?"

"None that I can think of. Unless I did it because I'm losing my mind."

"You don't strike me as deranged."

Strange what a relief that was to hear…that maybe I wasn't like my family. That maybe there was hope for me.

"By the way, you'll have to do a special knock so Atlene will know I sent you." I showed him on the door.

"Got it. I guess I'd better get to work."

"Maybe I should come with you, in case you forget the knock."

"I don't think that's a good idea. The villagers are already out for your blood. Remember what happened yesterday? No," he went on firmly. "I think you'd better stay here."

"But this is my responsibility!" *And I need to get out, do a little reconnaissance, get rid of this feeling that the walls are closing in on me.* My refuge was fast becoming my prison. On top of all that, I needed to know for sure who was doing this to me.

"It's not yours at all. You didn't do anything."

"But everyone thinks I did, and that somehow feels worse."

"Which is precisely why you need to stay here. I won't see you getting hurt trying to defend yourself, especially when you're innocent. Besides," he hurried on when he saw me about to protest, "I've a feeling my sister is behind this. So, really, it's *my* responsibility."

"That's like saying I'm responsible for ending the curse because my ancestor made it."

"Stop being so stubborn, Lorelle, and just let me do this."

I heaved a sigh. I did not want to let go of the reins on this horse, but I needed his help. "All right. Fine. You'll come back as soon as possible and let me know how it went?"

"Absolutely."

"Before you go, have you heard anything more about Hawthorn Lane's intruder?"

The pause before he spoke was miniscule, but noting the tiniest of minutiae is my specialty. "Nothing relevant." He quickly stepped back and gave me a bow. "I'll return as soon as I can." He sniffed at the air, which was dry and hot in the bright sun. "You're wearing a different perfume these days," he commented, and any questions I wanted to follow up on regarding his purposely vague response were forgotten. "I noticed it in the carriage the other night."

"Oh, well, I like to mix things up once in a while," I replied, thinking Kyran wasn't the only person who could be evasive.

"I like it, but I prefer what you wore before."

"Ah, well, how good of you to share that with me."

He laughed, and I felt its rumble in my chest. "Just thought you'd like to know my preferences."

I began backing away from him, slowly, casually. "Good luck, Kyran. See you soon."

"Soon." With one last bow, he turned and left me staring after him, my heart pounding a little too hard in my chest. What, after all, had I done wrong? Absolutely nothing. And yet, with Cutter's tattoo defacing my wrist and his scent forever following me about, I felt like I was being disloyal to Kyran, even though he had no claim on me. We were not dating, affianced, or married. I owed him nothing.

And yet I felt as though I did.

The day passed slowly. Edan woke up from his nap, went out for a flying excursion while I ate lunch, then returned to laze about and eat bugs under an apple tree as I worked in the garden. Since I'd used my powers to push back the stream, which had been threatening to flood my cottage after a storm a week earlier, the weather had been beautiful, not a drop of rain or a cloud in sight. The air was hot and dry, the heat of the sun almost oppressive as I weeded. This sunshiny weather set me on edge. Was it merely a normal weather pattern, all this blue sky and sunshine, or did it signal something more sinister? Had I permanently stopped the rain? If I had, I'd have to find a way to fix things. As if I didn't have enough problems.

Just enjoy the break from rain and storms, I scolded myself, though it wasn't an easy order to follow. I was so used to worrying about and analyzing every little thing, always being on the lookout for trouble. I didn't know how to be any other way. And now I had a bunch of new worries to add to my list.

I sighed and used the back of my hand to wipe the sweat from my forehead. *Where is he?* Kyran should be back by now. It was coming up on dinnertime; the sun was fast sinking and would soon drop behind the mountain. Had he run into problems? Maybe I should head into town and see for myself, angry mobs be damned. Besides, I was getting tired of waiting—hiding out—at my cottage. I was used to being out and about, watching, gathering, being a part of things.

I fed the chickens and ushered them into their henhouse for the night. Edan watched them with interest, but made no move to attack. Did he truly understand they were off-limits, or was he refraining because I was around? I hoped it was the former. Those chickens provided a lot of sustenance for me, yet would be a mere snack for the rapture.

"Do you need to feed?" I asked him as I put away my gardening tools.

"Braaah," he answered.

"You'd better go now, before it gets dark."

He nodded, then launched himself into the air. I made sure to leave the cottage door unlocked for when he returned, then decided to take an early bath, hoping Kyran wouldn't show up while I was in the middle of it. I didn't want to delay my ablutions, as I was hot and sweaty and dirt had climbed under my fingernails after all the weeding I'd done. It occurred to me too late that I should have tried out my magic on the weed infestation, then decided the physical labor had been much needed.

Kyran didn't show, and I was able to wash and change into a pale green gossamer evening gown, telling myself as I brushed out my hair that I was only wearing such a nice dress because it was lightweight and the cottage was still quite warm after the heat of the day.

I was halfway down the ladder when I heard pounding on the door. I hurried the rest of the way, and was just about to open the door when I heard, "Gragan, let me in!" My hand on the latch froze into a clawed version of itself. Damnit. I'd forgotten all about Berenea. Of course the reporter would come snooping. She'd likely heard all about my adventure in Wuthering Wood, and of course would still want to get my take on my role in removing the curse. I'd managed to avoid her all week, but today she'd caught me unawares. "I say, come out here and face me like a man!"

"I'm not a man, thanks be to Grim," I shouted back at her, "and if I were I'd be down at *Puck's Pub* drowning my sorrows in a pint of bitter. Come to think of it, a pint sounds just the thing right now."

A chuckle sounded through the door. "True, that." She cleared her throat, shifting into professional mode. "I know ye're hiding out, and I know ye ain't going to say a word about the curse, so I'll ask only this… Did ye save that boy's life?"

"Which boy?"

"Cut the crap, Gragan." A pause. "Wait, are ye saying there be more than one ye saved?"

"I'm not sure there was one in the first place, is what I'm saying."

"So ye admit there was a boy ye *might* probably have saved."

"You already think I saved a boy's life, Berenea, so I'm sure you're going to print exactly that."

"Only wanted confirmation, Gragan, so no need to get yer knickers in a twist. Anyway," she added haughtily, "I'm a reporter, not a fiction writer."

Could've fooled me. "Well, here's my official statement, Berenea… I can neither confirm nor deny the question for the simple reason that I'm not sure."

"Not sure? Were ye comatose when it happened?"

"I was wide awake, but who's to say that what I did resulted in his revival? I'm no scientist, but it sounds to me like a coincidence."

"Coincidence, my arse," she snorted. "I can say one thing's certain, Gragan...ye're still slippery as an eel. But not as ugly as one, I'll give ye that."

"Um, thanks?"

Another guffaw. "Ah, Gragan, toss me a bone here. I've a living to make."

"And I've a life to keep, Berenea. I can't commit, or people will start to think I can save anyone at any time, when maybe I can't do a damn thing. I won't get their hopes up, for their sake and for mine."

An unusually long period of silence followed my determined statement. "All right, then," Berenea conceded. "I'll just hint at a connection, as it's what folks're already saying."

"That's what I was afraid of."

"Well, ye know how it goes...news round here travels faster than a greased pig down a waterslide, and once moving, is twice as hard to stop."

"Now there's an image for you."

"Do ye at least admit to being there?"

"I do admit to that." I couldn't do anything but admit to it, or otherwise be called a liar, and rightfully so. "But that's all I'm saying, Berenea."

"Fine, fine," she grumbled. "Talking to ye is like trying to squeeze blood from a stone."

"So we're done here."

"I'll be back, sure enough. One of these days ye'll crack, and I'll be there to pick up the pieces."

"I so look forward to that day."

"Ha! I'll bring a bottle. It'll take the edge off yer sorry decline."

"Make it *Dark Spirits* and I'll give you an exclusive."

"I'll be holding ye to that, Gragan!"

"Goodbye, Berenea."

"Oh revoor," she said. "That means until later."

"Is that what it means?" I replied dryly.

"I've been working on me French."

Is that what that was? Out loud, I said, "How enterprising of you." It was. A number of fey could speak the language, which was considered something of a status symbol, and not knowing it put her at a distinct disadvantage when it came to eavesdropping. Berenea is a perpetual thorn in my side and I get my digs in, even if just in my head, when I can, but I had to give her credit for making the attempt.

"I do me best to better meself."

"Well, then I say to you in return, au revoir, Madame Battle."

"Say, ye're pretty good at that. Ye'll have to give me lessons."

"We'll start right after I give you my exclusive."

Another disbelieving snort. "Oh, ye're a real card, Gragan. Ta!"

I waited for the sound of her boots to fade away before relaxing, a small smile playing about my lips. Berenea was a giant pain in the arse, but I must admit that I enjoyed doing battle with her.

When I was sure she was gone—she was known to sneak back for one last question just when you've lowered your defenses—I bustled around the room, straightening up. I lit the candles on my spider web candelabra before starting up the old Victrola I'd bought a couple years back. I owned a paltry six records, borrowing one or two from Professor Ballylee whenever I was in the mood for a change. My favorite album was a compilation of haunting music, leading off with Edvard Grieg's *In the Hall of the Mountain King*. The song was a personal favorite, and written for Henrik Ibsen's fantastical play *Peer Gynt*, about an egotistical but charming man who avoids reality and the truth as a means of surviving. It was this piece that was playing when I heard the door opening behind me.

I spun around. "You're back!" I cried, a bit more enthusiastically than was my norm. But the visitor I'd been expecting was not who I saw. "Cutter?" His slim figure darkened the doorway, hovering half in and half out. "What are you doing here, and why didn't you knock?" And why hadn't I locked the door after Berenea's visit? Edan was smart enough to make some noise when he got home to let me know he'd arrived, and with the latest contretemps with the juvenile delinquents and the incident at Atlene's shop, I should be in hunker down mode, with the door shut and bolted, not inviting the whole world to enter. Was it because I was expecting Kyran? Perchance?

"What fitting music," the death wraith remarked, not bothering to answer my questions.

"Fitting for what?"

"My arrival."

"Because..." I prompted.

"I can relate to Peer Gynt."

"As a selfish narcissist?"

"Perhaps," he acknowledged with a serious nod. "But also as a man who does not truly know himself."

"Ah. Well, that clarifies things."

He gave me his one-sided twitch of a smile. "Which fits exactly with how Peer Gynt lived his life."

"Why are you here, Cutter?" I demanded again, since he hadn't answered me the first time. Kyran was bound to show soon and I didn't want the death wraith here when he came. "Much as I like skulls, I'm really not happy about that tattoo you gave me. I've found out that I have to make a great sacrifice to remove it."

He looked bewildered. "Whyever would you want to remove it?"

"Because I never wanted it in the first place!"

"You do not wish to be connected to me?"

"Are you surprised by that? For Grim's sake, Cutter! First of all, you wouldn't have given me the time of day before you found out I was Omni-Fey, so no, I don't wish to be connected. Second, you can't force people to be connected to you. It breeds discontent."

"I came to play for you," he said as he stepped all the way inside, apparently deciding to fully commit to the visit.

I threw my hands in the air. "Am I not speaking out loud?"

"I heard what you said and will think upon it at another time. Right now I will play for you." He pulled out a violin from behind his back, and its reddish wood glowed in the candlelight like hot coals.

"I don't have time for this. I'm expecting a visitor at any moment and—"

"Count Van der Daarke will not be coming to see you this evening. He is otherwise occupied."

"How did you know Kyran was coming? And how do you know he's not anymore?" Damnit, I knew I should have gone with him to deal with the Atlene issue.

"I know things. Too much I sometimes think." He looked a little sad at this.

"So how is he *otherwise occupied*, Cutter?" My heart had started doing weird things the moment he'd used that horrid phrase, and I needed clarification. *Otherwise occupied* could mean so many things, but typically it meant sex. "Perhaps I should go to him."

"That would be unwise and assist you not in the least."

"This isn't about me. He might be hurt…" or having sex. Though, come to think of it, I probably wouldn't want to see that. But if I could keep it from happening…

"He is not hurt, and is in no danger of being hurt."

"Then why can't he come to see me? He was going to update me on a certain incident that happened."

"Ah, yes. Mistress Atlene's shop. I had heard about that."

"And have you heard what happened afterward?"

"I can only say that Count Van der Daarke has been summoned to an Executor Assembly…to discuss the situation of the breach, I believe."

Well, that meant no sex. Hopefully. That crew was older than dirt. "Why is he attending a meeting of the Executors? He's new here. What use would he be to them?"

Cutter lifted up his violin. "What music would you like me to play?"

"You have an infuriating way of not answering my questions."

His emerald eyes met mine. "And you have an infuriating way of not answering mine, Lorelle Gragan."

I strode over to the record player and removed the record, nearly scratching it in my pique. "Play what you want. I don't care." I sat down on the chaise in front of the cold, dark fireplace and clasped my hands together in frustration.

"Then I shall play nepenthe music, for I sense we could both use some forgetting." He came to stand in front of the fireplace, facing me squarely, the light from a lamp behind him turning his figure to shadow. He settled his violin on his shoulder and raised his bow, readying himself with a deep breath. Then he began to play, and within a few notes I was lost.

The music was mournful, yet compelling. Quiet, yet full of dark energy. Listening, I fell into a sort of trance as he played on and on, the stream of notes flowing along like a deep and winding river. I forgot about everything. About Kyran, about my troubles, about dinner, about Edan.

Somewhere along the way, Cutter set down his violin and pulled me up to dance with him. The music somehow continued on, though maybe only in our minds as we twirled around and around the cottage.

Cutter murmured words into my ear as we danced, words that filled me with a heavy sorrow at the truth of them. "We are two of a kind, Lorelle, persecuted and punished by others, cut off and terribly lonely. I'm your haven now, as you are mine. Remember this when trouble comes, because it is coming."

"Trouble is always coming," I mumbled, my mind fuzzy as though drugged.

"This coming is worse than most." He stroked my hair with a strange sort of tenderness. "But I am here for you."

"You only like me because I'm an Omni-Fey now," I managed to push out through thick lips. "Before that you avoided me."

"I avoided everyone, Lorelle…because of who I am, because of what I do to those who attempt to get close to me, or whom I attempt to get close to."

A little alarm bell went off in my otherwise muddled mind. "What do you do?" I whispered, looking up at him. His features were sharp in the candlelight, almost demonic.

"I drain the life from the living."

Chapter Twenty-One

I awoke the next morning in my bed nook, disoriented and out of sorts. What had happened? I smacked my lips, but they weren't overly dry, nor did my head ache, so it wasn't a hangover making me feel this way. In fact, I didn't remember drinking anything last night, or even eating dinner, which would explain my growling stomach.

But I did remember some things…Cutter arriving at my cottage, Cutter playing the violin. In my mind, I saw us, *felt* us dancing together, arm in arm and chest to chest, like lovers do. I remembered him telling me something terrible about himself, but I couldn't recall what it was. After that, my memory was pretty blank. My eyes widened. What had he done to me?

I sat up quickly, saw I was still wearing the same dress I'd had on last night and breathed a sigh of relief. So *that* hadn't happened. I'd be royally pissed if it had…for all the obvious reasons, but also because if I had wanted to have, and did have, sex with Cutter, it appeared as though I wouldn't recall any of it. If I were going to break my dry spell…no, *drought*…I should at least be able to remember doing so. I stared down at the lightly throbbing tattoo on my wrist, then leaned down to sniff it. Cutter's scent flooded my body like an adrenaline rush, and I closed my eyes as images whirled through my mind—his hungry touch, his haunted eyes, the sound of his voice as he whispered in my ear—but everything was heightened as though magnified.

Someone tapped on the door downstairs, startling me, and I scrambled out of bed, slightly breathless. Edan! I'd forgotten all about him. How could I have done that? I was a terrible, terrible person, and a horrible mother.

Nearly killing myself, I shimmied backward down the ladder. When I reached the bottom, I turned around to face the door, then stopped and swung toward the conservatory. There was Edan, fast asleep in his eyrie, little breaths ruffling the fuzz around his neck. He was safe. The door, when I turned back toward it, was shut and locked.

So Cutter had put me safely to bed, survived an encounter with a very protective rapture, then ensured the bird was looked after.

Just who are you, Cutter Flint?

I unlocked the door and opened it to a rush of warm air, which lifted my dark hair into wings. Outside the door sat two packages, and inside the gargoyle knocker's mouth were three rolled-up notes. Typically I went months without receiving a message, and now had three in one morning, along with two mysterious parcels. Such abundance made me suspicious. Grabbing the scrolls and the packages, I shuffled back inside and locked the door. Despite being hungry, and almost painfully curious about the notes and parcels, I decided to get ready for the day first. With the way my luck was going, Berenea would show up with quill pen in hand and a sketch artist to capture my wild hair and wrinkled gown, to be splashed across the front page of *Thorny Issues* for the amusement of the villagers, and possibly to be used afterwards for darts at *Puck's Pub*.

After bathing, I donned a red blood silk gown, feeling the need to wear a power color today. I broke off all the *Dead Man's Fingers* for Edan's breakfast, then made my own meal. Eggs curry, Bayonne ham, and two cups of limoney tea later, I was as ready as I was going to be to face the notes staring up at me from the table. For some reason, I didn't want to read them, sensing they were trouble-laden. But I was curious, and curiosity is a siren call I cannot resist.

I opened the first scroll, which was pink, heavily perfumed, and undoubtedly from Avice.

Oh, Lorel! Whare wer u? I wated and wated yestrday for u too arrive for ar flyeng lesons. (Avice, to put it nicely, is a terrible speller—the result of skipping lessons to go shopping, then later, when she was older, from doing her instructor instead of her homework). I mised u soooo bad! I herd wat peple r sayin u did and I dont beleve it. Not for a minut. Not my Lorel I sed too any one who'd listin. Gud theng u hav Keerin too fix thengs. If I dont here from u soon Im comeng over. Hugs and kises and anytheng els u wil take from me.
♥ Your best frend <u>ever</u>, Avice ♥

It felt nice to be missed, though I wondered what she knew about Kyran and how he'd managed to fix things. If he didn't come by soon I would have to take the risk and head into the village to see for myself. While there I'd do some snooping around for any signs that my mother had been there, like patches of burnt grass or the lingering scent of evil, to either confirm my suspicions, or hopefully dismiss them. Afterward I'd visit Avice and convince her to stay sober long enough to teach me to fly. I needed to be able to defend myself from the attacks I felt sure were to come after the Atlene disaster.

The next note was from Renwick. I paused for a moment before reading that one, not sure I was up to dealing with his latest request. But again, I was curious, and Renwick held a certain measure of appeal for me, mainly because he wasn't quite the doormat I'd thought he was. Did I mention he's also easy on the eyes?

Dearest Lorelle,

I imagine you've heard by now what has happened to me. I've been flushed out by one of Melaina's spies. I know you meant for my stay with Matron to be a punishment, but she actually saved my hide, telling Melaina what's what and sending her off, no doubt with her tail tucked firmly between her long, lovely legs. I was actually working when it happened, so I missed the whole thing, damn the luck. Though I heard one of the dryads - Ashley? I think that was the name, rallied the troops and made sure she left the wood and couldn't return. I'm safe for now, I suppose, but probably not for long, even with the formidable Matron Thornback and those rather unnerving dryads on my side. Melaina isn't known for giving up on anything, and I hate bringing my problems to the wood fey here. They treat me rather nicely. I imagine I shall leave Matron's place sooner rather than later. Luckily the weather's been kind - it wouldn't be the first time I've slept out under the stars. Been thinking of you often, and not in the way you're currently imagining—your clothes off and lying in bed longing for me. Though I do think of you that way. (Cheeky bugger.) *I'll tell you all about it when I see you next. If I survive Matron that long... Ha.*

~R~

I set down the note, feeling frustrated. I, who was so used to being on top of all the latest news, had missed out on two major stories. Hiding myself away to avoid trouble, was I in danger of losing my effectiveness as a gatherer? I didn't like that. And what did Renwick have to tell me? What was he thinking about regarding me? It drove me bonkers not knowing things. Whatever was going on, I did know one thing: Renwick was hinting at staying with me.

Not in this lifetime, buster.

I picked up the third note, which was bigger than the rest by quite a bit, then unrolled the parchment and read through it with growing fury.

Under the order of the Dynast Overseer and the Executor Council, Lorelle Gragan has been placed under our protection from this day forward. Those who work against or harm Mistress Gragan work against and harm the Fey Demesne. Disobedience will not be countenanced and punishment for any transgressions against her will be severe.

Lady Vira Ansela Giselo de Faylan
Dynast Overseer of the Hawthorn Lane Realm

~Stay inside and lay low, Lorelle... For your safety and for the safety of the village. VF

"What the hell?" I threw the paper across the room. So this is what she was planning! To keep me out of the way so she could go after Kyran. Maybe there had never been an intruder in the first place. Maybe that's why she hadn't wanted Kyran involved after the breach. Perhaps she'd set the whole thing up as a means of pulling him to her. "I didn't ask for your help, you officious troll! And now you want me to stay hidden?" I slapped the table with both hands. "I don't think so!"

"Braaah?" Edan squawked worriedly, awakened by my outburst.

I rose and went to him, patting him on the beak. "Sorry, boy. Just bad news from an interfering busybody." I pulled his head down and leaned my forehead against his cool, hard beak. "And I'm so sorry I didn't see you to bed last night. I wasn't myself."

Edan nuzzled at my hair. "Is okay. He were here."

I straightened up, looking him in the eye. "Cutter Flint? He was here when you came home?"

"Yes."

"And you didn't think he was threatening?"

"Music too nice."

"I see." Not something I could argue with, being that Cutter's music had soothed the savage beast in me as well. "When did you get home?"

"Late. Got carried away."

"Carried away, hm? Sounds interesting. See anything good?"

He shrugged his shoulders, a strangely human-like action. "Lots."

"Your speaking has improved quite a bit, Edan," I noted, feeling inordinately proud of him...like I had anything to do with it.

"Was listening to voices many hours."

"Did you hear anything about Kyran and the shop?" He shook his head. "Did you hear anything important, then?"

"Many angry."

"With me?" I provided the words he didn't want to speak.

He nodded. "Sorry."

I sighed and rubbed his head. "I'm getting used to it."

I pulled away and Edan, after studying me for a moment, began cleaning his feathers. I returned to the table to tend to the parcels, wondering what they contained. Each package came with a little note telling me how important I was to the community, and how lovely I looked at the ball, and etc. and etc. Matron was right that I was going to be feted. But just how much? I was itching to find out.

The first package contained a variety of delicacies from one of my favorite little shops, *Posh Nosh*, which I generally can't afford to frequent. The second box held a bottle of perfume wrapped up in black tissue paper and came from Merceen Arie's perfumery, *Scentsibility*. I opened the stopper, took a sniff, and nearly gagged. The scent was overpowering, obnoxiously sweet, but with overripe undertones, as though it were rotten at the core. So that's what the patrician elf thought of me, eh? Next time I saw her I was going to take the skull and crossbones-shaped perfume bottle and shove it up her tightly clenched ass. Luckily I didn't hate the owner of *Posh Nosh*, as I was definitely keeping the food and preferred not to have it anywhere near anyone's ass.

After clearing the detritus and putting the treats away, I fetched Edan's bowl of *Dead Man's Fingers* and watched him wolf down his meal. It was still a bit strange seeing him swallow what looked like human fingers, and hoped he'd never mistake real fingers for the fungus variety. "Still hungry?" He nodded. "Then you'd better go hunt. You're being careful, right?" He nodded again. "Good. I don't want anything to happen to you." I patted him affectionately on the head. "Come on, then." He trotted after to me to the door, where I stopped and pointed.

"Braaah?"

"I want to see if you can do it yourself."

He stepped forward and after a bit of a tussle, managed to use his beak to lift the bar and unlock the door. One more manipulation and he was outside. I gave a mental sigh of relief. I didn't like the idea of him being trapped if something were ever to happen to the cottage, like getting firebombed by an angry horde of villagers. I watched from the doorway as Edan took off, enjoying the sight of him in full flight. He disappeared over the trees, and I was just turning to go deal with the chickens when I heard the sound of hooves galloping down the road.

Kyran.

My heart started to beat a little faster, and I smoothed my hair before realizing what I was doing and stopped myself. What was with me and this guy? I asked the question as though I had no clue, but I knew. He'd gotten under my skin, and I didn't know how to, or more accurately, didn't want to, get him out.

He slid off his horse, tied it up outside the gate, and strode down the walk like a man on a mission, an embossed leather bag around his torso bouncing with each step. When he was within a couple feet of where I stood, he stopped and looked me over very thoroughly. I felt a shiver go through me. "Damn. I was hoping to catch you in your nightgown again."

So he *had* noticed its sparse state.

"Where have you been?" I demanded, then instantly regretted showing my hand. Now he'd think I'd been worried, and that I cared about his welfare. Even though maybe I did, I wasn't quite ready to share that. Hell's bells, the man had a way of making me careless.

His expression grew wary. "Doing what you asked, Lorelle."

"It took you that long?"

"I had other business to attend to afterwards."

"Like a meeting with the Executors."

He frowned. "How'd you hear about that?"

"A concerned friend told me."

"How'd she know?"

"*He*, and I guess he has his ways." And I wondered what those were. Who did Cutter Flint know in the village that could and *would* feed him information like this? No one else in Hawthorn Lane seemed to want to have anything to do with the death wraith, go figure.

"You were with Renwick," he said in a tone of disgust.

"Wrong friend. So what did you talk about in your meeting?"

He looked like he wanted to pursue the 'friend' angle, but he refrained, if only just barely, judging by his clenched fists. "We talked about the breach and what to do about it."

A breach that might never have happened, if my theory about Lady Faylan is correct.

"Why did they include you? You're new here, and you definitely don't know our ways."

"I know enough, for now anyway. I got a crash course on the subject."

"From whom?"

He began to look a little uncomfortable, a reaction that didn't fit him very well. "From Lady Faylan."

My throat grew tight and I had to fight to maintain my typical calm, cool demeanor. "Ah. The very person you warned me to be careful around."

"It's not what you think. I was worried about you after what happened to Atlene, and wanted to make sure Lady Faylan knew exactly what was going on so she could do something about it."

"That's why she and the Executors issued that decree?"

"You know about that, too?"

"She sent me a copy."

"Oh."

"Right. Well, I'm glad you two are best buddies now. Maybe you can set up a play date and practice magic together."

He shook his head, as though disappointed in me. "You're making something out of nothing."

"You told me you'd update me on what happened *as soon as possible.* Did it occur to you that I might be a little worried?"

"It did occur to me, but this opportunity presented itself and I couldn't pass it up. Lady Faylan offered you her protection. How could I say no?"

"Like this. *No.* See? Simple."

He hunched his shoulders in frustration. "Can we go inside and talk about this? I need to sit down."

I realized then that he looked completely washed out. "I guess so," I muttered, trying not to feel like a heel when I wasn't the one in the wrong here.

I turned back inside, leaving him to follow. "Could I have some of your bread?" he asked my retreating, no doubt stiff-looking, back.

"Hungry so soon?" I said over my shoulder. "Breakfast wasn't all that long ago."

"I haven't eaten since I saw you yesterday."

I turned to face him, reluctantly admitting defeat—it left such a bitter taste in my mouth. "Damnit, Kyran! You do have a way of making me feel guilty. Sit down and I'll fix you something."

"Thank you." He took off his bag and set it carefully on the floor, then sat in the rocking chair that I was beginning to think of as his.

I had started up the kettle and was about to ask him what he wanted to eat when I realized he was fast asleep. I would have to wait to learn my fate, and unfortunately for me, I was not good at waiting.

Chapter Twenty-Two

Edan returned an hour later and still Kyran slept on. The rapture crept up to where Kyran was sitting, plopped down next to him, and maneuvered his head so that Kyran's dangling hand rested on it. Edan shifted a few times, then slipped into a doze himself. Once in a while Kyran sleep-petted the bird, which was amusing to watch.

While the two of them napped, I tended to the chickens, then I baked and baked and baked, maybe not the best thing to do in this heat, but I was out of chores to do. I made ham, cheese, and asparagus pasties and Russian teacakes, cream-filled blueberry muffins (a.k.a. creamkins) and chocolate bon-bons. I had a lot of nervous energy to wear off. Did I mention that I don't like not knowing things? I also didn't like the idea of an intruder creeping around the village, and no one acting particularly worried about it—that my fellow Hawthornites seemed more intent on hating me than figuring out who was threatening their safety. I should be out there doing something, not sitting here waiting. Unless, of course, no breach had occurred, and they all knew that. But why leave me out of the loop? To make me suffer? Or was this all part of a bigger plan, one I had no idea about? It was a disturbing thought.

While the creamkins cooled on a rack, I washed the dishes, then began scrubbing the floor with ferocious intensity. A noise at the door halted my work, and I was grateful for the distraction. I hate scrubbing the floor. It's murder on the knees.

Throwing down my rag, I scurried to the closed door. "Who's there?"

"It's Avice, of course! Since you didn't come to me, naughty thing, I decided to come to you."

I unlocked the door and opened it, then placed a finger to my lips.

Giving me a funny look, Avice tiptoed inside, her hands wrapped around a dark package. When she saw Kyran, her eyes widened in dismay. "Why is he sleeping here? I offered him my place!"

"Are you talking about Kyran or the bird?" was my less-than-subtle response.

Her eyes lowered and she stepped back, hand to her chest. "What in Grim's name is that?"

I couldn't hide my smug smile. "That, my friend, is a rapture, and his name is Edan. He's my new messenger-slash-attack bird."

"I've never seen one in person. Where on earth did you get him?"

I shrugged. "Someone left him on my front stoop. I've no idea who.

I take it you didn't send him as a gift?"

"Are you kidding me? He's a beauty. If I could get my hands on one of those I'd definitely be keeping him for myself."

"Nice to know where I lie on your list of priorities." She smirked. "So if it wasn't you, then who sent him?"

"The Count, I imagine." Her tone was bitter. "To protect you."

"He said it wasn't him."

She looked pleased at this. "What *is* he doing here, by the way? You never answered me." She sniffed the air. "Are those creamkins I smell?"

"They are." I glanced at the parcel she was holding. "Making deliveries now?"

"What?" She looked down. "Oh, this. It was on your doorstep." She handed it over to me. Wrapped in black parchment, it felt like a picture frame. "Well?" she prompted when I hesitated. "Aren't you going to open it?"

"I suppose." I went over to the table and set the package down to untie the string binding it. Pulling back the paper revealed a black mahogany-framed mirror, each corner displaying a delicately carved rose, connected to the next by a spiky stem.

Another gift.

Avice peered over my shoulder. "A mirror?"

"Looks like it," I said dryly.

"Who's it from?"

"No note." While some of my gifts came with notes, others did not. So someone out there didn't want any credit, which meant the anonymous presents were given simply to please me. I rather liked that.

"Well, if that's from the Count, he's got no imagination. I mean, a mirror? Dime a dozen those are. Not like the old days when it meant something to get one as a gift."

"If it were from Kyran I think he would've given it to me directly when he showed up at the door."

She rolled her eyes, already bored with the subject. "I suppose."

I leaned the mirror against my bookshelf to hang at a later time. "Go sit in the conservatory, and I'll make us lunch and fill you in on what I know."

"I won't say no to a free meal, especially one of yours." She scurried into the conservatory and sat down on the settee, arranging her skirts around her. Her eyes flicked to the kitchen and her nose twitched like a hungry rabbit. "Can I have two creamkins?"

"Of course. I baked enough to feed an army."

"Then make it three."

I began to prepare our lunch. Wanting to heat the water quickly, I used magic; a flick of the wrist shooting sparks down the kettle's spout, which immediately sent it into a whistling frenzy. I was pleased at my success, and wished everything could be handled so easily. I'd have to try my hand at using magic to scrub the floor next, though hopefully I'd have better luck than poor Mickey in *Fantasia*. I certainly didn't need any more floods.

Tray in hand, I joined Avice on the settee, using the nearby stool as a table. "I really don't know much, Avice," I said as I served up our tea, "but I'll share what I do know." I told her what had happened with Atlene, how she'd thought it had been me who'd destroyed her shop, and Kyran's role in setting things straight. "He was going to report back to me last night, but he didn't show. He arrived this morning, sat down, and promptly fell asleep."

"So I know something you don't?" she said coyly as she bit into a creamkin, her eyes never leaving mine. She was obviously enjoying her power immensely. Her tongue flicked out and snapped up a crumb attempting to take refuge on her plump lower lip.

"I suppose that you do."

"And I imagine you'd like to know what I know?"

"I would."

She leaned forward, revealing a good portion of her breasts. "What would I get in return for my information?"

"Nothing from me, you shameless hussy," I scolded. "Unlike you, I possess a strange little virtue called patience, which means I can wait to ask Kyran when he wakes up."

She scowled. "You ruin all my fun, Lorelle." She sighed and took a sip from her cup. "Your tea is different today." She wrinkled her nose, then giggled. "Like it's filled with bubbles." It well might be, I thought, thinking back to how I'd warmed it. Had I somehow infused it with energy? Come to think of it, I was feeling a bit more bubbly myself. Avice took another drink, longer this time, and I copied her. "You know, it's really too bad you missed out on the show, luv, because the Count was amazing. We were all gathered outside the shop when he arrived because Atlene had locked the door and wouldn't let us in. When she saw him, she opened up." Avice set down her teacup. "We tried to follow, but he ordered us to stay outside, so forcefully and manfully, too." Her eyelids fluttered lustily. "We were able to watch through the display window, though, and it was a sight to see!" She clasped her hands together. "He was so powerful, so skilled, Lorelle. Like a master sorcerer. He certainly doesn't need my help in magic training." She paused and gave me a triumphant smile. "And yet he continues coming to lessons. Fancy that."

"Yes. Fancy that," I replied. "So everything's fixed? Atlene's store is all right?"

"More than all right. After what Kyran did, people flocked into the shop and nearly bought her out. Everyone wanted a souvenir."

"Including you?"

She dimpled prettily. "I needed a new set of wine goblets. I keep breaking mine." Avice had a bad habit of dashing her glass into the fireplace after making a toast, and she made a lot of toasts…mostly to herself.

"So I'm off the hook?"

"Oh, no. Not in the least. The villagers still believe you did it, even though Atlene said she now knows it wasn't you. She made the mistake of telling them she'd talked to you after it happened and Merceen out-right accused you of spelling Atlene to get her to change her story."

"They really still think I did it? All of them?"

"Some didn't believe it." Avice scooted toward me, grabbing my hand in her warm one. "I don't."

"Thank you, Avice," I said distractedly. "Your loyalty means a lot to me."

"Does that mean I get some sort of thank you?"

"Hm? Well, I suppose it does." Feeling a bit lightheaded from the tea, I leaned forward, meeting her halfway, and recklessly pressed my lips to her soft ones. "Thank you."

Her eyes were wide when I pulled back, her mouth open in surprise. "You've never done that before."

"Because I've never been that grateful to you before." And I've never drunk magic tea before, either.

Her eyes teared up. "Oh, Lorelle. I'm worried for you."

I stood abruptly. "I'm afraid I rather share your sentiment, Avice, but I'll be fine. One way or another I'll sort this out."

"Not if Merceen and Melaina have their way. When we were in the shop they kept stirring things up, making snide comments, accusing you of things…but subtly, of course."

"Well, at least I have you on my side."

"And Lady Faylan, too. I can't believe she released that decree giving you Executor protection. But she did take you under her wing all those years ago, so it makes sense that she's protective of you. Plus, you saved her sister, so I suppose she feels she owes you."

Boy, does she ever.

"I don't think we should be seen together," I told Avice. "Until all this blows over," I added hastily, seeing her wounded expression. "I'm grateful you're on my side, and that you're not afraid to show it, but I don't want people turning on you, too."

She drew herself up. "They wouldn't dare."

"There are a lot of people in Hawthorn Lane who are jealous of you, Avice, and would love to see you brought down a notch or two. You supporting me gives them a weapon to use against you. If you got hurt because of me, I couldn't live with that."

"Do you really mean that?"

"I do."

She rose and gave me a long hug, and I let myself enjoy the warmth of her body, physical contact I'd been starved of for far too long. Well, not that long, I belatedly remembered. I'd danced with Kyran only days ago and that had been wonderful. And then, last night... Last night? A memory niggled at the back of my mind, something about last night. A flash of Cutter stroking my hair came to me, followed by the heady sensation of intoxication bubbling in my veins. Or was that the tea?

"Lorelle?"

I shook my head, returning to the room. "Sorry." I slowly disengaged myself from her embrace. "Just trying to figure out what to do next."

"I have some ideas," she said coquettishly, running her finger down my cheek and ending at my chin, which she tapped twice.

"I'm sure you do, you harlot." I took her arm. "Come on. You need to go home. I'm not saying you have to hide out, but I am saying you need to be careful." I wanted to add, *There are things going on that I don't understand, and they're all happening at once, and that worries me.* But I was too used to keeping my troubles to myself. "Have you noticed any-thing different about yourself lately?" I asked her as we neared the door.

She tilted her head. "Different?"

"Your magic. Has it grown?"

Her smile was coy. "How did you know?"

"I think it's happening to everyone."

She looked put out. "Everyone?"

"That dampening spell Lady Faylan used to stifle the curse? Well, I think it dampened our magic powers, too. Now I think it's lifting."

"But if it's lifting on magic, wouldn't it also be lifting on the curse?"

Oh, wretched. "I hadn't thought of it that way." No wonder the vil-lagers had been so vile, why Carius and his friends had attacked me, maybe even why Ilia was so angry with me. It was easier for them to take out their anger on me than on each other. I was a relative new-comer with no known family to support me, and an Omni-Fey, too. I generally kept to myself, and knew things, secret things, about every single villager, and it didn't help that everyone believed my great-grandmother had created the curse. Put all these things together and you have the ingredients for a perfect blame stew.

"Thank Grim I still feel the same way about you," Avice said, taking my hands.

"And I you."

She beamed. "No silly old curse is going to tear us apart." She peered up into my eyes. "You'll come for flying lessons soon? I'd like to try again, and this time I promise I'll stay sober." She crossed her heart, then frowned. "Well, as sober as I can stay anyway."

"I'll come tomorrow night, under the cover of darkness."

"Oooh! How intriguing." She wrapped her arms around my neck. "I'll be waiting." Before I could react, she kissed me hard on the mouth. Then she was gone, out the door, while my mind whirred with stunned disbelief. Avice was always trying things on me, but she'd never gone that far. Well, not while we were both awake. I reminded myself not to ever make her magic tea again…or myself, for that mat-ter, since I'd been the one to kiss her first.

Behind me, I heard the sound of clapping. "Bloody good show," Kyran said, his tone low and seductive. "Would you like to try that on with me?"

Chapter Twenty-Three

I turned around to face Kyran, catching a provocative smile lighting up his tired face. Despite my anger with him for leaving me in the lurch last night, I felt my blood warm and my body tingle. Edan shifted, looked blearily about, then settled back into slumber.

"Glad you liked it, cowboy, but it was only—" I had almost said the tea, but decided not to let on. It'd be interesting to discover how he'd react to its effects. *Oh, I'm a devious girl.* "It was only gratitude," I finished smoothly.

"That was a lot of gratitude." He stretched his arms up into the air. "How long was I asleep?"

"A few hours," I told him. "Are you hungry?"

He rubbed his flat stomach. "Famished." He sniffed at the air. "You've been baking."

"I needed something to do while you slept. I don't like waiting."

"Sorry about that. I really did mean to come last night, but Lady Faylan waylaid me. When I realized what she was trying to do, I decided it would serve you better to know more about what was going on."

"And what did you learn?" As I waited for his reply, I went about making him a tray, deciding against magicking the water. I felt quite sure the tea had worked its magic on me, as well, and I needed to keep my wits about me. I could only hope the effects had worn off by now.

"I learned a lot about the politics of this place," he took his time answering. "How Lady Faylan runs security with her Mage Patrol, who lives here in Hawthorn Lane and why. It was quite an education." I glanced over at him to see a hint of satisfaction lifting one corner of his mouth. Apparently Lady Faylan had gotten over her unwillingness to share with him.

If she'd ever been unwilling in the first place. I realized I'd made the mistake of taking him at his word at *Chez Chantilly* when the facts didn't really jive. I just couldn't see Lady Faylan giving up an opportunity to spend time with Kyran. Or maybe this was all a part of her plan.

"The governing faction is a bit of a mess," he went on, "and frankly, antiquated as bloodletting, but there's potential."

"Potential for what?" I couldn't help asking, even though he was veering off topic.

"Potential for change."

I kept my eyes on my work to hide my dismay. I'd been right. He did want to take over the governing of the village. He did want to become

more than a Count. He wanted to be a hero. "Well, don't let Lady Faylan hear you say that. She isn't exactly a revolutionary, more of a tradi-
tionalist, I'd say."

"Traditions have their places," he admitted. "But as you mentioned
before, so do revolutions."

"But aren't you against revolution?"

"I am, for most things."

"Hm." I set the tray before him, then sat down on the chaise. "So
what's your plan?"

He poured his tea, then raised the cup to me with a roguish glint in
his eye. "I'll let you know when I figure it out."

Yeah, right.

"Did she mention anything about the intruder? Does she know who
it is?"

"She has her suspicions, but would only say she needed to do more
reconnaissance before she could know for certain."

I didn't like the sound of that. "Lady Faylan is a master at stonewall-
ing." She certainly was, and if she'd faked the breach, she was delaying
for a reason. What that was, I didn't know. Giving me yet another motive for getting out of this cottage and taking a look around.

"I'm beginning to see that," he said dryly.

"She's also quite good at misdirection, avoidance, making threats, and
carrying out personal attacks."

"She'd make a good businesswoman back in the Alterworld."

He sounded almost admiring, and I wanted to kick him in the teeth.
"I'm sure she would."

"Do you want to hear about what happened at Atlene's?" he quickly
changed the subject, perhaps noting me giving said teeth an appraising
look.

"Avice said you were a hero. That afterwards there was a run on the
shop for souvenirs. Good show."

He looked up from his pastie. "You don't sound very happy about
that."

"She also told me that Merceen and Melaina were agitating against
me."

"I wasn't aware of that. I'd expect it of my sister, but Baroness Arie is
a bit of a surprise." I was irrationally annoyed he remembered Merceen's name, and that he hadn't quite caught on yet how awful she was.

"So how did it go down—your saving my hide? Avice was a bit light
on the details."

"Avice? Light on the details? Imagine that." He gave me a small smile.

"What's to add, though? The shop was a complete disaster, and when I went inside, the proprietor, Ms. Stoneham, was looking at me with such hope in her eyes. All I could think of was that I couldn't let her down." He leaned forward, as though confiding in me. "I wasn't sure if I could do it, Lorelle, but once I began, well…" he paused, gazed up at the ceiling. "Well, it was the most amazing thing I've ever experienced." He lowered his gaze to meet mine and I had to inhale deeply to keep from shivering. "All that power flowing through me, the sensation of righting a wrong. Heady stuff." He sat back in his chair. "I think I liked it a bit too much."

"Doing magic can be a bit addictive," I admitted. Even now, I could feel the pull of my sparks. I hadn't been wearing gloves around the house, so could only hope my magic behaved itself.

"The more you do it, the more you want to."

"Exactly."

We sat there in silence as we contemplated this—what it could mean. "In the end, I was simply grateful I could help set something right," he said after a few moments.

"And afterwards?"

"People rushed into the store, wanting to buy something as a souvenir, some of them even wanted my autograph, if you can believe it. I felt like a rock star." He gave a small laugh. "I think I actually signed someone's chest."

Avice's, no doubt.

"Which reminds me…" He leaned down and picked up his worn leather bag.

"I don't need an autograph, thank you."

He laughed as he opened the satchel and pulled out another bag with the label, *Crystalline Vessels*, on it. He handed it to me. "For you. Autograph free."

I took the bag from him, letting my fingers touch his. I got my shock, welcome as a mouthful of *Dark Spirits*, and breathed in deeply. "How sweet of Atlene," I said as I opened the bag and pulled out a crystal goblet, one of six in a box. Beautifully shaped and cut, the glass featured raised crystal on the outside, which formed a spider web. "It's exquisite."

"You like it?"

"I do." I looked at him, caught his expectant expression. "Wait… You got this for me?"

"Well, yes. It's another reason why I was so late. I had Atlene make it for me, special order. She was more than happy to do so after what I did. She wouldn't even let me pay."

Fancy that, he had a new admirer. "Well, thank you," I said stiffly and set the glass aside, feeling stupidly hurt. There was no reason for him to get me a gift, so what was this? Getting in good with the Omni-Fey? I had foolishly thought he'd be above that sort of thing. "So," I briskly changed the subject, "what were the villagers saying about me? Avice mentioned they still believe I destroyed Atlene's shop."

"I tried to explain to the crowd that you'd been set up, but they weren't having it. They only wanted to know how I'd managed to do such complicated magic." He stared at his hands as though trying to answer that question for himself.

"Apparently Merceen was telling people that I'd spelled Atlene to get her to recant her story."

He nodded thoughtfully. "That would explain their behavior, though I didn't get much of a chance to change their minds. Those rumors must be why Lady Faylan wanted to issue that decree."

"But why would she support me? As you warned, she's not my friend."

"She's not—" He stopped abruptly and his eyes fastened on the conservatory behind me. I resisted the urge to turn around and look, not wanting to be distracted. I wanted to know what he really thought of Lady Faylan, and his ruse wasn't going to get him off the hook. At last he looked away from the conservatory, arched his back slightly as though stretching, then relaxed. After a second or two, he returned his attention to his meal. "You know," he said slowly, after taking a sip of tea, "maybe I was wrong about Lady Faylan."

I stared at him, a cold sensation creeping through my chest. "What do you mean?"

"I mean, perhaps I, and you, have gotten the wrong end of the stick about her."

"I see." I stood abruptly, glancing quickly back at the conservatory. There was no one there. "Would you like anything else?" I kept my voice light, as though I hadn't a care in the world. Inwardly, though, I was seething. Wrong about her? *Wrong* about her? Didn't he see that she was evil incarnate?

"I'm good," he replied, finishing off the last of his creamkin. "Thank you. That was amazing." He sounded surprised.

"Well, it's the least I could do for the man who helped a friend of mine." I gave him a grateful smile, which was mostly sincere. "Atlene didn't deserve this, though I'm glad it turned out to be the best thing for her."

Kyran stood and grabbed the tray before I could. I sidled away from him like a spooked horse, wanting him gone, wanting space to think, needing time to figure out what was going on with him and Lady Faylan. Could I trust him? It certainly didn't feel like it. And if he wasn't for me, he was against me. Which means he had to go.

"I'm only saying that maybe you should give Lady Faylan the benefit of the doubt," he went on, returning to the topic like a dog at a femur. "She does seem to want the best for you."

I smiled to hide my true feelings…utter disgust. "I'm sure you're right, Kyran. And thank you, again, for fixing Atlene's shop, and for the glasses." I nodded at the box.

He grinned at me. Actually *grinned* at me. "It was my pleasure." He followed me to the sink and set the tray down on the counter. "I want you to know we're doing everything we can to track down the intruder. That you're not to worry."

We?

"Why do you think *I* should be worried?"

"Well, Lady Faylan has hinted that the intruder might have something to do with you."

Oh, no. "How would she know that?" I asked, working hard to keep my voice even, to not betray my alarm. "Did you tell her about my mother? That she could be here? Please tell me you didn't."

"I didn't tell her anything of the sort. I wouldn't ever do that to you." He reached out as though to touch my cheek—the same spot Avice had chosen—and I jerked back before his fingers could make contact.

"Because if you tell her things about me, Kyran," I said fiercely, my hands in fists, "I won't ever speak to you again. Hawthorn Lane can rot under the curse for all I care. I won't be a topic of discussion with that witch."

He regarded me with amused eyes. "I only want the best for you, Lorelle. That's all I've *ever* wanted." He paused, then added, almost maliciously, "As does Lady Faylan."

I stared at him. "I just don't like being talked about," I said in a calmer voice. I needed him to think we were okay, to not be aware that I was on to him, that I knew him for the traitor he was. "Now," I said briskly, clapping my hands together. "I need to get Edan out to feed and exercise, then I have a million chores to catch up on. I didn't get much done yesterday. I couldn't concentrate waiting to hear back from you, then my friend came over…" I trailed off. That last part had slipped out, and I wondered what my subconscious mind was playing at.

Kyran stiffened. "This friend of yours…do I know him?" Oh, yes, now I know what it was playing at.

"Maybe." I started the water to fill the sink.

"What was his name again?"

I frowned in thought. "Why, I don't think I ever said."

"Can you say it now?"

"Braaah!" Edan squawked, looking put-out, and I mentally praised the bird for his excellent timing. He stood and flapped his wings a few times, stirring up the ash in the fireplace.

"Looks like I'm needed," I said, shutting off the water. "It was good of you to come, Count." I headed for the door and opened it wide. "I'm sure I'll see you around."

"Have you thought about giving Lady Faylan a chance, Lorelle? I heard her story last night, and it was worse than I thought. I misjudged her at the ball, and I feel I owe her for that."

"It doesn't matter, Kyran."

"Why not? Don't you want to get along with the people here?"

I smiled at him, sweetly, innocently. "I used to, but I'll be leaving in a few days and then it won't matter anymore."

I started to close the door on him, but he stopped it with his hand. "You promised me one week." His voice was harsh, as though struggling to come out.

"I didn't actually *promise* anything, and anyway, that week is up in a few days." I gave him a stern look. "You haven't said anything to Lady Faylan about me leaving, have you?"

He looked away, *guiltily*. "I have not."

Why did I not believe him? "Say hello from me the next time you see her."

"You won't leave before the week is up?"

"I'm certainly tempted to. Might be better for everyone if I got out of Dodge. This village is like a tinder box and I'm the match."

"We don't want you to go, Lorelle."

That cold feeling again… "*We?*"

"Well, Lady Faylan, myself, the Executors…"

Oh, dear Grim, you need to leave.

Without thinking, I brought my hand down across the tender bones of his wrist with a sharp crack, and when he withdrew his arm in surprise, I threw my weight against the door, pushing him out. When it was shut, I slammed down the bar and leaned against the door, waiting to see if he'd try to gain access.

He didn't try. But I could feel him standing there, as though contemplating whether or not to. His retreating footsteps, which came only after some time had passed, told me he'd given up…for now.

I groaned and pushed away from the door, my head spinning. Edan was busy grooming himself, so I washed the dishes, including the goblets, resisting the temptation to throw them all at the wall, and thought hard about what had just happened. Here I was, beginning to think that I might want to be with the man, give this curse breaking a try, and maybe get rid of my awful tattoo in the bargain, and afterwards very likely have mind-blowing sex. *So what if he's ambitious*, I'd been telling myself. *That's not a crime.* Being as gorgeous and provocative as he is…now that should be a crime.

But then he had to go and screw things up.

Only three things could explain Kyran's change of heart about Lady Faylan. One, he was a gullible eejit and had fallen for whatever sob story she'd told him. Two, he was as awful as she was and had been lying to me the whole time. And three? He'd been spelled by that scheming witch, exactly as I worried would happen.

I wasn't sure which one I wanted it to be because none of the options were the least bit appealing, but I knew one thing for sure—no matter what I'd said to Kyran about staying for a week, I had to leave this place. The sooner, the better.

Chapter Twenty-Four

Edan flew off to feed, and I used that time to compose two letters. When he returned a couple hours later, I sent him on his way again with the notes, one of which went to Professor Ballylee, thanking him for his kindness over the years, but making no mention of my intention to leave, though I knew he'd figure it out. I also knew he wouldn't say anything to anyone about it. Being very old and very wise, he understood there were times you just have to let things happen in their own way. I wasn't quite sure how Edan was going to deliver the notes without being seen, but I had faith he could figure it out.

I had just finished putting together a shrimp stew, which was now fermenting on the stovetop, and was up on a stool tending to my conservatory plants when I spotted them coming. I hurried to the front door, swung it open, and quickly stepped outside to hold them off. It was late afternoon, but still quite hot. Shading my eyes, I watched the group trooping down the road and wished they'd hurry it up. In a short amount of time, my fair skin already felt as though it were burning. Maybe I really had done something to the weather. If it didn't rain soon, we'd be in danger of a water shortage. First a flood, and now a drought. I sighed. Could this place ever do anything without going to extremes?

My visitors marched through the gate, looking quite determined. "Hello, Juletta," I greeted the first of them warily. I liked the ex-Desolate, but as Lady Faylan's sister, I wasn't sure I could fully trust her. "What brings you out my way?"

Dawn stepped forward. "This is my doing, Lorelle."

"So what exactly is it that you're doing, Dawn?"

She thrust out her flat chest importantly. "Showing you that we support you, you mook."

I raised a surprised eyebrow at her, then let my eyes take in the small contingent of blue bloods standing behind her. Ilia was one of the group, though judging from the obstinate expression on her face she was still mad at me and hadn't really wanted to come to 'support' me at all. Next to her stood Enchanté Iverich, Charlton's younger sister. This was a surprise. Enchanté had always seemed nice enough, if a bit bland, but therein lay the surprise. She was too nice to be here, and as a faerie she shouldn't be seen siding with a non-faerie, especially being that I apparently was now persona non grata. She was going to get into big trouble if people found out that she was here.

But then again, maybe not. I remembered how some of the villagers at *Devil's Cakes* had seemed to support me, and pretty much all of them had been high-borns. Was that why Enchanté and all the rest had come? To curry favor with me? The thought made my stomach clench up.

Gemma Fiersen, next-door neighbor and one of the help Kyran had hired to work at Castle Daarke, was the outlier in the group before me. As wood elves, the Fiersens weren't even close to being high-born. However, she did work for one, who seemed to want to cultivate my goodwill.

"And why do I need your support?"

Dawn looked astonished. "Because of who we are!"

I turned my scrutiny on the others. Enchanté blushed when I looked at her, though Gemma met my gaze with a forthright one of her own. Today her out of control red curls seemed electrified, encircling her head like the halo on a medieval angel. Ilia stared at her feet, her thin features scrunched up and sour, and Juletta simply looked amused.

"Because we like you, Lorelle, and because we're bored," Juletta answered more diplomatically. "Some of us more of the former, some of us more of the latter. But probably a bit of both for everyone."

"Right," Dawn reasserted herself, throwing a thumb at Juletta. "What she said." She smirked. "But just to be clear, we support you in spirit only."

"Ah. So you're saying the moment things go bad you're gone?"

"Oh, Lorelle, I do like that you get me so well," Dawn replied matter-of-factly. "By the way, Fan doesn't know I'm here, so can you keep this quiet?" She snorted with amusement. "Sorry. I forgot who I was talking to. Of course you'll keep it quiet. You're like a grave full of secrets."

"How poetic, Dawn."

She tilted her head to one side and gave a little shrug. "Yeah, I know. Weird, huh?"

"We believe you're being unfairly accused," Juletta clarified. "Something we all know a bit about. So we wanted you to know that some of us in the village can think for ourselves."

I turned to Enchanté, curious to know her opinion since I wasn't sure when she had ever been unfairly accused of anything. She was a soft-looking thing, soft brown curls, soft brown eyes, vapid as a cow's, soft voice. While she was attractive, she looked nothing like her mother or brothers, with their silver eyes and chiseled features. For that matter, I'm not sure she resembled her father all that much, either. "Is that what you think, Enchanté?"

"My mother and my brother, Charlton, say we're to show we're on your side," she answered, trying to meet my eye and failing, "so that's good enough for me." I sighed inwardly. So much for thinking for herself.

I looked around. "Avice didn't want to come?"

"She was going to," Dawn replied, "but then something came up and she had to send her regrets. She was quite mysterious about it all." At least I didn't have to worry about her feeling like she'd missed out. She had a social life that would put a celebrity to shame, and yet any time I did something or something happened without her, she acted like I'd betrayed her.

"Well, I appreciate you coming out here and telling me yourself that you support me *in spirit*. But now you have to go." I made a shooing motion toward the gate. "It's too dangerous to be seen with me, and I have things to do."

As in, packing and fleeing.

"Like you're getting off that easily." Dawn smoothed down her rose petal dress and looked over my shoulder at the cottage, her tiny nose twitching. "We came all the way out here, and I smell food, so you're feeding us, Gragan. Deal with it."

I watched in silence as she strutted past me and into my cottage as though she owned it. I rather regretted urging her to get out from under her sister's thumb and do her own thing. "Really, ladies," I tried again. "I mean it. Get out while the getting is good." I absently touched the cut on the back of my head, remembering just how quickly things could get out of hand.

"I'm a big girl, Lorelle," Juletta replied, eyeing my gesture. "And while I'm not wearing my big girl pants, or *panties*, for that matter"— she waggled her eyebrows at me—"I can still fend for myself. Come on, girls." She followed after Dawn, disappearing into the darkness of my cottage.

Ilia was the last to go inside, avoiding my eyes as she passed hurriedly by me. I didn't understand what was going on with her. If she was mad at me, why was she here? It made no sense. Everything was backwards. The people I had thought I could trust, like her and Kyran, I couldn't, and people I'd thought were my enemies, like Cutter and Dawn, were rallying around me.

Admitting I wasn't going to win this battle, I trudged inside and set about preparing dinner for my uninvited guests, all of whom were milling about, either talking to each other or studying my little cottage and its contents as though viewing a strange new species. While the stew bubbled, I filled my new glasses with *Dark Spirits*, using up the last of it with a feeling of sadness, and set the crystal goblets, barely filled, on the table.

When the dinnerware was set and the food ready, I called everyone to the table, wondering how, in showing me their support, I was the one who ended up feeding them. I was beginning to think the price of friendship was awfully high. Ah, well. I could look at this dinner as my final goodbye to Hawthorn Lane and a way to use up all the food I'd baked this afternoon. This was to be my last supper, so to speak, though I certainly didn't plan on getting crucified.

There were oohs and ahhs of delight as people sat down and leaned over their bowls to inhale the thick stew's robust, spicy scent. Then everyone tucked in, going at the meal with the avidity of starving wolves. The wine soon disappeared, and when I went to hold up the bottle to show with regret that it was empty, I found it filled. I stared at it, but decided not to question my good luck, likely the result of someone's magic.

I refilled everyone's glasses, and Juletta raised her crystal goblet in the air. "To Lorelle…who's brave enough to do her own thing, and take on a Desolate, as well."

"Hear, hear!" Dawn shouted. "All this," she waved her glass around the room, which she had once shown disdain for, "and the most eligible bachelor to hit Hawthorn Lane for a century. Lucky snot."

"Lucky snot, is right," Enchanté agreed, and I stared at her in surprise. Gone was the softness, at least in her eyes. "I'd kill for a place of my own, and for a chance to bed Kyran Van der Daarke, too." She fixed her narrowed brown eyes on my stunned expression. Was this really Enchanté, or was she, courtesy of the curse, merely unleashing the darkness that resides in us all? "You don't know what you have, do you?" I sat there frozen, not sure how to respond. I didn't think I was easily taken aback, but here I was, mouth gaping.

Dawn screeched mirthfully, breaking the tension. "Holy Grim! Did anyone else see that coming? Enchanté, you minx, you!" She raised her glass to the faerie, then took a large gulp, and I was grateful not to be the only one in shock. "Kyran's a definite rouser," she went on. "I'm not afraid to admit it, especially after that show he put on in Atlene's shop. Ooh…la…*la*!" She fanned herself, then looked around, her eyes bright with mischief. "Did anyone see Merceen there? She looked like she was about to tear off his clothes and go at him right then and there! *Ewww!*" She turned to Gemma and nudged her. "And you get to live with the man, you lucky wench. What's that like?"

"I can't really say anything," Gemma replied, a little unsteadily, though her grip on her glass was firm. "Me da and Sinead threatened to cut out me tongue if I breathed a word about milord, but"—she placed a strong, freckled hand to her breast—"I will say this...I wish he'd go without a shirt *all the time.*"

"Oh, ho!" Juletta hooted. "How often does he?"

"Not nearly enough." Gemma leaned forward confidentially. "Truth is, I only saw the once, when I were fetching him some water to clean up after I accidentally spilled wine on his shirt at dinner, and what I saw, it were like a gift from the gods."

"Accidentally, my arse," Dawn crowed and Gemma gave a mischievous laugh.

"So we're all curious," Juletta turned to me, "why you haven't snatched him up, Lorelle."

"It's not like he's a cookie I dropped on the floor," I replied warily.

"But if you were with him you could end the curse," Ilia said softly, though a hardness edged her words.

"Not according to Lady Faylan," I argued. "She isn't convinced I'm the one to make it happen."

"That's because my sister wants the Count for herself," Juletta pointed out.

"How do you know that?" I asked.

"Because she manages to bring him in to every conversation we've had over the past week and a half. I know Vira, and when she sets her mind to something, she'll do whatever it takes to get it."

"Right," I replied airily. "So why bother trying? No matter what I do, I can't win." I stared at Ilia as I said this and she quickly looked away. "So," I went on casually. "How's Josepha been?"

Her head swung back to face me. "You know exactly how he's been!"

"Well, I know he won some money the other night. Other than that, I'm afraid I'm not in the loop anymore."

"How can you say that? You know I like him. You know—"

"You like a wood elf?" Enchanté interrupted, her eyes wide.

Ilia tensed. "What's wrong with liking a wood elf?"

"Yeah," Gemma chimed in, looking ready to pop Enchanté in the mouth.

Enchanté shrugged, seemingly unaware of the tension she'd created. "Oh, I don't know. Nothing really. I guess I'm just so used to hearing Mother speak poorly of them, of everyone, really..." She trailed off, her brown eyes darkening to black. "She ruins everything for me," she went on in a low voice. "Friendships, romances, anything I might possibly want to do to improve my depressing life. There are days when I imagine different ways of ending it all. It's the only thing that seems to bring me happiness lately."

Gemma didn't look impressed, but Ilia pulled out of her snit and threw her arms around the miserable girl. "Oh, Enchanté! Don't kill yourself!"

The faerie gave a mirthless laugh, a sound reminiscent of shattering icicles. "Oh, I'd probably just hag it up anyway."

"Listen to me, Enchanté," I commanded. When she turned to face me, reluctantly, I looked her directly in the eye. "Your mother is an unhappy woman, and she shares her misery like a virus, spreading it as though it were her own personal plague. I believe she loves you"—much as I disliked Coriana, I always had the impression that she lived for her children—"but she'll take you down with her. Don't let her do that."

"Easy for you to say," she flared, showing a spirit I didn't think she possessed. "You're an Omni-Fey, you have your own house and business, you can do whatever you want, whenever you want. You're *strong*, Lorelle, where I'm weak. I can never be you."

"That's the problem, Enchanté. You can't be me, you can only be you, and I think there's more to that person than you realize."

"Pretty words, Lorelle," she said dismissively. "But meaningless, because you've never been in my situation, living with a mother like mine."

"That's where you're wrong," I said recklessly, liking her more and more. "My mother makes yours look like an angel."

"You have a mother, Lorelle?" Dawn interjected. "Because I thought you'd materialized from a dung heap." She giggled, and I was grateful for her distraction. The last thing I wanted to do was talk about my mother. "Now come on, you tarts! I'm drunk, away from my sister, and rebelling, just like you told me to do, Lorelle. So if the two of you don't stop harshing my vibe, I'm going to go all bedlam on you!"

I couldn't help myself, I laughed. "You and whose army?"

She held up her hands. "I've got these ten soldiers right here!" She pointed them at me, and grinned evilly. I looked down in awe as one by one the buttons on my bodice began to pop off. "Not exactly an impressive skill," she admitted, "but more than I could do before."

I lifted my own hands and threw a shower of sparks at her. "Hey!" she cried, batting at the hail of light. I threw more sparks into the air, and before I knew it, we were all doing magic. It got messy—Ilia broke open a bag of flour and Gemma knocked over a potted plant—and nonsensical—Juletta made Gemma's curls stand on end and Dawn kept making our clothes fall off, but it was fun.

We were all laughing and giggling, and I found myself having a surprisingly wonderful time. I was beginning to understand the allure of having friends. Though the wary side of me wondered what the cost would be... There's always a cost.

I was creating a light show with my sparks when music started to play, filling the whole room as though the musician were standing inside the cottage, playing right before us. But there was no one there.

"Is that you, Lorelle?" Gemma demanded, her eyes wide as she peered around her, slightly breathless from attempting to catch the sparks.

I shrugged helplessly. It wasn't me, but I knew where the music was coming from...Cutter Flint.

The toe of Gemma's faerie-tipped shoe started to tap. "Because if it is, it's absolutely delicious!" She threw her hands in the air, and before I knew it, we were all whirling and twirling about the cottage. My chaise and table were pushed to the side, and soon we were dancing together, synchronized as though we'd done these steps together a million times. The rhythmic beat was mesmerizing and we danced and drank wine for what felt like a long time. Hearts beating in unison, breaths coming in tandem, we were connected as though one mind and one body.

My ancient grandfather clock, never very reliable, began to strike, a sound that barely penetrated my foggy mind. When the last chime tolled, I realized it was midnight. The Witching Hour. *How appropriate.* As though under a spell, Ilia floated toward the door and opened it. She stepped outside, I heard a delightful whoop, then silence. Ten minutes later, Gemma made her way, spinning and singing, toward the door.

When it was Enchanté's turn, she grabbed me in a hug. She was as soft as I'd thought she would be, squishy in all the right places, and I rather liked hugging her, until she whispered in my ear, "My mother and a certain person of high standing are scheming against you."

"What are they scheming?"

"To set you up with Charlton." So I was right. Coriana was plotting to manipulate me, very likely with Lady Faylan's encouragement. But was Kyran in on it, too? After his strange behavior regarding the overseer earlier today, I had a bad feeling he was.

"Me with Charlton? But he's faerie, and I'm most definitely not."

"You're an Omni, Lorelle, and that trumps everything. My mother consulted Professor Ballylee. But..." She giggled wildly. "That's not all. Charlton, like my brother and myself, isn't exactly a pure-blood, if you get my drift. So that's my gift to you, Lorelle, for giving me the best time I've *ever* had." She pulled away with an impish smile, then spun out the door, laughing softly. I watched her go through hazy eyes, my mind unable to fully comprehend what I'd just heard.

Dawn was the last to leave, and she was singing happily off-key as I followed her, vaguely curious as to what was going on. Outside I found the yard bathed in moonlight, the glow turning everything to ghosts. On the silvery lawn stood Edan, his feathers reflecting the light like a mirror. He delicately lifted one leg, then bent it to form a sort of step. Dawn climbed onto Edan's knee, hauled herself onto his back, and gave me a tipsy salute. "I hope you told Renwick I want him desperately."

"I told him you're a rebel, and that you don't need him or his charm."

"I *am* a rebel!" she cried, then hooted loudly.

"But I mean it, Dawn. You don't need a man to get by."

"Tell that to my loins!"

"Because you have friends now," I persisted, my voice echoing in my mind as though I were speaking to myself.

She sobered a little. "Yeah, I guess I do. Never had those before. Not real ones, anyway. But now I have an Omni criminal, an ex-Desolate, a skinny patrician, and a low-born elf for my besties. Aren't I the lucky one?" She was trying hard to sound cynical, but couldn't quite manage it, her wondrous expression getting in her way.

"And we have you…a psychotic cyborg with homicidal tendencies."

"Exactly." She lifted her fist into the air and pumped it, crying, "Best… party…ever!" summing up the evening perfectly. Then she screeched in delight as Edan took off, flapping high into the silvery sky. I watched them go, feeling awed.

"What a magnificent bird he is," a voice from the darkness spoke out.

"Yes," I agreed in wonder. "Magnificent."

Cutter grabbed hold of my arm. "I will take you to bed now." Together we headed back into the cottage, and each step felt as though I were floating on air. "I am your sanctuary, Lorelle," the death wraith whispered into my ear as I flopped down onto my bed, my head spinning. "And when the time comes, you will be mine."

"I will be yours, Cutter Flint," I agreed sleepily, then was lost to the darkness.

Chapter Twenty-Five

I awoke once again to a hangover. What was going on with me? I never indulged like this. *Ever.* It was too dangerous to lose control. And yet it had been really fun, with no harm done. Except to my aching head, I realized when I sat up. Grumbling to myself, I made my way downstairs, glad but not surprised to see Edan tucked into his eyrie, fast asleep.

I was thrilled to find the cottage had been set to rights, with not so much as a footprint of flour remaining. Cutter had cleaned up after us, and he'd done it well. Hmmm… There was something to be said for a man willing to do housework.

I shook my head. Absolutely not. Just because Kyran was acting strangely didn't mean I was going to turn to Cutter for comfort. Yes, I felt betrayed by Kyran and his ostensible defection, and I had every right to throw up my defenses. But if he'd been spelled, was it fair to blame him for his behavior? Probably not, but a part of me expected him to be stronger than that. In fact, I wanted him to be infallible. An unrealistic standard? Maybe. But why not? Was perfection too much to ask of the man people wanted me to spend the rest of my life with? I think not.

Not even all that deep down I knew I was just making excuses to protect myself from getting hurt again. And even though I was upset with Kyran, I wasn't getting involved with Cutter Flint. He was an intriguing man, and yes, I found myself attracted to him—had been feeling the Cutter vibe even before Kyran had arrived on the scene—but I knew he was not for me, and I was not for him, much as he wanted it to be so. But why did he want it to be so? I felt quite certain it had nothing to do with me as a woman.

As I pulled on my wellies to go do chores, something crucial tugged at my mind, like a child pulling at a balloon string, something about last night, and something about that first night when Cutter and I had danced together. Whatever it was felt important, but it wouldn't come to me.

I remembered dancing with the girls, how good it felt to let loose and have fun. I remembered the laughter and the many raunchy jokes. I remembered feeling a part of something bigger, a rare occurrence for me. I'd never done anything like what had happened at last night's gathering, and I found myself wondering when we could do it again.

Then I also remembered that I was leaving Hawthorn Lane soon, and a chill of regret took hold in my chest. I'd meant to make preparations to clear out last night, but Dawn and the others had shown up, blowing that plan out of the water. Was their visit a coincidence, or had Kyran somehow brought it about, sensing through his connection to me that I was thinking of bolting? Or had he gotten it out of our conversation when I'd basically said I was thinking of bolting? Or maybe it was that karate chop I'd delivered to his unsuspecting wrist to get him out of the cottage and far away from me. So many possibilities…

I sighed and headed outside to feed the chickens. Whatever the case, whether Kyran was up to something or not, I had to go from this place. If my mother were here, intent on destruction, I needed to draw her away from my home and my newfound friends, even from Kyran, who I believed that, unlike myself, remained the key component for removing the curse.

In leaving I'd be killing yet another bird, as well. Making this sacrifice should serve to remove the tattoo Cutter had bestowed upon me, and thereby release me from his thrall. And what a relief that would be. Just thinking about him made the tattoo throb, and each little beat released his scent into the warm, dry air like a fan. I closed my eyes and let the irresistible fragrance of vetiver fill my senses.

I drain the life from the living, whispered a voice in the wind. My eyes flew open, though I remained still, looking about. No one was nearby, not even the chickens. Who had said that, I wondered, and what did it mean? Who drained the life from the living, and why?

With great caution I made my way back to the cottage. Nothing happened, and I got myself inside, swiftly locking and barring the door behind me, my prison instantly transforming back into a refuge. Edan slept on, and I headed to the bathroom for a long soak that would hopefully clear my mind and pull the ache from my body so that I could concentrate on figuring all this out.

Twenty minutes later, I was beginning to feel better when a loud crash rattled the bathroom door. Edan's furious squawks followed soon after.

I leapt out of the tub, grabbed my robe, and pulled it over my dripping torso. Not stopping to think, I yanked open the door, ready to fight whoever was hurting Edan. But my bird, I soon discovered, could take care of himself. Massive wings flapping strong enough to make a breeze, he charged toward a gaping hole in the conservatory, hissing and screeching like an angry goose. A dark figure darted past his flapping wings and jumped through the hole, disappearing before I could see who it was.

I raced toward Edan, but his wing flicked out and stopped me just before I ran over the thousands of broken glass shards littering the floor. I bolted toward the door. It took me entirely too long to raise the bar and undo the lock, and by the time I raced outside, whoever had broken in was out of sight. I thought about sending Edan after our intruder, then decided against it. I'd rather him be around if the person returned to finish the job, whatever that might be.

Back inside, I rushed to Edan, looking him over with a practiced eye. He had stepped away from the glass, and I was able to get close enough to see blood smeared on one of his massive claws.

"You're hurt!" I bent down to examine the wound.

"Not mine," he croaked.

"Oh." I stood back up. "Well, good job." I patted him on the head, then threw all caution to the wind and wrapped my arms around him. His body was thick and muscular, and I reveled in its strength. "You saved me, my prince."

"Braaah," he wheezed happily.

After a few moments, he started getting antsy. I released him and stepped back, feeling slightly embarrassed. It wasn't like me to be so demonstrative. But if ever there were a time for emotional gestures, this was it, right? Was it sad that I didn't know the answer to that?

I looked around at the destruction, forcing myself to focus. "Did you see who did this? Was it Kyran?"

Edan shook his head. "Not know person."

"You've never seen him before?"

"Two of them," he corrected. "I follow."

"Don't bother. They're long gone."

"Blood trail."

I considered this. If Edan left, I'd be on my own, but I'd been taking care of myself for a long time now. This time wouldn't be any different, except for the angry mob/intruder/break-in thing going on right now.

"All right, Edan," I decided. "Go quickly then, and be careful."

"You safe?"

"I'll lock the door." He swung his head toward the hole in the conservatory. "Ah, yes." I gave a shaky laugh. "Forgot about that. Well, maybe I can get Kyran to fix it."

"You do it."

"Me?" I shook my head. "I don't think I can."

"You do it," he repeated stubbornly.

I wasn't sure if he was confident in my abilities or didn't want Kyran coming here, the latter being a little worrying. "I'll try," I promised. "Now you'd better go. Blood trails don't last long around here." The earth in Hawthorn Lane has a way of absorbing blood quickly, something I'd learned whilst tracking a wounded charlatan one time.

I opened the door for Edan, and he shuffled outside. "You'd better hunt afterward," I told him, and he nodded, his steely eyes on the sky. With a pat on the head, he was gone, and I went back inside to survey the damage. It didn't look good—a jagged hole in the conservatory wall, glass everywhere, a knocked over fern. Other than the fern, I had no idea how to fix the mess, but Edan was right. I needed to try. I couldn't always be relying on Kyran to come to my rescue, especially if he was Team Faylan now. I wondered how Edan had sensed my magical ability, and why he believed in its potential. Could others sense it too? Was this why I'd always felt like I never fit in—because others treated me differently for being an Omni-Fey? Or had their reticence been of my own making? Was I always holding back because I never thought I'd be accepted? It was quite possible it was my own fault, but preferable to blame others. Then I wouldn't have to fix myself.

Realizing I hadn't yet dressed, I climbed up to my loft and quickly pulled on a lightweight Viennese gown, then ran a brush through my hair before wrapping it up in a loose chignon. My stomach was grumbling and my head bore the burden of a slight ache, so I knew I had to eat before I tried doing any magic.

I was crossing the floor to the kitchen when I saw them…two white roses flung onto the table, and I knew instantly they were a message from my visitor, delivered just before Edan had attacked. The white rose represents purity and innocence, and new beginnings, as well, and that sounds lovely, doesn't it? But I felt pretty sure those roses were not meant to convey good tidings. Both looked as though they had some sort of disease, the edges of each petal rimmed in curling black. When I picked up a flower, a nasty slug oozed out of the center like spit-up. Grimacing, I grabbed both flowers and threw them into the fireplace. Heaping a handful of kindling on top, I lit the fire and watched the nasty things burn.

When the flowers had been reduced to ashes, I turned toward the kitchen, my stomach gurgling loudly, only to be met with a second surprise. On my chaise lay a thick book, leather-bound with gold filigree writing on the cover. I hadn't noticed the book before, my attention focused on ridding myself of the roses. Though now that I saw it, I couldn't imagine how I'd missed it. I picked up the slender volume and saw that it was *Paradise Lost*, John Milton's poem about Adam and

Eve's fall from grace.

My visitor had given me rotting white roses, surely meant to convey that my life here was about to come to an end, one way or another, and a poem about two humans banished from their beloved home. The message seemed clear... This place is no longer yours. Leave or be punished dearly. *Paradise Lost* had always been a favorite of mine, but now I could only see the epic poem as a sinister threat.

But who had left the 'gifts'? A random villager trying to scare me? Lady Faylan wanting to get rid of me? My mother? It could be her. The message behind the roses and poetry book—that my escape, my stay here, was over—fit perfectly with her agenda.

But then I remembered Edan had mentioned that two people had been here. A cold chill ran through me when I realized that if it were my mother who'd broken in, then she would likely have brought my aunt Nimair to help her. My mother was cold and ruthless, but reasonably predictable. Aunt Nimair was chaos incarnate; one never knew where she was coming from or when she'd strike. In fact, her best weapon was her inconsistency. There were times when she'd be nice, then turn on you, just because she was bored. Together the two sisters were extremely dangerous.

I had to leave, the sooner the better.

But not quite yet. I would meet Avice tonight for my flying lesson to say goodbye to her. Then I'd summon the caretaker I'd chosen to look after Edan. When I felt sure I'd tied up all my loose ends, I'd leave Hawthorn Lane. If the intruders were indeed my mother and aunt, then hopefully my leaving would pull the two demon hags with me.

Rialban would undoubtedly try to stop me again, but he would fail. I had a plan to rout him that he wouldn't see coming, and I was quite looking forward to putting it into play.

Chapter Twenty-Six

As I waited for Edan to return I readied the cottage for my absence. But this time felt harder, this time I was leaving behind someone who depended on me. Edan might be physically all grown up, but that didn't mean he was ready to face the world on his own. I'd made plans for him, though I wasn't sure they'd be adequate, and I felt like I was abandoning him.

I also, rather annoyingly, felt a twinge of conscience at leaving before a full week was up. Kyran had been adamant that I stay the whole time, and I had sort of committed to that. But what if he'd wanted me to stay because he and Lady Faylan were plotting against me? Then again, if they were, what exactly was their plan? I mean, why keep me here? She wanted him, and he appeared to like her now, so they could be together if they wanted. I certainly couldn't stop them. Something else must be going on, maybe something even more diabolical. But what that something might be, I hadn't a clue, though it seemed to involve me. So while I felt uncomfortable about leaving, it was the best thing to do.

As I went about my chores, I couldn't help glancing at the broken glass and gaping hole the intruder had left behind. The damage obviously wasn't going to fix itself, which meant I had to do it. When there was nothing left to do, I made my slow, reluctant way toward the wreckage. Standing just outside the ring of glass shards, I studied the hole. Whoever had made it hadn't done it with brute force—the hole was far too large for that. So I had to guess it had been done by magic. But if that were the case, then how could it have been my mother? She didn't know she had powers. Or did she? Perhaps she'd known about her abilities all along, had developed them for decades, and here I was, supposedly an Omni-Fey, and unable even to undo what she'd done.

Discovering I was fey was turning out to be both a blessing and a curse. I could now live in this world without fear of being found out, but with that newfound freedom came the knowledge that I was supposed to be something really great. What if I wasn't really great? What if I turned out to be a miserable failure? Even though I'd controlled the elements to end the flood that had threatened my cottage, and then potentially saved a child's life, those might have been isolated incidents, never to be duplicated.

So what? I demanded, despising how uncertain and namby-pamby I'd grown lately. *How does that make you any worse off than before?*

Simply put, it didn't.

Admittedly, it was a little more complicated than my simply being afraid of failure. I'd already invested hope into the belief that I might be something more than what I was, when I'd felt so inferior all my life. I didn't want to give that up.

Too bad, I told myself sternly. I was simply going to have to find out what I could do, and better to do that now than in a dangerous situation. The best way to know my limits was to try and duplicate what I'd already done. Anger and the fear of losing my home had driven me to push back the water, and compassion for a suffering soul and fear of getting mobbed had driven me to help Jaimen. Maybe what I needed to do here was tap into my most powerful resource…my emotions. Perhaps they were my glister, my spark.

Girding myself, I pictured my mother in my cottage, defiling my home with her evil intentions, fouling the air with her bitterness and malevolence. *How dare she? This is my world, my haven, and she has no right to sully it with her nasty presence!*

Rage boiled through me and I lifted my hands as though to strike her away; sparks popped from my fingertips, eager to be set free. Pulling in a deep breath, I pointed my fingers at the ruined glass wall. In my mind's eye, I saw the shards rise, watched them fly backward, melding together to become whole once more. Then I focused my entire essence on the gaping hole and released my energy. The sparks leaped from my hands and flew toward the empty space, pulling the shards of glass with them. Like a puzzle, the jagged pieces connected together, one after the other. There was a sizzling noise, like hot iron being dipped in water, and then silence.

I blinked. Before me stood the reunited glass, looking as it always had, thick and whole. Then I noticed something was different. I went up to a pane and rapped on the still-warm surface. Not only did it look like glass, it sounded like glass, and yet I couldn't shake the feeling that something had changed. I picked up a nearby stone frog, held it tight, then smashed it against the panel. There was a dull thud and the frog jumped backward off the glass as though catapulted. I tried again, harder this time, but the glass remained solid beneath my assault. I moved to a section that I hadn't magically fixed and tried again. The glass immediately splintered.

I took a step back and viewed my work with awe. The magicked glass was stronger now, hard as a diamond. I had made it better. I quickly fixed the splintered part, then aimed my sparks at the remaining window panes, hardening the glass to indestructibility. When that task was complete, I took aim at the rest of the cottage, using my fear to strengthen the wood and stone so that I need never worry about anyone breaking into my place—literally—ever again. Not that it mattered for me anymore, but the new owner would appreciate the added security.

I sighed and let my arms drop. Nothing about my decision to leave was going to be easy, and I wondered what I'd done in a past life to deserve this fate. *Probably beheaded a few innocent people.*

Ah, well. There was no hope for it. I had to leave, and for more than one reason now. Not only did I need to make things right with Dallen, it was imperative that I lure whoever was stalking me, be it my mother and aunt or a fey-hunter, far away from this place.

A thump sounded on the door, and I hurried to let Edan in. By the slump of his shoulders as he shuffled past me, I could tell his hunt had been unsuccessful. To cheer him up, I gave him an awkward pat on the head, then showed him what I'd done. When he saw my handiwork, he gave a satisfied squawk and I felt a surge of confidence. I demonstrated how I'd made the glass stronger and he spent a few minutes testing out my work by pecking with great energy at various spots, which easily held up to the force of his powerful beak.

"There's something I need to tell you, Edan," I said when he'd tired of his pecking game. I couldn't just walk away from him without an explanation, though it might be easier on me.

"Braaah?"

I hesitated. "I have to leave Hawthorn Lane."

He blinked a few times, as though trying to take this in, then his intelligent eyes peered into mine. "Why?"

Oh, murder. This was awful. I felt like I was abandoning my child, and maybe, for all intents and purposes, I was. "For a couple reasons, actually," I finally said, and explained them to him as best I could. Though none of my excuses sounded as pressing out loud, especially my determination to make things right with Dallen. If it weren't for the potential that it was my mother and aunt creating havoc, I might be tempted to send my ex a postcard saying I was sorry and wished the best for him, yours etc. Hugs. "You can't tell anyone that I'm going or why, all right?" I finished my atypically long-winded explanation.

"Will not tell."

"You don't approve of my leaving, do you?"

"None of it your fault."

That got me. "I suppose it isn't," I said breezily, trying to hide my distress, "but that doesn't excuse me from doing something about it."

"I come with you."

My laugh had a bitter edge to it. "I wish you could, Edan. But you'd stand out way too much in the Alterworld. Your kind doesn't exist there."

"Not even one?" He looked shocked, an emotion I had no idea birds could convey, or feel. Of course, this bird could hold a conversation, so I should be beyond shock by this point.

"Sadly, not even one. We have smaller birds of prey, and we have large birds, like ostriches and emus, neither of which can fly, but nothing like you. You'd be a rarity. People would come after you with pitchforks."

"Pitchforks?"

"They wouldn't be nice to you," I translated, then changed the subject. "So the blood trail disappeared?" I didn't want him getting it into his head that following me into the Alterworld was a good idea, and besides, this conversation was making me want to bawl.

"Found one drop. On leaf," he croaked. "Familiar."

"What's familiar?"

"The blood."

Ah. There it was...proof. My whole body felt like ice. "Well, I guess that shows it was either my aunt or my mother who broke in here, or both. That's why I have to leave. It seems they're getting bolder and more destructive with every passing day, and I have to do something to stop them."

"Did it again."

"Did what again?"

"Pretending to be you."

I felt like someone had punched me. "What did they do this time?"

"Hurt a boy."

Oh, blast. "Is he going to be all right?"

"Not sure."

"Which one got hurt?"

"The mean one."

"Carius?" My fingers curled into fists. "Oh, this just gets better and better, Edan. So someone who looked like me attacked the boy who attacked me... When did this happen?"

"Short time ago."

"Did anyone see it happen?" He shook his head. "Is the boy conscious?" Another shake. "So I'm safe until he wakes up." *If he wakes up...*

"Brah."

A pounding on the door startled me and I swung toward it, reaching for my dagger. "Who's there?" Had they come for me already? I motioned for Edan to stay back.

"It's Renwick, luv. Open up!"

I ran across the room. "I never thought I'd be glad to see you," I said as I flung open the door. He looked good, his beard filling in nicely. The facial hair gave him the appearance of a rakish bandit, which I suspect was why he was growing it out.

"Well, that terribly complimentary greeting just set my heart a-flutter."

I grabbed his arm and dragged him inside, re-barring the door. "You got my note." I hadn't been expecting him to come this soon, but his timing was perfect.

"I did. You said you needed my help?"

"I don't have a lot of choice in the matter. You're it."

"Please, stop it with the flattery. I can feel my head swelling as we speak."

"I think that chicken has already flown the coop, big head."

"Maybe you should check it out?" His eyes dropped to his belt buckle.

"We'd better be talking about the head on your neck, cheeky bugger."

He grinned. "So what is it that you need?"

I turned and gestured toward Edan. "A babysitter."

Edan took a few steps forward, and Renwick jumped back, clapping a hand to his chest. "Holy hell! What is that beast?"

Edan hissed at him, not pleased. "That is a rapture, and you've not gotten off on the best foot with him. His name is Edan. Edan, this is Renwick Van der Daarke."

Edan gave Renwick the stink eye.

Renwick, sensing he'd mucked things up, gave a low bow. "My apologies, Edan. You're quite an impressive sight, and frankly you scared the crap out of me."

Edan relaxed slightly. "Impressive sight," he echoed.

Renwick turned to me. "He can talk, too?"

"And better than you can."

Edan gave a squawk that sounded suspiciously like a laugh.

"Obviously. So your note said you needed my help and had a proposal for me." I nodded. "And while I was hoping you were asking for my hand in marriage, I'm guessing it has something to do with this guy."

"I want you to stay here and look after my place and Edan while I'm gone." At this reminder of someone else living here, I felt a little sick to my stomach. This was *my* home, a building I knew every inch of, every creak and every crack. There was no way Renwick could love it like I did. But at least in allowing him to stay here I wouldn't be defaulting on my loan to Lady Faylan. No way was I going to let my beloved cottage become hers. I'd rather burn it to the ground.

"Gone?" He looked baffled. "Where are you going?"

"I have to go to the Alterworld."

Renwick eyed me warily. "When are you coming back?"

"As soon as I can," I answered vaguely.

"Which might be never," he shrewdly guessed. "What's going on here, Lorelle? And don't give me the run around. I got enough of that sort of thing from Melaina, so I know when it's being done to me."

I suppressed a sigh. "Have you heard what's been happening?"

"I've picked up things here and there at *Chez.* That's why I said in my note that I've been thinking about you. It sounds like someone is trying to make you look bad."

"Someone whom I'm fairly sure is Melaina."

He rubbed a tired hand over his face. "She's like a blight, isn't she? Everything she touches turns to rot."

"Including you?"

He turned his hand over and looked at it speculatively. "I sometimes wonder."

I decided to take that reply with a grain of salt. "When do you have to be at work?"

"I've got an hour."

"All right. Sit down. I'll fix you lunch and explain everything. But what I tell you must be kept confidential. If certain people find out, everything will be ruined."

"I may not do many things right in my life, Lorelle, but I can keep my mouth shut."

"I hope so. Lives depend on it, Renwick."

"If yours is one of those lives, then know I'll take this as seriously as can be."

I peered into his golden-brown eyes, and Grim help me, decided to believe him.

Chapter Twenty-Seven

While we ate lunch, I told Renwick everything—about the Haw-thornite delinquents who attacked me, about my mysterious visi-tors and strange gifts—none of which, he said regretfully, he'd sent, about what had happened at Atlene's store. Well, I told him mostly everything. I said nothing about my family's possible involvement, not because I wanted to protect them but because I felt ashamed of them. Even though Renwick probably would have understood better than anyone the burden of family ties. I ended by saying that I needed to get away, leaving out Dallen's role, as well. I also left out that Kyran had asked me to stay for a full week for reasons unknown, and that I thought he might be conspiring with Lady Faylan. I might have ne-glected to mention that a death wraith had made a claim on me, as well.

No need to overcomplicate things...or scare the guy off.

When I finished talking, Renwick wiped his mouth with a black silk napkin and leaned back with a happy sigh. We were sitting at the table, and had just finished our bacon and cheese potato pie, which is as deli-cious and heart attack inducing as it sounds. "Why are you telling me all this, Lorelle?" he asked after a sip of cider.

Hm. He was not exactly jumping at this opportunity like I thought he would. Was Matron Thornback losing her coquettish touch? Or did he like her coquettish touch?

I suppressed a shudder and answered his question. "Because I need someone I can somewhat trust to make this work. You need a place to stay, one that's safe from Melaina, and I need someone to keep an eye on Edan for me since I don't know when I'll be coming back."

"If ever."

"If ever," I reluctantly admitted.

"Why me? Why not my cousin?"

Damn. He really wasn't going for this. "I'm not sure I can trust him."

"Not trust the saintly Kyran, while you 'somewhat' trust me? What-ever is this world coming to?"

"Is that how you see him? Saintly?"

He shrugged. "I suppose I do. It's quite annoying to have to compete with such virtue."

I decided not to follow up on why he needed to compete with Kyran, saying instead, "Well, he's been awfully chummy with Lady Faylan as of late, and I hold the same sentiment toward her that you do."

He smiled. "Interesting. So we're to be partners, eh?"

"I wouldn't go that far."

He gave me an amused smile. "All right. I'll do it."

"Really? You're not messing with me?"

"Truly. Seriously, Lorelle. Get my own digs, and an awesome attack bird in the bargain? How could I say no?" From his eyrie Edan burred softly in agreement. I'd fed him some fungus and he'd settled into his nest to watch us with one eye open.

"So we have a bargain?"

He stuck out his hand. "We do indeed."

I reached out and he clasped my hand in both of his, which were warm and dry and oddly comforting. A feeble part of me wanted Renwick to keep holding onto me and never let go. I bit my lip in annoyance. Funny how I'd gone from distrusting him greatly to relying on him... I wasn't sure I liked the change, but I also wasn't sure that I could do anything differently.

I pulled my hand from his and stood abruptly, vexed at my moment of weakness. "Your hour is almost up, so I'll have to show you everything you'll need to know some other time. When can you come? It'll have to be soon."

"Tonight?" He peered at me from under hooded lids as though setting up a rendezvous for making love.

I paused, thinking of my flying lessons. "Late, then," I replied, ignoring the provocative tone of his voice. "Half past midnight?" It shouldn't take more than half an hour, and then I'd leave right after that.

"That should work for me. I get off around then."

"Perfect," I said crisply.

He rose, pushed in his chair. "I'd help you with clean-up, but I have to run or I'll be late. And I'm never late."

"You?"

His eyes darkened. "I know what you think of me, Lorelle, but you must remember something. I'm a Van der Daarke, and a poor relation at that. I've learned the hard way that I'm going to be judged more harshly than most, and have taken great pains to never give people reason to judge."

"You made your cousin believe someone was trying to kill him," I pointed out, my tone as dry as the dust I still needed to clean up before I left.

His right eyebrow twitched. "That was simply a little payback."

"For what?"

"For being such a perfect specimen."

"I'd hate to see what you'd do to a real enemy."

"If you were that enemy, then yes, you would hate it."

I studied him for a moment, wondering if I'd made a mistake offering my home to him. What, after all, did I really know about Renwick Van der Daarke, other than that he and his ex-girlfriend had tricked and trapped me? Not much. In fact, I had the feeling that Renwick was, like myself, a consummate actor, a skill we'd both gained as a means of surviving in a harsh world.

But again, what choice did I have? There was no one else in Hawthorn Lane I could depend upon to this extent, not even Avice. Renwick and I were two people in need, and to get what we needed, we had to rely on each other. It wasn't an ideal situation, but it was all we had.

"You say that like you're some kind of warrior assassin," I challenged, my voice light, "and yet you play the role of ineffectual rake so perfectly."

He cocked a mischievous eyebrow at me. "Don't you think that role suits me?"

I laughed. "I suppose it does." I pushed in my chair. "Do you know what you're going to tell Matron?"

"The truth."

I regarded him skeptically. "Really?"

He feigned shock. "Of course."

"And how do you think she'll take it?"

"With her typical courage and aplomb."

"Ha! She's not going to let you go without a fight, you know."

"I'm very aware of that, Lorelle." He grinned charmingly. "That's why I'm leaving a note and sneaking out in the middle of the night."

"Coward." I pushed him toward the door. "Now go on. Mustn't be late. I don't want the downfall of your principles on my head."

"Until tonight, then." He nodded at me, then dashed out the door.

"I say there!" an elegant voice called out.

"Sorry, old chap!" Renwick apologized. "In a hurry."

I leaned out the doorway to see Charlton looking back at Renwick, a displeased expression marring his patrician features, which, according to his sister, might not be so patrician. Could it be true that Charlton and his siblings weren't their father's children? Or were they his, but birthed by another woman? I wasn't sure if I could believe Enchanté, but it was knowledge I would certainly bear in mind for the time when, or *if*, I returned to Hawthorn Lane.

"He has to get to work," I explained.

Charlton spun about. "Oh, Lorelle. I didn't notice you there." *If you had, I wager you would not have let me witness your obvious displeasure at seeing Renwick coming out of my cottage. But what business is it of yours, faerie?* I had to wonder. *Why would someone like you care about what someone like me does?* Because you want me to marry Kyran and end the curse? Because you want to get in good with the Omni? Or is there some other, less obvious, reason? Like the fact that your mother is plotting with my enemy to hook us up.

And then it hit me. Coriana didn't just want me for Charlton, she wanted Kyran for Enchanté. That's why she seemed so on edge around Lady Faylan. She was double dealing with her. *Oh, Coriana, you are messing with the wrong witch.*

"You had a visitor, I see," Charlton said when I didn't speak.

"How astute of you to notice. What can I do for you, Charlton?" Despite the growing heat of the day I kept my voice cool. I wasn't about to forget that he had been quite eager for me to sacrifice my own happiness to undo the curse, especially when I was quite sure there were other recourses. Plus, he had yet to meet Edan, and for some reason I wasn't ready for him to do so.

Judging by the nervous twitch in his left cheek, he had caught my coolness, even in such heat. "I wanted to see how you were doing."

"I'm fine. And you?"

"I, too, am fine, though concerned for your welfare. I heard about what happened at *Crystalline Vessels.* I wanted you to know that not for one moment did I believe the rumors about your involvement. I could never see you being so destructive. You're much too refined for such behavior."

"If you think that about me, Charlton, then you obviously don't know me very well."

His silvery eyes widened in surprise. "Excuse me?"

"Do I need to repeat myself?"

"No...it's just that I don't understand."

"I didn't destroy that shop, Charlton, but if I'd wanted to, I would've done it and not missed a wink of sleep over it."

He looked slightly taken aback. "I see."

I watched him for a moment, gauging his mood, his intentions, and decided it was time to take control of the conversation. Last time we'd spoken I'd lost hold of the reins; I would not let that happen again.

"So, Enchanté says that I have your family's support. I find that a bit odd, don't you?"

"You spoke to Enchanté?"

"In the flesh. It was an enlightening conversation."

"I see," he repeated himself, though I wasn't sure he saw as much as he claimed to. "Well, the thing of it is, Lorelle, we, the Iverich family, want you to know we are behind you one hundred percent."

"Why would your family support me?"

He stiffened. "Well, because you are our friend."

I gave a very unrefined snort. "Since when?"

He tugged ineffectually at his high white collar, as though the stiff cloth was trying to choke him. Granted, we did live in a magical place, so maybe it was. "Since you helped me at the ball, I suppose, saving me from numerous unwanted advances." He tried a self-deprecatory smile on me that I didn't buy for one second, and I certainly didn't return it. I wanted to know what he was up to, and I wanted to know now. "And for a long time you've assisted Hanover with his, uh, affliction," he went on, "and said not a word. You have always been kind to us." So he knew more about that than I'd thought.

"I've been useful to you, Charlton. There's a difference." I took a step closer to him. "Tell me the real reason your family is backing me like this." I'd already guessed the real reason, but it wouldn't hurt to have it confirmed.

To his credit, Charlton didn't shrink from my challenge this time, standing up straight and proud as he spoke. "For myself, I consider you a friend simply because you helped me at a time when I was in, shall we say, a weak position. For my father and mother, you are to be considered an asset because you're an Omni-Fey. They have proposed to myself and to my siblings that we do everything in our power to cultivate a relationship with you."

"Well, thank you for being honest, though I think it was more an order than a proposal."

"In that I fear you are right. My parents can be somewhat imperious."

"What a nice way of putting it."

His smile was genuine, and it momentarily humanized his controlled features. "And how would you put it, Lorelle?" He leaned forward, almost avidly, to hear my response.

"I'd call a spade a spade, Charlton. Your parents are overweening, overbearing, dictatorial prigs."

A delighted laugh slipped out of him and his hand rose to his mouth to block it, then dropped as though understanding the futility of the gesture. "That's one way to put it."

"In my mind, the only way." I paused and looked him over. "Now, can we get to the real reason you're here, Charlton? There are some things I have left to do today that cannot wait."

The laughter in his eyes slipped away, back into the darkness, and he gave me a slight bow. "Of course. I didn't mean to be a burden to you."

"Oh, stop playing the martyr, Charlton. I really do have things to do, and I need you to get to the point so that I can do them."

"I will do my best."

"I expect nothing less. Now chop, chop!"

His brow lowered and he said quietly, "I sense that you're angry with me."

"What was your first clue?" I sighed. "During your last visit you made it quite clear that you felt I should sacrifice myself for the good of the village. A village that has never exactly embraced me, and has since set out to blame me for something I didn't do. Your insensitivity didn't exactly endear you to me."

"I'm sorry for that, Lorelle. You're right that I came here for a reason. I knew I was in error and wanted to apologize for my mistake. I also wanted to explain why I said what I did."

I crossed my arms and regarded him suspiciously. "Go on."

"You know why I want you to end the curse, Lorelle? I want you to do it not for me, but for my family. It would be the saving of them. My parents would stop fighting, Hanover wouldn't flee to the Alterworld every chance he gets, and Enchanté would at last find meaning to her life."

"And you, Charlton? What would you get out of this?"

"I don't think I'm made to be happy, Lorelle."

"Again with the martyrdom."

He gave me a sad smile. "We all carry burdens."

"We do, and I wish relieving your burden was that simple, Charlton. You want me to marry a man whom I hardly know to fix a problem not of my making. Like you, I carry burdens and have since the day I was born. And I understand that sometimes we need to make sacrifices, and I've done that many times in my life. But when does it stop? When do *I* get to be selfish? When do *I* get to choose the life I want?"

Charlton sighed. "I've wondered these very same things, Lorelle."

I threw up my hands, feeling angry, helpless, and worse, trapped. "Then you of all people should understand what I'm saying!" If a person is to make a sacrifice, it should be done willingly, not forced on them. As mad as I was at the villagers right now, in the end, if sacrificing myself was the only answer, I'd probably do it. But not yet, not this way.

"My understanding changes nothing," he said, his voice tired. "We're still cursed. All of us, you included, and until that curse is removed, none of us will have what we want, what we *need*. We will all continue to suffer." He rubbed his forehead with two long, elegant fingers. "But that is neither here nor there. I came only to apologize and warn you, Lorelle. Please believe that. I know you do not trust my family, or myself, but I promise you I'm speaking the truth."

At last I caught on. "What is it that you're trying to tell me, Charlton?"

"There are forces here in Hawthorn Lane working against you, Lorelle, and you must take care."

"What forces?"

He looked around for a moment, his gaze seemingly unwilling to settle on mine. Then, at last, he met my eyes, his own glittering with tightly controlled anger. "The very man I wanted you to marry…Kyran Van der Daarke."

Chapter Twenty-Eight

"You're telling me Kyran Van der Daarke is working against me. What proof do you have?" I demanded, working hard to keep my chaotic feelings under control. It wasn't easy. Anger is a slippery beast, writhing and fighting with all its might to break free, and honestly, I was at a point where I would happily loose the beast. Though I wasn't sure if I'd aim it at Charlton for being the bearer of bad news, or at Kyran for betraying me.

"I possess only what I've heard with my own ears. Right before coming here, I visited the castle to check on a delivery of Effervescence and was waiting in the Great Hall to talk to the Count to assure myself he was satisfied with our services. I was studying a tapestry when I heard Lady Faylan speaking. I never saw her, mind you, but I'd know her voice anywhere. It is quite unmistakable." A cross between school marm and prison warden, it certainly was. "She was saying that it was time they made their move, that it was time to take care of their problem." He paused. "And then she said your name, Lorelle."

"So I'm the problem that needs to be taken care of, and soon, it seems."

"That's what it sounded like to me."

"Did you hear anything more?"

"No. But a minute later Kyran arrived in the Great Hall, and he looked distracted, as though something were weighing heavily on his mind."

"I see." Oh, for Grim's sake. Now I was saying it, though unlike Charlton I think I saw all too well which way the wind was blowing. "Thank you for letting me know, and for your apology."

He brushed this aside. "You know what this means, don't you, Lorelle? You can't marry Kyran Van der Daarke."

"I thought you wanted me to, no matter the cost to me."

His gaze slipped from mine. "I never wanted you to marry him. Not truly."

"Well, rest assured I don't plan on marrying anyone for a good long while, if at all."

My words didn't seem to soothe him as I intended; his eyes when they returned to mine were fervent. "So long as you don't marry *him* you'll be fine."

"I cannot—"

"Then do not." That was not what I'd been about to say, but Charlton hurried on before I could clarify what I meant. "I'm going to the Alterworld on business." He glanced at the sky. "In fact, I'm already running late. But I needed to tell you what I'd heard, and I needed to warn you. Promise me you'll be careful, Lorelle."

"I can only promise—"

Behind him the gate opened to admit yet another visitor, and I cut off what I'd been about to say, groaning inwardly. Really, with the exception of paying customers, I'd had more people dropping by my cottage in the last couple weeks than I'd had in my entire time living in Hawthorn Lane. Seeing who it was, I quickly, and with calculation, placed a hand on Charlton's arm. "Thank you so much for coming, Charlton. You're a life saver." I gave him my most charming smile, then nodded my head at Kyran, who was fast approaching.

Charlton spun about. "Count Van der Daarke," he greeted with a slight bow. "We meet again."

Kyran gave him a dubious look. "So we do. Twice in one day. What a coincidence." His tone was dry, his eye assessing.

"I thought I'd stop by and see if Lorelle needed anything before I headed home for the day." *Home for the day...*so he really didn't trust Kyran. Not enough to mention that he was leaving town anyway.

I gave Charlton's arm an affectionate squeeze. "You're so thoughtful, Charlton. What you've told me has been quite illuminating, and I'll most definitely consider it. I'll keep you updated on what I decide, as well."

"It was my pleasure, Lorelle." He reached out and lifted my hand from his arm, then bowed over it with the reverence of a subject toward his majesty. He surprised me as he placed his cool lips on the back of my hand, lingering just a tad too long for proper social etiquette, or maybe just proper Charlton etiquette. "Until we meet again?"

"I look forward to it. Stay safe, all right?"

"With all the intrigue going on these days, I will certainly try." He gave me a short bow, released my hand, then turned to Kyran. "Sir."

"Charlton."

Charlton shot me one last meaningful look, then strode down the walk. When the gate closed behind him, Kyran turned on me. "What was that all about?"

"Business," I said shortly. "What do you want? I thought I made it clear at our last parting that I was not happy with you."

He frowned. "You did?"

"Uh, yes. I was not subtle about it."

The frown deepened. "I don't recall that."

"Well, it happened."

"Being that it doesn't take much for me to ruffle your feathers," he said dryly, "I guess I shouldn't be surprised. At any rate, I came to warn you."

"Warn me about what?"

He looked around. "Can we go inside?"

I hesitated, not wanting to commit to a longer visit, or to being trapped inside with him, then relented. I didn't like being exposed like this, either, for the messenger birds to see, for Berenea to pounce, for the riff-raff to start throwing rocks. Plus, it was bloody hot outside.

"Fine. But just for a bit. I've things to do." I waved him inside, then followed, making sure to lock and bar the door behind me. The cottage, while warm, was at least a little cooler than standing in the glare of the sun.

"You're not still thinking of leaving early?" He indicated my to-do list for Renwick, which was on the table, as he sat down in the rocking chair by the fireplace.

I took a seat on the nearby chaise. "I'm not feeling the safest right now, so what do you think?"

"I guess I can't exactly blame you."

"Really?" He was giving in too easily, which meant he was up to something.

"Really. But I didn't come to talk about that. I came here to tell you about my sister."

"What about her?"

"She's up to something big, but I'm not sure what it is. She's taken over the west wing of the house"—*how appropriate*—"yes, I know," he said, as though reading my mind, or at the very least the expression on my face, "and has closed it off to myself, Ilia, and the staff. In fact, I think she might have hired her own staff. I hear her talking up there, and while I wouldn't put it past her to talk to herself, finding her own voice irresistible, I'm pretty sure the answering voice is different than hers. At any rate, I think she's planning to do something even worse than what she's already done."

I thought of my injured attacker, Carius, and wondered if that was Melaina's doing, and not my mother's. "What does Lady Faylan think about your theory?"

He glanced up, startled. "What do you mean?"

I kept my face blank. "I'm sure you've told her. Aren't you and she collaborating to save Hawthorn Lane?"

"Collaborating?"

"Braaah!" Edan squawked, and I nearly jumped ten feet in the air. I turned about to see him hopping down his ramp and coming toward us as fast as his four-toed feet could go.

"Do you need to eat?" I asked him.

"Brah," he replied in the affirmative, but instead of heading for the door, he waddled straight for Kyran, who reached out and patted Edan's bowed head.

"I think you've grown since I last saw you."

"He should pretty much be done with all that," I commented, looking the bird over.

"Then he's filling out. That's it. All muscle, right, Edan?"

"All muscle," Edan agreed, puffing out his chest proudly.

I stood and unbarred the door before opening it, and after one last pat from Kyran Edan followed. "Out you go. Just knock when you get back."

"Gone long time."

I lifted an eyebrow. "How long?"

He shrugged his winged shoulders. "Must explore."

"Don't tell me you've already got cabin fever?" But why not? I had it.

"Need to be ready," he croaked, and I felt a tingling sensation along my spine.

"Ready for what?" I whispered.

"For what comes."

That sounded ominous. "Be careful out there, Edan." I petted his downy head, letting my fingers slide through the soft patch of feathers. "And come home to me."

"I will."

As I watched him go, tendrils of doubt began to crawl through my body. What if something happened to him? What if someone connected him to me and hurt him to teach me a lesson? When he was gone, I reluctantly closed the door and barred it, wondering if this was the last time I'd see him.

"It's like you've had a crash course in parenting," Kyran noted when he saw my face.

"Would Melaina hurt him?"

"She might try, but I think Edan would be too formidable an opponent for her. Melaina prefers to go after the weak."

"*I'm* not weak."

"Not yet."

I grimaced. "What is she hoping to do? Scare me into marrying you?"

"It wouldn't be the first time a couple was forced into marriage."

"But I don't want to marry you!"

"I told you not to dwell on that part," he said calmly, as though unaffected by my words.

"I don't want to marry anyone right now," I felt compelled to explain, "and besides, I have an obligation elsewhere." He frowned at that, as though he didn't believe me. "I'm stuck, Kyran, between two worlds. It's not how I want it, but it is what it is."

"Don't go yet, Lorelle. I'm close to having an answer for you, at least regarding the curse, but I need more time."

"What are you going to do?" *Marry Lady Faylan?* Had it come so far so soon?

"Two more days," he said, his eyes going over my head, toward the conservatory. He shifted uncomfortably in his chair, then settled. "And then everything will become clear." I stared at him. The dark tone of his voice seemed a promise of extermination rather than illumination.

"You were just about to explain yourself," I said, watching his face, which had grown strange and tight, "and now you can't?"

"Something has come up. Suffice it to say that Lady Faylan and I are working on a way to fix everything."

So Charlton was right. "You need to stop saying that name in my presence."

"Lady Faylan will be quite upset to hear that you don't trust her, but you will come around, I feel quite sure of it."

My whole body started to tremble with a rage that felt like a volcano about to blow. Sparks began to leap from my fingers, quick as popping corn. "You need to leave."

He stood, patted my shoulder. "Two days, Lorelle." He pushed the words out, as though he hadn't wanted to speak them at all.

"Two days, Kyran, but this had better be good." I was lying through my teeth—I planned on leaving tonight—but he'd forced me into a deception by having the gall to invoke Lady Faylan's name in my home. *Again.* He knew how I felt about her, and I'd once thought he'd felt the same way. But his own words and actions, along with what Charlton had claimed to hear Lady Faylan saying in the castle, were working against him.

"I will leave you to your work." He hastened toward the door, lifted the bar and undid the lock. Suddenly he was in a hurry. "Keep yourself safe, Lorelle."

"You, too," I replied automatically.

He blinked slowly. "I hope you mean that." And then he was gone, out the door and very likely out of my life. I would probably never see Kyran Van der Daarke again, and the realization made me absolutely, and unsuitably, dismal.

Chapter Twenty-Nine

I spent the remainder of the day putting the personal papers in my study in order, hiding important documents, and clearing away anything that might possibly incriminate me or titillate Renwick. I couldn't pack my undergarments, but I wasn't about to leave them lying about for anyone to root through. When all that was done, I took the opportunity to practice my magic, using it to dust the entire cottage in a matter of minutes, then regretted doing so. Now I had time to spare before heading to Avice's for flying lessons, and I didn't want to spend it thinking about leaving the home I loved.

So I searched for more things to do. I edited my list for Renwick and spruced up all my plants for the tenth time. Then at last it was time to go. I left my door unlocked for Renwick, and my gloves on the table, deciding it might be prudent to have my sparks ready for release at any time. Besides, I was sick of hiding my true self. I had wanted to take Edan into town for protection, had been looking forward to riding him, but he'd yet to return.

After scanning the sky one last time, I set off for the village. Perhaps it was just as well that Edan didn't come with me, safer for him anyway. And there'd be no long, uncomfortable goodbyes, either. Still, I hated how this was ending. I didn't want to leave Hawthorn Lane, and I didn't want to leave Edan. I would miss the big lug. Really miss him.

The streets were quiet as I passed along them; most villagers were indoors at this time of night, either in the pubs, or home fast asleep. I hoped they'd stay there. While I was excited to learn how to fly, I was feeling more than a little jumpy about venturing into the village. I felt no inclination to meet up with an angry mob, but the idea of coming face to face with my mother was even more disturbing. Despite the evidence, I couldn't quite accept that she was here, defiling my home. Yet I wouldn't reject the idea, either; that would not be smart.

As I scurried along, the air felt dry and hot on my skin and in my lungs; the absence of the sun had done nothing to lower the temperature. Like a soldier on recon, I kept to the shadows, and my eyes open. When I at last made it to Avice's flat, I felt like the quarry who'd just outwitted her hunter.

For now, anyway.

Ensign opened the door to my knocker knocking. Peering up at me, his eyes rimmed with red, he stepped back without a word. "Everything all right?" I asked the obviously upset dwarf.

"That remains to be seen," he replied cryptically, then led me up to the ballroom where Avice was pacing the floor, her silken skirt swishing with every step. When she saw us, she stopped pacing, but made no effort to come forward to greet me. Her eyes were slightly puffy, a bit bleary, too, and I wondered if she'd been drinking. Probably. But her apparent weariness might also be from the oppressive warmth of the room. For being so hot-blooded, Avice was surprisingly not good with heat.

"Is it too late for our lesson?" I asked her as Ensign shut the doors behind him. "I didn't want to come too soon and risk running into all my adoring fans."

Avice regarded me with peevish eyes. "Do I look tired to you?"

"Frankly, yes."

"Oh, that's nice, Lorelle."

"Don't get all pissy with me, Avice. You asked the question, and I answered honestly. If you're tired, then we don't have to do this. It's very warm in here, you know. But I didn't want to risk coming any earlier when people were out and about and could see me. These days it's hard to tell who's friend or foe."

"Don't I know it."

I regarded her more closely. "You're mad at me."

"I am *not*. Are you ready to begin? Because I don't have all night. You're not my only friend, you know."

I studied her for a moment, a trickle of sweat sliding down my back. She was obviously angry with me…her pursed lips and dagger eyes made that apparent, but it seemed she was going to make me play a guessing game. What she didn't get is that I didn't have time for games tonight. "I'm ready when you are."

Avice met my eyes steadily. "Flying depends a lot on faith, you see. If you don't believe you can do it, then you can't."

"Makes sense."

"I'm surprised that makes sense to you."

I tamped down an irritated sigh. Avice was in a terrible mood, I could see, as could anyone with eyes, and she was aiming her ire at me. Something I'd done some time between now and when I'd seen her at my cottage had angered her. And it could be anything, from not kissing both her cheeks to being one second later than she thought I'd be.

"Of course it does," I snipped back. "It's not exactly rocket science. What else do I need to know?"

Her lips tightened. "You have to have absolute confidence in what your teacher—that's *me*—is telling you. If you cannot trust me, then we might as well quit right now." She crossed her arms over her chest, which was thrust forward as though readying itself to take a blow.

"I do trust you, Avice."

Her eyes simmered with doubt. "Do you, Lorelle?"

"Absolutely. So tell me what I need to do and I'll do it."

She scowled. "All right, fine. You must be able to imagine you're lighter than air, that you can swoop and soar like a bird." She turned her hands into wings and fluttered them up and about. "If you cannot see it, you cannot be it."

"I have an excellent imagination, Avice. In fact, my ability to imagine the worst has kept me out of all sorts of trouble."

Something spiteful pinched her flushed features. "We'll see about that. Close your eyes."

I did as I was told, keeping my other senses on high alert. Something was off with Avice tonight, and damned if I was going to let her get the drop on me. "Eyes are closed," I pointed out when no further instruction came. I heard her soft footsteps as she approached, felt her arm slip around my waist and her soft breath on my neck. She was slightly damp and warm, like a feverish child.

"Now imagine yourself growing lighter and lighter," she whispered seductively into my ear. "Like a feather caught in an updraft, you are rising upward and upward." I felt her grip tighten as she began to rise. I did not go with her. "Think light as a feather, Lorelle, and then you'll soar."

Light as a feather, light as a feather.

"It's not working," I said after numerous seconds passed without so much as me rising a centimeter. "I'm more like stiff as a board."

"Try harder," she urged. "And relax."

"I was trying hard enough, and I am relaxed. This isn't working for me."

"Stop being such a baby," she snapped, sounding a little more like her old self. "Try thinking of something else, then."

"Fine. And I'm not being a baby."

"Yes, you are, and by rights, I should let you figure out how to fly on your own," she grumbled, but she didn't let go of me.

"I said I'd try."

She didn't answer, and I breathed out through my nose, hoping to clear my mind of all its clutter. I'd never been one for doing yoga or relaxation techniques. My mind never allowed me to participate. But I had to come up with another way to imagine myself flying or stay earthbound for the rest of my life.

And then it came to me…an image of Edan shooting up into the sky, swift and sure. *That* I could imagine myself doing.

"Agh!" Avice cried out as we shot upward like a rocket. Her cry made me lose my concentration, and I opened my eyes to find us plummeting from several feet up in the air. Avice tried to slow our descent, but we were dropping too fast and we hit the floor hard. My knees buckled under our combined weight, and I fell backwards onto Avice's sprawled form. For several long seconds, we lay like that, unmoving, simply breathing in and out, mentally assessing the damage.

"Are you all right?" I finally asked, afraid of the answer, or lack thereof.

"When I pictured you in my arms, it was never like this."

"What?"

"Oh, you heard me." She shoved me off and sat up. "What were you trying to do?"

"I was doing what you said…thinking of something that would make me feel lighter."

"And nearly killing us in the process."

"It was an accident." I rolled over and sat up, facing her. "What's going on, Avice? You look like you want to spear me on a spit and roast me."

She looked away. "Lady Faylan stopped by this afternoon."

"Lady Faylan came to see you." I laughed. "No, seriously. What's really going on?"

Avice's eyes swung back to meet my gaze. "Why shouldn't she come see me? Am I not important enough or clever enough to warrant a visit from the village overseer?"

"That's not what I meant and you know it. Why would she come visit you, Avice? You two have never gotten along and everybody knows that, the two of you best of all."

"Well," she stuck her chin in the air, "it appears as though I was wrong about her."

"What do you mean?" I felt suddenly breathless. Kyran had said pretty much the same thing.

"She told me a few things about you, Lorelle."

"Listen, I can explain—"

"I don't want to hear your excuses," she interrupted, her voice nearly a screech. "Vira warned me you'd try to manipulate me with your smooth words."

Vira?

"Just what exactly am I being accused of, Avice?"

"All those men, Lorelle. How many do you need? First you try to take Kyran from me, from all of us in Hawthorn Lane, then you have to go after Renwick and Charlton? Even that walking scarecrow, Cutter Flint, isn't safe from your designs. You've gotten gifts from them. Visits. You were seen *dancing* with them!" Lady Faylan had been spying on me, though I couldn't help wondering how I had not seen this coming. "How could you?"

"What part are you mad about, Avice?" I asked coolly. "That I was getting attention from men, and you were not? Or that I never said anything to you about it because I knew you wouldn't like hearing it?"

"You never say *anything*," she accused. "I used to think it was because you had nothing to tell, but now I know it was because you had everything to hide. You kept things from me because all this time you've been using me."

"Using you? As you might recall, Avice, I was quite happy to keep my distance from you. You were the one who sought me out."

"More fool me," she replied bitterly.

"And those visits? You're making way more out of them than there is…" Except for the visits from Cutter. There was definitely something behind those, but I hadn't invited him to my cottage. He'd come himself, with nefarious intentions, I felt sure. But I would not, could not, let on to Avice, or to anyone, that I'd been caught by him, that he held power over me. I had my pride, though I felt quite sure it was going to goeth before my fall. "Listen, Avice…let's not argue. I'm leaving Hawthorn Lane. Tonight, actually, and I came to say goodbye."

"Goodbye?" For the first time this evening, her angry mask slipped. "What do you mean, Lorelle? Where are you going?"

"I'm going back to the Alterworld. I don't want to go, but I have to. All these things you think I've done to hurt you have nothing to do with you. They relate only to what's going on with me. The curse, the attacks, that impersonator pretending to be me. Someone is trying to bring me down, and it's time I left before somebody gets hurt, either myself or someone I care about."

Her lower lip jutted out. "You're lying."

"I'm not lying. I have no reason to. There's more, Avice. Being in danger isn't the only reason I'm leaving Hawthorn Lane. There's something I have to make right with someone in the Alterworld."

"Who?"

"Someone I once loved."

"Loved?" She looked staggered. "You love someone else?"

"Not anymore. But I did him a wrong and now I need to make amends.

Someday, when all this blows over and I no longer have to fear for your safety, I'll return and tell you everything. I'm sorry if I hurt you before. You've been a good friend to me."

I leaned forward, my intent to share one last embrace, but she pulled back from me, her eyes burning bright. "You're lying to me, just like she said you would."

I checked my movement. "I'm sorry you feel that way. I'm telling the truth, and one day you'll see that. I hope that my leaving will save Hawthorn Lane. Lady Faylan and Kyran can marry and break the curse and you can all be happy."

She pushed herself to her feet and backed away as though I'd suddenly sprouted fangs. "I won't let you go, Lorelle."

"I'm afraid you don't have a choice."

Her features twisted. "Oh, really?" She ran to a window and flung it open, letting in a warm waft of dry air. "She's here! Lorelle Gragan is here!"

"What are you doing?" I hissed, wishing I'd waited and brought Edan with me after all.

Avice turned to face me. "It's time to pay the piper, Lorelle. It's time to make up for all those years you spent pretending to be someone else. You thought you weren't fey, but you pretended to be one so that you could trick us into liking you. Your great-grandmother cursed this village, and you act like you're entirely innocent!" So Lady Faylan had told Avice about my deception. She had broken her promise to me.

I heard shouting out in the streets, and I joined Avice at the window. Lights were turning on, doors were slamming. The mob was gathering. "They'll tear me limb from limb," I said in a low voice.

Beside me Avice stiffened. "No, they won't. They'll simply see to it that you do what you're supposed to do."

"And what is that, Avice?"

"Marry Kyran and break the curse, of course."

"I thought you wanted Kyran for yourself."

For a moment she looked confused. "No. I want you. I mean, I want to be happy!" she quickly amended. "She said I'd be happy, that if you did this I could finally settle down and be content with one person. She promised me!"

"So you decided that I was expendable? That our friendship means nothing to you?"

"It means nothing because you lied to me, and don't you pretend otherwise!"

"Don't you understand that I don't want to leave? I love it here, and

I don't want to be anywhere else but Hawthorn Lane."

Her lower lip trembled. "I don't believe you."

"But you'll believe Lady Faylan, who has never had a kind word for you ever. She's looked down on you for years, and now suddenly she's your friend? Don't you find that suspicious?"

Avice's eyes darted about. "I don't know! She said so many things. She made you look so hateful!"

I stared at the crowd gathering down below and was reminded of every Frankenstein movie I'd ever seen. Only this time I was the monster.

"They're going to kill me, Avice."

"No, they won't. They need you to stop the curse."

"Do you really think Lady Faylan wants me to have Kyran?"

"She promised," she said feebly.

"She wants me out of the way, one way or another, so that she can have him for herself."

"But she came here," Avice insisted. "She said you had to make things right."

"It wasn't her who came," I said grimly.

She rolled her eyes. "I think I know what Lady Faylan looks like, Ms. Know-It-All."

"There's already been one incident of impersonation."

Her mouth gaped open. "No. It's not possible."

"It's very possible. I didn't damage Atlene's store. I had no reason to do it."

"All right, if it wasn't her, then who was it?"

"I think it was Melaina Van der Daarke."

"No way. Whoever this was had to be quite gifted. I've heard Melaina is only third-rate, magic-wise. She couldn't have done this."

Then who? My mother? My aunt? Were they this talented? If so, why hadn't they ever shown their magical abilities before now? Perhaps to keep me ignorant, and my powers limited. But how could they have resisted using magic all that time? I just couldn't believe they could, and I would've noticed them doing it some time during the eighteen years I'd lived with them.

So maybe they weren't the intruders, and that made me nervous— better the devil you know, right? So if it wasn't them, who was it? Fey-hunters? If that were the case, Lady Faylan would have captured them by now, or at least put out a stronger warning. Something was terribly wrong about all this, but I couldn't put my finger on what it was. Someone was setting me up, but who? The entire village?

"You have to get me out of here, Avice." The scene I'd witnessed in

Cutter's lair—the one showing the French Revolution—came back to me. How prescient that had been, almost too prescient. Cutter must know something, too, maybe even was in on it. "The villagers won't be thinking clearly," I went on. "They're angry with me and want me to pay for their misery. If my best friend can turn on me, what do you think they'll do?"

"Am I still your best friend?"

"That remains to be seen," I said coolly. "You chose to believe Lady Faylan over me, *and* you sicced a mob on me."

Her eyelids flickered with guilt. "I'll get you out of this, Lorelle. I'll do it."

"How?"

"How else?" She pushed the window open wide. "We'll fly."

Chapter Thirty

"I'm not exactly an expert at flying, remember?" I reminded her as I looked down at the gathering crowd. A number of them were looking up at us, peering through the darkness as they attempted to make us out.

"You aren't going to do the flying," she said. "I am."

"How are you going to lift me?"

"I'm stronger than I look, and besides, I told you I've been getting more powerful lately. Magically speaking, that is. I can do this." She pulled back her round shoulders determinedly.

"So you're going to lift me up and fly out of here? Just like that?"

"Why not?"

"Because it's crazy."

Avice's head swiveled back toward the door to the ballroom. "Do you hear that?"

I did hear it. A shout, followed by another. "They got inside. Any other way out of here? An attic, maybe? Or a back staircase?"

"Nope," she responded, more smugly than the situation warranted. "You've no choice but to fly out of here." She threw her thumb at her ample chest. "With me."

"I guess you're right," I said grimly, thinking back to all the different times I'd had to fight just to keep from getting screwed over by everyone who came into contact with me. "I was never given any choice in any of this, was I, Avice?"

Her blue eyes welled with tears. "I didn't mean to betray you, my love! I was"—she snapped her fingers—"I was bewitched! Lady Faylan was so believable. You wouldn't believe how believable she was! She said all these things about you that sounded so real."

"And all of them lies."

"And all of them lies," she repeated in a wobbly whisper, and I hoped she included my deception about my fey in her statement. "That means I have to make things right with you. I have to save you, Lorelle, or I'll never forgive myself. I'll die from it. I'll drown myself in Watery Grave Pond and end up in Atermorte Cemetery, my lovely flesh turning to bones and dust, and what a waste that would be."

"What a waste that would be," I echoed.

The sound of feet pounding up the steps drifted down the corridor, into the ballroom. "All right, Avice, we'll give it a try. But be quick." In two swift strides, I was behind her. I wrapped my arms around her corseted waist and pulled her to my chest. "I hope you can hold me, but if I get to be too much to carry, then tell me, and I'll let go."

"I can't just let you fall, Lorelle. You'll die!"

"Better than both of us."

"She's not in here!" a thick voice rumbled.

"Ready?" Avice asked, sounding excited.

"She must be in the ballroom!" another voice shouted, and footsteps rushed our way.

"Ready," I said, as the doors opened behind us.

"There they are!"

Avice took a deep breath, exhaled, and with it, we lifted off the floor as easily as though a giant had picked us up. Light as dandelion seeds, we floated out the window. A hand reached out to grab my skirt and I shot sparks at it. There was a yelp and the arm withdrew.

Avice maneuvered us farther out, and when I looked down at the twenty-foot drop I tightened my hold. "Oh, I like that, Lorelle," Avice gasped. "Though if you could move your hands a little higher."

"Focus, Avice!" I exclaimed as we began to drop.

"I'm trying to," she answered in a low, seductive voice.

"Wrong subject."

"Oh, fine," she grumped. She breathed in once more, exhaled, and we rose higher into the air. I looked about, impressed; the view over the lit-up village was amazing. If we weren't being hunted, I'd find it rather nice up here, especially as it was a bit cooler.

"Up there!" a young woman screeched from the street below. "They're flying!"

"Oh, murder!" Avice cursed. "They've spotted us."

"I'm letting go," I said as we swayed precariously. "Get yourself somewhere safe."

"Don't you dare," she growled. We straightened out a bit, then rose higher, just barely clearing a chimney on the next-door building. "I mucked things up with you," she pushed through gritted teeth. "It won't happen again." *Yeah, right.* "It won't!"

"Stop reading my mind."

"I did just do that, didn't I?"

"I'd applaud, but my hands are a bit occupied."

"Not really. They aren't even doing anything."

"They're keeping me from falling."

Big sigh. "You aren't any fun, Lorelle. So where do you want to go?"

"My place, I suppose. I have to make sure Edan's all right, then make a run for it."

"I don't want you to go."

"I don't want to go, either, but right now it looks as though the Alterworld is the safest place for me."

We cleared the next building and came out on the other side. A piercing voice cried out from below us, "There they are!" then a whistling noise whizzed past my ear.

"Someone's shooting at us," I warned Avice.

"A pox on them and their snotty children!" she howled.

Swerving back around toward the building we'd passed, she began to fly over the rooftops. In front of us a dormer window opened and a pointy-eared figure leaned out. Spotting us, the elf tried to grab my leg as we passed. I kicked at her reaching hands, making Avice wobble and throwing off her steering. The elf missed her target, but we ended up veering toward a chimney. Unable to adjust in time, my left shoulder smacked against the brick, sending shockwaves of pain through my body, and I let go of Avice.

Avice screeched as I hit the roof with a thud. I began sliding down, rapidly picking up speed. I kicked out, hoping to catch onto something with my feet to slow my descent, but no such luck. Seconds later I shot off the roof and plummeted to the cobblestone street below.

I landed hard, my knees crumpling beneath me as I let my body collapse. I tucked into a roll, ending up on my hind end, ankles stinging and shoulder throbbing, but alive, and no broken bones. I looked up to see where I had landed and groaned when I read the sign for *Fawn's Fashions*.

Higher up, Avice peered over the edge of the roof. "Are you all right?"

I waved her back. "I will be. Stay out of sight."

The door to the shop swung open. "Well, well, well," Dawn drawled, peering down at me. "Look what the pussy dragged in." She glanced up. "Go hide yourself, Avice. I've got this."

"But I'm supposed to be rescuing her, Dawn."

"And a fine job you're doing of it, you bird-witted bit of baggage," she muttered. Then, louder, "They know she's with you, so you need to split up. I'll take it from here, all right?"

"But—!"

"Just go, Avice," I urged her. "I can't let you get caught up in this." With great forbearance I refrained from mentioning that *she* was the reason *I* was caught up in this.

"When will I see you again?" she asked plaintively.

"As soon as I can get away," I replied, keeping my answer vague. The sound of voices grew louder. "Now go before we're both caught."

She nodded, then blew me a kiss before pulling back from the edge of the roof and disappearing. The voices that had been growing nearer suddenly veered off. "She's going that way!" several cries went up at once. Grim bless her, Avice had set herself up as a diversion.

Taking advantage of the villagers' mistake, Dawn reached down and grabbed my arm, yanking me to my feet with surprising strength. With all the 'operations' she'd gone through I had to wonder if maybe they'd replaced a majority of her body with robotic wiring. "I locked my sister in her room so she won't get in the way. It was the best I could do on the spur of the moment." She cocked her head. "They're heading that way," she nodded down the street, "which means you need to go that way." She pointed toward Savage Mountain and the castle. "Now go before you drag my innocent self into your scandalous affairs." She turned me around and aimed me at the road toward the castle.

I looked back at her. "I thought you were going to help me only in spirit?"

She grinned wickedly. "Lucky you that I got drunk tonight."

I studied her for a moment. "You've changed, Dawn."

"I'm simply taking your advice, Lorelle. Let's hope it doesn't get me killed. Now get out of here before we both go down for your trespasses."

I took a step, then turned around. "Just so you know… I'm leaving town for a while and Renwick will be staying in my cottage. Perhaps you should pay him a visit. It can get quite lonely out there."

"Loneliness is a terrible thing."

"It is. Good luck, Dawn."

"What's luck got to do with it when I look like this?" She ran her hands over her model-like torso.

"Just know that he's not all he seems."

"I like that in a man. Now get out of here before I turn you in myself for the reward money."

Reward money?

There was no time to ask for details; I had to move. "I'll see you later."

"Only if I'm in hell, cause that's where you're going, you bloody reprobate."

"Oh, goody. I've always wanted to see where you were born."

"Ha, ha. Very funny. No, wait." She snorted. "Actually, that was pretty funny…and true." She stepped forward and shoved me. "Now go, you bobble-headed bimbo."

I went. It was dark out, but I could see well enough to find the road leading up to the mountain, and I made my way toward it. At any moment I expected to hear someone cry out that I'd been spotted, and yet it was still a surprise when someone did.

"She's heading to the castle!" an old witch sounded the alarm, damn her eyes.

I thought about taking a right turn and dashing into the woods, but changed my mind when I saw movement amongst the trees, keeping pace with me. Friend or foe, I couldn't say, but if it was Rialban, I wanted nothing to do with the centaur. If he caught me, he'd carry me off to Kyran, the last person I wanted to see right now.

But it seemed I was being given little choice in the matter, my escape routes cut off by the mob and my forest stalker. I was heading into Van der Daarke territory whether I liked it or not, and wondered if I was ever going to be able to leave this place.

I glanced back to get a feel for how many people I was dealing with, and came up with fifty or sixty villagers marching my way. Several were carrying torches, and I wouldn't have been surprised to find a few pitchforks amongst the rabble. Someone on horseback joined the pack, and in the firelight I recognized Merceen Arie. The proud woman looked to be in her element, leading an angry horde of howling Hawthornites to take me down.

Now was the time to skedaddle. I picked up my skirts and began to sprint up the steepening dirt road. I'd always been really fast, but now that I knew my uncanny quickness came from being fey, I figured I could go even faster if I put some thought into it. I concentrated on sending energy waves to my feet, to my legs, to my pumping arms, and felt an exhilarating burst of speed push my body forward.

A few backward glances told me I was putting considerable space between myself and the mob. At this rate, I could outdistance the villagers and my stalker, and at some point would be able to veer off down the path through the woods that led to my cottage.

But then the story changed. I felt rather than saw a presence high above me, and with a quick glance confirmed what I'd sensed. Overhead flew several witches and warlocks whizzing along in tight formation on their brooms. It seemed a most uncomfortable way to travel, but they managed it quite efficiently. The only group I could imagine showing such skill was Lady Faylan's Mage Patrol. Which meant she was not only aware of where I was, but was preparing for some sort of action on my part. She knew I was going to run. But why try to stop me? It was in her best interest to let me leave Hawthorn Lane. So maybe she had something else in mind, something painful.

I was going to have to brave the forest and hope for the best. If I en-countered Rialban, I'd put my original plan into place, flying right over that bastard's bald head and to freedom…and hopefully not dying in the process.

I turned slightly, then picked up speed, racing toward the trees. Only a little farther, I told my heaving chest, and I'll be in. But then a light-ning bolt shot from the sky and smashed into the ground only a few yards from where I was heading, sending up a heat wave of sparks. I turned at the last second, skidding and sliding, but managed to stay on my feet, and kept moving forward. Ten yards to the tree line. I could make it…

Another bolt, closer this time. Then another. Soon the white-hot spears were raining down on me, heating the air and turning the black of night to near-day. When I turned back toward the road the deluge slowed. I ran for twenty yards, then tried again to make it to the woods, a move that set off a fresh storm of hot bolts.

I was being herded like a stray calf.

Right toward the castle.

So much for my brilliant plan.

Chapter Thirty-One

I had no choice. The only place left to go was Castle Daarke, where very likely a trap set by Lady Faylan and Kyran awaited me. Accepting my fate, I sprinted toward the massive building looming in the distance. I picked up speed, hoping to outrun the mage parade, but they kept pace with me, some even passing me to go on ahead. I thought about trying to fly, then decided against it. Being that I wasn't even sure I could do it without leaving orbit, it was something I'd resort to only if I was keenly desperate, and right now, I was only mildly desperate.

The castle gates were open, as though expecting me. I raced under the archway and into the courtyard, my labored breath hissing in my ears. The anguished rasping of my gown echoed across the wide-open space, and the pressing warmth of the air surrounded me like a steam bath.

Halfway across the cobbled yard, I pulled up straight, nearly skidding to a stop. Someone was coming out of the castle, and I stood still, waiting to see which way to run. Around me the mages jumped from their brooms to the ground, and the sound was like dud bombs landing on grass. Dressed all in black, my uninvited escorts blended into the night, even as burning torches illuminated the darkness. They kept their distance from me, but I was trapped within their ring of twelve. I could guess who number thirteen of their little coven was…Lady Faylan.

For it was her coming outside, descending the steps as though lady of the manor. Her movements were swift and light, completely unlike her usual ponderous step. She must be happy to see me here, happy to have corralled me like a wild animal, happy to have won.

"So glad you could make it," she addressed me. "Though it took some doing to pull you here. You're a stubborn one."

I used the back of my hand to wipe sweat off my brow. "I'm not one of your lackeys, Lady Faylan. You can't just order me about like a mindless monkey."

A slight shifting rippled through the troops, as though my words rankled, exactly as I'd meant them to. "Don't overestimate yourself. You always did find yourself superior, didn't you?"

"Me? Superior? That's a laugh." Behind me, the din of the mob grew louder. Soon they'd be here.

"Do you see me laughing? You always lorded it over me, always had things I never did, always acted like you were better than me. And now you're in this exalted position that by rights should be mine. I'm sick of it."

"What are you talking about? You live in a mansion. You're Dynast Overseer. You practically run this place. Other than having Kyran Van der Daarke as a suitor and being an Omni-Fey," I added maliciously, "what could I have that beats all that?"

A wariness flashed across her features and she straightened as though suddenly remembering that people were watching. She indicated the mob. "You're obviously no longer welcome in Hawthorn Lane. It's my time now. I've waited long enough for this moment, and I expect to make the most of it."

I stared at her in disbelief. "Have you lost your mind, Lady Faylan?"

She threw back her head and released a long, seductive laugh that echoed ominously about the courtyard. "Au contraire. I've finally found it."

The door to the castle swung open and a strident figure stormed out, stopping on the landing and peering about. Melaina Van der Daarke had arrived. Behind her trotted Ilia, her face wet with tears.

"What's going on here?" Melaina demanded, facing Lady Faylan. She was starting to take on the Hawthorn Lane accent, but somehow it didn't sit right with her. "Lady Faylan, what are you doing here? If I've told you once, I've told you a thousand times, my brother is not for you, you harpy. Now leave this place before I have you thrown out!"

This was unexpected.

"You and whose army?" Lady Faylan drawled, then swept her arm toward the circle of mages.

"Oh, please. They might be your toadies, but they wouldn't dare anger a Van der Daarke."

Melaina caught sight of me. "So you've finally come to your senses, hm, Lorelle?"

"I'm not here of my own accord, Melaina."

She smirked. "Oh? How odd."

"I know what you've been up to. You were the one who impersonated me, weren't you? You made people think I'd destroyed Atlene's shop when I hadn't. That I'd hurt Carius when I wasn't anywhere near him."

Her laugh was malicious. "That wasn't me, you brainless twerp. When those things happened, I was at home." She threw a manicured hand back at Ilia. "Just ask my daughter. Speak up, darling. One would think you didn't have a tongue. Or a brain."

"It's true," Ilia said softly, not looking at me. "She was here."

"At any rate," Melaina went on, "I'm not the one on trial here. Your ancestor made the curse, Lorelle, not mine."

I had loads to say about that, but kept my counsel. I looked over Melaina's shoulder, deciding now was the time for a diversion. "Where's Rennie?" I asked, using her pet name for her ex-lover.

Her lips flattened into two disapproving lines. "I heard I have you to thank for his little disappearing act. I know you're responsible for his leaving me, Gragan, you and that hag friend of yours. But get this straight, he's not yours, nor will he ever be. Rennie and I have a connection between us that nothing can break. He might have left me, but I hold no anger toward him." *Yeah, right.* "You doubt me, but who do you think made sure the villagers treated him right when he'd taken that horrible job?" *So that's why they'd been okay with him working as a waiter. I thought they might actually have moved beyond all that judgment stuff. Silly me.* "I'm sure he simply wanted to prove his manhood. No man likes to be kept." She took a step closer. "He loves me, Lorelle, and only me, and as soon as this damn curse is broken we'll be together again. I won't let it happen any other way." Her face, which had hardened to granite during her little speech, softened a little and her voice turned wheedling. "You and Kyran are meant to be. I suggest you take him and run." She looked me up and down. "You'll never get a better offer."

I drew myself up. "You can't make me marry your brother, Melaina, not through your tricks or coercion or lies."

She nodded in the direction of the gate. "Oh, but they can."

Before I could turn around, Kyran strode out the door, his expression thunderous. "What the devil is going on?" His eyes found me. "Lorelle? I thought I felt your presence. What are you doing here?" He took in the sea of torches approaching the castle, the mages encircling me like prison bars, then Lady Faylan, looking triumphant, and the pieces fell into place. "What have you done now, Melaina?" he growled at his sister.

"I simply applied a little pressure," she replied breezily. "The rest happened on its own."

"A little pressure? You pretended to be Lorelle and created havoc in the village."

"As I've already told Lorelle, I impersonated no one." Her expression grew sour. "I'm not yet at that level of skill."

"Then who did it?" I turned to Lady Faylan. "Was it you?"

She shrugged. "What if it were?"

It was in that moment that I realized something that I hadn't understood before, but now that I did, I couldn't believe I hadn't seen it sooner. "You're not really Lady Faylan, are you?"

The mages closest to me straightened up. "What is she talking about, Dynast Overseer?" the young warlock to my left dared to ask.

She wrinkled her nose. "I haven't the slightest."

"Liar!" I cried. "Show your true self, or I'll do it for you, and you can imagine how that might turn out from an untrained Omni-Fey. I could end up turning you inside out."

Lady Faylan laughed, though it sounded forced. "Oh, fine, though it took you long enough, Lori." *Lori?* So it really was my mother who'd been the troublemaker all this time.

A shimmering effect hazed over Lady Faylan's form, and like wax her features melted away, replaced one part at a time with a variation on the theme. Her hair uncoiled, her clothes transformed from severe to revealing, and a fresh cut, which she'd undoubtedly gotten from fleeing through broken glass, could be seen on her now bare right arm. The shape of her face changed, though the derision in her shrewish brown eyes, the contempt curling her pencil-thin, pink-glossed lips remained. I took in her new womanly figure, slender yet shapely in a pink spandex dress. She remained taller than me, especially in the black stilettos she wore, but only by a bit. Her brown hair reached nearly to her waist, and was all one length, with chunks of blond highlights that seemed more brassy than classy. Her fake eyelashes and heavy eye makeup made her look more like an anime character than a real person. I'm not sure what look she was going for, but tramp came to mind.

"Eudrea?" I had *not* seen this one coming.

"You always were quick, Lori," my sister sneered at me, her close-set eyes filled with contempt. She looked me over, head tilting to one side, showing off her chin dimple to its best advantage. "You're wearing your hair long now. Looks like I blew it on that one. It's always the details that catch you up, am I right?" She appealed to the mages, who were all looking at her with matching expressions of dismay and confusion.

"Why, Eudrea?"

"I even tried to make you think you'd done it, you know, sending you that dream," she replied, treating my question like she treated most of them, as though she hadn't heard it. "I mean, wouldn't that have been the goddamned icing on the cake? Set you up, then make you believe you were guilty, too? Ummm, sweet as sugar. Your greatest weakness always has been your conscience. Get rid of that, Lori, and someday, in the distant future, you could be someone."

Kyran stepped forward, taking care to shield Ilia from this stranger. I envied her a bit. "Who are you?"

Eudrea nodded at me. "Care to make the introductions?"

No, I did not care to make the introductions. But better from my mouth than her lying one. "This is my sister, Eudrea," I spoke through dry lips. "She must have been the intruder who triggered the breach. She was also the one who pretended to be me and destroyed Atlene's shop. I'm pretty sure she hurt Carius, too. She was setting me up, though I'm not sure why." But I did know it was comforting that this hadn't been a conspiracy involving the entire village. Yes, there was a mob of villagers out for my blood, and they probably still wanted to blame me for everything, but they had been bewitched by Eudrea. And that made all the difference.

Kyran turned on Melaina, his expression fierce. "Did you bring her here?"

She pouted a little. "I might have suggested she pay us a visit. She was only too happy to comply when she understood what was at stake."

Oh, she'd done more than suggest Eudrea pay a visit...she'd conspired with her. They'd put on a little show for Charlton, making him believe Lady Faylan was planning something so he would come tell me all about it. *Time they made their move, time to take care of the problem.* Though Melaina had screwed up, because Charlton had assumed she was talking to Kyran, and Melaina wouldn't want to put me off Kyran.

Yes, Eudrea, it's the little details that can ruin everything.

"Did you bring Mother or Aunt Nimair with you?" I demanded, remembering that someone else had been with her when she'd broken into my cottage. I looked around, dread growing inside me. I did not want to be caught off-guard around any one of my relatives. "I know you had a partner."

Eudrea's smug complacency slipped a little. "Why would you think I had someone with me?"

"I saw her."

"Her? Your eyes have grown weak, Sister. There was no *her.*"

My mind spun. Eudrea always lied through her teeth, even about inconsequential things, but she also always kept an element of truth in her lies. When she'd said, 'no *her*,' maybe she was telling the truth. "It was a him, then," I deduced. "I didn't get a close look at whoever it was, just assumed it was Mother and Aunt Nimair coming to make my life miserable. Now I'm thinking it was you and someone else."

Someone who knows me, I didn't add, remembering what Kyran had said the first time my cottage had been breached. *I feel that one of them is connected to you by blood, the second, I'm not sure about. There's seems to be a link, but in some other way.*

Some other way. That was the key.

Eudrea took a subtle step backward, then another. "You were imagining things." An edge to her voice made each word sharp as a blade to the skin. "As usual."

"Like when I imagined you having sex with my boyfriend?"

"It wasn't like that!" a voice cried out, and I looked up to see Josepha push past Ilia and run down the steps, stopping just outside the ring of mages. He held out his hands in a pleading gesture. Ilia's face was pale and somber, but she did not look surprised to see him doing this.

"Josepha? *You* were Eudrea's partner? How could you?"

"Well, you see, that's just it. I'm not Josepha." A moment passed, and then, quick as a blink, a nearly transparent figure separated from the elf like a shadow coming to life. Slowly the outline of the body solidified, and with every passing second it grew more substantial. Ilia let loose a little scream when Josepha sank to his knees, holding his head. But she didn't move to go to him, standing frozen like the rest of us as we watched the strange scene unfold.

"Dallen?" I whispered, recognizing my old lover. He looked a little older, his cheeks a bit more hollow, his jaw more defined and his blue eyes shadowed. He was less of a pretty boy now, more mature. "What are you doing here? How did you get into Hawthorn Lane?" I paused, remembering I'd just witnessed him walk out of Josepha's body. "You're fey," I said in a cold, hard voice. "That's how."

"Do you think your mother would've allowed me to be with you if I weren't, Lorelle?"

"I don't know what to think anymore." I glanced back over my shoulder. Judging by the tremors beneath my feet and the increasing noise outside the castle walls, I had about a minute tops before the angry horde arrived. Really, they should already be here—the road to the castle was not terribly long—and I wondered what or *who* was delaying them. The image of my forest stalker came to mind. Rialban? Perhaps. If so, I just might have to forgive him for taking me hostage. "Why are you here, Dallen?"

"I came to bring you home, Lorelle. I never stopped loving you. You thought I'd been with Eudrea that day, but I truly thought it was you. I told you that, begged you to believe me." My cheeks warmed as I remembered refusing to even consider any other alternative. "What I didn't realize until years later was that she'd tricked me." He turned to glare at Eudrea, his nostrils flaring. "As you can see, she's quite adept at impersonating people."

"Shut your trap now, Dallen," Eudrea hissed, her fist raised. "Or I'll shut it for you!"

"She made me forget for a good long time," he went on, ignoring her. "But I remember everything now."

"You always knew!" my sister screeched at him.

"Lorelle?" Kyran called in a commanding voice, and I swear I could feel it in my chest. "Are you all right? Who is this boy?"

I peered up at the man the entire village wanted me to marry. He stood at the top of the steps looking so proud and impossibly strong that I felt tempted to run to him. But I couldn't trust him. He was with Lady Faylan now, and that I couldn't forgive or forget. I should never have let myself feel anything for him, and now I was paying the price for it. I knew better. Get close to someone and they will burn you... even if they don't mean to.

"I told you I had to go home to take care of something, Kyran. This is it. I have to make amends to Dallen for not believing him all those years ago."

"You were coming back to me?" Dallen said, his eyes alight. "You know I wasn't to blame?"

"I must make amends," I repeated dully. "But now you're here, with Eudrea, who's trying to ruin my life. *Again.* Why are you with her, Dallen, if you know she tricked you?"

"She only thinks I'm with her," he said quickly. "Once she told me where you were and what was going on with the curse, I agreed to help her. But really, baby, I came to rescue you."

"Liar!" Eudrea screamed at him. "You love me, and you know it. We've been together ever since that day," she declared triumphantly to me. "Ask Mother, or Aunt Nimair. They'll tell you." Again, I had to sort through the words to find the truth. Dallen might not love her, not like a woman would want, but I sensed he had been with her all this time. Thinking I'd abandoned him why not go with the person who would hurt me the most? Then again, he claimed not to remember the incident with Eudrea because she'd messed with his memory of it. And he had said that when he'd confronted me all those years ago.

"You loved him?" Kyran had left the landing and was coming down the stairs at a rapid pace. "Do you still love him, Lorelle?"

"I don't know why you care about my affairs," I replied coolly. "You have Lady Faylan now."

"Lady Faylan? What does she have to do with any of this? You know I don't care for that woman."

"Drop the act, Kyran. I'm not buying it."

"It's not an act," he growled.

"It seems you're surrounded by liars," Dallen rushed to say. "I'm the only one who never lied to you, Lorelle." He held out his hand to me. "Return home with me, and we can pick up where we left off. I'm a lawyer now. I make good money." He gave me the dimpled smile I remembered, the one that used to melt my heart. "We'll have a good life."

"Now see here, *boy*," Kyran snarled, coming to stand by my side. I could feel his intensity, his electric presence, and wondered how I was going to live without it. I'd already grown to miss it. "Lorelle isn't going anywhere."

"I think that's up to Lorelle," Dallen said in a threatening voice.

The roaring of the mob suddenly intensified, as though a muffler had been removed, and we all spun around in one choreographed movement. Whatever had been delaying the villagers was no longer doing so. The increased noise was making it hard to hear, hard to think straight. I had to get away, had to work all this out before I committed to anything. But I was trapped, and these people weren't going to let me go anywhere.

"It's her!" a voice screamed, that same old witch who'd spotted me in the village. It was a voice I was starting to hate. A mass of villagers poured though the gates, led by Merceen on a massive silvery white charger. The mages, realizing their leader wasn't who they'd thought, decided now was the time to get out. In unison, they lifted into the air, leaving me exposed to the rampaging crowd. Hovering on the fringe, riding her ratty old broom, was Berenea. Pipe clenched between her snaggleteeth, the oversized witcharazzi somehow managed to fly, smoke, and write, all at the same time, though her capotain hat sat somewhat precariously on her head, likely knocked askew in her race to get here for the story of the century.

Merceen, spotting Kyran, pulled her horse up, then turned it around so that she remained toward the back of the crowd. The elf wasn't entirely stupid, and didn't want to risk angering Kyran, even now, in the midst of chaos. She would bide her time, then pounce when he wasn't looking.

Kyran stepped in front of me so that he stood between me and the horde. "Stop right there!" he boomed, and his voice echoed all around us like cannon shot. Startled, the mob skidded to a halt, the ones in back pushing into the ones in front, knocking rows to the ground like fat dominoes. From the chaos emerged one figure…Lady Faylan; unscathed, she glided across the courtyard as though floating, as perhaps she was. "What is the meaning of all this, Count Van der Daarke?"

"You mean this little party you and he cooked up?" I accused. "I know you two are conspiring against me."

Kyran spun around, his expression furious. "I don't know where you got that idea, Lorelle. I've only been trying to help you."

"And yet here I am, at Castle Daarke, run to ground like a wild animal. Melaina and my sister might have instigated the mobs, but you and Lady Faylan were planning something, too. Charlton overheard you talking about it."

"Your sister is *here*?" she hissed, ignoring my accusation.

"I'm afraid so. She made the breach."

Lady Faylan grabbed my arm and pulled me away from Kyran's side. "Tell me everything you know."

"You were right when you said the intruder was obsessed with revenge. My sister hates me, has always hated me, and was probably furious that I escaped and left her behind with my mother and aunt. So she hunted me down."

"I should've known. Your family can't keep their hands clean, can they?"

"And yours can? *Please.* Your hands are about as clean as a politician's."

"How dare you!"

"Quite easily. Somehow she knew something about me, *Lady* Faylan. Something she passed along to Avice while pretending to be you."

"Pretending to be *me*?" Her obvious astonishment nearly made me doubt her role in all this.

"That's what Eudrea does. She dares to do what the rest of us only dream of doing. If it's any comfort, she pretended to be me, too. She created all sorts of problems in the village, leaving everyone to think I was responsible. She did it by conspiring with Melaina. But how she was conspiring with you, that's what I'd like to know."

"I conspired with no one," Lady Faylan replied haughtily, and I wondered how I'd ever thought Eudrea was her. They were nothing alike. "That's not my style, as you should know. And I certainly wouldn't conspire with a Gragan."

"Oh, no? Then how did she come to know something about me that only you and I know?" She looked blank. "That I kept quiet about my perceived lack of fey?"

"Oh, that," she said dismissively. "I've no idea." Her expression darkened. "However, I was talking to Kyran at the castle, and I might have let something slip about it to him. Completely unintentional," she lied without batting an eye. Lucky for her he already knew my little secret, or I'd have cracked her one. "But he and I were alone. No one could possibly have heard me."

I glanced over her shoulder at the villagers pushing themselves to their feet and brushing off the dirt from the courtyard. Red-faced and pumped full of indignation, they looked even madder now. Merceen rode in and out amongst them, working to reignite the crowd's ire without being too obvious about it. No doubt if discovered she'd claim she'd been trying to stop them. She wouldn't want to be caught out supporting the wrong side, now would she, the conniving bitch. Though I think I had my answer about who had offered the reward money.

At some point the fire inside the mob would catch hold once more, and I'd have to be ready to move. No way were the villagers going to listen to reason now. They were furious with misery, some had been for decades, and wanted to take that anger out on me. A forever outsider, and a link to the curse.

Strange as it might seem, I couldn't entirely blame them. This curse was awful, and like a hurricane it seemed intent on destroying the happiness of everyone in its path.

"If you're sure no one heard you, then it sounds like Eudrea pretended to be Kyran, too."

Lady Faylan went still, as though turned to stone. "That's not possible. It was him. I know it was him."

"Did he happen to confess his love for you?"

Her cool façade faltered. "H-how did you know about that?"

"I told you. That's what Eudrea does. She finds your weakness and exploits it. She says doing so gives her such delightful shivers." I took a step backward, then another, making my way toward Kyran. He might not be on my side, but he was big and at the very least would make a good shield. "We had a bargain, Lady Faylan, and you broke it. You'd better hope to Grim I don't let anything slip about you and the curse, though by rights I certainly should."

"Don't do it, Lorelle," she ordered, trying to regain her imperious demeanor. "We must talk this out—"

Anything else she might have said was drowned out by the roar of the mob. They had remembered why they'd come in the first place. Intent on making me pay for a crime I didn't commit, they began to run toward me, a river of fury and pain, and I had nowhere left to hide.

Chapter Thirty-Two

They were only steps away when Kyran threw out his hands, creating an explosion of fire and smoke, then he grabbed my arm and pulled. "Into the castle!" His touch set off shockwaves throughout my body, instantly clearing my mind, and I began to run with him. Not wanting to be left out, Dallen seized my other arm and together they hauled me up the steps double-time. Because apparently I wasn't capable of doing it myself.

Kyran steered me toward an open door. "We need to get you inside."

"Oh, no, you don't!" Melaina stepped in front of us, cutting off the way. "Lorelle needs to face the music."

"She needs to do nothing of the sort. Now move out of the way, Melaina, or I'll make you move."

She raised her hands and pointed them at me. "If you do anything to me, brother of mine, the girl gets it. I might not be very powerful yet, but I'm good enough to turn her into ash."

"Step aside, Melaina," he ordered, tightening his grip on my arm and angling his body to protect me. "At this rate, they're going to kill her, and then what? You'll be without your precious antidote, and the curse will continue."

"They won't kill her," she sneered, though uncertainty darkened her eyes.

"Right now they want blood," he stated grimly. "And they want hers."

I shook off my two protectors. "I can speak for myself, you know."

"You!" Melaina spat. "Because of you and your ancestors I can never be happy, never find love. You're going to fix this, and you're going to fix it *now*."

I pushed Kyran out of the way and faced his sister straight on. "Don't blame your relationship problems on me, Melaina Van der Daarke. You're a sour, prune-faced, judgmental bitch, who's jealous of her own daughter, and I don't see how lifting the curse is going to change any of that!"

Her jaw tightened as she stepped forward. "As soon as you end this curse, Gragan, I'm going to kill you myself."

"More reason not to go through with marrying your brother, you plague on humanity."

"We'll see about that." She pushed around me, crying out in her strident voice, "She's up here!"

Most of the fallout from the explosion had cleared, and the villagers soon spotted me at the top of the steps.

"Here I am!" a strangely familiar voice called out, and when I looked toward where it was coming from I realized why I recognized it. It was me…or Eudrea as me. How surreal to see myself outside my reflection in the mirror. I eyed my duplicate critically, thinking I looked rather severe with my hair done up like that. More like Lady Faylan than a woman who wanted to have sex again some time in her life.

The crowd, uncertain what to do, stopped at the bottom of the steps and peered up, their heads swiveling back and forth between us. Berenea hovered nearby on her beat-up old broomstick, ready to fly in whichever direction was likely to elicit the best view.

"What are you doing, Eudrea?" I hissed at her.

She gave me a wink full of spite, then cried out with relish, "Who's the real Lorelle?" She never could stand it when I got more attention than her. Though why she wanted this sort of attention was beyond my ken. "That's right, you ignoramuses. Take a good hard look. Try to figure out which one of us is the person who fooled you for years, who walked amongst you as though by right, who garnered your friendship to use against you. Lorelle number one?" she indicated herself. "Or Lorelle number two?" She flung her hand at me. "Well? Which one?"

The crowd remained silent, their eyes darting from me to Eudrea and back again.

"You know, I hope I killed that elf brat," she went on when her little show failed to produce the desired results. "I hope he's dead and that the rest of you all go straight to hell with him!"

I sighed. Eudrea never knew when to stop.

"You rotten bitch!" shouted a rough-looking elf, wiry and dangerous—a grown-up, meaner version of Carius. "If we be going to hell, then you can get the place ready for us!" He lifted his arm and a loud twang reverberated through the air. Eudrea's eyes widened in surprise and her smile flattened. She looked down at her chest where an arrow pierced it; a bloom of blood darkened her dress, and she dropped to her knees, her mouth opened in silent appeal.

Dallen raced toward Eudrea, and I was right behind him. He grabbed hold of her and she sank against him, her eyes dim with pain as she fought to pull out the arrow.

I kneeled before her and grabbed her arm, wrenching it away. "You'll just make it worse."

Her hand dropped to her side. "I was trying to get them to go after you, and yet here I am with an arrow through my chest. Oh, the irony," she slurred.

"Everyone here knows I wouldn't make such a speech, you idiot. I never was one to bring attention to myself. And if you actually knew me, you'd have figured that out a long time ago. No, you can only see the world through your warped and self-centered point of view. That's why you got my hair wrong—you couldn't fathom that other people might change without your permission. You think the rest of us live and breathe thanks to your exalted presence." I leaned closer. "But get this straight, Eudrea…when you die, the rest of us will carry on as though you never existed in the first place."

"I really hate you, Lori. Really, really *hate* you." Losing her strength, she also lost her ability to hold her impersonation, and slowly her features transformed back into her own.

"Just hang in there, Eudrea," Dallen coaxed, his face pale. "We'll fix this."

"Fix this?" She laughed angrily and blood bubbled from her lips. "I have a goddamned hole in my chest."

Kyran kneeled down beside me, and despite everything, I was glad for his solid presence. "We need to get her inside."

"Be the girl dying?" Berenea shouted from her broom as she approached our little group. Her bright eyes told me exactly what she hoped I'd say, and so I obliged her.

"Yes, she is."

Eudrea shuddered. "I don't want to die."

"Ain't too many who do," Berenea observed. "But it be what's coming to ye after what ye did to Atlene, and to that Carius, even though he deserved it, the little sheit."

"Is he going to be all right?" I asked Berenea.

She shrugged. "May never walk right again, but he'll live."

"The brat attacked me," Eudrea barked. "He got what was coming to him."

"Go on," Berenea coaxed, rapidly scribbling with her quill pen. "Get it off your chest, dearie." She eyed the arrow. "No pun intended."

"You looked like me when he went after you, didn't you?" I said to Eudrea. I don't know how she did it, but even while dying she still managed to look sullen in response to my question. "I'll take that as a yes." I glanced up at Berenea. "A couple days ago Carius and a group of youngsters attacked me at my cottage. His excuse was that I wouldn't remove the curse."

"Is that so?"

"Can you tell the others all that, and what Eudrea did when he attacked her?"

She squinted at me. "If I get an exclusive from you after all this is done."

I didn't even hesitate. For the first time, I wanted my story told. "It's a deal."

She looked surprised, and pleased, and maybe a little suspicious of her good fortune. "Well, isn't this a day for the books?" She tipped her hat to me, then zipped down the stairs to talk to the villagers on my behalf. Having Berenea serve as my mouthpiece was a risk. She would very likely put things a bit more dramatically to, as she liked to call it, "create a moment" so she could sell more copies. But I needed her gone, so she couldn't witness what I was about to do next.

"I don't want to die!" Eudrea cried suddenly, grabbing my hand. Her fingers were cold and sweaty, and I could sense she was losing her battle. For a brief moment I was glad.

"Then you shouldn't have pretended to be me, Eudrea," I said, mainly because I can be an asshole myself sometimes.

"You always were a cold-hearted bitch," she spat, and more blood gushed from her mouth. "Oh, *shit*," she screeched, realizing what it was. "I thought that was spit." She giggled hysterically. "I just made a rhyme." Her face crumpled and her grip tightened. "I'm not ready to die, Lori."

"You're not going to die."

"Don't lie to me. You told that witch I was dying."

"You are."

"So you lied!"

I pulled my hands from her cold, wet grasp. "When have I ever lied to you, Eudrea?"

Her lower lip jutted out. "That time you took my candy."

"That was Aunt Nimair. She was always stealing from us, and you know it." I reached out and wrapped my fingers around the arrow. "You are dying, but you're not going to die. Now close your eyes."

"I'm not closing my eyes around you! You'll kill me."

"As I told you," I said patiently, "you're already dying. And besides, if I'd wanted you dead, I would've killed you a long time ago, and in a very painful way. Now I need you to stay still, so that means you're going to have to trust me."

"I'd sooner trust the devil."

I let go of the arrow's shaft and made to stand. "So be it."

She grabbed at my hand. "No. Don't go, Lori! I'll do it. I'll do what you say."

I stooped back down and grabbed hold of the arrow, not caring if I hurt her. "Close your eyes," I ordered, allowing a small fiendish gleam to show in my own. If I was going to save the ungrateful wretch's life, the least I could do is get some pleasure out of it. She gave me one last distrusting glare, then did as she was told.

I stared at the arrow, saw it turn to ash in my mind. The shaft began to glow, heating up in my hand, but I hung on despite the pain. Eudrea shrieked, but I didn't let her distract me. Moments later the wood dissolved in my hand as quick as paper exposed to a hot flame, and I was left with black powder on my fingers. When the arrow was gone, I covered the wound with the palm of my hand and sent my sparks into Eudrea's body.

She shuddered, then her eyes flew wide open. She looked down at her chest, then up at me. "You actually did it."

"I did." Though I didn't tell her I left the arrowhead lodged inside her chest. She wouldn't die from it—I'd encased it in muscle—but having spelled it, it would serve as a means of always knowing her, no matter what form she tried to take from here on out.

I stood up. "Take her inside the castle," I told Dallen. "And hide her."

"But Lorelle—" He stood up, leaving Eudrea to fall back. She howled indignantly, but he ignored her. He grabbed my arm and pulled me away. "I don't want to be with Eudrea. I came here for you."

"She was telling the truth, wasn't she, Dallen? You stayed with her after I left."

He looked away, his pretty boy features darkening. "I was very angry with you, Lorelle."

"I don't blame you, Dallen, since my sister messed with your memory, but your being with her means that I can't be with you."

His head swung up. "Why not?"

"The first time you were with Eudrea was not your fault, I know that now, and I'm sorry for not believing you. But after that, you made a choice. You knew I despised my sister, but you went with her anyway."

"I thought you'd left me, Lorelle. I thought you were dead!"

"Yes, and I'm sorry about that. I didn't know until recently that you were innocent." Even if I had known, would I have returned? Risk it being discovered that I wasn't fey? I wasn't sure that I would…and what did that say about my feelings for Dallen? Not enough.

"I'm not giving up on you," he said through gritted teeth, his jaw hard. "I've yet to lose a case, I won't lose you."

I sighed. "You're wasting your time."

"I deserve a second chance. You owe me that for not believing me."

"What do you even see in me anymore?"

His eyelids lowered slightly and his nostrils flared. "You've turned into a beautiful woman, Lorelle. And you're different now. Powerful. We'd make a great team, you and I."

My fists clenched. "You know, I've about had enough of you men. Where were all of you when I had no one? For six whole years?"

"Six whole years?" Kyran echoed, and I realized he'd joined us, very quietly and sneakily. "You haven't been with a man for six years?"

"Oh, shut up." I left them and kneeled down before Eudrea, who was looking quite smug now that she was no longer dying and still had Dallen in her clutches. "Just remember, Eudrea, as I giveth, so can I taketh away. You might be my sister, but you make my enemies look innocent as baby seals. My advice is that you leave Hawthorn Lane, and quickly. The prole elves are not a forgiving bunch. Nor am I."

Her smug expression grew stubborn. "You can't tell me what to do, Lori."

"I just did. Now go before I melt all your skin and leave your bones for the crows to pick over."

She opened her mouth to sass me, then closed it when she saw the look on my face. I'm pretty sure she read from it exactly what I was feeling about her. I'd about had it with everyone right now, and woe be to the idiot who pushed me over the edge. Eudrea knew the old Lorelle; she had no idea what I'd become.

"I'm not leaving," she stated firmly, letting Dallen pull her to her feet.

"It's your funeral. Now get out of my sight."

Taking a risk, I turned my back on her. A slight scuffling sound ensued and I had a feeling Dallen was holding her back from attacking me. She gave a yelp, and I glanced back to see her struggling in Dallen's arms as he carried her away.

"You're so predictable," I mouthed to her. She lunged, but Dallen jerked her back and kept on walking, barely breaking stride.

I turned back to face the crowd down below. Berenea saw me and flew up to hover by my side. Her eyes went to where Eudrea had lain, the spot obvious by the large pool of dark blood still remaining. "Where'd the little vixen go?"

"Into hiding," I stated succinctly. "Did you tell them what I said about Carius?"

"His da weren't so believing of it, but the rest were. Carius Dal is a troublemaker if ever there was one. No one's particularly sad to see him reduced to a hobbling cripple, to be sure. A right bully, that one, just like his da."

"Do they understand that I wasn't the one who destroyed Atlene's shop, and that I wasn't the one who hurt the boy?"

"They do."

"But…" I pushed.

Her protuberant, probing eyes slid over to Kyran, then back to me. "There still be that cursèd curse to deal with."

"Exactly!" Melaina spoke up behind me, and I nearly jumped out of my skin. "No time like the present. Right, Lorelle?"

I turned around to face her at the same time Kyran said, "Leave her alone, Melaina."

"No, it's all right. It's time everyone heard this."

Melaina looked triumphant as I turned to face the crowd. Everyone looked hot, sweaty, and thoroughly disgruntled, and I could only hope they'd be open to hearing me out. "I've something to say to everyone," I shouted, and the talking amongst the villagers gradually faded. I found Lady Faylan amongst all the avid faces and gave her a meaningful look. She gave me a speculative one back, as though considering how much trouble she'd get into if she shot me dead right then and there. My eyes nearly missed Avice, surrounded by beaus, her hands clasped and her eyes wide with fright. Nearby stood Dawn and Juletta, both looking concerned, yet also calculating. And then there was Asherley Rowan, standing off to the side, aloof and watchful. What was the dryad doing here?

"Are ye finally ridding us of this awful curse?" Gorn, a busybody dwarf, shouted.

"Fellow Hawthornites, if I could, I would." Boos filled the air. "I know, I know," I soothed when the shouting died down. "But there's something you need to understand. You've been misled, I'm afraid. Kyran and I cannot be the ones to end the curse. At least I can't be the one to do it with him."

"Why not?" Gorn persisted, swiping a thick hand across his sweaty forehead. "We know you've feelings for him. Plain as the nose on me face."

"And that's quite plain, Gorn." The villagers chuckled. "But my feelings aren't the point. Remember what Lady Faylan said at the ball? That the lovers must be from two different worlds? Well, we are not. We're both high-born. But even if I weren't a high-born," I went on, not daring to look at Kyran, "I cannot marry Count Van der Daarke."

"Lorelle is right," Lady Faylan called out before the villagers could protest, and numerous heads, mouths frozen open, swung toward her. "I have thoroughly reviewed the situation, as well as garnered feedback from the Executors, and we've come to the conclusion that she cannot be the one to break her ancestor's curse. Someone else must do it in her place."

There was much less muttering and protesting than I expected.

"And who might that someone else be?" Berenea queried, pen poised.

"That remains to be seen," Lady Faylan replied, while at the same time several voices volunteered their services, feminine *and* masculine.

Hence the reason for the lack of protest.

"It has to be Kyran and Lorelle," Melaina insisted. "You're both the descendants of the parties who were originally wronged. I think we need to determine what exactly 'from two different worlds' means because I'm quite sure these two are the only ones who can break the curse."

"I don't agree." I turned to Kyran, arms crossed. "You and Lady Faylan could try it on. See what happens."

"Lady Faylan is high-born, too," Berenea pointed out. "Or is she?" she muttered half to herself as she scribbled this down.

"Her family lost a lot due to the curse, and she was a wronged party, as well," I went on, ignoring Berenea's point. "So she fits the profile. Besides, maybe Melaina is right and being from two different worlds means something different than what we thought." For some reason this gave me hope when hope was the last thing I wanted right now.

"I don't want to marry Lady Faylan," Kyran said to me in a low voice. "Why do you insist that she and I are conspiring, Lorelle? That I'd want to be with her?"

"Because you as good as admitted it to me," I ground out.

"What are you talking about?" He looked genuinely puzzled.

"When you visited me…you said—" I paused, confused. Something was wrong with this picture, but I couldn't figure out what it was. The answer was right in front of me, but when I tried to grab it, it disappeared like fog.

"I said what?" he prompted when I remained silent, and I shook my head, frustrated.

"If being from two different worlds means something different than what we thought, then Lorelle could still be the one," Melaina proclaimed, saving me from replying, but putting me right back where I'd started.

"We need time to study this thoroughly," Lady Faylan stated decisively. Of course she wanted more time. Time to sink her claws further into Kyran's hide. Time to plan and maneuver. Time to come up with a spell to make Kyran hers. "Who knows what kind of damage could come about if we get it wrong?"

Her announcement set off a fresh wave of anxious murmuring

through the crowd, and I looked about, feeling a sense of déjà vu. This exact same scenario had happened at the ball, and it was happening again. I had to end this now, once and for all, or be doomed to repeating this scene for the next several months.

"There's more," I announced, my voice loud and clear. "Something else is stopping me—" I broke off, searching my mind. There was something else, I realized now. But what was it? The scent of dust and vetiver and cinders surrounded me. *I am yours…* the wind whispered in my ear. I tilted my head, hoping to hear more, but there was only silence. "Something else is stopping me from marrying Count Van der Daarke," I went on, my voice growing less sure with every word. "Something I do not understand." My tattoo began to throb like a heartbeat, and darkness seeped into my mind, making it hard to think, to focus.

"We can marry them right now," I heard Melaina say, her voice as distant as an echo in a far away canyon.

"Without the banns?" Lady Faylan argued. "Without the celebration?"

"We'll celebrate afterwards."

Lady Faylan swiped her hand through the air. "Impossible."

"Nothing is impossible," Melaina countered. "Especially here in Hawthorn Lane."

I had to go. I had to escape, and there was only one way to do that. I'd fly out of here. I didn't know if I could actually do it, didn't know if I could pull it off without killing myself. But it was my only option. I was finally keenly desperate.

Pulling in a deep breath, I imagined myself as Edan, soaring high into the air. When I shot up like a rocket, I couldn't believe how easy it had been, and how wonderful it was to be free of gravity's grip, to get away from the villagers and my supposed responsibilities.

"Lorelle!" Kyran called after me, his head tilted back, his eyes wide with disbelief. "Come back!"

"I don't know how!" Exhilarated by my success, I rose higher and higher, the crowd below me dissolving into dolls. I'd done it. I was flying, and the cool air felt wonderful on my hot cheeks. Turning my upper body, I managed to change direction so that I could fly over the castle walls to freedom, and as my confidence grew, I picked up speed, the walls getting nearer and nearer.

Just when I thought I was safe, that I had finally escaped from my tormentors, something painful zapped me in the ribs. My hands clutched my chest, my mind went blank, and I began to fall.

Chapter Thirty-Three

I felt him before I heard him. The beating of his wings stirred the air all around me, and I knew it was Edan even though I couldn't see him. He wouldn't make it to me in time, though. He sounded too far away. I clutched at my ribs and tried to buoy myself, if only for an instant. But the pain, and the fact that I was free falling, made it too hard to focus on a skill I'd only just learned.

The dark ground rushed up to greet me and all my muscles tightened in anticipation of certain death. And then Edan was beneath me, catching my body with only seconds to spare, swooping back up into the sky like a hang glider. I clutched at him and held on for dear life as we soared over the treetops of Fell Forest. I still couldn't see him, though, which was odd. It was dark, but not that dark. I should at least be able to see something. It was like Edan was in stealth mode. Perhaps he was. It would explain how he'd managed to remain undetected all this time. If he'd been sighted, I'd have heard about it. So it looked like I had a bird who could make himself invisible. Was I a lucky girl, or what?

I saw we were heading for home and felt a wave of relief wash over me. Magically reinforced, the cottage should keep the mob out until I figured out what to do next. Edan began to show himself as we swooped into the yard, where I was surprised to see pinpoints of light escaping from the conservatory. Then I remembered my meeting with Renwick and quickly dismounted.

"Come on, Edan!" I urged when he didn't follow. "We have to get inside."

He shook his head, indicating the sky. "Keep watch."

I frowned. "But they're coming here, I'm sure. We need to get inside where it's safe."

"Keep watch," he repeated stubbornly.

"All right," I reluctantly conceded. "But come in when you see something. I don't want you getting hurt."

He didn't respond, and I could only hope he'd do what I asked.

"Sorry I'm late—" I began as I burst through the door, then froze when I saw the strange scene before me. Cutter was standing behind Renwick, who was sitting on a dining room chair, arms crossed and mouth mutinous. Seeing me, Renwick tried to stand, only to be pushed back down by Cutter.

"Cutter? What are you doing here?"

"Who the hell is this guy, Lorelle?" Renwick demanded. "He forced his way past me, like he owned the place, and hasn't let me move since."

"This is Cutter Flint, the cemetery caretaker. I told you about him when we were crossing the moors on our way to Matron's house. Remember what I told you?" I hoped he would remember, specifically that Cutter and I were not the best of friends. Or were we? The scent of vetiver rose up around me, distracting me.

"This is him?" Renwick looked up at Cutter, and his jaw tightened. "Why is he here?"

I shook my head, trying to clear it. "I don't know." I faced Cutter, whose expression was benign. "Well?"

He held up a black bundle, which had been lying on the table, and the length of it cascaded to the floor like an ink waterfall. "I brought you something, Lorelle."

"You brought me a gown?"

"Not just any gown."

"Then what kind?" I asked warily.

"This is to be your wedding dress."

"You want me to marry Kyran, too?" He grimaced slightly, then shook his head. "Then who?"

"I would think the answer is obvious." A pale hand rested on his chest. "Me, of course."

"Now just hold on!" Renwick sprang up once more, and once more was pushed back down as though a mere child. Cutter was thinner by far, and resembled a scholar more than a body builder, and yet he seemed to possess more power in his little finger than Renwick had in his entire body. I must admit his show of strength appealed to my darker side, and I had to suppress that side rather forcefully. "What is he talking about, Lorelle?"

I stared around me, searching for an answer I knew I had but could not produce. "I don't know," I finally answered.

Renwick's ordinarily carefree features hardened. "Something's wrong with you."

I pressed my fists to my temples. "I can't seem to think straight right now."

"It is time to go, Lorelle." Cutter left Renwick and glided toward me, hand held out before him. "Before the others arrive."

"Am I to get visitors?" I asked, confused.

"Those who work against us are coming for you. I would rather not be here in this place when they arrive. As I warned you, trouble is coming, and that time is now."

I blinked at him. "Where are we going?"

"Home."

"Home?" I looked around me. "Isn't this my home?"

"What have you done to her?" Renwick cried out. "This isn't the Lorelle I know."

"Lorelle has promised herself to me, and now we must flee from those who wish her harm."

I felt a throbbing in my ribs, the pain reminding me that I had been shot at by a fire bolt, and hit. "Cutter is right. They're after me, Renwick. They mean to make me marry Kyran even though he betrayed me."

"Kyran betrayed you? Are we talking about the same man? I mean, he's not my favorite person, I do admit, mainly because it's so damn hard to live up to Mr. Perfect. But I do know one thing. Kyran wouldn't betray you."

I rubbed a hand across my forehead. "He and Lady Faylan are together," I said uncertainly. That didn't seem right, but I couldn't figure out how. "They're working against me," I tried again, but that wasn't right, either.

"Events conspire against you, Lorelle," Cutter said gently. "They always have. You are a victim of your birth, of your brethren, and of your village. I offer you another way." He pulled me toward the door. "Just come with me."

I glanced back at Renwick, who was struggling to stand and failing, as though he'd been glued to his chair.

A screech sounded outside the door and Cutter stopped. "Their arrival is nigh. Edan will hold them off."

"I don't want him involved in this. He'll get hurt!"

"He will not, Lorelle. Trust me in this." He glanced behind him. "We will have to go another way."

"There is no other way. I magicked the cottage. We can't even break the windows."

He gave me an approving glance. "Good. That will give us time."

"How do you know about Edan?"

"I gave him unto thee."

"You did?" So that meant Cutter had saved my life, or at least saved me from getting hurt. Twice now.

"As I did the hawthorn and blackthorn. I made offer of the book of poetry, as well. I brought you friends, and now the dress," he went on. "Is that not what prospective grooms do for their lovers?"

"But we aren't lovers!" I knew this much for sure.

"Not yet." A promise of unearthly delights lay waiting in the undertone of his voice. I shivered in anticipation, then shook my head. This wasn't right.

Or was it?

"I don't remember saying I'd marry you, Cutter Flint. I hardly know you." I stared down at my wrist, wondering what the skull tattoo meant. I'd known at one time, but couldn't quite recall at the moment. Everything kept shifting about. One moment sliding in close, but when I went to grab hold, slipping back out of reach, elusive as a wild bird. I rubbed the tattoo hard, as though to erase it.

Renwick spotted the action. "What's that on your wrist?" He glared at Cutter. "What have you done to her?"

"It is what she would have wished for if she'd known to ask for it."

I frowned. "It is?"

"Of course, ma belle."

He tugged me away from the door, then turned to Renwick. "This grieves me, but it must be done." He snapped his fingers and Renwick's head fell forward as though Cutter had snapped his neck.

Fear surged up inside me, pushing back the waves of befuddlement. "What did you do to him?"

"I sent him into a long sleep."

I jerked away from the death wraith, not sure how I'd managed when his strength seemed insuperable, and ran to Renwick. "Renwick?" I cried, shaking him. "Renwick!" He didn't respond, didn't even seem to be breathing. Cutter swiftly left the door he'd secured with the wooden bar, and was immediately at my side, taking my arm and pulling me away. His touch muddled my mind once more, making me dizzy. "We go this way." He drew me to the trapdoor that led down into the cellar.

"You want to go down there? But then we'll really be trapped."

"In it lies a way to what hides beneath Hawthorn Lane." He lifted the trapdoor and held it up for me. "Down you go."

"It's dark." I hung back. "I don't want to go," I added stubbornly. "Something's not right."

"'Light thickens; and the crow makes wing to th' rooky wood,'" Cutter quoted *Macbeth*. "Good things of day begin to droop and drowse, Whiles night's black agents to their preys do rouse. Thou marvel'st at my words: but hold thee still. Things bad begun make strong themselves by ill. So, prithee, go with me.'"

The beautiful words swirled around and around inside my head, making me feel as though I were spiraling down into a vortex. Without consciously deciding to do so, I began to descend the wooden steps leading down into the cellar, feeling as I did so that I was entering my grave.

The coolness of the underground space was welcome after the close heat of the cottage, and I thought maybe Cutter was right. I must follow him. I must do as he told me.

"I will keep you safe," he said in a low voice, as though reading my mind. "From your wretched sister. From the untrustworthy Van der Daarkes. From all the vagaries of the world, Lorelle, I will keep you safe." Cutter closed the door on us, and the darkness was complete. And then, just as quickly, there was light.

"Hello, Aber," Cutter greeted, and the little orb bobbed a curtsy. "Lead us home."

"I know you, don't I?" I asked the round light floating before me.

The orb made a noise that sounded almost sad. "She is fine, Aber," Cutter said, his tone slightly impatient. "What I am doing will be her making."

Aber gave a little shrug, as though not quite believing Cutter, then turned about and floated toward a corner of the cellar, a corner I always avoided, feeling there was more in that dark space than the eye could see. When the orb disappeared as though swallowed I wasn't entirely surprised. Cutter's hand on my arm pulled me forward, and I spotted something I'd never noticed before—an opening, narrow and difficult to see, even with a light, but there all the same.

"How did you know this was here?" I asked as we stepped into a passage resembling an abandoned mining tunnel, though it was surprisingly free of cobwebs. When Aber spotted us, he zipped on ahead, leaving us to catch up.

"I told you," Cutter said patiently as he motioned me to follow. "It leads to my tangled web."

Tangled web. So the rumors were true...a labyrinth of passages lay below Hawthorn Lane, and likely all of them led to Atermorte Cemetery, the giant spider in the middle, and where, ironically, we'd eventually all end up.

"I don't like the sound of that."

A dry rasping noise filled the air. Cutter was laughing. "Oh, Lorelle. It is merely a way to get around the village without being discovered." And also a way to deliver gifts without being seen... *Very clever, Cutter Flint.*

"Is that how you knew about the attack on Atlene's shop?"

"Oh, no. The spirits of *Chez Chantilly* apprised me of that." Ah. I remembered now seeing Gangus, the werewolf, creeping about, listening in on conversations.

So that's how he learned about the happenings in the village. He could speak to the dead, and make them answer. Of course he could. He was mostly dead himself, and I was here with him, underground. And yet I couldn't quite make myself turn and run. *He has a hold on me,* a distant part of my mind warned. *The trick is to figure out how to undo it.*

But I couldn't concentrate on that now, or on much of anything really. We were moving faster to keep up with Aber and I could only focus on tracking the glowing orb as we turned this way and that.

At last we came to a grand door shaped like a gravestone and Aber stopped before it. Cutter produced a key to unlock the door. It opened easily, and he indicated with a flourish for me to step through. I looked at him, then crossed the threshold, into Cutter's world.

Chapter Thirty-Four

I was back in the cave-like room I'd been in a couple days earlier. It looked different, though. Neater, maybe.

My mind had cleared a bit on the walk and I was able to process things better now. I faced Cutter, who had turned from locking the door. "Why am I here?"

"The multitude has gathered against you. I brought you here to keep you safe."

"Is that the only reason?"

He looked away, his sharp chin cutting through the air. "No."

"Cutter—"

"Would you like something to refresh you?" he interrupted.

"I'm good. Tell me why you brought me here."

His dark eyes, when they met mine again, glittered with excitement. "I sensed our connection before, your first time in my lair, but I did not realize the true meaning of it until afterward, when I heard the rumors. Why did you not tell me you restored a child's life?"

"It wasn't something I thought worth mentioning to a *death wraith*."

My words brought no response. "You are a Resurrectionist, Lorelle. Did you know this about yourself?"

"I didn't, Cutter, because I'm pretty sure I'm *not* a Resurrectionist, even though I have no idea what one is." Though, admittedly, I could make a fairly educated guess.

"Resurrectionists, so very rare, are revered by my kind. You are indeed one, and you understand what it means, I am quite sure of that." His thin, pale hands gestured in the air as he spoke, like a conductor in an orchestra. "But perhaps not entirely, so I shall tell you. You can bring the dead back to life."

"No, Cutter," I firmly corrected him. "I've never done that. I only save those who are close to death. There's a difference. An important one, I'll bet."

He shrugged this off. "Have you ever tried restoring life to the *completely* dead?"

"I tend to avoid that sort of thing if I can help it." I'd read Stephen King's *Pet Sematary*, after all. I sighed, feeling betrayed and confused and displaced, all at once, and wanted only to return to the haven of my cottage, especially now that I wouldn't have to leave Hawthorn Lane. The thought warmed me. "You still haven't told me why you brought me here."

"I must relate to you a story, which I believe will help you to understand everything."

I crossed my arms, skeptical. "I'm listening."

"To put it succinctly, I am currently living in exile as punishment by the Lord Reaper for extending the life of a dying woman. We are forbidden to do this, you see."

I stared at him. "But that's what I did to that boy." I left out saving my sister. If Cutter, or the Lord Reaper, whoever that might be, didn't know about that, I certainly wasn't telling them.

"That is why you are so very special. You extended life and were not punished for doing so. You are one of the gifted ones, and that makes me so very pleased."

And here we go... "Why would that please you?"

"I shall tell you more of my story, and then it will become as clear as the air around you." I wasn't sure I agreed, but I motioned him to continue. I was anxious to get back to Edan and see if he was all right. There was something else wrong that I needed to attend to, but I couldn't place what it was. "I knew better than to do what I did, as love of a mortal by a death wraith is not allowed. As you might imagine it compromises our ability to do our job. But I could not resist the allure of aligning myself with such a life force. She was much like you, Lorelle, so very lovely, so very much alive. I never once touched her, in actuality loved her only from afar, but when it was her time, which came much too early, I couldn't resist attempting to alter the tides of fate. As punishment for my misdeed, I was sent here, and for every minute my love survived beyond her time I received one hundred years of penance."

Now I knew that he was here in Hawthorn Lane, not because he was running from something—like so many of us—but because he'd been condemned to come here.

"How long did she survive?" I asked, my voice no more than a whisper.

"Ten precious minutes."

"You got a thousand years of exile? Isn't that a bit harsh? You were only following your heart."

He drew himself up, like a soldier facing a firing squad. "It was what I deserved. I did wrong and needed to be punished. I will face my sanction as I was meant to do, however difficult."

"Well, at least you ended up here. There are far worse places than Hawthorn Lane." Like my house back in the Alterworld.

"I agree. But banishment is only part of my punishment. It is the other part that makes my life more trying."

"What could make your punishment *more* trying?"

"If I were to try to unite with another mortal, I would drain the life from them. My love for them would be their death sentence. It is a case of *auribus teneo lupum.*"

Holding the wolf by the ears...in other words, damned if you do, damned if you don't. He was right about that. Now I understood why he'd given me *Paradise Lost*. In his strange and serpentine way, he was trying to share his pain with me.

"Why are you telling me all this, Cutter?" I asked softly, though I already had a creeping sense of where this was going, and I didn't like it.

He reached out and grasped my hands in his cool, dry ones. "Because only a very powerful fey can withstand such a poisonous effect."

"And that powerful fey is me." My words were stilted, my skin cold.

"You cannot understand the relief I feel knowing I will not be alone for the next nine hundred years."

"Oh, Cutter," I breathed, taken aback. "You've already gone a hundred years without love? That's awful." I paused, looked him in the eye, and took a deep breath as I pulled my hands from his. I didn't mind being blunt to protect myself, but what I needed to say next wouldn't be easy. "I am sorry for you, but I cannot be the one to stay with you. I can't be with anyone right now. There are things happening in Hawthorn Lane that make my life complicated, and that complication means you and I can't be together."

"You have already promised yourself to me, Lorelle. We need only announce the banns for the required three weeks, and ever afterward together we shall be."

"I don't remember promising myself to you."

He touched a finger to my temple, setting off a series of images in my mind, ending with my saying one damning sentence...

I will be yours, Cutter Flint.

"Now do you remember, ma belle?"

That was me, that was my voice, but I didn't remember speaking the words. And yet, and yet they did seem familiar.

"What about the curse?" I demanded, feeling increasingly trapped. "I'm supposed to marry Kyran to break it. If he and I unite, we can end it and the suffering of the villagers." Never mind that I'd rejected that option only an hour ago. Marriage to Kyran was now a lifeline, one I was struggling to grab hold of to pull myself out of this mess.

"You are free from that obligation, ma belle. You and I come from two entirely different worlds...the living and the dead. Rest assured, we fit the required standards to break the curse. You shall have your cake, and eat it too." One corner of his mouth rose up in pleasure.

"I suppose you're the cake?"

"If you like." His gaze bore into mine. "It does summon up quite the image, does it not?"

I swallowed. It certainly did. "But I don't love you, Cutter."

"You will. In time."

Nine hundred years of time?

"Do you love me?" I asked, certain he would answer the same as I had.

"My attraction to you grows stronger with every meeting, with every moment we share, with every breath you take."

His words were the epitome of romantic sentiment, and yet I felt only a chill burrowing deep down inside me like a mouse made of ice. Had I really said those words? I didn't remember speaking them, didn't remember saying much of anything to Cutter. And they certainly didn't seem like anything I would say to anyone, *ever*.

"You are tired, ma belle. Come with me, and I will show you your new room. I feel quite certain it will suit you."

He took my hand, and I let him guide me across the open space to an opening at the far side of the chamber. We climbed a set of spiraling stone steps to a cavernous room lit by what seemed like a thousand candles. In the middle of the room loomed a four-poster bed bedecked in black velvet curtains. There was a wardrobe and a desk, a dressing table and mirror, a fireplace even. It all looked perfectly normal, though in this place, this tomb of sorts, a coffin seemed more fitting for my resting place.

"We aren't sharing that bed, are we?"

"Only if you want to."

I felt a shiver take hold of me. "I sleep better alone."

"As you wish." He walked over to the wardrobe and flung open the doors. Inside hung gown after exquisite gown, all in dark colors, like shadows at dusk, all beautiful and elegant. "I have been preparing your trousseau these past few days. The Ravenna sisters were quite intrigued when I placed my order."

"They know about this?"

"They know nothing beyond what I wished them to know. They know not yet of you."

Not yet. My relief quickly soured. "When do you announce the first banns?"

"On the morrow." He pulled out a dark nightgown, reminiscent of an outfit a Goth princess might wear to bed. Low-cut bodice, tight at the waist, long, flowing skirt. Cutter Flint might be a death wraith, but he certainly wasn't dead. Not if he chose a gown like that for me to wear. "I shall leave you now. If you wish to wash up, you may use the room next door."

I didn't. Nor was I changing into that nightgown. I took it from him anyway. "Thank you."

He bowed to me, smooth and elegant. "It is a pleasure to service you, Lorelle."

Oh, the way he phrased things.

Then he was gone, and I was alone. I sat down on the bed, soft as downy feathers, and looked around me. What was I going to do? My mind seemed to be growing clearer with every passing second, and for a brief moment I wished it would fog up again. I had to find a way out of this, but it was tempting to simply forget everything and just go along with Cutter's plan. A wave of exhaustion washed over me and I laid back, lifting my legs up and curling them close to my body. I would plan my escape tomorrow. For now I needed to sleep.

As soon as I closed my eyes, the candles whooshed out, leaving me in total darkness. The dark, rather than soothing me, stimulated my mind, and thoughts began to come at me fast and furious. Kyran. What would he think about all this? Would he realize I'd been kidnapped? Where was he now? Was he coming for me?

Why should he? I thought bitterly. He was conspiring with Lady Faylan. But if that were so, why had he seemed so vehemently opposed to my every word when I'd confronted him about it?

An image of Dallen entered my mind—the one in which he'd separated himself from Josepha's body and come to me. I frowned in thought. I'd read about this somewhere, observed an illustration. Ah, yes. *Fey or Foe.* That's where I'd seen it. Dallen was a possessor. According to Professor Ballylee, possessors take over people's bodies and control them—not completely, but enough to manipulate them.

And that's what he'd done to Kyran. It all made sense now. Dallen had taken over Kyran's body. *Twice.* The first time he must have slipped inside the cottage when Avice had left after her visit, and the second time he'd come in when Edan had gone out to hunt. Dallen had influenced Kyran. That's why he'd acted so strangely, why he'd actually *grinned*, why there hadn't been a shock between us when he'd patted me on the shoulder or when I'd struck his wrist, why sometimes it seemed as though he had to force himself to speak what he really wanted to say. Dallen had made him say those words about Lady Faylan, because Dallen wanted me to hate Kyran. His greatest revenge on me for leaving him was to force me to lose someone I cared for, just as he had lost me.

It was now clear why Ilia had been so mad at me. She must have seen Dallen as Josepha, and Eudrea as me, in an embrace, or caught them in an act even more intimate, and had justifiably blamed me for trying to take her man. She had come to my cottage with the others in the hope of making me change my mind about Josepha, maybe to beg me to back off. She'd hinted at things, but perhaps had lost her nerve to directly confront me when I'd acted like I had no idea what she was talking about—because I didn't. She must hate me, and this grieved me. I had believed she would get over whatever snit she'd been in, which is probably all it had been at *Chez Chantilly* because I hadn't come to see her, but she wouldn't get over this, not if she couldn't figure out what Dallen had done, not if I couldn't go back and fix things.

I sat up suddenly, sending a wave of pain through my chest where the fire bolt had hit me, and the candles whooshed back on. I wasn't sure how much time had passed, but could only hope Cutter had gone out, that he wasn't in the main area working on whatever it is death wraiths work on—his epitaphs, perhaps. If he were still here, I'd have to wait for him to leave, and who knew how long that would take. As a death wraith, he didn't really have to ever leave his lair, unless someone died.

I tiptoed down the stairs and peered into the large room. My heart sank. There he was, sitting at the table, hunched over and scribbling on a parchment.

I lowered myself into a crouch, preparing to wait for as long as necessary for him to leave. I doubted death wraiths had to sleep; I would likely have to wait until he decided to attend to some task above surface. In which case, I might have a long wait. I sat down on the step, one hand on the railing, ready to move.

A whirring sound filled the room and Cutter looked up from his writing. "What is it, Aber?" He leaned toward the obviously agitated orb. "You think you heard something?" He waited. "You are not entirely sure?" He sighed and set down his quill. "I will go check. Will that calm you?"

The orb bobbed up and down. Cutter stood and headed for the stairway opening that led to the crypt, moving swiftly to keep up with a quick-moving Aber. This was my chance. I waited a count of twenty, then slipped down the remaining steps and across the floor to the door that led to Cutter's labyrinth. I tried the handle only to find it locked. I thought maybe it would be, but I had to be sure. After waiting a few more seconds, I headed for the stairway. Glancing up, I could see nothing and hear nothing. I set my foot on the first step, paused for a moment to listen, then started up the stairs.

I hadn't gone far when one of the mirrors flashed on, the same grand one with the odd faces that had shown a scene from *Fawn's Fashions* on my last visit. I was about to pass it by when four familiar figures, all huddled together on the steps of Castle Daarke, caught my eye. They looked slightly off, as though reflections of themselves. Reflections. Of course. I was seeing them through a mirror. Cutter must use mirrors as yet another way to gather information, and had somehow managed to stash one, or more, mirrors at Castle Daarke. Even more disturbing was the plethora of mirrors that could be found in Hawthorn Lane. Then I remembered the mirror I'd received from an anonymous admirer, and felt myself grow cold. It had been from Cutter, of course. Funny he hadn't mentioned a mirror when listing his gifts to me. He must be out of his mind to think spying on me like that was okay. Although perhaps I wasn't in a position to judge, being that spying was what I did for a living.

Hearing faint sounds coming from the mirror, I leaned forward to listen. "So she's really gone?" Avice said in a shaky voice. "She told me she was going to go."

"We aren't sure she's the one who left," Juletta amended. "The alarm that signals when someone has left Hawthorn Lane went off not long after Lorelle flew away. My sister set one as soon as the unauthorized breach happened, so she could track who was coming and going. She thinks it was Lorelle, but there's no proof."

"She did a runner," Avice stated flatly, her lower lip trembling.

Dawn rolled her eyes. "Oh, come off it, Avice! She did what she had to do. She made a run for it, and I don't blame her. She had a mob chasing her."

"Don't you get it?" Avice sniffed and pressed a hand to her chest. "Lorelle abandoned me. She abandoned all of us!"

"Leaving us with the curse," Ilia added, her words quite clear despite her chattering teeth and pronounced lisp. Her too-skinny arms were wrapped around her narrow torso and strands of hair straggled around her wan face. I searched for Josepha, but he was nowhere in sight. "I thought I knew her."

"What happened between you two?" Dawn demanded. "I thought you were besties."

When Ilia didn't answer, Juletta wrapped her arm around the girl's shaking shoulders. "What did Lorelle do to make you so upset?"

Ilia hesitated, looking around at each of them, then took the plunge. "Well, first I was just mad because she hadn't come to visit me like she said she would and my mother was making me miserable and I was so lonely and scared. But then I saw something awful, and I realized she'd only been pretending to be my friend."

Dawn leaned forward with an avid expression on her face. "Go on."

"I saw her kissing Josepha, and not just any old kissing. It was like they couldn't get enough of each other." Her mouth turned downward. "She could have anyone, and she took him."

"No!" Avice cried. "It's not true. Not my Lorelle."

"I know what I saw, Avice," Ilia stated defiantly. "I might not be very smart, but I'm not blind." So Ilia hadn't made the connection like I'd been hoping she would. Rather than put two and two together, like most Hawthornites, she'd rather be angry with me.

"That sly dog," Dawn purred, her tone admiring. "Definitely didn't see that one coming." She cackled gleefully. "I'm so glad I drugged my sister and slipped out of the house to go gambling. Otherwise I might have missed out on all this." She looked around, pleased.

"I hate her," Ilia growled, and her whole body started to glow with emotion. "I'll never forgive her."

"Me, either," Avice howled, throwing her arms around Ilia.

The scene dissolved, and I felt sick inside at what I'd witnessed. They had it all wrong. I had to get out of this place. I had to explain, set them straight.

But then again, if they really knew me, they'd know I wouldn't do something like this. Avice had been my friend for six years, and yet she'd been willing to believe the worst of me. It seemed I was doomed to never have a good relationship with anyone. I was cursed, and not just by Lady Faylan's magic, though that certainly wasn't helping.

After a moment of darkness, another scene appeared in the mirror. I realized it was inside my cottage, and there was Kyran, pacing back and forth, looking like he wanted to demolish something. He'd come for me! Sitting at the kitchen table was Renwick, who looked groggy and out of sorts, but not dead. I sucked in a gust of relief. Cutter had not been using a metaphor; Renwick really had just been asleep. Until this moment, I'd forgotten what had happened to him, and I cursed Cutter's easy ability to control my mind.

"I just tell you a mob was here to hunt down Lorelle, and you can only stare at me like an idiot. You did not pick the best time to get drunk, Cousin," Kyran admonished, his expression thunderous.

"I do not remember doing so," Renwick claimed, shaking his head. "I remember entering the cottage, and then nothing. Besides, I wasn't here long enough to find anything to drink."

"Then you were drunk before you came."

"I was working at *Chez Chantilly*! Alindra would kill me if I so much as took a sip."

Kyran ignored Renwick's protest, though I knew Renwick was telling the truth. Alindra would kill him. Kyran marched toward the fireplace, then spun around. "Why are you here in the first place? How did you get in?"

"Lorelle invited me." Kyran's shoulders stiffened and his fists clenched as though they wanted to punch Renwick in the face. "She asked me to watch her place and to keep an eye on Edan while she was gone."

"She asked *you*?"

"I know. Insane, huh?" When Kyran didn't return his grin, Renwick sobered. "I believe she thought you were compromised."

Kyran's face twisted into a grimace and he sunk down onto the rocking chair. "I suppose that's why she didn't tell me about saving that elf boy's life."

"I only found out about it from Matron, who heard a neighbor talking about it. She likes to eavesdrop, among other things."

"Well, you know more about it than I do. Ilia mentioned the incident, but wouldn't say anything else. Lorelle obviously doesn't trust me enough to tell me what happened." He looked beaten by this admission, and I wanted to bust through the mirror and explain everything to him. "But I thought she'd at least say goodbye."

"From what you've told me, it sounds like she didn't have a choice in the matter. Are you sure she's gone, though?"

"Rumor has it that someone left Hawthorn Lane an hour ago. After Lorelle tried to leave several days ago"—I hadn't told Renwick about my first attempt to escape, though he didn't seem surprised to hear about it—"I set that centaur I told you about to keep an eye on her. He got distracted by news of an incursion in the forest—which, miraculously, dissipated the moment he arrived to handle it—and when he went to track her down, he couldn't trace her."

"That sounds rather suspicious." Renwick looked around the cottage. "She obviously isn't here, and since Rialban can't trace her, perhaps she really has left us. We were to meet and discuss what needed to be done around the place, but she didn't come. She left a list—" He broke off, and I cursed the conclusion he was drawing. Like Avice, he thought I'd cut and run.

"I see," Kyran replied coolly, and I knew he'd drawn the same conclusion. He closed his eyes for a moment, then opened them. "I suppose Lorelle thought I was conspiring with Lady Faylan because I was trying to delay her from leaving. I'm sure that made her suspicious."

"Lorelle is a naturally suspicious person," Renwick said, trying to be fair.

Kyran nodded wearily. "She has good reason to be. But I wasn't conspiring with anyone. You see, I had hoped to remove the curse myself. I've been working on my powers, improving them, controlling them, and I thought I could do it. I really did. I did my best to get all the information about the curse that I could from Lady Faylan, pretending to be intrigued by her, but she was only interested in sharing my bed."

Was this the truth? Lady Faylan wanting to share his bed was believable, but the part about him cozying up to her? It could be. I knew now that Dallen had made me think Kyran was in league with Lady Faylan for his own purposes, so maybe Kyran was innocent in all this. Edan had always trusted Kyran, and wouldn't have if Kyran were the enemy. The rapture would have made short work of him, and yet he hadn't. Could it be that I'd gotten Kyran Van der Daarke all wrong?

"I asked Lorelle to give me a week," Kyran went on, his voice tired, "but I made the mistake of insinuating that my request might have something to do with you, just to throw her off. She doesn't like not knowing things"—*very true*—"and I thought I'd better mislead her to keep her from finding out my plan too soon." He glanced at Renwick and his cousin shrugged, as though he understood perfectly. I wasn't sure I liked how well they seemed to know me. "But I played it a bit too carelessly and my scheme backfired. She's gone, Renwick. I sense it." How could he sense it? I wasn't gone. I was still here! "She must have left with that boy."

Tell him the truth, Renwick, I urged. *Tell him what really happened to me.*

But Renwick only frowned, and I knew with chilling certainty that Cutter had erased his memory. "Are you going after her?" he asked after a few long moments had passed.

"She's made her choice, and it was not me she chose. I cannot force her to come back. I will not."

"No!" I reached for him. "Don't give up on me, Kyran!"

Strong arms encircled my body, pulling me away from the mirror that was already darkening. "It shall be all right, Lorelle," Cutter soothed. "You will forget all about him, and he you, and together we shall be happy. I promise you that."

My mind started to grow dark and my thoughts turned hazy as the smell of vetiver grew stronger. "You're right, Cutter," I murmured softly. "I shall be happy with you."

"You will be my bride." It was not a question.

"I will, Cutter. I will."

With a half-smile, he swooped me up into his arms, and as my world grew dark, he carried me away from the mirrors, away from Kyran and my old life.

And I felt nothing but relief.

About the Author

Feeling Witchy

When author, Kristina Schram, was growing up she wanted to be a star. When that didn't turn out quite like she expected, she turned her mind to achieving other goals: Earning her Ph.D. in Counseling Psychology, working as an Artist-in-Residence at local schools, being a free-lance editor and reader, coaching parks & rec basketball, protecting the earth through recycling and using green products, and publishing her first novel, a YA fantasy called The Chronicles of Anaedor: The Prophecies.

Knowing what it's like to struggle with self-doubt and lack of confidence, her biggest dream (in addition to owning a castle) is to stamp out low self-esteem for everyone, especially young people. She lives in beautiful, wooded New Hampshire with her husband, three boys, and various pets, and can also throw a tomahawk, if need be. One of her favorite things to do is walk with her dog in the woods, where she searches for the impossible around every corner. Sometimes she finds it.

For more information on Kristina Schram, feel free to make a trip to her website: www.kristinaschram.com. She's also on Facebook, Twitter, and Pinterest.

Other Books by Kristina Schram

Tales From Hawthorn Lane

Bewitching Hawthorn Lane

Paranormal Gothic Romance

The Wrath
I Shall Return
Moon Dweller

YOUNG ADULT

The Pandora Belfry Adventures

Mayhem at Nepenthe Manor
The Labyrinth of Lunacy
The Eldritch Affair

The Forest Immortal Saga

The Changeling's Tale
Oswald's Revenge
Meltdown

The Chronicles of Anaedor

The Prophecies
The Return to Anaedor
The Lost Ones
The Uprising